When Rose reached the doorway, Jim leaned over quickly and shut it before her. Taking her in his arms he pressed her body to his and drew her face to him. Fervently, deliberately, he kissed her soundly on her lips. Closing her eyes, she gave herself up completely to him, as they savagely kissed again and again.

It was ecstasy being in his arms. For a fleeting moment she remembered why she came, but still pressed her body even closer to his. Then suddenly, quickly, she forcefully pushed him away.

"Jim," she said, her face flushing, "this is madness."

Slowly he opened the door. "As usual, my sweet one, you are correct. But don't forget me, Rose."

"I shan't ever, Jim. But this—this cannot be."

And as she walked away, he said, "There is only one Rose O'Neal . . ."

FICTION FOR TODAY'S WOMAN

EMBRACES   (666, $2.50)
by Sharon Wagner
Dr. Shelby Cole was an expert in the field of medicine and a novice
at love. She wasn't willing to give up her career to get married—
until she grew to want and need the child she was carrying.

MIRRORS   (690, $2.75)
by Barbara Krasnoff
The compelling story of a woman seeking changes in life and love,
and of her desperate struggle to give those changes impact—in the
midst of tragedy.

THE LAST CARESS   (722, $2.50)
by Dianna Booher
Since the tragic news that her teenaged daughter might die, Erin's
husband had become distant, isolated. Was this simply his way of
handling his grief, or was there more to it? If she was losing her
child, would she lose her husband as well?

VISIONS   (695, $2.95)
by Martin A. Grove
Caught up in the prime time world of power and lust, Jason and
Gillian fought desperately for the top position at Parliament
Television. Jason fought to keep it—Gillian, to take it away!

LONGINGS   (706, $2.50)
by Sylvia W. Greene
Andrea was adored by her husband throughout their seven years of
childless marriage. Now that she was finally pregnant, a haze of
suspicion shrouded what should have been the happiest time of
their lives.

*Available wherever paperbacks are sold, or order direct from the
Publisher. Send cover price plus 50¢ per copy for mailing and
handling to Zebra Books, 21 East 40th Street, New York, N.Y.
10016. DO NOT SEND CASH!*

A WOMAN OF DESTINY

BY
GRANDIN K. HAMMELL

ZEBRA BOOKS

KENSINGTON PUBLISHING CORP.

ZEBRA BOOKS

are published by

KENSINGTON PUBLISHING CORP.
21 East 40th Street
New York, N.Y. 10016

Printed in the United States of America

To

Kay
Joan
Karen
Skipper
and
Mike

who maintained faith
the twenty-two years
it took to write
this book.

I

The Grand Ball

Spring 1833

Rose O'Neal looked out upon the misty streets of Washington from her bedroom window and, arms stretched high, threw her head back in utter abandon. "Someday this city will be mine!" she declared, smiling fiercely. Completely bare to the waist, she brought her hands to her fully blossomed breasts that belied her nineteen years and firmly pressed the soft flesh against her body. Swinging to the full-length mirror, she spoke to the reflection in a cold, steely voice, "Nobody out there knows me now. But they will. Everyone in Washington will pay homage to me. Someday!"

Her eyes became soft with a sultry, unbridled passion. "No man will resist me. And the women—I don't care about them. It's the men who control this city. And it is they who determine the destiny of this entire nation. And I will control them!" She flounced gaily to the window and watched the steady procession of horses and carriages. She was happy in the knowledge that men considered her beautiful, and that her exceptional intelligence and shrewdness gave her an almost mystic ability to judge them and quickly determine their weaknesses. "And I have never in my whole life seen so many handsome men—and so attentive."

The animated conversation at her aunt's dinner table enthralled her, and the constant anticipation of gay dances and thrilling balls in honor of some visiting dignitary from a faraway country made her tingle with excitement. It was so unlike the little town of Poolesville, Maryland, from whence she had come that it was impossible to compare the two. Nothing ever happened in Poolesville, while this—"This is the center of a rising, great nation," as Mr. Calhoun had said to her.

Her reverie was abruptly interrupted as her sister Ellen burst into the room. "Oh, Rose, I expected you to be ready and just look at you," Ellen exclaimed in anguish as she pointed to Rose calmly leaning on the windowsill in nothing but her lace pantaloons. "Don't you realize that our gentlemen will be here any minute?"

"And I shall be ready."

"But you know how James hates to be kept waiting—" Ellen's voice turned to panic as the door gong sounded downstairs. "They're here! Oh," Ellen wailed, "how could you do this to me?"

Rose laughed. "You look so frightened, Ellen. If you are this afraid of James before you are married, what will you be like afterward?"

"How can you joke when you—oh, look at you."

Rose smiled calmly. "I shan't tease you anymore, Ellen. I'll let you in on a little secret." Taking her sister's arm she led her to the bedstead where her dress hung supported from the canopy. Lifting up the lower hem, she disappeared beneath it only to reappear almost instantly with the dress draped about her. "Isn't that tricky?" she laughed as she fastened the dress behind her. "The dress and bodice and all my petticoats at one fell swoop. My own little invention."

"Amazing!" Ellen gasped in surprise as she started toward the door. "I shall tell the men you will be right down."

Calmly biding her time, Rose dabbed powder on her shoulders and neck and added the faintest touch of red rouge to her cheeks.

Presently, Rose appeared on the broad stairway looking older than her nineteen years. Her black hair glistened in the yellow light and her eyes fairly sparkled as the others stood in the hallway watching her. Her entrance was truly in the grand style, and well-timed, as if it had been deliberate, which it was.

"James," she smiled broadly. "You look absolutely handsome in your full dress tonight."

"And you, my dear Rose, look ravishing," James replied bowing and kissing her hand. Then turning to his companion, he added, "May I present my very good friend, Lieutenant Gerald Faulkner."

Rose demurely lowered her eyes and curtsied. "This is indeed a pleasure," she said breathlessly, taking in the tall masculine figure, the broad shoulders, and the handsome aquiline profile of this young man who was to be her escort for the evening. "And now we must be off," she said gaily, taking Lieutenant Faulkner's arm and starting toward the door. "We mustn't be a moment late," she smiled mischievously, making the others forget that it was she for whom they had been waiting patiently for a full fifteen minutes.

Ellen and her beau followed down the brownstone steps of their house and got into the carriage drawn up at the curb.

"I'm so excited," Rose said as they started off. "I have heard it rumored that President Jackson himself may put in an appearance."

"It is quite possible," agreed Lieutenant Faulkner. "I know he is in town."

"Yes," Rose commented, "he has just returned yesterday night from New York City."

Lieutenant Faulkner raised his eyebrows. "How did you know that?" he asked admiringly. "That was supposed to be a matter strictly for the military."

"He was there to place his approval for the terms of the 'Black Hawk' war," she said knowingly.

Lieutenant Faulkner's eyes widened in astonishment. "You truly amaze me, Miss O'Neal. How did you ever—"

"Oh, I think the affairs of state are fascinating." She smiled beguilingly. "And we are fortunate to hear such matters discussed freely by so many important men of the government who are boarding at Aunt Hattie's."

"Oh, now Rose, let us not fill the evening with politics and the country's business," Ellen remonstrated.

"Ellen is right, you know," Rose remarked gaily as she drew Lieutenant Faulkner closer to her. "There are more important matters close at hand, such as learning more about you. Where do you come from, lieutenant?"

Lieutenant Faulkner's face reddened as he felt her warm body so close to his. He hoped no one would notice how ill at ease this gay, intriguing girl made him. He did so want to make a good impression on her. He laughed lightly. "I hail from way up north originally—Montpelier, Vermont. I doubt if you have ever heard of it."

"I must confess that I have not. But that is no matter. Father used to joke about our little town of Poolesville. He said it consisted mostly of the O'Neals, the Morehouses, whom he married into, and one other family."

All of them laughed. Rose looked out the window of the carriage and noticed they were passing an enormous building only partially constructed. "I wonder what that is?"

"It is the new Capitol building," James volunteered hurriedly, trying valiantly to become a part of the conversation. "When it is completed I believe the lieutenant will be working there, won't you Jerry?"

"I indeed hope so."

"Oh, wonderful," Rose enthused. "And may I visit you there?"

"I would be delighted. It is not very often—" he broke off suddenly as the carriage drew to a halt.

James leaned out the window and shouted to the driver, "Why are you stopping, Willie?"

"We is here," Willie replied.

"But this isn't the National Hotel," said James.

10

"It's as close as we can get, Master Cutts. We'll have to wait our turn in line."

"But that will take forever to get to the ball," Rose pouted.

"Oh, be patient, Rose," Ellen remonstrated.

"It shouldn't take very long for those coaches to discharge their passengers," James commented in resignation.

"It will indeed take entirely too long. I am anxious to get to the ball," Rose remarked firmly. "Move on, Willie."

"I can't, Miss O'Neal. We got this long line."

"Move out alongside. I'll show you where to go."

Willie leaned down to catch the eye of his master who seemed resigned and merely shrugged his shoulders. Shrugging his own shoulders, he pulled their coach out of line and drove on ahead to exactly where he did not know.

As they drew up beside the massive front entrance of the National Hotel Rose commanded, "Stop. Don't attempt to draw up to the curb."

As the coach halted and the others looked at Rose in amazement, she remarked matter-of-factly, "Well, aren't you gentlemen going to help us out, or do we have to manage by ourselves with these ungainly hoop skirts?"

Lieutenant Faulkner quickly sprang to his feet and, followed by James, jumped out of the coach and stood by the door, his arms extended.

"But the mud, lieutenant," Rose said simply, "our dresses will be ruined."

"You wanted to get to the head of the line," Ellen remarked.

"I don't want your arm, lieutenant, I want you. Won't you please carry me over to the steps?" The lieutenant looked at his companion half in amazement, half in wonder, as Rose stretched out both her arms. Quickly he regained his composure and, beaming with admiration, grabbed Rose by the waist and carefully carried her across the muddied road through the line of coaches and set her safely down on the steps of the hotel.

"Aren't you going to join us?" Rose shouted back to her

sister, whereupon James gingerly picked Ellen up and followed.

As Ellen came up to her she spoke in a low voice. "I've never been so embarrassed in my life. Everyone is staring at us."

"This is known as the Grande Entrée."

As the men walked ahead of them to open the mirrored double doors, Ellen whispered to her, "But think of our gentlemen . . . having to bodily carry us like—"

"That is what they are for, my dear." Rose patted her older sister's cheek, and taking the arm of her lieutenant, strode grandly into the foyer of the hotel.

The hall was decorated magnificently for the grand ball. American flags and bunting hung gaily from the bandstand and around the walls, paper lanterns were strung across the ceiling, and the mahogany-paneled doors leading into the ballroom were covered with more gaily colored bunting. A rich red carpet led from the entrance directly to the edge of the dancing area.

"Isn't it magnificent?" Rose breathed softly as she gazed wide-eyed about the room. A matronly lady curtsied as they entered and they were each handed a dance reservation card. "Twelve dances," Rose murmured happily. "This will really be a ball."

"It is truly breathtaking," Ellen agreed as she handed James her dance card. "You may fill out my dance card, James."

"I am so fortunate that you reserve every dance for me, my dear," James said happily, hastily writing his name on her card.

Lieutenant Faulkner reached for Rose's card. "May I?" he asked impatiently.

"Of course," Rose replied, handing him the card. "You may place your name opposite the first dance."

"Only one?" he asked, unable to conceal his disappointment.

"There will be others," Rose assured him, "but let us first see how well we dance together," and then she added casually, "and note what other fine ladies and gentlemen are here this evening."

The music began to play a lively mazurka and partners were forming opposite each other. Ellen and James had already taken their places on the ballroom floor.

"Shall we, Miss O'Neal?" the lieutenant asked eagerly.

"Oh, I would love to," Rose replied excitedly and added, "this is going to be a wonderful evening. I just know it. I'm so excited."

As they commenced the formations of the dance, it soon became apparent that Lieutenant Faulkner was an excellent dancer, a fact Rose complimented him upon when they came together. However, when they were apart, Rose quickly focused her attention on the other partners about her so as to learn what important personages were present.

"Everyone of importance is here tonight," she smiled as they came together. "Do you recognize any of them?"

"Oh, but of course," Lieutenant Faulkner remarked importantly. "The gentleman who just brushed by us is Mr. Vincent, first assistant secretary of state. I have had occasion to speak with him several times. And that is Senator Williamson from New York standing by the punch bowl."

"You are familiar with so many of the great men of our country," Rose marveled. "Have you been in Washington long?"

"Nearly a year now. And when I think how pleasant my stay could have been if I had only known you sooner."

"Oh, but I only came to live with my aunt a few weeks ago. I know hardly anyone as yet."

"You need not worry about that. It's said almost all the important persons in Washington have boarded at your aunt's boarding house at one time or another."

They were close to the edge of the ballroom when Rose stopped momentarily and waved. As he followed her gaze he suddenly stood at attention and bowed stiffly as Rose said, "Good evening, Senator Calhoun."

They broke away from their dance figuration as Senator

Calhoun came up to them. "How nice to see you, Rose. I didn't know you were coming."

"I couldn't miss this wonderful evening, sir. May I present my escort, Lieutenant Faulkner. Lieutenant, this is Senator Calhoun."

Lieutenant Faulkner shook the senator's hand gingerly and murmured, "This is an unexpected honor, sir."

"Thank you," the senator smiled and turned to Rose. "I trust you have saved a dance for me, Rose."

"The very next one," said Rose extending her card.

Hastily Senator Calhoun scribbed his initials on her card and then said, "I must not interrupt your dance any further." He smiled and turned away adding, "I shall see you later, Rose."

Rose and the lieutenant again took their positions on the dance floor. "Oh, Rose," he chided her, "how could you let me brag about the people I know when you know *him?*"

"But he is only one man, surely he is not that important."

"Only a former vice president of the United States and now the senior senator from South Carolina."

The music ended and they walked arm in arm off the floor.

It was a glorious evening for Rose. She danced with Senator Calhoun and smiled mischievously as she noted the envious look of several of the other ladies. Rose laughed as she told him of the awe of Lieutenant Faulkner upon meeting the former vice president of the United States.

"The office is highly overrated," Calhoun commented. "Actually he is a nobody with nothing to do save keep his tongue in his head and wait for the president to die while he is still in office."

"I am happy to know one vice president who did otherwise."

"You are undoubtedly referring to my maneuvers to get the Nullification Act passed in South Carolina."

"I am."

"I could not stand idly by while the rights of our states are jeopardized." Calhoun sighed. "You are learning a lot at your

14

Aunt Hill's boarding house."

"I try, senator. To me it is fascinating."

"It really isn't fair, you know. Those poor politicians are feeling at home, and are so lonely for their families far away, it is only natural that they should discuss the day's excitement on Capitol Hill."

"I am learning, senator. Honestly I haven't heard such heated arguments since Mrs. O'Neale's arrival."

"That poor woman has split poor Jackson's Cabinet by her notoriety."

"I understand she is to be here this evening. I should like to meet her."

"You must not."

"But senator, you were never one to snub her."

"It is different with you. You are young and only now are forming your associations. Never hitch your aspirations to anyone whose reputation is questionable."

"But Mrs. O'Neale is famous. The whole capital is talking about her."

"Infamous is more the word, and believe me she can do you no good. Better that you foster the acquaintances you meet at diplomatic receptions and White House levees."

"But I have not attended any."

"More the shame, young lady. And why not?"

"Because no one has invited me."

"Oh." Senator Calhoun stopped in the middle of a quadrille, pursed his lips and rubbed his chin. Rose took his arm and glided him through the balance of the steps so they would not collide with any of the other couples. The music stopped. As they walked off the ballroom floor arm in arm, he turned to her, saying, "Mr. McLane has just been appointed the new secretary of state. The State Department is planning a reception for him next Thursday evening at Georgetown. I shall have you included in the guest list."

Rose hugged the senator's arm closer to her. "Oh, senator, would you really?"

15

"Better still, there's a young man connected with State that might make a fine escort for you."

"I would be forever grateful to you."

"He is here tonight," the senator murmured absently as he looked about the ballroom. "There he is now if I could catch his eye—" He stopped as the man of his attention looked their way and the senator beckoned to him.

As Rose watched the young man coming over to them she felt the blood gradually rushing to her cheeks. She had never seen a more handsome man before in her life. Although he was dressed as a civilian he walked with trim, almost military steps. His tall, lean frame and jet-black hair and eyes made him stand out most emphatically from the rest of the men about him.

As he came up to them Rose noticed that his eyes twinkled in merriment. His captivating smile made her feel that she already knew him, although she had never seen him before in her life. When he looked at her it was with a deep, penetrating stare, which was not at all assuming. It made her believe that he knew her every thought—and this made her even more uncomfortable.

"Robert, I believe you have heard me mention Miss Rose O'Neal."

Robert bowed grandly and took Rose's hand in his. "You did, sir, but I never dreamed that the young lady would turn out to be as lovely as she is."

"Thank you, sir." Rose smiled her prettiest smile as she curtsied.

"Rose, this is Dr. Robert Greenhow, chief translator and interpreter for the State Department. You won't be able to say anything behind his back, young lady, for he speaks five different languages."

Dr. Greenhow's lace ruffles and embroidered waistcoat seemed to accentuate his extreme height. Rose laughed coquettishly to cover her embarrassment. She had never felt this way before. A strange uncertainness welled up within her as she felt a magnetism drawing her closer to this strange, impressive man.

"We were speaking of State's reception for Mr. McLane," Senator Calhoun was saying. "Miss O'Neal remarked how delighted she would be to attend—that is, if she did not have to go with some old fogy like myself."

Rose giggled. She hated girls who giggled but she couldn't help herself. "Oh, senator, I never said any such thing."

"I should be happy to accompany you, Miss O'Neal," Robert said, looking at her intently with deep, penetrating eyes. Rose did not reply. She could think of nothing to say. It was not like her to be speechless. Whatever had come over her?

II

The Accusation

Before Rose could collect her wits about her, Lieutenant Faulkner came up to them. "I hope I am not intruding," he said stiffly, "but I believe I am to have the next dance."

Rose was glad that he had come. It seemed to break the spell that this handsome young man had cast upon her. She could think clearly and quickly once again. "Oh, I am so sorry, lieutenant," she looked up at him innocently, "but surely there must be some mistake. I have just promised this dance to Dr. Greenhow."

Dr. Greenhow interrupted hastily, "Oh, I wouldn't—"

"Of course if you don't care to, Dr. Greenhow, I shall of course permit the lieutenant to exercise his option."

Dr. Greenhow's broad grin reflected his admiration. "I would be very happy to dance with you, Miss O'Neal."

"Well, that settles it then, lieutenant," Senator Calhoun broke in. "Come join me in a brandy." As the two men walked away the senator turned and winked at Rose. She could have kissed him. "I can't stand that punch they have, can you lieutenant?" the senator remarked throwing his arm over his companion's shoulder as they moved into the crowd.

The music started and couples were taking their places upon the floor. "Well, doctor," Rose said quietly, "what are we waiting for?"

They danced silently together for a few moments as Dr.

Greenhow smiled at her. "I find that my new acquaintance has a way of letting her wishes be known in no uncertain terms."

"You did not wish it otherwise, did you, doctor?"

"I am truly delighted. It is just that I had been promised this dance by Miss Benton and I was not quite prepared for the change of events."

"Miss Jessie Benton?"

"Yes, do you know her?"

"I should say so. She comes from Poolesville, the same town as I."

"Well then, you must have a great deal in common."

"I think not, doctor."

Dr. Greenhow could not escape noting the disparaging tone of her voice and hastily changed the subject. "Are you familiar with many persons here this evening?" he asked.

Rose was not listening to him. "Do you know her very well, doctor?"

"You mean Jessie?" He could not understand how this beautiful, vivacious young girl could so suddenly change her mood.

"Yes."

"I accompanied her here this evening. We have known each other only a few weeks. I have been abroad until—"

"What do you think of her?"

"Well, she seems likable enough."

Rose uttered a short, hard laugh as they parted and swung to the partners next to them. When next they came together, Rose said coldly, "Jessie will be furious when she learns you have danced with me."

"I gather you and she are not the best of friends."

"She is a spoiled, selfish girl. If you have not determined that for yourself, it only goes to prove the old adage: 'Men are blind where women are concerned.'"

"I—I like frankness, Miss O'Neal."

"So do I. We should get along splendidly together."

Dr. Greenhow was a fine dancer and Rose leaned as close to

19

him as her hooped skirts would permit as they met at the close of a formation. It was so pleasant being with this tall, masculine man, she thought to herself as they danced away from each other. Dr. Greenhow seemed to add strength to her own being. She liked him. As a matter of fact, she liked him more than any man she had ever met. Could she be in love with him? This was impossible. She had only known him for a few moments. But that made no difference—not to Rose. When next they joined hands, they danced silently for a moment. Then Dr. Greenhow pressed her arm. "We are suddenly so quiet," he chided her. "Surely I have said nothing to offend you."

"Oh, no. My goodness, you must think I am a terrible bore."

"If you wish to know what I really think, you are a very exciting and beautiful young woman."

"Why, Dr. Greenhow."

"You said that you liked frankness."

The music stopped and Dr. Greenhow bowed grandly. "Thank you for the most wonderful dance of my life." He turned partly away. It was obvious that he was anxious to return to Jessie.

"It's terribly warm in here," she said quickly. "Couldn't we have a cup of punch?"

"Certainly, Miss O'Neal. I'll get it for you."

"I will go with you." She smiled her most bewitching smile as they walked over to the refreshment table as the music started to play again. "Do I detect a southern accent, Dr. Greenhow?"

He laughed. "You are most observant. I am from Williamsburg. But I thought that I had been in Europe for so long that I had completely lost any southern accent. In law school—"

"Oh, you are a lawyer."

"That is where I met—perhaps we should not talk about it tonight."

"You know Jessie's father? He is a lawyer, too."

"Yes, he taught at law school when I—"

Rose suddenly interrupted. "Couldn't we talk while we dance?" she asked as she noticed Lieutenant Faulkner coming over to them.

"I suppose so, but I really should go over to—"

Hastily she took his half-finished cup of punch, placed it on the table and swung him toward the dance. "If you wish to continue our conversation, we must dance, for my lieutenant is coming over to claim me."

"So I notice. He seems most disturbed that we are dancing together again. Have you known him long?"

"Heavens no. I only met him this evening." Rose smiled as she detected the disappearance of a slight frown from Dr. Greenhow's features. "He seems to be a most understanding young man, though. Well trained in military discipline."

"I daresay Jessie will not be quite so understanding."

Rose cast a quick glance to the sidelines where she spotted Jessie seated, impatiently tapping the floor with her slippers and trying unsuccessfully to appear unconcerned. Rose could not refrain from smiling impishly at Jessie as she caught her eye. The doctor and she danced away from each other, and when they were once again together, Dr. Greenhow said hastily, "Before we are separated for the evening, I must know where I can pick you up next Thursday."

"I am staying at Mrs. Hill's boarding house. It is on Clay Street."

"Everyone knows where Mrs. Hill's house is. But I didn't know that she took in young ladies."

"Oh, she doesn't. She is my aunt. My sister and I are staying with her."

"Then I am most fortunate to have you agree to go with me to the reception, when you could go with any one of the important personages who dine at Mrs. Hill's."

"I do not know many of those politicians. Aunt Hattie is very strict with us. Which reminds me, would it be possible for my sister and her gentleman friend to accompany us to the reception? Auntie will never permit me to go without a chaperone."

"It can be easily arranged. I shall pick you up about eight, then."

As the music stopped, Dr. Greenhow looked at his gold watch and whistled softly under his breath. "I didn't realize how long I had been away from Miss Benton. I am really being a cad." He pressed her hand as he walked with her arm in his. "It has been so enjoyable, Miss O'Neal—I mean, the time has passed so quickly."

"It has been wonderful, Dr. Greenhow. It is regrettable that it must end so soon."

"Yes, well I—I—" he sighed unconsciously. "I see your lieutenant friend coming over." Dr. Greenhow bowed as Lieutenant Faulkner came up to them. "We were looking for you, lieutenant." Turning to Rose he bowed deeply and took her hand in his. "I thank you ever so much, Miss O'Neal, and if I do not see you again this evening, I shall come for you next Thursday at eight. That is to say," he corrected himself quickly, "you and your sister and her friend."

"I shall look forward to it, Dr. Greenhow." She watched him walk away from her, paying no attention to Lieutenant Faulkner standing by her side.

"Tall sort of a fellow, isn't he?"

"What did you say, lieutenant?"

"I said he is rather tall, isn't he?"

The music began to play a lively tune and Lieutenant Faulkner took her arm. "Shall we dance, Miss O'Neal?"

"Oh, I must rest a bit, if you don't mind."

"But you said you loved to dance."

"I do, but—lieutenant would you excuse me for a few moments while I freshen up in the retiring room?"

"But of course. Only I—well, I had hoped that we could have this dance together. It seems half the evening is gone already and I have only had the pleasure of your company for one dance."

"I'm sorry, lieutenant. To make up for my thoughtlessness you shall have the next two dances."

"Is that a promise, Miss O'Neal?"

"Write your name on my card so there will be no question."

Eagerly Lieutenant Faulkner scribbled his name on her card and she turned to go. "I shall be only a short time."

"I can hardly contain myself until your return."

In the retiring room Rose hummed gaily as she surveyed herself in the mirror. The other women in the room seemed so much older than she. Feverishly, earnestly, they tried unsuccessfully to cover up the wrinkles that the strenuous evening had made so evident.

Ellen came in and sat down beside her. "Rose, what in heaven's name have you been doing? Lieutenant Faulkner has been almost beside himself. Frankly my dear, I think he is quite stricken with you."

"Ellen, I have met the most wonderful man!"

"I could not help but notice you dancing with him."

"Isn't he handsome?"

"Who is he? I hope you met him properly."

"Senator Calhoun introduced me to him. He is a doctor—Dr. Greenhow, and he is a lawyer, and he works for the State Department—and he speaks five different languages. Oh, Ellen, don't you think that he is wonderful?"

"I haven't met him yet. Goodness, he certainly must have made an impression on you to go on so."

"Oh, he did, Ellen. He did. And I am going to the State Department reception for Mr. McLane next Thursday evening with him."

"Rose! You can't be serious. You know Aunt Hattie will never allow you to go without—"

"But you and James are to go with us. He is arranging an invitation for us all."

"Well, I am most thankful that you let James and myself know of our plans in advance."

"You will go, won't you, Ellen?"

23

"I shall have to ask James. I hardly know how I will explain it to him. Neither of us even know the man."

"Oh, but you will like him, Ellen. I know that you will."

"I'll do my best to convince James to go since it obviously means so much to you. Rose, I have some news also. I too am excited."

"What is it? Tell me."

"James has proposed marriage to me!"

"You are engaged!"

"Well, I did tell him he would have to talk to Aunt Hattie. But that is only a formality. You know how she likes James."

"Yes, and James Madison Cutts's family even better." Rose patted a bit of starch powder on her cheeks. "My sister married," she mused. "It is difficult to believe. When will it be, Ellen?"

"Next spring."

"Next spring? That is nearly a year from now. I could never wait that long. Whatever possessed you to—"

"There are so many things that have to be done. And James is going abroad late this summer to look into something about his family interests."

"If you were married, you could go with him."

"Now Rose don't try to run my marriage as you do everything else. This is my wedding and please permit me to plan it when and as I wish."

"I shall not interfere. I only wish—"

Rose stopped in the middle of her thought, aware that someone was standing behind her. As she looked up she saw Jessie Benton smiling sarcastically down at her. "Up to your old tricks, I see," Jessie said coldly. "You haven't changed a bit since leaving Poolesville."

Rose furiously patted her nose. "What are you talking about?"

"You know what I am referring to all too well. Robert Greenhow came with me this evening."

"Oh, it's Robert is it? He refers to you as Miss Benton."

24

"Whatever it is, I expect to dance with him the rest of the evening."

"Is his name on your card?"

"He will gladly agree if you keep from butting into our association. I can read you like an open book, Rose O'Neal, and Robert would never have treated me so shabbily if you had not cajoled him into it. I'm giving you fair warning, Miss O'Neal, I like him. Leave him alone."

Jessie flounced over to a dressing table and swept a comb fiercely through her hair. The room suddenly became strangely quiet as the two girls raised their voices.

"You hardly know him," Rose shouted. "He told me so himself."

Ellen touched her sister's arm. "Rose," she whispered, "do be quiet, you will start a scene."

"I don't care. She needn't think—"

"Please," Ellen begged, "you are wrong. I did not dream that your friend came with anyone. Imagine how Jessie must have felt sitting alone while she watched you dancing with her escort."

"I cannot imagine any chit admitting that some other girl had taken her escort away from her."

Jessie slammed the comb on the vanity shelf. "That's not true and you know it. You aren't interested in Robert. He's just a passing fancy to you. You're just like your father!"

Rose jumped up as if she had been slapped. Ellen tried to restrain her but was brusquely pushed aside as Rose strode over to Jessie.

"Leave my papa out of this!" she retorted hotly. "He's dead and I'll thank you to show proper respect for him!"

"I would do it gladly if he were entitled to it."

Rose savagely swung Jessie around to face her. Jessie, on the other hand, seeing that she had finally succeeded in upsetting Rose's composure, stood squarely before her, a sneering smile on her face.

"Stop making insinuations and explain yourself," Rose

muttered through tightly pressed lips.

"I was merely referring to certain circumstances concerning your poor papa's sudden departure from this earth."

"My poor papa died of pneumonia and I won't have any chit of a girl saying—"

"All I was referring to was that he would probably be alive today if—"

"If what?"

"If he hadn't caught cold leaving Mrs. Maybelle Reid's house in such a hurry!"

"You take that back. I don't know what you are referring to but I won't have you insinuating—"

"I'm not insinuating anything. I'm only repeating what everyone in Poolesville knows to be true. Your poor papa caught his death of cold runnig out of Maybelle's house in his underwear when her husband came home unexpectedly and trapped him in her room without any clothes on."

"You lie!" Rose screamed as she grabbed Jessie and shook her. "Say that you are lying or I'll—I'll kill you."

"Take your hands off me!" Jessie grabbed the back of Rose's hair to pull her away but she could not. To defend herself she slapped Rose and each girl grabbed the other's dress. A woman in the room screamed and Ellen's voice could be heard shouting, "Rose, Rose! Stop it! Stop it!!!"

As the two girls fell against the dressing table bottles scattered and broke, the bench fell over, and Rose sobbed in her rage, "Admit that it is a lie! Admit it!"

Jessie, pushing Rose away, caught her bracelet in Rose's dress and the delicate cloth ripped. "Let go of me, you gutter wench. It is the truth, and you can't deny it."

Ellen sobbed aloud as Rose yanked Jessie's head down by her hair, throwing both girls off balance and sending them to the floor locked in each other's grip. They rolled back and forth on the floor, lace petticoats and flounced ball gowns flying in the air. Rose savagely scratched Jessie's face. A mad grab by Jessie caught Rose's dress at the shoulder and ripped it to the waist, taking with it her bodice and underthings. Her firm, bare breast lay fully exposed as she rolled over into a sitting position atop Jessie's prostrate figure. Undaunted by this challenge to her feminine modesty, Rose grabbed Jessie's head by the hair with both hands and bounced the poor girl's head against the floor. Both girls were crying, as were most of the women huddled in a corner of the small room.

No one of the onlookers dared to attempt to tear the two girls apart. One of them was able to slip out the door into the main ballroom to seek help—masculine help. Presently three or four men rushed into the room, one of the few instances when any man had ever dared to venture into the inner sanctum of the ladies' retiring room. As they grabbed the two girls and tore them apart, Ellen, crying, quickly threw her shawl over Rose's exposed body, but not before Rose had violently bitten one gentleman on the finger and scratched the face of another in her uncontrollable rage.

Completely unconcerned about her lack of attire, she shouted, "Say that you lie! Tell them all that you lie!"

But Jessie was in no condition to say anything. She had truly received the worst of the bargain, although she was not physically hurt beyond a bloody scratch or two and a welt on her arm where Rose had hit her with a buckle. Her hair was in complete disarray and her hooped skirt had been pulled apart at the seams, exposing her pantaloons and part of the silk underclothing beneath them. One of the other women pulled her lace tulle from about her and wrapped it around Jessie's exposed legs.

"Get their carriages quickly," one of the men said, quietly taking command of the situation. It was obvious that neither of these young ladies would be attending any more of the ball this evening.

Ellen sent word to James, explaining that Rose had met with an accident and it was necessary that she take her home at once. The two sisters made a hasty exit through a rear door and shortly they were in the safety of James's carriage.

27

"Drive us to our home as quickly as you can," Ellen instructed Willie. As the horses pranced along the girls sat slumped in the corners, neither speaking. Occasionally Rose would emit a forlorn sob, as she gradually became calmer.

Presently Ellen looked at her sister's torn attire and said quietly, "Your behavior was abominable, Rose O'Neal."

"You heard what she said about poor Papa."

"Yes."

"She is a vicious, evil girl to speak thusly about the dead."

"She is that."

"Then why did you not tell her so?"

"What good would it do?"

"We could have made her deny it."

"I doubt it."

"Why not? Or was this no surprise to you?"

"Jessie is right, Rose."

"Do you mean that Father was having an affair with Maybelle Reid?"

"No one ever knew for sure. I had heard the rumor before. I have also heard Jessie's version of the story."

"Then why didn't you tell me?"

"I thought I could save you the embarrassment, the heartache which Mama and I were forced to bear. Of course, I did not hear of it until after papa's untimely death."

"But you said yourself it was only a rumor. You should have proven it beyond all doubt—you owed that much to Papa."

"I was afraid."

"Afraid?"

"Papa loved life. He always had a fascination for women. You know how he indulged himself to the extreme in any sport that took his fancy."

"He loved all of life that was active and violent."

"Can you understand why I never pursued these ugly stories?"

"Yes." Rose winced as she touched her face and felt a scratch across her cheek. "Whether it is true or not, I wager

Jessie Benton will never repeat that story in my presence again."

"You were terrible, Rose. Auntie is forever telling us that no matter what happens we must always behave as young ladies should. I don't know what I am ever going to do with you."

"You won't have to worry about that for long. You will be getting married."

Ellen sighed. "If James ever wants to see me again after tonight."

"He will marry you, wait and see. It would be hard for him to forget you for the land and dowry that father left you."

"I would hate to think that he was marrying me for that reason." Ellen put her head on Rose's shoulder and patted her hand. "Jessie was correct about one thing, Rose. You are just like Papa. You must beware of that and exercise some restraint."

"Yes, I will have to be very careful, won't I?"

III

The Marriage

Spring 1835

Time passed rapidly in Washington for Rose. She missed the company of her sister at Aunt Hattie's, but Ellen's marriage to James Madison Cutts had opened many doors for Rose. As the wife of Dolly Madison's nephew, Ellen had been brought into the magic circle of that great lady's friends. And Dolly had been magnanimous enough to include Ellen's sister in her invitations to her soirees and levees. Between the statesmen who dined at her aunt's boarding house and the people she met at Dolly Madison's affairs, Rose was fast becoming acquainted with everyone of importance who was building the young nation into a great country.

It was a cold day in March 1835 when Rose awoke as the first rays of the lazy sun came drifting into her room. Hurriedly she jumped out of bed and rushed to the wide open window. She took a deep breath of fresh air.

In spite of the cold, she stood for a moment looking out on the narrow, muddy street. Although it was after seven o'clock, there were few signs of people moving in the street below. She smiled as she noticed a cow grazing among the grass and weeds beside the road. How incongruous, she thought to herself. The capital of a great nation, and still cows graze beside its busiest thoroughfares. She slid open the shutters and closed the blinds. Quickly she shut the window with a resounding bang.

She slipped off her flannel nightgown and ran her hands over the velvety skin of her slim body. "Still all mine," she murmured seductively, "shared with no man." She nodded to herself. "No small feat for any young girl after three years in this fast-moving city. And while I am in full control of my body, it will remain slim, too." She remembered how Ellen had begun to fill out not too long after her marriage, even before she started to show signs of the baby developing within her, which was due to come into the world in early September.

Of course she was open to certain compromise, she admitted to herself as her thoughts turned to handsome Robert Greenhow. She would gladly share her entire being with him. Capturing him would be worth any price, and besides, it would surely make many of the young single girls in Washington society extremely envious, including that nasty Jessie Benton. Then she frowned. She was not too sure that she had captured Robert. She firmly believed that he thought a great deal of her, since he was constantly paying her his respects. But she had not seen him in over a week. Certainly not too good a sign from one supposedly madly in love with her.

As little goose bumps began to appear on her bare body she hastily put on a chemise and a heavy petticoat. Then she slipped into the rest of her attire in one fell swoop. Her under and outer garments had been carefully put together the night before in her own little private invention which she had hung at the foot of her canopied bedstead.

Her head emerged above the fluff in a bright red taffeta dress with full sweeping lines well to the floor. Hastily she wrapped a black satin waistband about her and buttoned the few buttons at the top that brought the dress tightly around her firm breasts. She surveyed herself in the mirror and smiled. It was a bit dressy for morning, but she was planning a visit to the Senate for a good part of the day and was not to be outshone by the other fine ladies who would undoubtedly attend before the day was out.

She did not linger long at her boudoir table, brushing the

31

faintest flow of red rouge to her cheeks and covering them softly with rice powder. Breakfast was at seven-thirty sharp and Aunt Hattie did not permit tardiness at any of her meals, least of all by her own niece.

Rose selected a wide-hooded velvet bonnet and started downstairs. She hung her bonnet on the ornate umbrella stand at the foot of the stairs just as a loud gong rang announcing breakfast.

Already she could hear men's voices and boisterous laughing. She smiled bewitchingly as she entered the dining room. Those men who had already seated themselves rose graciously. They were all there in their accustomed places: Senator Calhoun, Henry Clay, Daniel Webster, Thomas Hart Benton, Chief Justice Marshall, and others. Aunt Hattie was seated at the head of the table, as was her custom.

"Good morning, gentlemen," said Rose as she took her place to the right of her aunt.

"How lovely you look today," commented Mr. Clay.

"And at this hour of the morning," Mr. Webster added as the men seated themselves. "I don't know how you do it."

"That's my Wild Rose," Senator Calhoun volunteered. "A beautiful young woman at any hour of the day and always dressed in the latest fashions."

Aunt Hattie frowned ever so slightly as she passed her niece a bowl of stewed fruit. "A little overdressed for this hour of the day, I might say."

"Oh, Auntie," Rose admonished teasingly. "It promises to be such a beautiful day, I just had to put something gay on to celebrate the passing of a bleak, savage winter."

"More than likely you are brewing some special plans for the day about which I have not been consulted," snapped Aunt Hattie.

"You wrong me, truly, Aunt Hattie."

"I know you."

Rose's dark eyes twinkled and her face flushed ever so

32

slightly. Aunt Hattie was a very perceptive woman. She was not only knowledgeable in the ways of political conspiracies, but she astounded her niece by her anticipation of Rose's thoughts long before she had put them into words. Rose decided it would be best to change the subject. "Please do not permit me to interrupt your discussion, gentlemen."

"A pretty girl is always a pleasant interruption," Senator Calhoun said.

"Flatterer," Rose smiled, then added in quite a businesslike fashion, "What affair of state is being discussed this morning, gentlemen?"

"These men have just been raking me over the coals, Rose," Justice Marshall said. "I'm glad you came in."

"We've been doing nothing of the kind," explained Mr. Clay. "You see, Rose, we expect the Senate will vote on the bill to control states' commerce today."

"Yes, and I am to give a dissertation on the legal aspects of the proposal," added Justice Marshall. "And these great orators are—"

"All we're suggesting is that you eliminate some of the legal details, John," interrupted Mr. Webster, as he passed a large platter of roast duckling and potatoes after helping himself to a generous portion. "Your advice on this matter can be very influential. We don't want you to sacrifice any of its import with too lengthy a discussion."

"That's right, John," Mr. Benton commented as he sipped his mug of coffee. "You know the public has a very short interest span, to say nothing of the senators, present company excepted, of course."

"Thank you, Tom." Senator Calhoun smiled, then addressed Justice Marshall. "Just what is your position on this bill to try and control states' commerce, John?"

"There is no question," said Justice Marshall, "that the Constitution intended for the federal government to extend its power to control commerce between the states."

"If this is done at the expense of the states' rights, I warn you, justice, that I will vote against it," Senator Calhoun replied.

"It is not at the expense of the states," argued Justice Marshall. "Our forefathers could see that such matters as commerce affected every state equally. That is why they felt it must be kept under the control of our federal government to avoid any one state's taking unfair advantage of another."

"It sounds exciting," Rose commented, "and more than likely it will be voted on today. I should truly like to witness the event."

"So, that is your plan," Aunt Hattie interrupted. "You cannot have the carriage, Rose. I have some shopping to do later in the day."

"Oh, I can walk down, Aunt Hattie. It's only a little more than a mile, and if I'm to be cooped up in the Senate gallery all day, the walk will do me good."

"You'll not walk down there by yourself. What will people think?"

"Oh, please, Auntie. After all, I am twenty-one years old. Most girls my age are married and on their own by now."

"Well, we'll see. You just can't be too careful, you know."

The pros and cons of the commerce bill continued to be discussed throughout the morning meal much to the delight of Rose, who eagerly listened to the conversation. Finally Justice Marshall, pulling his gold watch from his vest pocket, exclaimed, "The damn day slips away from you when you're in good company." He pulled back from the table and rose. "I've got to get down to my office and rewrite this speech. Or perhaps I should say, cut out most of it."

Mr. Webster rose quickly. "Wait until I finish my coffee and I'll ride down with you, John. Perhaps I might be able to help you with your speech, that is, if you don't mind."

"I would appreciate it," the justice replied. "Come along." The two men started out of the room.

"I'll drop by later myself, John," said Senator Calhoun. "I'd like to get as much advance knowledge on the subject as I can."

"You're more than welcome, senator. I'll be in my office in the Senate basement all morning. If you wish to come now, there's room in my carriage."

"No, I'll be in later." Mr. Calhoun looked at Rose and smiled. "As a matter of fact, I'll walk down with Rose, if she has no other plans."

Rose's eyes brightened. "Oh, would you, Senator Calhoun?" She turned to her aunt. "There you see, Auntie. Now, you will have nothing to worry about."

"It's lucky for you the senator is gracious enough to have you accompany him." Aunt Hattie nodded her head seriously at her young niece. "Be sure you return well before supper."

With the departure of the two great men, the meal continued with a leisurely discussion of the events of the day. Finally Senator Calhoun said to Rose, "I'm ready to adjourn to the lion's den whenever you are, my dear."

"I'm ready now," Rose said excitedly as she jumped up. "I'll return directly after the vote has been taken, Auntie." She kissed her aunt lightly on the cheek and added, "You're sweet. You're so understanding."

Rose gaily took her bonnet from the umbrella stand, hastily adjusted it in the hall mirror, and slipped her arm in the senator's.

He put his tall silk hat on and they went out into the fresh spring air, Rose taking long steps to keep pace with her escort.

They had gone only a short distance when Senator Calhoun looked at her quizzically. "You seem exceptionally cheerful this morning, Rose. Almost the way of a young girl in love."

"I—I believe I am in love, senator."

"Could it be that good-looking Greenhow fellow over at State?"

"It could be and it is." Rose squeezed his arm in her enthusiasm.

"An excellent choice, Rose. He has a most promising career at State. Vice President Van Buren speaks highly of him."

"It isn't a matter of choice, senator. Rather it is the dictates of my heart. To be truthful, I cannot help myself."

"Does the gentleman in question reciprocate?"

Rose frowned. "It's so difficult to determine what he is really thinking."

"Of course it is. He is a diplomat."

"I should imagine even diplomats show their true feelings when they are in love."

"I do not consider myself an expert in the field, my dear Wild Rose, but shouldn't a young lady in such a position embolden herself, coyly, of course, in order to force the issue?"

"Why, senator, whatever do you mean?"

"No offense, but to paraphrase a current slogan: 'Faint heart never won a battle.'"

"I have thought of that, senator. Of course I don't want to frighten him away."

"I'm sure there must be devious means a pretty young girl can employ to determine a young man's true intent."

"There are many ways as old as the history of man and woman, but ofttimes the consequences do not justify the risks that are taken. Of course, Peggy O'Neale was one of the more fortunate ladies."

"Good heavens, Rose, I would not recommend living with a man before you marry him, as was her choice."

They came to the end of G Street and turned into State. Senator Calhoun helped her step over the ruts in the street and grunted, "I'm sure you can find a more worthy example than that tavernkeeper's unfortunate daughter."

"You forget, senator. I am the daughter of a steeplechase rider and a gambler."

"But you have not besmirched your reputation. If you are wise, my dear, you will not mention her name in the presence of any other ladies, for you will truly suffer dire consequences."

"She is an important person. Her husband is the secretary of

36

war. I am sorry, senator, but I think that she is a very fine woman. I know that your wife has been the leader in snubbing this poor woman, but I think it is most unjust."

Senator Calhoun patted Rose's hand, which rested in the crook of his elbow. "It does not behoove a young girl to sit in judgment of her elders. Whether they are right or wrong is really not the question. If you wish to retain your popularity in proper Washington society you must go along with the majority without a single comment that can be considered detrimental to your character. Forgive me for being frank, my dear, but you will undoubtedly thank me someday."

Rose's face reddened at the peak of her cheekbones, and her dark eyes flashed arrogantly at the senator. "I am sorry, but this country is based on freedom of thought, as well as action. I believe I have every right to think as I please and say what I please and I will do so for the rest of my life."

"You will do well to heed my words." Then, as if abruptly to change the subject, he nodded toward a tall, distinguished man in a white beaver hat walking toward them along the side of the road, picking his way between the ruts with his tasseled cane. "Look yonder, approaching us."

"Why, it's President Jackson," Rose exclaimed excitedly, then immediately changed her attitude and smiled broadly as they came up to him. "Good morning, Mr. President."

"Why, good morning, Rose. And Senator Calhoun." Both men tipped their hats and bowed. "I see you have brought the young lady down to witness the passing of the commerce between the states bill."

"Rose has come to view the debate of the commerce bill, Mr. President."

"Oh, I see. I take it that you are planning a negative vote on the issue."

"I have stated my position many times on the sovereignty of the states, sir. I believe this bill will jeopardize our inalienable rights."

Rose laughed. "Justice Marshall's speech will need to bring

up some very salient points to convince Senator Calhoun to vote for this bill, I fear."

"Is he delivering a speech on the commerce bill today? Well, goddamn—pardon me, Miss O'Neal—but the good justice was in my office just yesterday telling me he was delivering a speech next week before the combined Congress on another legal interpretation of the Constitution. He believes his court has authority to review all federal and state laws to determine their constitutionality. Gad, he's a busy man these days."

"We all are, sir." Senator Calhoun poked out his chin in the gesture that had become so famous with him. "There's a lot to be done."

"Yes, and oh by the way, senator, you were absolutely correct about the tobacco juice stains in some of the White House rooms. They are most unpleasant. I want you to know that I have ordered twenty spittoons for the state parlors. They should be put in place no later than next week."

"Very wise of you, Mr. President. I am sure any visiting ladies will be grateful to you."

"Well, I'll let them know that they have you to thank for it. I never would have thought of it."

"Frankly, neither would I, Mr. President. It was my good wife who brought it up."

President Jackson grimaced. "Just another one of the advantages a married man has over us poor widowers. Speaking of the ladies, I assume that I will be seeing you at Dolly Madison's levee this weekend."

"I sincerely hope so. Mrs. Calhoun and I have a very busy schedule, but we will certainly make an effort to attend."

"I am advised that Secretary Eaton will be inspecting fortifications at Fort Washington in New York so, of course, Peggy O'Neale Eaton will not be attending."

"Thank, you, Mr. President. I shall convey this information to my wife."

"Good." President Jackson sighed. "I do wish you could convince your lovely wife to take a less vigorous stand against

38

Mrs. Eaton, senator. Frankly, she's making such an issue of this it is raising hell with my government. It's practically splitting my Cabinet in two."

"I am sorry, Mr. President. But there are certain basic issues that—"

"Yes. I know—I know. There are certain issues that are worth fighting for as one sees fit." The president chortled. "Gad, battles on the fighting front were never like this." He turned to Rose. "I trust you will be attending, my dear."

"Oh, yes, I am going with Dr. Greenhow."

"Good, I shall see you there, then." President Jackson started to pass by. "Remember me to Mrs. Hill."

"I will, Mr. President."

"I'll be over for one of her marvelous meals someday soon."

"I'll advise her. She will be delighted to have you, sir."

They walked on toward the Capitol steps. "I didn't know you were going to Dolly Madison's levee with Bob Greenhow, Rose. Congratulations. Apparently all is not lost."

"I'm not too sure. You see, Robert doesn't know he is escorting me yet."

"Oh?"

"That is one of the reasons I am so anxious to see him. I don't want to go with anyone else."

Senator Calhoun smiled. "My Wild Rose."

"You wouldn't have me any other way, would you, senator?" She started to climb the long stretch of massive steps. He stopped her.

"I must see Justice Marshall to learn when he will be free. If you will come with me, I shall be glad to take you to the Senate gallery and escort you to the section reserved for senators' families. You will be sure of a seat there."

"That is most gracious of you, Senator Calhoun."

They walked under the steps leading to the main entrance of the Capitol and went down into the basement of the cavernous building. So few rays of the sun filtered through the narrow slits of windows that the hallway leading to the chief justice's

39

office was nearly dark. Although it was broad daylight outside the corridor was dimly lighted with spermaceti candles. Rose made herself comfortable in one of the cushioned sofas placed at intervals along the walls while Senator Calhoun went into Chief Justice Marshall's office. Rose smiled cheerfully at two or three senators' wives who she recognized.

She watched longingly as statesmen walked in and out of the doorway at the end of the hall. It didn't seem fair that only men could enter the Hole in the Wall—the inviting Capitol pub where senators could sustain themselves at any hour by a stiff drink of potent corn or rye whiskey. I'm sure no woman has ever been inside those hallowed portals, she thought to herself, and I think it is grossly unjust. Perhaps one of my friends will someday rectify such a slight to all ladies.

She was interrupted in her thoughts as Senator Calhoun rejoined her. "The justice will be free in fifteen minutes. He is scheduled to deliver his speech at noon. Apparently an attempt is being made to vote on the commerce bill before noonday break. You shouldn't have too long to wait for a decision," he said as he took her arm. They walked up the long double flights of stairs, first to the main Senate chamber, then to the Senate gallery.

Senator Calhoun escorted Rose into the chamber and whispered instructions to the page at the entrance. The senator bid her a cheerful goodbye and watched as the page escorted her to a seat in the front row of the gallery.

The sun had not warmed the spacious Senate chambers as yet and it was cold inside. Rose shivered as she looked down upon the senators huddled in hats and blankets to keep themselves warm. Two rusty wood stoves gave off a sparse amount of heat at each end of the Senate floor. As usual, several senators were standing beside the stoves, their backs to the fire, rubbing their hands. At frequent intervals a page would hastily open the grated iron doors and throw a quantity of split logs into the belly of the stove.

The senator from New Jersey was expounding the virtues of

40

the proposed bill. When he had finished, the senators moved back and forth exchanging comments, some of them furiously waving their hands in the air to emphasize a point. Shortly after the senior senator from Virginia had taken the stand to talk, Rose spied Senator Calhoun entering the chambers. He turned and looked up at her. She leaned over the railing and waved. Senator Calhoun smiled.

Precisely at noon, Justice Marshall entered. A polite round of applause followed him as he strode majestically to the front of the great hall.

His speech was surprisingly short, and Rose strained to hear every word. Justice Marshall described the pending bill in glowing terms and gave his legal opinion that the Constitution as written assured the federal government's control of all commerce between states. As he finished, there was another round of applause. Rose noted that Senator Calhoun was only lightly applauding.

During another lengthy pause, the senators scurried back and forth to speak to their colleagues and argue among themselves, calling to pages from time to time to run errands for them. Finally Vice President Van Buren, as presiding officer of the Senate, tapped his gavel and called for a vote on the proposed legislation. The senators' voices could plainly be heard as each cast his vote when his name was monotonously intoned by the clerk. Senator Calhoun voted a resounding "Nay" when his name was called. Rose noted that neither the justice's speech nor the persuasions of his colleagues had changed his mind.

It was nearly an hour later that the clerk announced the results of the vote: "Voting Aye, thirty-one, voting Nay, seventeen. The proposed bill extending the power of the United States government to control all commerce between any and all of the states becomes law."

A loud cheer arose from the Senate floor, augmented by many voices in the gallery. The will of the people had been accomplished. The southern senators had voted almost unanimously against the bill. Once again a sovereign right of the states, defended so vigorously by the South, had been soundly defeated. In celebration of the rapid passage of the bill, Vice President Van Buren adjourned the Senate for the balance of the day.

Rose walked slowly out of the gallery, being pushed along toward the exit by the departing crowd. As she came down to the main lobby, she caught sight of Senator Calhoun and waved to him, but she could not get his attention and in the crowd it was impossible to reach him.

Once again outside on the Capitol grounds, she stood watching the departing crowd. It was thrilling to witness the evolving of the laws that were to govern the country. She turned and gazed at the Capitol, with its flag of thirteen stripes and twenty-four stars waving in the breeze. In spite of its rapid expansion, Rose thought to herself, those congressmen can move swiftly when they are of a mind to. It generally took many days of quibbling and negotiating to secure enough votes to pass a bill. The Commerce Bill today was introduced and voted upon before noonday break, as Senator Calhoun had predicted.

It is most encouraging for the country, Rose thought, but almost a disaster for me. She was confronted with still half of the day and nothing of import to occupy her. She casually walked down the street beside the Capitol and stopped at a small cafe. She ordered a small plate of a special mixture of terrapin and fried oysters covered with a spicy sauce. It was one of her favorite dishes and she ordered it often, despite its exorbitant cost of thirty-five cents.

She finally finished her delicacy and was about to start for home when a sudden thought struck her. Her wandering had taken her to within a block of the State Department building. She would surprise Robert Greenhow with a visit! Of course, it was unheard of, for no lady was ever seen in any government office, except on rare occasions when business demanded it. But she was so anxious to see Robert, and if he really did care

42

for her he would be glad to see her. What was it that Senator Calhoun had said? "Faint heart never won a battle."

She did have some misgivings as she walked into the massive hallway of the State Department. Robert might be so shocked by her boldness that his embarrassment would cause just the opposite effect to what she had intended. She forced herself to approach the young man sitting at a desk beside the double doors at the entrance.

"Can you advise me where the office of Dr. Robert Greenhow is located?" she asked boldly.

"Oh, yes ma'am, he is on the second floor. If you will take those stairs and turn left, you will find his office off the first door to the right."

She thanked him, and trying to act casual, started up the marble steps. Her self-assurance was slightly disturbed as she climbed the winding stairway and caught a glimpse of the young man below watching her progress in utter amazement.

She entered the first door to the right and found herself in a large room with several desks occupied by men of all ages, most of them wearing dark green shades over their foreheads. The room was completely paneled in oak, with an occasional door opening into a private office. A short, balding man looked startled as he noticed her and hastily came over. Squinting behind heavy gold-rimmed glasses, he asked, "May I be of any assistance?"

"I should like to see Dr. Greenhow," she said, hoping that he could not detect the weakness in her voice. He looked at her so forcefully that she cast a quick glance at her dress to be sure it was in order.

"What country may I say is involved?"

"I beg your pardon?"

"What country may I tell him you are representing?"

"Oh, I—I am representing myself."

"I understand," the gentleman said in a manner that indicated that he did not understand at all. Obviously this wizened little fellow had never before been confronted with a young lady "representing herself" in the many years of his tenure at the State Department.

He politely pointed to one of the paneled private offices and said quietly so no one could hear him, "That is Dr. Greenhow's office on the right, but he isn't in at the present time."

Rose smiled her most bewitching smile. "Would you know where he is at the present time?"

The man cleared his throat and ran his finger around his stiff collar, which was not at all tight. "I think he is with Mr. Forsythe." The little man indicated by his tone that he considered the statement sufficient excuse not to interrupt Dr. Greenhow for any reason.

Rose had not gone this far to be deterred in her mission. She came closer to the man and adjusted her bonnet. "Oh, the secretary of state. I am so glad to see that Dr. Greenhow consorts with the most important people. Would you be so kind as to tell him that Miss O'Neal is here to see him?"

"I—I don't know whether I should, Miss O'Neal. You see something has come up that necessitated his conferring with the secretary of state. I know that it is urgent."

"It is also urgent that I see him, Mr.—"

"Doaks. John Doaks. You see, I work for Dr. Greenhow."

"How interesting, Mr. Doaks. You may rest assured that I will tell Dr. Greenhow how considerate you have been of me."

"That will be very nice, Miss O'Neal. I shall see if I can find him." He turned and started to go.

"Mr. Doaks," Rose called quickly. As he stopped she asked sweetly, "Do you think Dr. Greenhow would mind if I waited for him in his office?"

"Oh, no. Not at all." He turned back and bade her follow him into Robert Greenhow's office. Pulling a cushioned armchair around he gestured for her to be seated. "Please make yourself comfortable, Miss O'Neal. I shall be gone only a short time."

He went to the door and turned around just before he disappeared from view. His worried look indicated he was hoping that Rose would change her mind, that perhaps she would give him a reprieve from his unofficially assigned duty, but she continued to stare sweetly at him. Smiling weakly, he departed.

Rose was not too sure that this was such a good idea. Mr. Doaks's actions did not encourage her in the least. She brushed the wrinkles out of her dress. She looked around the room. It was a spacious room, evidencing the importance the State Department placed in Robert. She was glad of that. She could never fall in love with anyone who was mediocre. A large mahogany desk behind which there was a high leather upholstered chair commanded one corner of the room. There were several papers on the desk, spaced in neat piles. She had known this was the way Robert's desk would look.

Only a moment or two had elapsed since Mr. Doaks had left, but it seemed an interminable time to Rose. She got up and walked to the large, heavily draped window. A beautiful view of Washington formed a panorama before her. She could clearly see the massive Washington Monument, half-completed, rising majestically over all the buildings. From this distance she could still see the different shades of granite stone. She remembered that there was a stone from every state in the Union represented there and wondered which one of them was from her beloved state of Maryland. She also recalled hearing the politicians at Aunt Hill's discuss the problems that had arisen in financing the monument, so that it was still not completed.

As Robert still did not put in an appearance, she began to feel nervous. She thought for a moment of leaving but her desire to see him quickly overcame that idea. Turning back to the office, she glanced once again at Robert's desk. Trying to control her nervousness, she walked over and sat in his chair. It was most comfortable, despite the fact that when she leaned back her feet could not touch the floor. Robert was much taller than she and that was good. She picked up a group of long, clearly handwritten papers and looked furtively at them. The heading

45

intrigued her: *Conte Federico Confalonieri.*

She eagerly read on. Conte Confalonieri was apparently a noted Italian nationalist. After the Piedmontero revolt, the Austrians had arrested him. There was proof that he had been tortured in prison. None of this affair involved the United States. The Austrians had indicated they would pardon him, but only into exile. He was requesting permission to come to the United States. Rose was so deeply engrossed in the story that she did not realize it was nearly fifteen minutes before Robert finally came in.

As he entered, he looked at Rose in amazement. "Rose!" he exclaimed, surprised.

Dropping the papers she quickly stood up, and coming over to him took his hands in hers. "You seem surprised, Robert?"

"I am."

"Didn't Mr. Doaks tell you that I was here?"

Robert laughed. "He did that. The poor man was beside himself. But he said that it was Miss Peggy O'Neale who wished to see me, John Eaton's wife. I couldn't imagine what she would want of me."

"It must have given you a bit of a fright."

"It did. I shall have to tell Mr. Forsythe which Miss O'Neal wanted to see me, so he won't be getting any wrong ideas."

"*You* had better not get any wrong ideas either about that woman, Robert Greenhow."

Robert laughed. "You don't think I'd have anything to do with that hussy, do you?"

"I note you have been listening to Mrs. Calhoun's stories about that poor woman."

There was an awkward pause as they stood opposite each other.

"Well, Robert," Rose finally said as she looked up at him. "Aren't you glad to see me?"

"You can be sure that I am." He bent down and kissed her hand. "Oh, Rose, I've thought of you so often these last few days. It seems an eternity since I last saw you."

"It's been over a week. I had begun to think you had forgotten all about me."

He looked deeply into her eyes and took her chin in his hands. "No man who ever knows you can ever forget you," he said affectionately.

"But they say actions speak louder than words, Robert, and I've been so lonesome waiting at home."

"I know, Rose. It's only that something important has come up and the whole matter has been dumped in my lap."

She brushed a stray hair from his coat. "The Confalonieri affair?"

"Yes, how did you—" then he remembered she had been at his desk when he came in. "Rose, you were reading my file on this case."

"Is it unforgivable, Robert?" she asked coyly as she sat down in the chair Mr. Doaks had offered her. "You were so long in coming back to your office. And I was getting more nervous by the minute. The papers were out in plain sight and I—well, frankly it was most intriguing reading. Please forgive me."

He placed his hand tightly on her shoulder. "There are none of my affairs that you cannot have free access to, if you wish." He looked at her seriously and leaned closer. Suddenly he realized that his office door was open and quickly drew himself away from her.

He went to the door and started to close it, then turned to her. "I suppose being in my office behind a closed door might compromise a young lady."

"Not if it is by mutual consent." She smiled at him roguishly.

Quietly he closed the door. But he did not go to his own chair behind his desk. Instead he came over beside Rose and sat on the arm of her chair.

"You don't know how happy I am to see you, Rose."

"I'm so glad. Believe me, it took a great deal of determination to come here. While I was alone in your office, I

47

almost decided to leave."

"I'm certainly glad that you didn't." He put his arm around the back of her chair. "But tell me, what is the occasion that is sufficiently important for you to ignore all proprieties and traditions?"

"Well, the first item is Aunt Dolly's levee this Saturday evening."

"This Saturday evening. My, this is rather short notice."

"It would have been much longer notice, Dr. Greenhow, if I had seen you before!"

"Touché, Miss O'Neal. I shall make it a point to accompany you there."

"You may drive by for me about three o'clock."

Robert drew out a small pad from inside his waistcoat pocket and made a note. "I look forward to this with the greatest pleasure. What else do you have on that active little mind of yours?"

"Nothing else really, excepting—"

"Yes, Rose?"

"Oh, Robert, you said I have been on your mind so much throughout this week that we have not seen each other, but I have no way of knowing this unless you tell me."

"I know, Rose. It is true I have thought of you constantly. I wish there were some way we could rectify the situation, but honestly, Rose, Secretary Forsythe is giving me more and more responsibility. I'm flattered, but it's become necessary for me to be working here all hours of the day and night. I haven't done any writing in nearly a month and you know that is— well, that is my second love. I want to see you more. I'm miserable every day that I don't see you. I honestly don't know what I can do about it."

"There is one thing that you can do." She laid her hand gently on his arm.

"What is that? Tell me."

Rose impatiently drew her arm away from him and looked away. "Good heavens, Robert, must I be the one to make every

48

suggestion . . . even those that could affect the rest of our lives?"

Robert slapped his leg soundly. "My God, Rose, how utterly stupid of me." Softly he turned her head to him and leaned close to her. "I love you, Rose." He drew her closer to him and kissed her gently on her upturned cheek. Then more swiftly, he crushed her to him and kissed her again fully on her lips. His passion quickly roused her as she closed her eyes and put her arms around him.

"Oh, Robert, if you only could know how I have dreamed of this moment for so long." Slowly she stood up and he followed her, never releasing his hold on her. Instead he drew her against him until their whole bodies touched.

"Rose, my darling, will you marry me?"

She was tantalizing as she smiled up at him. "I'm so glad that you didn't force me to ask you."

He put his arms around her and their lips met. Passionately, almost savagely, he pressed her closer to him and kissed her hungrily. The pent-up emotions that had been suppressed so long inside him were suddenly released. He could feel her body giving in to him. They kissed again fervently, with a passion which Rose had never experienced before. They stood for a long time with their breasts pressed together. Slowly, tenderly his hand dropped to her breast. His hand shook as he pressed it feverishly. Then he bent down and kissed her breast.

Suddenly he pulled away from her. "My God, Rose, what am I doing? This is the middle of the day. I am in my office."

Rose's only response was to smile tenderly and stare languidly up at him with a faraway, transparent look in her eyes. "It is so sweet, I hope that it will never end."

"We shall have the rest of our lives together, my sweet." Then he looked at the closed door that shut them away from the rest of the world. "I shall have to marry you, you know, now that you have been so boldly compromised in my office!"

"Is the thought distasteful to you, Robert?"

"No, excepting you have never told me you loved me as I

49

have you."

She drew his head down to hers and her lips parted as she pressed them to his. Her cheeks were flaming as they met in a passionate embrace. Without moving away from him she unbuttoned the three top buttons covering her breast. Gently taking his hand she guided it inside of her dress and pressed her bare breast to his hand. Then she savagely threw both her arms about him and pressed herself so close to him she could feel the tenseness of every muscle in his body. They swayed back and forth, her lips inside his, her body in perfect motion with his until in one estatic moment she could feel him rigidly press against her in one final spasm. Their fast breathing came in short gasps. For one beautiful moment they were one. They stood motionless, exhausted, until finally he drew himself away from her. Slowly, unashamedly, she buttoned the three buttons of her dress and looked up at him with adoration in her eyes.

"Does this tell you how much I love you?"

"Yes, my loved one," he said, his voice shaking. Then he kissed her again soft, gently.

IV

The Election

Robert Greenhow had been uncertain about requesting Mrs.
Hill's permission to marry Rose. Rose assured him that there
would be no objection. She was correct. Aunt Hattie was
delighted to have Rose marry. She liked Dr. Greenhow, but
more than that she was relieved to have Rose settle down. Rose
was such an impetuous girl. She loved life and lived it to its
full, just as her father had done all his life. More than once
Aunt Hattie was disturbed to note the similarity between them.
Obviously, Rose was going to drain every bit of pleasure from
life that it could hold for her, just as her father had done before
her. But he was a man, and Rose's being a woman made the
situation an entirely different matter, and while Rose was
under Aunt Hattie's roof, she was Aunt Hattie's responsibility.

When Dolly Madison learned of Rose's intended marriage
plans she insisted that Rose and Robert be married at her
country home, the Hermitage. She also offered them her
mansion for their honeymoon, and she herself returned to
Washington so they could spend blissful hours in complete
privacy.

They had intended to stay two weeks, but Rose was so
anxious to set up housekeeping that Robert finally agreed to
return to Washington after the first week of their honeymoon.
Rose was determined that the seat of the federal government
would be the center of her activities, and she found a cozy little

house on F Street much closer to the Capitol than Mrs. Hill's

Her marriage to Robert Greenhow gave Rose the most enjoyable years of her young life. They entertained extensively. John Calhoun was a constant visitor; and many members of the Senate, the House of Representatives, the Supreme Court, and President Van Buren (who had succeeded Jackson in the presidency) and his Cabinet were known to enjoy the Greenhows' gracious parties.

Rose made it a particular point to entertain any of the foreign dignitaries who visited the United States.

"It will help you rise in the State Department, Robert," Rose remarked as they sat on the divan in their parlor on one of those rare nights when they were alone and Robert was not working.

"I'm satisfied doing just what I am."

Rose was astounded. "Robert," she replied aghast. "Where is your ambition?"

"Ambition has killed many a person."

"It will not kill me. I won't stop until Robert Greenhow's name is on the lips of every important person in Washington. And they will also know that Rose Greenhow is his loyal, energetic helpmate."

"And ambitious, my pretty little coquette."

"Ambition is not a crime, Robert."

"I wonder." He put his arm around his beloved wife and sighed. "For my part I will be satisfied just to have more time for my writing."

Rose snuggled up to him. "I read your work on Tripoli today, Robert. It is an exceptionally fine treatise."

"Thank you."

"Would you mind if I made a suggestion?"

"Please believe me—I am not one of those egotistical, vain writers who flies into uncontrollable rages when anyone suggests that a word he has put on paper for posterity could possibly be in error. I welcome criticism."

"I believe there could be more description of the port in

52

Tripoli and its importance to the rest of the countries of the Mediterranean."

Robert's brow furrowed in deep thought as he contemplated her suggestion. Presently he pinched his lower lip and smiled. "You know, Rose, you are correct. Tripoli is so familiar to me I forget that a certain amount of description is necessary for the average reader to picture the area I have in mind." He put his hand on his wife's lap. "You have a keen analytical mind, Rose. You can be of great assistance in my projects."

"I would love to do that, Robert. I have studied the English language considerably, and I could correct your grammar and edit your works. At least," she added enthusiastically, "you will have another person's opinion before you take your book to a publisher. Tell me, Robert, what are you working on now?"

"I have two projects equally advanced. Kendrick's passage through Ruca'a Strait, and the seizure of the *Argonaut* voyages of La Perouse, based on my visits to those places."

"It must be wonderful to travel to foreign countries."

"It's fascinating, Rose. It gives you an entirely new outlook on life."

"I hope we may visit some other countries someday, Robert."

"I will let you in on a little secret, my darling. President Van Buren is anxious to clear up the Mexican border disputes. He has instructed John Forsythe to send someone to Mexico to investigate all territorial boundary claims. Since the president knows I have an extensive background in boundary research, he has recommended that I go."

"Oh, Robert, and if you do go, may I accompany you?"

"By all means."

Rose threw her arms around her husband. "Wouldn't that be exciting? I have never visited Mexico. I shall do my best to make it happen."

Rose had every intention of inviting the president and John Forsythe to her next soiree to influence their decision in favor of sending Robert to Mexico. But it seemed that the country had many more pressing problems and Robert advised her that the settlement of the Mexican boundary disputes was indefinitely delayed.

Finally, as Van Buren's term of office drew to a close and no action had been taken on the Mexican boundaries, the matter was once again brought up. When Robert mentioned it, Rose decided immediately that she must waste no time in seeing that he would be the one selected for the mission.

Shortly afterward an ideal opportunity presented itself. Conte Federico Confalonieri had been granted asylum in the United States and she quickly volunteered to host a reception in his honor to which she invited both the president and his secretary of state.

The reception was a success, described by the Washington *Daily Morning Chronicle* as one of the finest social events of the season. But it proved a personal disappointment for Rose. She had taken particular pains to talk to both the president and the secretary, individually and together, impressing upon them Robert's expertise in resolving disputed land claims.

Mr. Forsythe not only agreed that Robert Greenhow was one of his most able men, he described his abilities in glowing terms. As a matter of fact, he assured the president that Dr. Greenhow could not be spared from the State Department, since trouble was brewing with both France and Great Britain because of the boundary disputes in the far western Pacific territories.

Rose was extremely disappointed, but Robert assured her in his calm fashion that it was for the best and that something better would surely come along.

Rose was determined that she was going to make something better come along and confided her plans to Robert one night when she had invited their good friend, John Calhoun, to their home for a small private dinner.

"As you know, Robert, John Calhoun is becoming an extremely important man in our government. One to whom we an hitch our wagon and succeed in receiving important rewards. Such as going to Paris, or some other European capital, not to resolve boundary disputes, but as ambassador."

"He is important, Rose, but hardly in a position to dictate who will be ambassador to any European country."

"He would be if he were president."

"Oh, Rose, that's impossible."

"Nothing is impossible, Robert darling. With the election coming up next year it will behoove us to become active in the campaign. The new president cannot help but show his appreciation by granting us some little favor we might request."

"But Rose, Van Buren will undoubtedly run again. They do not call him the Little Magician—"

"Shhh, quiet," Rose interrupted him as the door gong sounded. "Let us wait and see."

Rose went to the door and graciously ushered John Calhoun into their parlor. "Please sit down," she said. "My goodness, John, you do look exhausted."

"I am," he said wearily as he slumped down on their sofa. "I've lost another battle with Van Buren over the United States Bank. When Jackson throws his support behind Van Buren they make a combination that can't be beaten."

"Politics can be so unnerving. But I have just the antidote for you." She went to a large silver container and poured three tall glasses of a dark, frothy concoction. Handing two of the glasses to the men, she said, "This will make you forget the cares of the world."

"What is it?"

"A Queen Charlotte Cocktail. It is my new specialty."

As Calhoun quaffed a long, hefty draft of the drink, he smiled. "This is delicious. You shall have to show me how they are made."

"I shall be glad to. But best be careful of them, John, they are potent."

"And relaxing. I could stand a bit of relaxation after my

constant battle with the administration. It gets discouraging.'

"But promise me you will never give up."

"I won't."

"What are they pressuring you about now?" asked Robert

He drained his glass and smacked his lips. "It's the damn Tariff Act again. As you may recall, I sponsored an ordinance in my state of South Carolina nullifying the loathsome tariff burden in our state."

"A marvelous piece of legislation," Rose commented. "It placed the state in a position to resist the federal government if they attempted to implement that horrible act."

"Unfortunately the president has succeeded in having a force bill introduced into the Senate authorizing the use of the armed forces if necessary to enforce the laws."

"Why, that is unconstitutional," said Rose indignantly.

"What countermeasures do you plan?" Robert asked.

"Why not suggest that the state convention adopt a resolution nullifying the force bill?" volunteered Rose.

"That's exactly what I have proposed. But Henry Clay got wind of it and introduced a new tariff bill that is acceptable to South Carolina."

"Then it's a victory for you," Rose said.

"Only temporarily. They will come back with more legislation some day, again limiting states' rights."

"It is a vicious circle," Rose commented as Calhoun stared silently before him.

"It's gotten so bad that my wife, Floride, has left Washington with all of our nine children. She says she needs the quiet of Fort Hill to keep her senses about her and tells me I had better do the same."

"Oh, how dreadful."

"In a way, I can't blame her. Fort Hill is much to be preferred for bringing up young children."

At that moment their house slave, Randy, appeared to announce that dinner was ready, whereupon the three of them

56

retired to the dining room to feast on roast of mutton, kidney gravy, creamed potatoes, and little white onions and green peas sautéed in a deep butter sauce. All of this was appropriately washed down with an ancient vintage of imported Madeira wine.

But the move to the dining room did not conclude their political discussion, as was Rose's plan.

"John, there is only one way that you can gain sufficient strength to carry out your program. You must run for president next year."

Calhoun shook his head. "No, I do not have sufficient backing. It would be impossible to defeat Van Buren."

Rose cast a hasty glance at her husband. "Nothing is impossible. The country is ready for a change, which you can provide."

"God knows I want to, Rose, but—"

"We'll help all we can," Rose replied.

"I know you will. And you can give me a great deal of help. I'll need an organization. I'll have to have a good number of papers in every state behind me."

"I could help there," volunteered Robert. "After all, I am editor of the *Petersburg Republican*. That's one paper you can count on immediately."

"Damned helpful of you, Robert. Forgive me, but that is only one paper. I need a paper in every major city."

"I'll approach them for you."

"How could you?" Calhoun interjected. "You are too tied down at State."

"I'll take a leave of absence."

Rose gasped in amazement. "Robert, would you?"

"Of course I would. I can begin next month."

"We could be sure of support in Arkansas," Rose said enthusiastically. "They are below the Mason-Dixon line, and this is the first presidential election they have had an opportunity to vote in."

57

A gleam of enthusiasm shone in Calhoun's eyes. "By God, it's worth a try!" Calhoun banged his fist on the dining room table.

"Of course, it is. I told you the people of this country need a change," said Rose, elated.

"Yes, but do the people know it?"

"Perhaps not now," Robert interjected, "but they surely will when we get through telling them about your program." Calhoun reached his hands across the table and grasped each of theirs. "It does a man's heart good to have fine friends such as you."

"Since Floride is in South Carolina with your children, I know it will get terribly lonely for you in your house," Rose remarked.

Calhoun grimaced. "It's like a morgue already, and they've been gone only three days."

"You must come and live with us. It will be simpler to keep in touch with each other and discuss our problems."

"I couldn't impose on you like that."

"It doesn't have to be permanent. Only a few weeks. And I assure you that it is no imposition to house the future president of the United States."

"All right, I'll do it. But I don't know how I can ever repay you."

"Don't give it a second thought. We'll find a way, won't we Robert?"

"I'm sure we will." They smiled at each other as Calhoun looked at his watch.

"Goddamn, do you folks realize it is nearly eleven o'clock? I must be going. I have a big day tomorrow." Calhoun sighed. "We all will be having big days ahead of us."

They saw Calhoun to the door and bade him goodnight after making arrangements to meet the following day to lay plans for Robert's proposed visits to other states.

As they were undressing for bed Rose asked quite casually, "Robert, do you anticipate any difficulty in being granted time away from State?"

"I don't give a damn, Rose. I need some time off. I had no vacation this year. I have only had our three annual holidays and very few Sundays."

He lay on his back for a moment staring into the darkness. "I guess this is the end of my writing career. Perhaps forever."

"It will only be a delay, Robert, and it will be worth it. This can open up a whole new world for us."

"I don't want a whole new world." He put his arms around her and drew her close to him. "I have you, and I am well established in the State Department. And I have my writing. Only I don't have my writing anymore. As my friend Lord Byron once said to me, 'The only way one can succeed in writing is to write. There is no other way.'"

"Robert, were you friendly with Lord Byron?"

"Intimately, Rose. I stayed with him at Newstead Abbey while he worked on *Don Juan.*"

Rose sat up in bed, breaking herself away from his grasp. "Robert, what are you saying?"

"Darling, my knowing Lord Byron is no cause for you to be so upset."

"Robert, you know better. Lord Byron is a roué. It's common knowledge even here in America that he has had attachments with many women."

"Is that a fact?"

Rose found his hair in the dark and tugged at it roughly. "Robert Greenhow, don't you tease me so. Tell me, did you ever go out with him on any of his notorious escapades?"

"My goodness, Rose, are you jealous?"

"You can be assured I am jealous. I damn well better know about your relations with that man's several concubines."

Robert laughed. "Darling, I have never before heard you swear an oath. Actually, I believe it becomes you." Then he added seriously, "To be sure Lord Byron had a dreadful reputation, but that was before I knew him. When I stayed at his estate, he had formed a liaison with Contessa Teresa

Guiccioli, and actually she's been his mistress ever since."

"But he's not married to her."

"No, I'll admit that, but he's as faithful to her as if he were."

Once again he drew her to him and slowly pulled the straps of her nightgown down below her waist. Softly, gently he held her breasts in his hands, and leaning over her, kissed them both. "Now let's forget Lord Byron and everyone else in the wide world, and tell me that you love me."

"Yes, I love you. If men were only a bit more observant you could see how much I love you."

"What do you mean?"

She took his hand from her breast and lowered it beneath her nightgown until it rested on her bare stomach.

"Feel this, Robert." Suddenly there was an unmistakable movement beneath her flesh. Startled, he drew his hand away.

"Rose, are you telling me—"

"Haven't you noticed that I have been getting fat all in one place?"

"We're going to have a baby!"

"Of course we are, silly. Are you glad?"

"Oh, Rose, you've made me the happiest man in the world!" It was Robert's turn to sit up. Then he took her in his arms and kissed her over and over again tenderly, feeling her warm body pressed so close to him. Suddenly he stopped and turned his back to her. "What am I doing? I shall have to be more careful. I don't suppose we'll—well—I assume we won't be able to show our love for each other until after the baby is born."

Rose turned his body to her and pulled the pants of his pajamas apart so vigorously she tore off his waist button. She pressed her body to his and squirmed ecstatically against him. With sudden added strength, she pushed him over on his back and placed her body on top of his. Searching in the dark she found what, at that moment, was the most important part of him and deftly placed it inside of her. With complete, utter abandon, she moved her whole body up and down until he picked up her rhythm and moved in time with her. Her firm

60

breasts pressed hard against him, her round buttocks brought him ever deeper and deeper within her, gyrating continually faster and faster until in one glorious moment they became rigid and the fruits of his passion became marvelously intermingled with her own. She lay on top of him for a short while, panting and feeling his hot breath against her face.

It was several moments after they had both been delightfully satisfied that she rolled away from him and, in complete exhaustion, whispered in a hardly audible voice, "Don't you imagine for an instant that you can deprive me of the greatest pleasure of my life because I am having your baby." She kissed him gently on the mouth and ran her tongue fervently between his warm lips and added quietly, "Do you want a girl or a boy, my sweet?"

"I should prefer a girl, darling, but I understand that there is an equal chance it might be a boy."

"I shall make every effort to deliver you a bouncing baby girl."

Suddenly he turned to her again. "Rose, how could you have sat there at the dinner table this evening and made all those plans to promote John Calhoun for the presidency when you knew all along that you would not be able to participate?"

"But why not?"

"When ladies have babies don't they retire from all outside activities until well after the baby is born?"

"Yes, some women do. But, Robert, don't you know that I am not that kind of woman?"

He smiled in the darkness, put his arm around her and kissed her gently. "My Wild Rose," he said fondly.

The next few days were busy ones for Rose. Hurried preparations were made for Robert to start on his journey in behalf of their good friend's quest for the presidency. It was with a bit of difficulty that Robert secured a leave of absence from the State Department for three months. Robert was the foremost authority in the United States government on boundaries, the natural features of North America, its coastlines, mountains, climates, and rivers. Such information was becoming more and more important as the country began to grow and additional states were carved out to take their places in the Union. He finally succeeded in securing his leave be agreeing to contact the State Department at least every two weeks, and consenting to stay there for a day or two if any problems of an emergency nature should arise.

It was not until the very day Robert was scheduled to leave for Virginia and then a brief tour of the Southwest, after John Calhoun had temporarily moved into their home, that Robert became aware of what was actually happening in his household.

"Good glory," he said to Rose as he was packing his valise. "I will be gone from here for a week at a time—sometimes more."

"I'll miss you dreadfully, dear," Rose said, longingly putting her arm around his shoulder. "I don't care how busy you are, I expect you to write every day, or at the least every two days."

"I will and I'll miss you. But that isn't what I am referring to."

"I don't understand."

"Do you realize that you will be all alone with another man in our house?"

"Oh, John Calhoun is old enough to be my father."

"Fathers have been known to have affairs, you know."

"Why, Robert, I do believe you are jealous."

"I'll admit it. I only repeat your own words, I damn well better know what your relations are with that man."

"You can put your mind at ease, Robert. The Senate will be in recess for two weeks and John is planning to go back to Fort Hill for a visit with his family. Then he is going to tour some of the southern states to get their reaction to his running for president."

"Good!"

"He will only be at our house for one or two nights the entire time you are gone. If it will make you feel better I could go over to Aunt Hattie's when he is here."

"No, I'm being foolish, Rose. It's just—well, I know what I've got, and if any other man realizes how wonderful you are, he might want to share some of my happiness."

"You're sweet, Robert."

"Some people will talk, you know."

"Let them. We will know the truth."

They embraced and Robert was off. John Calhoun was not at Rose's home for one single night while Robert was away. As Rose had anticipated the senator was on the road feeling the pulse of the public—his public in his beloved southern states.

It was nearly three weeks before the three of them were to meet at the Greenhow house again, and a great deal of the enthusiasm and joy for their project had waned.

"It was the same everywhere I went," Robert sighed, weary and worn from his trying journey and the excruciating schedule that he had maintained for himself.

"What was it, Robert?" asked Rose.

He looked at her with haunted, hollowed eyes from lack of sleep. "None of the papers would come out and say that they would back John Calhoun for president."

"But that is incredible. They know what he has done for our country."

"They were polite enough. They would listen attentively to what I had to say, then, almost without exception, they would say, 'What is wrong with Van Buren?' Or if they believed we needed a change their comment was, 'Why not elect a Whig?'"

"I can't believe what you are saying."

Calhoun leaned back in their comfortable parlor chair and sighed. "I can. I got the same reaction in the South. People who voted for me in my own state told me frankly that I could do more for them as their senator than if I were president of all the states."

"You're not giving up, are you?" Rose asked increduously.

"No, but I'm getting damned discouraged," Calhoun frowned.

63

"Let's try once more to see if there is a more agreeable feeling in the western states," Robert suggested.

Trying to bolster each other's morale, they began to make plans for Robert's next foray. "I'll go to Arkansas and then swing over to Missouri and through Illinois and Indiana," Robert said pointing to the states on a map he drew from his pocket.

"Good," Calhoun agreed seriously. "By then we shall be able to tell where we stand and what my next move should be."

"Believe me, I will do my utmost to convince them." Robert shook his head for emphasis.

"I know you will, Robert." Calhoun smiled wanly.

The following morning Robert fondly kissed his wife goodbye and was off again on his second tour of the country in behalf of John Calhoun. After a little more than a week he cut his journey short and returned home.

"It is no use, Rose," he said solemnly. "The papers will not budge. There wasn't one of them I approached who did not have the greatest respect for John Calhoun and his dedication to the country, but most of them are still satisfied with Van Buren. They claim they know their readers and what the people want. Consistently those who really want to see a change say the only way that this can be accomplished is by voting a Whig into office. When I ask them which Whig, they can't suggest a likely candidate." Robert bowed his head in his hands and moaned a tired, helpless groan.

"Have you seen John since you returned?" she asked with a certain bit of resignation.

"I saw him this morning. He is going to announce his candidacy for another term as senior senator from South Carolina."

"Then it is final."

"I have already been down to State and told them I am cutting my leave of absence short and will return to work the beginning of next week. They knew what I was doing. I did not tell them, but it would be a rather inefficient State Department if they didn't know what was going on in their own country as well as everywhere else in the world."

Rose sighed. She had learned a very valuable lesson that would stand her in good stead the rest of her life. She vowed she would never again try to influence the thinking or the politics of the unfathomable voting public. She would let them choose whomever they wished. Then she would become friendly with their choice and thus accomplish her own ends.

"I shall go down tomorrow morning and offer to assist President Van Buren in his upcoming campaign."

Tired and worn as he was, Robert could not conceal his astonishment. "Rose, you can't do that!"

"Why not?"

"The elections are still four months away. You're pregnant, Rose. You'll be having the baby just about the time the presidency is decided. People will laugh at you."

"People will not laugh at Rose O'Neal Greenhow. Not if they know what is good for them," she said as she drew her lips firmly together and a sparkling, flashing look came into her dark eyes.

"All right, Rose. But be careful. I don't want you to do anything that will be harmful for you or the baby."

Rose smiled determinedly. "It will be good for the baby, Robert. It will give it early training in what can be expected from its mother and what he or she can look forward to while growing up."

So it was that the next morning Rose dressed hastily and left the house before Robert was up.

Instead of going to her beloved Senate chambers, she went directly to the White House. She was able to see Angelica Singleton Van Buren, the president's daughter-in-law and official White House hostess in the absence of the president's wife, who had died before he took office.

"This is an unexpected pleasure, Rose." Angelica greeted her warmly, trying vainly to conceal her astonishment as she ushered Rose into the Green Room of the White House.

"Thank you, Angelica. I would like to see President Van Buren if it is at all possible."

"That will be difficult this morning, Rose. You see he i meeting with a group of constituents from New York who ar forming a club on his behalf to help him seek another term o office."

"But that is what I wish to see him about. I want to join hi campaign."

"But I thought—"

Rose smiled casually. "You have heard that Senato Calhoun is thinking of running for president. Of course, if h did, our friendship would demand that I support him. But h has decided that the people of South Carolina need him as thei senator and he is bowing to their wishes. Under th circumstances I can think of no one I would rather see at th head of our government for another four years than you father-in-law."

"This is quite a surprise, Rose. And I'm sure papa Van Buren will be most happy to hear of your decision." She glanced at her watch which dangled from a delicate gold chain around her neck. "It's nearly ten o'clock and that is the time they were scheduled to meet." She got up abruptly from her chair. "Will you excuse me for a moment? I shall see if I can catch the president before he begins his meeting."

She disappeared into the hall and Rose caught a glimpse of her going up the spacious stairs to the president's private living quarters. Rose looked about the ornate room and sighed. It was beautiful and so stately. Truly, it was an appropriate reception room for visiting ambassadors and heads of state from the older countries of Europe, as well as for the rough and ready men who came to the Capitol from the backwoods states of Oklahoma, Kentucky, and Tennessee, and the territories of the far West. She smiled whimsically to herself as the thought struck her that only a few days ago she had been planning to visit the White House in the fall with one of her closest friends ensconced there as head of this great country. Quickly she brushed the thought from her mind. What was to be would be and she was determined to make the best of it.

She was interrupted in her thoughts as Angelica came into the room.

"Papa Van Buren was delighted to learn that you will join his campaign, Rose, as I was sure he would be."

"Very good. May I see him?"

"He thought it might be well if you joined the group this morning. They are assembling now in his private office adjoining his bedroom. Would you care to come?"

"I would be delighted," Rose said as she stood up. She followed Angelica into the hall and up the stairs.

"This is just an informal meeting. Papa is giving his friends a tour of the White House."

They went into the upstairs office where the group was seated in a semicircle. President Van Buren was speaking. At first glance Rose thought the group consisted entirely of men, but then she noticed one lone woman seated at the far end of the room.

"Come in, Rose," the president greeted her affably and beckoned to a chair in front of him. As Rose sat down President Van Buren continued, "Gentlemen, and lady," he bowed to the previously lone woman in the group, "I want you to meet Mrs. Rose Greenhow, one of the loveliest hostesses in our fine capital."

The men rose and bowed graciously as President Van Buren introduced each one of them by name. "This is a group from New York State down here to form a club on my behalf, Rose. Gentlemen, and lady, I have only recently learned that Mrs. Greenhow wishes to assist us in our proposed campaign. I took the liberty of inviting her to join us this morning!" As the group smiled at Rose, President Van Buren continued. "I suggested that we have our initial meeting here because I thought that you might enjoy getting a personal view of the White House—*your* White House, before we get down to more serious business. Now, if you will follow me I shall show you a little-known secret."

The group rose and followed him to, of all places, his private bathroom. Rose smiled at the astonished look on some of their faces as they stood huddled beside the President of the United States in this seldom seen room.

President Van Buren pointed to a large tank above him extending upward to the ceiling. "Of all the achievements of my administration, folks, this may go down in history as one of my greatest accomplishments. This, my dear friends, is a tank I have had installed for water which is heated from a small stove in the next room. Henceforth,,the president and his family will be able to have hot bath water without having it brought up by the pailful from the kitchen."

The group laughed and the ice was broken. After a rather hasty tour of the private quarters of the president, he led them back into the Green Room where chairs had been set up. Then the president announced to them, "I have a meeting with the Cabinet this morning. I shall now turn over the organizational part of this group to Mr. Sikes."

The president bowed himself out and Mr. Sikes took over as chairman. Almost immediately he looked at Rose and commented, "It isn't quite clear to me what your position is in this group, young lady."

"I wish to join you in your activities to support President Van Buren in his quest for a second term for president."

"But we are all from New York. We are only down here for a week and then we will be returning to our various precincts where we will work for President Van Buren."

"It might be well to have a member of our committee stationed in Washington to act as liaison with other clubs which are being formed throughout the country," said the other lady, a Mrs. Wentworth.

Mr. Sikes frowned and pursed his lips. "Well, liaison work is pretty difficult for any woman, even in New York, Mrs. Wentworth."

"I can see that Mr. Sikes is from the old school who believes hat a woman's place is in the kitchen where she shall remain at, barefoot, and pregnant," Rose smiled brightly.

Some of the members of the committee snickered with a strained expression on their faces as Rose continued. "It might please you to know, Mr. Sikes, that I *am* presently pregnant. But I also wish to advise you that I can tell you more about what is going on in Washington and can introduce you to more important people than most of the members of the president's own Cabinet."

Mr. Sikes hurrumphed and cleared his throat. "No offense was intended, Mrs. Greenhow, and I can see that we should be grateful that we have you as an active member of our club." No more questions were brought up concerning Rose's qualifications. They went on to discuss the formation of the club. It was to be semisecret, to enhance its mystery. "We shall simply call ourselves 'The New York Democratic Club.'"

"There already is a New York Democratic club," objected one of the group. "We want to make ourselves different."

"That's right," another volunteered. "I'm from Old Kinderhook, President Van Buren's birthplace. Let's call it the Democratic Old Kinderhook Club."

"It might be well to use only the initials," Rose volunteered. "You wish to establish a certain bit of mystery about our club, why not call this the Democratic OK Club, without revealing the meaning of the initials to anyone save our members?"

The rest readily agreed. "It should encourage membership," another commented. "If for no other reason than to learn what the secret letters stand for."

Thus, the "Democratic OK Club" of New York was formed, with Rose an active participant out of their Washington headquarters.

V

The Inauguration

Spring 184.

The "Democratic OK Club" was a huge success, and true to Rose's prediction, the mysterious letters aroused tremendous interest and curiosity. Members of the rival party, the Whigs, were unusually disturbed to note that the letters were being quoted by members of both major parties, and letters to papers throughout New York began to appear, surmising what OK actually stood for.

Shortly after William Henry Harrison—who had received the greatest number of electoral votes against Van Buren in the previous election—was selected as their presidential flag bearer, the Whigs decided that some action must be taken to counteract the tremendous interest that the Democratic OK Club was generating. One of the members of the OK Club sent two clippings to Rose. One, taken from the *New York Herald*, surmised that "OK" stood for "Ole Kurrek." The other New York paper stated that it had heard on good authority that the letters stood for "Oll Korrect," which only signified how incompetent the Democratic Party was in office. "What should we do now?" the sender had scribbled in a note at the bottom of one of the clippings.

Hastily Rose sent off a reply. "Don't do anything. Don't admit to the explanation or deny it. Such complete unconcern will only make our club seem more mysterious and effective."

Again Rose was correct, and she was delighted to overhear a

70

promising member of the Whig Party in Washington say, "That damn OK Club in New York is raising hell with our campaign. Somebody has got to do something about it."

It was only a few days later that Rose discovered what the Whigs were going to do. By word of mouth and in letters to editors comments began to surface to the effect that the letters O and K really were being used incorrectly. If they were reversed—KO—it could be seen that they stood for "Kick Out Van Buren"!

President Van Buren mentioned it to Rose one evening when he was dining at their home. "OK was a great idea, Rose, but it has backfired. We've got a monkey on our backs now that we can't get rid of."

Rose smiled. "Let us admit that the initials OK really stand for 'All Correct' and see if we can't rectify the damage that has taken place."

The explanation was readily accepted. Within two weeks nearly everyone in New York City was using the new phrase, "OK," and associating it with the incumbent president. Van Buren was delighted. "I'm forever grateful to you, Rose," he said, beaming.

When the senator from Vermont used the phrase in one of his speeches and a newspaper in Ohio quoted the OK symbol as standing for "All Correct Van Buren," President Van Buren said to Rose, "If there is ever anything that I can do for you or your husband, just let me know."

Rose smiled delightedly. "Let us wait until after you are reelected, Mr. President."

In spite of her impending childbirth, Rose helped considerably with Van Buren's campaign for reelection. He was selected as his party's candidate at the Democrat Convention in Baltimore that summer with few dissenting votes. The official start of the campaign late in the summer of 1840 was a welcome excuse for Rose to initiate informal gatherings on Van Buren's behalf. Although their home was fairly small, it was surprising how many people Rose could accommodate at one time. There were few weeks that went by that she did not entertain with a reception or garden party to raise funds or to welcome important people who traveled through Washington and acquaint them with the benefits to the country of reelecting Mr. Van Buren as president.

As a result of her activities, she was included in nearly all of the public functions associated with the administration. She and Robert attended theater parties and, although she did make one concession by not actively dancing because of her condition, they were seen at many of the balls and receptions given in honor of state dignitaries.

The party slogan, "OK," standing for "All Correct Van Buren," swept through the states until it was on nearly everyone's lips. It was becoming a household word, and Van Buren was profuse in his praise of Rose's brilliant idea and her work on his behalf.

When Robert was involved in his writing and could not attend one of the public functions, Rose was never at a loss for a companion to escort her. John Calhoun, Daniel Webster, Henry Clay, and the newcomer on the Washington scene, James Buchanan, were constantly vying with each other to accompany her.

A month before the November elections Rose's first baby was born. In accordance with the preference expressed by the father, it was a darling, rosy-cheeked little girl. They named her Florence. Robert Greenhow was beside himself with joy. For once he abandoned his staid, conservative manners in announcing the event to everyone he came in contact with. They received congratulations from members of both parties, from the Capitol, and from several states, including far-western Michigan, which had just recently joined the Union.

The blessed event was perfectly timed, in that it permitted Rose to be fully recovered and back at social functions well before the presidential election. She plunged into her round of entertainments, soirees, balls, receptions, and garden parties with a renewed vigor. So sure was she and her closest associates of Van Buren's reelection that she found time to reinstate herself as unofficial hostess of the State Department. So, the news was received with particular delight when Robert brought home word that the famous author Charles Dickens was planning to visit the capital.

"We must plan a reception in his honor, Robert," she announced immediately.

"But, Rose, do you feel equal to the occasion?"

"I don't understand."

"So soon after Florence's birth, I mean. Surely this must have left you in a weakened condition."

"Nonsense. Who is better qualified to introduce Mr. Dickens to the important people of Washington than you and I?"

"But, Rose, this is a singular occasion. He has been welcomed with a lavish parade in Boston, as well as in the City of New York."

"That is ridiculous. What that man needs is to personally meet the leaders of our country and learn about them at first hand. Please have an appropriate date which coincides with his visit approved and I shall commence to make plans."

"I only hope you do not overextend yourself, Rose."

Rose smiled and her husband recognized the gleam in her eye as evidence that, regardless of any handicap, his beautiful wife was about to reenter the stage of unofficial diplomacy which had been so much a part of her life.

When Rose advised Angelica Van Buren of the pending reception she was planning for the famous author, Angelica suggested, "You may wish me to arrange for a ballroom in one of the hotels."

"On the contrary," Rose replied, "we shall have the reception in our home. The evenings are still warm enough for us to entertain in our garden as well as our house. We shall have the garden lighted with Japanese lanterns and we'll add large torches reminiscent of medieval England. That should make Mr. Dickens feel quite at home."

"Very well then, I shall be glad to help you in any way that I can."

"Robert is having invitations printed at State. You may wish to assist me with the guest list."

"Your garden party will be scheduled two days after their arrival, if that is agreeable with you."

"Their arrival?"

"Oh, yes, Mrs. Dickens is traveling with her husband. We shall allow them the first day to rest up from their arduous travels. The following evening they will be honored with an official reception at the White House."

Rose plunged with vigor into her extremely important task of preparing for her informal reception for Charles Dickens. The guest list read like a roster of the leaders of the government of the United States and their wives. There was, of course, President Van Buren and his son and daughter-in-law, Angelica; Vice President Richard Johnson and his wife; Secretaries of State, John Forsyth; Treasury, Levi Woodbury; War, Joel Poinsett; Navy, James Paulding; Attorney General Henry Gilpin, and Postmaster General, John Niles.

As the evening drew near, Rose was elated to note that her reception for the Charles Dickenses was being considered the social event of the season, second only to the inaugural which would follow the upcoming election. The *Washington Evening Star* had requested permission for one of their reporters to attend, which in itself was almost unheard of. Outside of official state business, personal names were never included in the published events of the day, excepting on the occasions of births, weddings, or deaths.

The evening of the reception was unusually warm as the guests began to arrive. The Greenhow house was filled to overflowing as was the well-lighted garden. Charles Dickens arrived with his wife well after all of the guests had put in an appearance, and they took places in comfortable chairs in the Greenhow parlor.

Rose tried in vain to strike up a conversation with Mr.

Dickens. She was chagrined to note that he apparently was overcome with a strange sense of bashfulness or plain orneriness; she could not decide which.

Seeing that neither his wife nor himself partook of any of the lavish food that had been prepared, Rose selected a few pieces of each of her finest delicacies and carried them over to Mr. Dickens.

"You must be famished after your journeys around our country," she said, smiling, as she handed the famous author a plate.

"It has been tiring," he replied in a noncommittal tone.

"My husband writes on occasion," she remarked hopefully.

"Everyone writes on occasion. Has he ever had anything published?"

"Oh, but to be sure." Rose mentioned several of Robert's publications.

"Never heard of them," Dickens commented gruffly.

At that moment Mr. Newmier, the reporter from the *Washington Evening Star*, came up to them with notebook and pencil in hand. "I was wondering, Mr. Dickens, if you would care to state your views and reactions to our country."

"Oh, but Mr. Newmier," Rose quickly interrupted, "Mr. Dickens must be quite tired of delivering his reactions. Perhaps you could arrange—"

"On the contrary, Mrs. Greenhow," Mr. Dickens countered, "I have been waiting for someone to ask me this question. I would be delighted to tell you."

"But there are so many people who are clamoring to meet you this evening, Mr. Dickens."

"Bring them over to me and introduce them—one at a time."

"Oh, very well," Rose replied, crestfallen. She turned to address Mrs. Dickens and was appalled to see her calmly concentrating on sewing a button on a ruffled shirt.

"I hope you will forgive me, Mrs. Greenhow," Mrs. Dickens said casually, in a cockney drawl that was most disconcerting.

"This gallavanting around has left me behind in my sewing. I declare, Charles does not have a single shirt to his name with a complete set of buttons on it."

"I—I—" For a moment Rose was speechless, then she hastily gained control of herself. "May I be of assistance to you?"

"Nope."

"Would you care to retire to my dressing room where you will have more privacy?"

"No, thank you. I'll do just fine here. I might miss something off by myself. I hope you don't mind."

"Not at all," Rose replied graciously, as if it were a daily occurrence to encounter someone sewing at her most elegant reception.

"You might get me a bit of something to eat, if you would be so kind."

"I would be delighted." Rose excused herself and bowed to Mr. Dickens, but she could have saved herself the trouble, for he was deeply engrossed in a lengthy discussion with the reporter, Mr. Newmier.

And so the evening progressed. Generally speaking, the reception for the famous Charles Dickens was a tremendous success judging by the pleased reactions of those in attendance. However, she was chagrined by the uncooperative actions of the guest of honor. Nothing Rose could say or do could break down the barrier that her guests of honor had drawn between themselves and all Americans present.

By the time the last guest had departed, Rose was almost in tears. "I have never been treated so rudely in my entire life," she said to her husband as they were helping to straighten up the house.

"He's an odd character," Robert consoled her. "He hates to leave his beloved England, I am told."

"Well, then, why did he come over here in the first place?"

"His publisher insisted on it. Actually, they are selling more of his books here than in his native England."

"I shan't buy one of his books, I can assure you."

"But the American public can't wait to read his serials. The story got back to Mr. Dickens's publisher that Americans were assembling on the wharf to meet the boat which brought his latest episode. They crowded around the gangway shouting, 'What has happened to little Nell?' The publisher decided that the great Mr. Dickens should honor this country with his personal presence."

"I wish he hadn't."

"Don't be disturbed, Rose. The reception was a tremendous success. Martin Van Buren thanked me profusely and said he was having an official letter of thanks sent to you."

"The great Mr. Dickens has set back the social life of Washington by a full season."

"The ways of the English are different, my dear."

"If every Englishman were like these two, I would gladly boycott them all."

"Come to bed, my dear," Robert smiled, taking his wife's arm. "Tomorrow will be another day." He knew from past experience that the next day Rose would rebound from her rebuff and once again be her usual, enthusiastic self.

Neither he nor Rose were prepared for the interview that appeared the following day in the *Washington Evening Star.*

Rose was complimented on the impeccable table and decorations that had made Charles Dickens's reception at her home a spectacular success. The balance of the article was devoted to a report of Mr. Dickens's reactions to American and specifically Washington society. "Washington is unhealthy and ugly," Rose read furiously to her husband as they sat at their evening meal. "With the faces of its politicians swollen with tobacco, their spitting habits disgusting, their costumes grotesque—"

Rose jumped up from the table in a rage, her dark eyes flashing, and she was actually shouting as she read. "Their tactics and manners are unspeakable!" She threw the paper on the dining room table and walked away.

"Come back and finish your dinner, Rose," Robert said calmly. "You know there will always be some bad connected with every bit of good."

"That insufferable monster!"

Robert could hardly conceal his amusement. "In days gone by, wars between countries were started over incidents such as this. In the reign of Henry II—"

"I don't want to hear about it!!!"

Even a letter from John Calhoun, who had returned to Fort Hill, lay on the mantelpiece unopened. Picking it up, Robert remarked, "You haven't read what news our good friend has to impart to us."

"It arrived at the same time as the evening paper," Rose fumed. "After reading the great Charles Dickens's latest masterpiece, I was in no mood for anyone else's writing."

"Do you mind if I open it?"

"Of course not."

Robert opened the letter and after hastily glancing over it announced, "John plans to stay at Fort Hill until after the election. He has invited us to come and visit him."

Rose returned to the table. "That is most gracious of him. Some of our British citizens could take much needed lessons in etiquette from our American statesmen."

"Let us go down, Rose. Both of us need a change of atmosphere."

For the first time, Rose smiled. "It would be pleasant. But of course we won't be able to go until after the election."

"Good; then let us plan on it. As soon as Van Buren is elected."

But as the days went by, Rose was destined for even greater disappointment. The presidential election was only a few weeks away when the Van Buren forces began to worry. There was nothing specific, except that major newspapers throughout the country seemed to be devoting more and more space to candidate Harrison and his proposed program. Robert was particularly worried, since a new administration would mean a new head of State. But Rose, with her usual exuberance, was as enthusiastic as ever.

"The people know what Van Buren stands for. They can see what he has accomplished in his administration. It would be foolhardy to advocate a change," she said with a marked degree of certainty.

Robert frowned. "Harrison garnered seventy-three electoral votes in the last election against Van Buren. The country has changed a great deal in these last four years. Two new states have been added and the infighting amongst the Democrats has not gone unnoticed by the thinking people of this country. Actually Harrison will only need to double his electoral votes to defeat Van Buren."

"Doubling the number of electoral votes is a herculean task."

Rose never went to bed the night of the election. She could have saved herself the effort, for only scattered returns dwindled into Washington. When the first noticeable returns were received the following day, Harrison showed a slight majority over Van Buren.

"These are only the results from the large northern cities. They cannot possibly be conclusive," Rose commented defiantly. This was true, for only the large industrial cities of the north had been connected by railroad ties to carry the recently invented steam locomotives. The locomotives were put to good use bringing in accounts of the first election returns. It was fully five days before results from the outlying districts and from the more western states began to drift into the nation's capital by stagecoach and private messenger riders to the papers. Rose spent a great part of each day at the White House.

It soon became obvious that Harrison could possibly win the election by capturing more than two hundred electoral votes in the states where he was forging ahead, leaving a paltry less than one hundred to be allocated to the incumbent president. When the full returns came in from New York indicating that a large majority had voted for Harrison, Rose, at last, admitted defeat. A decisive, undeniable voice of the people had been witnessed.

Rose was beside herself with grief. She remained in her household the entire day following the final results, a most unusual occurrence for the incessantly active Rose O'Neal Greenhow. "First Calhoun and now Van Buren," she said to her husband as they sat in their parlor that evening. "I hate politics and its unpredictable uncertainties."

"You chose to become involved, my sweet. You must accept the consequences regardless of the outcome." Robert put his arm around his wife and smiled. "The people have delivered their ultimatum."

"The people!" Rose replied contemptuously. "The people haven't sufficient good sense to know what is best for them. They would be better off as slaves with a few able citizens making their decisions for them."

"The free and honest vote of the populace has made this country what it is today, Rose."

"All of our plans, Robert, they have come to naught."

"A new administration doesn't mark the end of our country."

Rose's next words made Robert finally realize what was truly bothering his pretty wife. "But I will know no one in this new administration," Rose fretted. "There will be entirely new faces—unfamiliar Cabinet members and their wives. I will be on the outside, Robert, looking in. I will be an unknown in my own city. The city I love so much." She wiped a tear with the laced sleeve of her dress. Robert quickly drew out his handkerchief and handed it to her. She heartily blew her nose and somehow felt better.

Robert patted her shoulder. "Don't worry, you will make out. A minor matter such as losing a presidential election will not keep my Wild Rose down for long."

Rose smiled ever so faintly. Even she could not realize at the time how true a prediction Robert had made.

The following New Year's Day she paid her usual visit to the White House and forced herself to be charming and gay in spite of her heavy heart. She was glad to note that the Van Burens were taking their defeat bravely, with an almost devil-may-care attitude, knowing that life must go on.

Following her visit to the White House she went to visit Dolly Madison, as was her New Year's Day custom. She had not seen Dolly in quite some time.

Her visit was not lengthy, however, for she received some unexpected news which completely unnerved her.

"President Harrison has assured me that I will be his guest of honor at the inaugural ball," Dolly beamed.

"How exciting!" Rose exclaimed, as an unexplainable heavy burden seemed to be tugging at her heart. She was actually jealous of Dolly Madison, one of her most loyal friends. Using as an excuse that she must return home quickly because she had left Robert alone with their baby, she left hastily and went directly home.

She came into the house and throwing herself into Robert's arms began to cry. "I won't even be invited to the inaugural ball," she sobbed.

"If you do not attend the inaugural this year, Rose, you will assuredly be present at the next one. And besides, you don't know that you won't be invited. The inaugural is still nearly three months away."

"But I don't know anyone. Who would ever invite me?"

Hoping to change her mood, Robert quickly announced, "Rose, I had another meeting with Richard Pakenham last week."

"The British Minister to the United States?"

"Yes, he's a bachelor you know. And he raved so much about the wonderful dinners he has had at our house I took the liberty of inviting him over again."

Rose looked up at him through tear-stained eyes. "When?"

"This Thursday evening. I hope you don't mind."

"Oh, but Robert, that is only two days away."

"I realize that, but I am sure you will be equal to the occasion."

Rose smiled. "I shall make it a point to be. After all, we must continue our associations with any friends who are still on active duty in the Capitol, must we not?"

True to her resolve, Rose began more vigorously to entertain any foreign guests who visited the capital. She had several members of the Italian legation to her house for a reception on February 25, celebrating the birth of the Italian Republic in 1802. She eagerly sought to entertain as many members of any of the European legations as she could. Soon she was so busily occupied with planning and executing her many parties and soirees, that she was for once in her life completely separated from the internal political intrigues of the nation.

Then, one weekend shortly before the inauguration, it happened. A special messenger arrived at her home to deliver a message addressed to the Robert Greenhows. The letter was on White House stationery.

"What could it ever be?" Rose asked excitedly as she stared at the unopened envelope.

"Open it, my dear. That will readily eliminate the suspense."

With trembling, uncertain hands, she quickly ripped open the envelope and stared at the beautifully engraved paper which met her eyes.

"An invitation to the inaugural ball!" Rose breathed almost reverently.

"Read the message at the bottom," said Robert, looking over her shoulder.

There, scrawled in a heavy, masculine handwriting, were the words: "To the OK Lady who gave me the fright of my political life." It was signed William Henry Harrison, President of the United States.

"How sweet."

"You should be flattered, Rose. This is probably one of the first official acts of state."

So Rose and Robert Greenhow were part of the official party which attended the inaugural ceremonies capped by the inaugural ball in the evening. Nature's elements seemed to be outdoing themselves to make the inauguration day a particularly dismal one. It snowed all morning and later in the day, as it turned to a sleeting rain, the president and all of his party became thoroughly drenched.

Rose finally had to return to her home for a change of clothes. She came back in time to attend the dinner and reception which preceded the inaugural ball. She was chagrined to note that the president had had such a strenuous day he had not taken time to change his attire, which by now was showing the effects of the vicious natural elements. His formal coat and striped pants no longer had any semblance of creases and drooped baggily around his large frame. But, more than that, it was quite evident that, in spite of the umbrellas that had been held over the president all during the trying day, his black velvet-trimmed coat and even his waistcoat had become uncomfortably wet. An item Rose could not help calling to his attention when she was personally presented to him.

"My goodness, Mr. President, you most certainly have been subjected to our foulest weather on your first day in office. I declare, you do seem exhausted."

"I regret, Mrs. Greenhow, the crowded schedule of the day did not allow for any rest or change of clothing."

"You should have issued a presidential proclamation, Mr. Harrison, demanding sufficient time. Glory be, you will be lucky if you don't catch your death of cold."

President Harrison smiled. "I shall have to take my chances, Mrs. Greenhow. It will not be the first chance I have taken, you know." President Harrison winked at her and she moved along in the reception line.

"It is difficult not to like the man," Rose whispered to her

83

husband. "I believe we will be able to get along."

"I am sure of it, Rose."

Rose was not the center of attraction at the Inaugural Ball. That special position was reserved for the greatest living lady of the country, Dolly Madison. But Rose did not care. Rose was in attendance and that was really all that mattered.

That evening she was proud of her friend. Dolly wore an elaborate gown which flowed gracefully behind her as she walked. A wide gold girdle was wrapped tightly about her waist, touched off by a matching gold necklace and bracelet. She wore a feathered turban upon her head.

As the U.S. Marine Band played a stirring march, the president escorted Dolly across the ballroom to the dais set up along the side of the room. Rose applauded vigorously, joined by all present. Dolly Madison was truly a great woman. Tonight was her crowning glory. She seemed far younger than her eighty-one years. Rose hoped she would live so long and could do so well.

VI

The Beginning

Winter 1844

Rose did not realize how prophetic she had been when she told President Harrison on Inauguration Day that he would catch his death of cold. As the result of the long, hard day in the inclement weather, the president caught a bad cold that soon developed into pneumonia. He tried valiantly to continue working in his newly elected office, selecting the best men available for his Cabinet.

Robert was pleased with his appointment of Daniel Webster as secretary of state. "Webster is an extremely able statesman and has a good grasp of the international problems confronting the nation," he told Rose.

Rose was also delighted, for Daniel Webster had attended many of her socials and she believed his personal acquaintance with the Greenhows could give her husband a certain advantage over many of the other members of the State Department.

President Harrison's condition continued to deteriorate, and exactly thirty-one days after he had taken office, Rose and the rest of the nation were bewildered to learn that he had died. John Tyler, who had been elected vice president, was immediately sworn in as president, and the nation was plunged into a month of mourning.

Rose sadly shook her head in disbelief when Robert brought her the news. "Now there will be an entirely *new* set of faces in

Washington for me to become familiar with." Then, realizing how callous she might sound, she added quickly, "The poor man suffered greatly during his month in office. At least he has finally found peace. God rest his soul."

"The nation will never know what kind of a president they elected," Robert said sadly.

"Has President Tyler given any indication of his intentions where President Harrison's appointments were concerned?"

"He issued a brief statement to the effect that he would retain President Harrison's Cabinet."

"That is a relief. At least Daniel Webster will stay on at State."

"For a while, anyway. This is good for the department. Too many abrupt changes are demoralizing."

But Rose was not listening. "I wonder what sort of a woman Mrs. Tyler is?" she mused to herself.

"He is a widower, Rose. Mrs. Tyler was an invalid and died a short time ago."

"Oh, dear, another lone president in the White House. This will never do. It is so much easier to become familiar with the presidential administration through their wives. Now what available female do I know who would be a likely helpmate for our new president?"

"Good heavens, Rose, you can't possibly set yourself up as a matchmaker for the President of the United States?"

"Why not? He will certainly need companionship in his high office. Mr. Van Buren told me several times how lonely he was."

"But the president is fifty-one years old."

"He is in the prime of his life."

"Mr. Tyler has already distinguished himself as the first vice president to become president. Now, if you can arrange it, you will make him the first president to become married in office. A rather difficult assignment you have set yourself, my dear."

"Julia Gardiner is available," Rose mused, paying no attention to her husband. "She has many beaux but obviously

86

is not serious with any of them."

"But Rose, he is old enough to be her father. She is little more than a child."

"She is older than I was when I married you, my sweet. And look how happy we have been. She comes from a good family. Her father is wealthy and commands a great deal of influence and respect. I believe she would be an ideal woman in the White House."

"Rose, you should confine your activities to the domestic affairs of the government and not the private lives of the people who run it."

"The least I can do is see that he meets her."

"Which might prove a bit difficult since you have little more than a passing acquaintance with the president yourself."

"You forget, Robert, that we are on very friendly terms with one of his closest officials, the secretary of state."

Robert knew better than to argue with his wife when she had once decided upon a course of action regardless of how dangerous or incongruous it might be. He could only marvel at her audacity. "My Wild Rose," he murmured, shaking his head.

The opportunity that she sought to introduce Mr. Tyler to Miss Gardiner was not long in coming. A few weeks after Tyler became president he boldly vetoed a bill to reestablish the national bank, a key measure of the Whigs. Within three months a second bill was again passed authorizing the national bank, and he flagrantly vetoed it against the recommendations of all of his advisers. Almost immediately the president's Cabinet resigned en masse, with the exception of Daniel Webster.

It so happened that the day this tragic action took place, Rose and her husband had been invited to Daniel Webster's home for dinner.

When they first arrived, the seriousness of the day's events made their meeting a most somber occasion.

"My sympathies go out to Tyler," Webster said as he sadly

shook his head. "Today he is alone in a sea of vipers. He has hardly had time to learn the responsibilities of the presidency when he must face the many problems confronting the nation veritably single-handedly."

"Do you anticipate a national crisis, Daniel?" Rose asked, disturbed by his somber expression.

"Not if the president acts swiftly," Webster replied. "But he will need some sage advice before one of our foreign adversaries acts to take advantage of the situation."

"I have given you my recommendations on the Canadian border dispute," Robert reminded him.

Rose listened attentively as the two men entered into a serious discussion. "I have talked to Mr. Tyler and he is in complete accord. At his direction I have set up a meeting with Mr. Ashburton to acquaint him with your suggestions."

"It is only a stop-gap solution, but it will undoubtedly serve as the basis for a more permanent treaty in the future when the country is more prepared to deal with the situation."

"Let us hope so. But there is the matter of the Oregon territory."

"It could very easily lead to a war with England if it is not settled soon. Neither are our southern borders secure. With the present crisis, it would not surprise me if the Mexican government took action. Those fiery devils are ready to fight at the drop of a hat."

"But I have heard they are such poor fighters," Rose commented.

"Very true. However, at this point they are better organized and their administration is obviously more competent than our own."

The conversation was becoming much too serious for Rose, reminding her more of an official conference that she could imagine her husband engaging in at his State Department office. She was adept at handling such situations and soon had Webster and her husband in a happier frame of mind.

Rose was well aware of the pride Webster took in the meals

his black cook prepared. As the meal progressed she tactfully chided him, "These soft-shell crabs are done to perfection. Your cook has once again outdone himself."

"Why, thank you, Rose," Webster beamed.

"It is unfortunate he did not have a finer natural product on which to display his culinary talents."

"What do you mean?"

"It is readily acknowledged that the crabs from the Rappahannock are far superior to any other. I noticed a similar problem where his fried oysters were concerned."

"Rose, you are not serious. You cannot possibly discern the difference!"

"But I can, Daniel. Please do not misunderstand me. Your cook has accomplished wonders with these. It is just that the result could be even better if his shellfish had been brought up from the Rappahannock."

"I declare, you do get a particular pleasure out of goading me. But this time I think I have you cornered." He called to his cook, who promptly appeared in the doorway of the dining room.

"Chocko, Mrs. Greenhow wishes to compliment you on your preparation of the soft crabs and the clams."

Chocko smiled and said, "Why, thank you, ma'am."

"However she claims that they could have been better if they had originated in different waters. Do you know where these shellfish came from?"

"Oh, yes sir. I know how you and Mrs. Greenhow take pleasure in rapping each other over your foodstuffs. When you told me Mrs. Greenhow was coming to dinner I went to particular pains to get nothing but the best ingredients to work with."

"Aha!" Mr. Webster smiled triumphantly. "Would you advise Mrs. Greenhow of their origin?"

"I would be glad to, sir. I insisted that the market get them special for me. They obliged by having that shellfish brought in clear from Delaware Bay."

Rose laughed. "I shall let you in on a secret, Chocko. The best shellfish in the country are gotten right close by from the Rappahannock or where it empties into Chesapeake Bay."

"Is that right, ma'am?"

"Don't take my word for it. Try them yourself. And with your culinary magic the results will not be matched."

"Why thank you, ma'am. I shall try them the very next time and see if there is a difference." He bowed graciously and disappeared.

"When you dine at our house next, Daniel, I shall serve Rappahannock shellfish if you will promise to tell me truthfully if you notice any difference."

"I give you my word I shall judge them fairly."

Rose smiled coyly at Mr. Webster as she selected a few pieces of the concoction of crayfish mixed with tiny oysters. "I am rightly proud of the high esteem in which you hold my husband's opinions in foreign matters, Daniel. It is unfortunate that you do not share his and my views on certain internal matters which are so vital to our nation."

"You are undoubtedly referring to my comments which were quoted in the *Washington Daily National Intelligencer* yesterday evening concerning reinforcement of the Fugitive Slave Act."

"I am."

"I regret that I cannot share your opinion on this subject, Rose. It is wrong to return slaves to their masters once they have escaped and gained their freedom in the north."

"Are you saying that slavery is wrong?"

"I am, without equivocation."

"You, yourself, own slaves. Chocko is happy."

"I have seriously considered freeing him and the others. I then thought better of it. I will not take any action on behalf of my slaves until the government takes a stand on a national scale. To do so would only place them at the mercy of some unscrupulous white."

"You do not consider the advantages of being a slave," Rose retorted.

"Advantages? My dear Wild Rose, what advantages are there to being in bondage for your entire life?"

"They are fed and cared for from birth to the time they are able to work."

"True," Webster agreed, frowning.

"During their years of productive labor, they cannot be discharged—they are never at the mercy of the vagrancies of our economy." Rose's dark eyes sparkled in her seriousness. "From the beginning of old age and for the remainder of their lives they are not for a moment terrified by the—the specter of a friendless future of want and starvation. Honestly, Daniel, do you believe that such a condition should be outlawed?"

"You make a right good case for your cause, Rose." Webster slowly rubbed his chin. "You would have made an excellent lawyer. But you have grossly distorted the facts."

"How so?" Rose asked him, then before he could answer she quickly said, "Do not answer that question. It is not my intention to get into a lengthy discussion concerning our differences, of which there are many. On this you will undoubtedly agree."

"Most certainly," Webster replied, "but I assure you I thoroughly enjoy our discussions. I would consider it my loss if I were not a party to them from time to time."

"There is another reason that I wish you in a cheerful frame of mind this evening."

Webster smiled. "What favor do you wish?"

"As you know Richard Pakenham is leaving the British legation to return home."

"Yes, I am well aware of it!"

"Robert and I are giving him a farewell dinner to honor his many years of service to both our countries. You will, of course, receive an invitation. I trust we can count on your acceptance."

"Naturally I will attend. Certainly this is not the favor that you ask?"

"No, we are inviting the president as well. I wish you would urge him to accept our invitation."

"I shall do my best. But this is a most trying time for him. The selection of practically an entire Cabinet, all of the problems that confront him."

"That is why I need your help. I have a particular reason for wishing him to attend. If you would remind him that his presence will smooth our relations with England which are none too secure at the moment, I am sure he would listen to you."

"I shall. May I inquire what your particular reason is for wanting him there?"

Rose laughed. "You would be the first to suggest that a good diplomat never reveals her hand."

"I could be more enthusiastic in urging the president to attend if I knew the real reason why I was doing so."

"It is nothing of an official matter," Robert interjected, "but I must warn you, Daniel, my wife does have an ulterior motive."

"It is only that I am also inviting Julia Gardiner and I shall seat the president beside her."

"Is this wise? Does the president know Miss Gardiner?"

"If he does not, I shall make it a point to introduce him."

"Whether the president now knows Miss Gardiner or not is immaterial, Daniel," Robert hastily explained. "You see, Rose has decided Mr. Tyler would bear up better under the exigencies of his office if he had a comforting wife by his side."

"No!" Webster exclaimed in astonishment, then added thoughtfully, "This is beyond my diplomatic prerogatives, Rose. Such a matter might prove disastrous and I could regret being a party to it."

"You need not be a party to it, Daniel. You have only to assure us that the president will attend."

"A small matter." Webster laughed dubiously.

However, Mr. Webster did secure the president's assurance that he would attend the Greenhow's formal dinner for the departing British minister. It was Rose who had to do quite a bit of coaxing in order to fulfill her part of the plan.

When she invited Julia Gardiner and then informed her that she was intended to be the president's partner at dinner, that young lady became extremely flustered. "Oh, but Rose, the president of the United States! I just couldn't. I wouldn't know what to say. I would be tongue-tied. I would make an utter fool of myself."

"Nonsense, my dear. Just be yourself. Exercise your God-given womanly charm and the rest will take care of itself."

Julia did finally agree to accept her invitation. Rose made it a point to personally introduce her to the president. She was happy to note that during the course of the dinner the two were continually engaged in lively conversation.

Rose seated herself beside the guest of honor. She had taken exceptional pains to see that the dinner would be a memorable one. It began with lobster with truffles and fish pate with goose liver. There was a delectable lobster bisque followed by a thick mussel soup. A serving of swordfish specially prepared was followed by her own unusual mixture of crayfish and oysters.

When the latter was served, she took particular delight in Mr. Webster's comment. "You are correct, Rose. There is a difference in these Rappahannock shellfish. I have never tasted any quite as delicious."

Rose had included so many courses that she had had to borrow three extra servants from her sister, Mrs. Cutts, in addition to her own Randy for the serving. The four slaves were dressed in fine silk livery and were constantly coming in with an additional course and hastily retreating to the kitchen with empty trays and dishes. The entree was a rack of lamb and fine, plump, young squab. For dessert there was frozen soufflé with strawberries and apple tarts with brandy followed by several platters of petit fours, chocolate mousse, cake and chocolate truffles.

The British minister, whom Rose was well aware enjoyed fine food immensely, was in his glory. "I shall never forget this evening for the rest of my life. You have made my departure a memorable occasion," he told her.

"I'm so glad, Richard. Then perhaps you will always think kindly of us Americans."

"Not only that," he replied, "I shall alert my replacement that he has not completed his mission to America until he has dined at your home."

"Perhaps we can arrange a reception for him when he arrives. Do you know who it will be?"

"Oh, yes. It is to be Sir Henry Bulwer. A magnificent fellow. He is, of course, bringing his charming wife, Lady Bulwer, with him. As you know, she is the niece of the Duke of Wellington. You will like them both very much. I am sure they will ably continue to cement good relations between our two governments."

"That is most desirable," Rose commented, "particularly since the Canadian border is now being settled."

"It is being settled?" Pakenham asked in astonishment. "I hadn't heard about this."

Webster, overhearing the conversation, quickly interrupted. "There is nothing definite, Richard. I'm sure, Rose, that Mr. Pakenham is not interested in idle rumors that might be going the rounds."

"Oh, but I am, my dear fellow. I find that much of my information comes to me first via rumors. One of the strictest rules by which I live is to pay particular attention to all rumors. I am a firm believer in the trite phrase, 'Where there is smoke there is generally bound to be a bit of fire.'"

"But this is not exactly rumor, Richard. As a matter of fact, Mr. Webster is meeting with Dr. Ashburton to discuss the possibilities for a treaty that will be mutually advantageous."

"Oh, is that so? I shall have to pass this information along to my replacement before I leave."

Rose smiled importantly. Webster looked at Robert and

both men frowned. Webster made a mental note to advise Robert rather sternly that there were certain subjects at State that would better be made public by State, rather than by Rose Greenhow. Robert would agree wholeheartedly but could only sigh in reply. He knew that his vivacious wife would never change.

Another successful social affair was credited to Rose O'Neal Greenhow. She was delighted with the results. This, despite the firm word of caution which her husband had been officially directed to pass on to her. She must be more discreet in matters of state. There were many delicate situations of which Robert was an integral part. Since their relationship with each other was most frank, she would undoubtedly have knowledge of much highly secret information. None of this information should be made public until the State Department deemed it appropriate, if ever.

Rose pouted. They very seldom had any differences. She would do her best to comply with Robert's and Mr. Webster's wishes, but she really couldn't imagine being able to avoid temptation when she had information available to very few others. Neither could her husband. They laughed about it and kissed.

Rose was delighted to note that several times in the ensuing year, President Tyler could be seen at state functions accompanied by Miss Julia Gardiner.

Thus it came as little surprise to her when it was announced that President Tyler would be marrying Miss Julia Gardiner in the Green Room of the White House the following year.

It was with deepest regret that Rose was unable to attend the wedding of the first president to be married while living in the White House. Rose had other business to attend to, being prevented from taking part in any public gatherings by the birth of her daughter, Gertrude. Both Rose and Robert were as delighted as they had been when Florence was born.

When Rose was up again and once more in the social whirl of

Washington society, she was completely unprepared for the changes that had taken place in the receptions and parties held at the White House. She smiled, as she noted how the pretty young wife of the president—who had been fearful of being his dinner partner such a short time ago—had become a social lioness.

Julia Gardiner Tyler had stormed upon the Washington scene as a child might behave let loose in a candy store. Since Julia was thirty years younger than her husband Rose dismissed Julia's actions without a second thought, but not so many of Washington's elite. Much to the horror of many members of the Cabinet, and particularly their wives, Julia had set up a miniature court.

She became noted for her plumed white horses and beautiful hand-painted enclosed carriage which transported her wherever she was to go in the city. Six maids of honor accompanied her on all occasions, whether they were affairs of state or informal social functions.

Rose was particularly delighted to attend the first White House ball hosted by the president and his new wife. Over two thousand people were invited. Julia was beautifully dressed in a thick purple velvet gown with a long train. She was ensconced on a raised dais where she regally received each of her guests as they were presented to her. It was a time of royal pomp and ceremony that had not been witnessed in America since the nation had broken away from England and the British fetish for royal deference.

Rose had ceased being active in political campaigns. She found that it more suited her ends to let the people choose whoever they pleased to run the country. She would then espouse her various causes by working behind the scenes, dining, dancing, and promenading with leading statesmen and diplomats.

During the last year of Tyler's presidency, Daniel Webster was becoming more and more disenchanted with the manner in which the president insisted that diplomatic missions be conducted by the State Department. Finally, and quite abruptly, Webster tendered his resignation.

There were a few bad days in the Greenhow household as Robert worried about the man who would be appointed as Webster's successor. Rose did not share his worry. She had not brought the president together with his new wife for nought. Unbeknownst to her husband, Rose hastened to the White House and mentioned informally to Julia that she knew just the man, in fact, probably the most qualified to replace Mr. Webster as secretary of state. She hoped Julia would pass her suggestion on to the president, and Julia assured her that she would.

Less than a week later Robert came home overjoyed to announce that President Tyler had selected none other than John C. Calhoun to be his new secretary of state. Rose made every effort to feign surprise.

For the balance of Tyler's term in office, Calhoun, as could be expected because of their close relationship, relied heavily on Robert's advice on the Mexican and Canadian border disputes as well as questions about the Oregon territory, rights to which were strongly challenged by England.

As the presidential election of 1844 drew near, Rose was determined to stand by her vow not to become involved. This did not prove necessary, for once again the passions of her and her husband bore fruit, and late that year Rose gave birth to a third girl. Robert was no less overjoyed than he had been on previous occasions, and they named their latest daughter Leila.

John Tyler had so infuriated his own party by his unorthodox, independent attitude that the Whigs turned their backs on him, selecting Henry Clay as their nominee. Van Buren had been considered a likely candidate for the Democratic nomination. His opposition to the annexation of Texas, however, made Andrew Jackson, still a strong force behind the scenes, swing his influence to James Knox Polk, who was finally nominated on the ninth ballot. Polk barely won the election by a majority of sixty-four electoral votes. His victory was attributed in no small way to a slogan his campaign workers had developed: "54° 40' or fight." This referred to his firm promise that he would fight if the British government tried to force him to accept any other boundary for the United States-Canadian border.

When Rose heard the results of the election her only comment was, "At least another Democrat is in the White House, and I understand that Sarah Polk is a delightful person, although a bit staid."

Through elections, through changes in party administrations, the nation still continued to grow. The Texas territory had secured its independence from Mexico and had petitioned the United States for acceptance into the Union. What had once been a fervent cause for argument between party stalwarts had apparently been settled by the defeat of Van Buren and his followers in his own party. At the end of the year, Texas was admitted into the Union as the twenty-eighth state. That same year Florida was also officially accepted, after having been ceded by Spain twenty-six years earlier.

President Polk selected James Buchanan to be his secretary of state. The appointment was welcome news to Robert and his ambitious wife, for he had been a guest at several of their receptions and both believed they could count on him as a friend. Rose wasted no time in inviting the personable bachelor to a private dinner at her home. Buchanan was a handsome man, and although he was in his early fifties, he still maintained an impressive devil-may-care attitude with the ladies. This was not lost on Rose.

It so happened that the day before their proposed dinner engagement, Robert found it necessary to set off on a long trip to Mexico in order to learn more about the position of the Mexican government concerning their claims to the territory between Mexico and the United States.

Rather than change her plans, Rose decided to go ahead with her private dinner. Buchanan, who, having authorized the trip, had been well aware of her husband's intended journey, arrived at the Greenhow home slightly after the usual dinner hour.

"I thought that perhaps you would cancel our engagement because of your husband's sudden departure," he said as Rose took his top hat and overcoat and hung it on the hall stand.

"It was my intent, Mr. Buchanan—may I call you Jim?" she inquired as she ushered him into her parlor.

"All of my friends do," he smiled as he sat down. "I trust that I can consider you and your husband my friends."

"You may be assured on that score. As I was saying, I had intended to call our engagement off when my husband was forced to leave Washington so suddenly, but then I thought, why waste this opportunity to become better acquainted with Robert's new boss? Do you mind?"

"Not at all, I am delighted."

"After all, Robert confers with me on all decisions that State is called upon to make. Would it surprise you to learn that I know as much about State as any of your staff?"

"Not in the least. As a matter of fact, I had heard about you long before coming to Washington."

"Really? I had no idea our reputation was known outside the capital. Pray tell what sort of information have you heard about me?"

"That you were the loveliest hostess in our nation's capital. And that you were a beautiful woman. I cannot speak for your ability as a hostess, but quite frankly I can tell you they have certainly underestimated your beauty!"

"How flattering of you, Jim. May I serve you a drink before dinner?"

"I would welcome one. It has been a hard day."

"Robert tells me every day is a difficult one down at State these days." She rang a small bell on the table beside her and her house slave appeared.

"I have a special surprise for you. Randy, will you bring Mr. Buchanan and myself a Queen Charlotte Cocktail?"

As Randy bowed and disappeared, Rose asked, "Have you

99

ever had a Queen Charlotte Cocktail?"

"I generally drink my liquor straight. But I welcome the opportunity to try your special concoction."

"Wait until you have tried it. Actually, it *is* almost straight liquor. That's why you must beware of its effects."

Buchanan sampled his Queen Charlotte Cocktail when it was brought to him and was delighted with its taste as well as its potency. It was apparent that James Buchanan and Rose were going to get along marvelously.

As they sat across the table at dinner they laughed together over some of the anecdotes that Rose could tell about the State Department and its outdated protocol.

As they were sipping brandies after dinner, she said seriously, "Our friendship may prove of value to you in the trying times that lie ahead in international affairs."

"I am counting on it, Rose. I have been advised that your husband is the greatest authority on boundaries and natural resources available to State."

"He has spent his entire academic life studying them." She got up from her chair. "Shall we retire to the parlor?"

They brushed against each other as they walked leisurely into the parlor. Rose blushed uncontrollably. The proximity of this magnetic man thrilled her. She had not been so excited by any man other than her husband and the sensation was unfamiliar to her. Quickly she gained control of herself and smiled as they seated themselves on the living room sofa.

"You will learn that Robert has been a reliable council to Mr. Calhoun, your predecessor. He willingly followed Robert's advice on the Oregon situation."

"I received an informal letter from Mr. Calhoun only today wherein he advised me of your husband's recommendations concerning the Oregon territory." Reaching inside his coat he drew out a letter. "Mr. Calhoun gave me his opinions and made the comment that Robert had influenced him. Would you care to hear it?"

"I would be most anxious to."

100

"It is beyond the power of man to trace the consequences of a war between us and England on the subject of Oregon," he read. "All that is certain is that she can take it and hold it against us as long as she has the supremacy of the ocean and retains her Eastern dominions. The rest is left in mystery.

"We have been on extremely close terms with Lord Bulwer, and he assures us that England would not think kindly of any action that we took on behalf of the Oregon territory. The situation is extremely difficult at this time due to the critical stages of the Canadian boundary dispute.

"I have discussed this with President Polk and he has authorized me to negotiate a treaty with Britain on the Canadian impasse. We shall offer to accept the forty-ninth parallel as the boundary between the United States and Canada."

"But Jim," Rose said at this point, "President Polk's campaign slogan was '54° 40' or fight.' You cannot accept the much lower forty-ninth parallel as our boundary."

Buchanan shrugged his shoulders. "It is simply a matter of discretion being the better part of valor."

"But the people will not stand for this."

"We cannot go to war with Britain while we are in such a vulnerable position with our Mexican neighbors."

"You must prepare the people well for this turn of events."

"I see you are an astute student of the reactions of the masses."

Rose smiled sardonically. "I should be. I witnessed their behavior through many of our presidential campaigns. I have come to the conclusion that they can be led in any direction you desire as simply as a flock of sheep. Your only obligation is to thoroughly acquaint them beforehand with the reasoning behind your decision."

"You say that you have established a close relationship with Lord Bulwer, the British minister?"

"We are on excellent terms."

"Perhaps you could informally acquaint him with our

willingness to forfeit territory if his government is agreeable to signing a treaty."

"I would be glad to. I am sure you will find they will be most cooperative. They would be foolish not to. It is the American people who might not accept such a compromise."

"The president and I will be responsible for the American people. It will be your and your husband's responsibility to assure Britain's cooperation."

"That will be no problem," replied Rose confidently.

A few moments later Buchanan rose to go. "It is much later than I had anticipated staying, Rose." Buchanan smiled as he put on his coat and held his hat in his hand. "This gives you some indication of the high esteem I have developed for my charming hostess."

He took her hand in his and bowing low kissed it tenderly. Then, slowly, he drew her arm closer to him. Dropping his hat he took her chin in his hand, drew her face quickly to his and kissed her. The incident was over in an instant but it left an indelible impression on Rose. Her eyes widened, her cheeks flushed, she stooped to pick up his hat in an effort to conceal her emotions. She could not accept the thrill that his sudden kiss had given her.

"Forgive me, Rose. I was carried away by the magic of our evening together."

"I should be angry with you, but I am not!"

He left. Without turning back he got into his carriage and was driven away.

The Oregon Treaty was signed with Britain on June 15 of the following year establishing the boundary between the two countries at the 49th parallel!

VII

The Hostess

Spring 1846

Robert returned from Mexico in a most pessimistic frame of mind. "I cannot understand the Mexican government," he told Rose even before he had reported to the new secretary of state, James Buchanan. "They indicate there is nothing to discuss where our mutual boundaries are involved."

"Surely they would listen to your arguments concerning the valid land claims which you presented?" Rose asked.

"They would not. The first three weeks of my visit I spent in local city halls and halls of records, investigating claims and searching for titles to properties. It seems to me that the most logical boundary between the two countries is the Rio Grande. The Mexican government flatly refuses to recognize this. Some of the state officials of Coahuila claim that their state has title to lands as far north and east as the new city of San Antonio. I could find no validation for their claims."

"It must have been a most frustrating experience."

"It was. Particularly after the grueling trip I experienced going down to Mexico. I declare, Rose, the situation is hopeless."

"It seems to me the matter has become one for the president himself to undertake. It could require the backing of our military before a final decision is made."

"This is what I am going to recommend."

It was not necessary for Robert to make any recommendations. Matters were already being closely watched, not only by the secretary of state but by President Polk as well. Settlers and large landholders in the area of the Rio Grande had reported that Mexican authorities were threatening to oust them from their claims by force, if necessary.

At Robert's suggestion, President Polk took a very firm stand where Texas was concerned. It was now a sovereign state of the United States of America, and as such its citizens would be protected from encroachment by any foreign country. For the present the matter of Mexico and its boundaries with the United States were taken out of Robert's hands.

Much to his delight Robert announced to Rose that he had been given a new assignment. "Congress's commission on American claims to Oregon territory has commissioned me to write a pamphlet on the geography and history of the Northwest."

"You will be engaged in writing for the government. That should please you."

"Extremely. I shall start my research immediately."

"Will this require a visit to the Northwest territory?"

"I don't know at this point. It is uncertain how much data I can develop in the archives in Washington."

"If you journey to the Northwest territory, Robert, I should like to accompany you."

"But, Rose, that territory is still very rugged. Most of it is undeveloped, with only a few scattered settlers here and there."

"But I have not traveled nearly as much as I wish. I want to learn more about this great country of ours."

"There are our three girls to consider."

"Florence and Gertrude are both in school now. They could stay with Aunt Hattie or my sister Ellen. The girls love both of them dearly. And in a few months baby Leila will be old enough to stay with them too. I should like very much to go, Robert. I have not been away from Washington excepting to visit some of our southern friends. A change of scenery will surely do

104

me good."

"Perhaps the girls could do without you for a few months, Rose, but could the city of Washington?"

They laughed and nothing further was mentioned. Robert spent the next few months studiously delving into the archives at the Library of Congress and the National Hall of Records. Once he made a short overnight trip to William and Mary College which boasted one of the most extensive libraries in the South.

Rose was again busying herself with the unofficial affairs of government. She continued her parties and levees, inviting government officials and their wives. The secretary of war, William Marcy, and his wife; John Mason, who was first President Polk's attorney general then secretary of the navy, and his wife; and President Polk and his wife Sarah were frequent visitors at her parties.

She often included James Buchanan in her list of invited guests but made a particular point of never being alone with him for any length of time. It would be extremely dangerous if actions by either of them could be questioned. She could not explain the strange attraction this man had for her. Of course, it was one of the few subjects she could not discuss with her husband. Cave Johnson, the postmaster general, was also a frequent visitor. Cave had been an old beau of hers when she was a young girl, and she was delighted to note that he no longer held any attraction for her. As a matter of fact, it seemed to her that he had gotten much stodgier as he had grown older. Their differences in age were much more obvious now than when she had first known him. She was thankful that she was still young in thought and action. She hoped she was not deluding herself.

Rose became very friendly with Sarah Polk and enjoyed being a guest at White House receptions. Sarah Polk was against dancing, wine, horse racing, and cards, and the soirees and parties conducted at the White House were rather staid and solemn affairs. This was quite to Rose's liking, for she was sure her own receptions stood out as momentous occasions by comparison.

She was particularly pleased to have Sam Houston as a guest at several of her parties. She had become friendly with him when he was a frequent visitor to Washington after Texas had declared its independence from Mexico. During the negotiations which preceded that state's entrance into the Union, he had been a leader of the Texas delegation. She liked his frank, happy-go-lucky attitude so much in contrast to the atmosphere surrounding the pious Methodist president and his fervently religious wife. Sam Houston confided to Rose one evening at her house, "I do like the president; the only fault I have to find with him is that he drinks too much water."

"I understand," Rose agreed, laughing. "He has made one contribution to history. He has installed gas lights in the White House."

Rose also liked the British visitors who came to Washington, in spite of her unpleasant experience with the Charles Dickenses, and she became friendly with Sir John F. Crampton, the British chargé d'affaires. So friendly, in fact, that it actually stood in the way of Robert's official duties at State.

He came home one evening in a most disagreeable mood. "President Polk has offered to buy the California territory from Mexico."

"That will undoubtedly settle the issue once and for all, will it not?" she asked cheerfully.

"It will never work. I told Buchanan so when I learned about it."

"When you learned about it, Robert? But did you not send the message? As the State Department's interpreter—"

"I have not been interpreting the messages from the Mexican government of late."

"But why?"

"Senator Benton has been translating our Mexican dispatches."

106

Rose's dark eyes flashed in anger. "That is his daughter Jessie Benton's doings. She hates me. She has always been jealous of me. She has constantly attempted to snub me ever since she became Mrs. John Fremont. Now she is trying to avenge herself through your position."

"Senator Benton claims he has grounds for suspecting our objectives."

"How can the president believe such an absurdity?"

"You are on very close terms with the British Embassy, Rose."

"I am friendly with the ambassador and the chargé d'affaires, but that does not make a case against you."

"The president has been convinced that it makes a case against *you.*"

"Robert, what are you saying?"

"Jessie has said that you are so involved pulling strings that you are constantly giving confidential information to the British."

"What unfounded lies!"

"I have warned you, Rose. You must be more discreet in bandying about our confidential discussions at social gatherings you attend."

"I have tried to be more careful, Robert. It is impossible to keep affairs of state out of my conversation completely. But what would be the point of my passing confidential information to the British?"

"Jessie has accused you of being in the pay of the British."

"Robert! We cannot stand for this. Surely Mr. Buchanan will intercede in your behalf."

"Mr. Buchanan has not been consulted in the matter."

"He is the secretary of state. Doesn't the president trust him?"

"No."

"Does he believe that Mr. Buchanan is in the pay of the British?"

"It was a simple matter to plant the seeds of distrust in Mr.

Polk's mind because the president believes Buchanan has presidential ambitions."

"Has he?"

"Mr. Buchanan denies it. But perhaps he realizes it is too early to show his hand."

"Oh, Robert, what are we going to do?"

"Nothing."

"Do you mean to tell me you will do nothing when the honor of your wife and yourself is at stake?"

"My position at State is secure."

"But what about these unfounded charges that this vicious creature is spreading like poison?"

"On the surface she has grounds for her accusations, Rose. You have been extremely friendly with the British."

"Jessie has never been able to get any of the important people in Washington to her social affairs. But I could not imagine even Jessie Fremont resorting to this sort of underhanded, sneaking deviltry. OHHHHH, she will pay for this!"

"Rose, you will be wise to let the matter be."

"How can you possibly forget this?"

"I can't forget it any more than you, but as long as Buchanan is still secretary of state and I continue with my present responsibilities, nothing can be gained by an outright feud among government officials."

"We shall see about this. I'll stifle that brazen hussy if it is the last thing I ever do!"

But Rose was destined to turn her attentions to other, more pressing matters than her private feud with Jessie Benton Fremont. In the spring of the following year, events with Mexico moved so quickly that they brought the people's emotions to fever pitch. President Polk decided to send his own personal emissary, John Slidell, to Mexico with an offer to purchase the territory he had in mind.

"I hope he has better luck than I had in Mexico," Robert commented.

"I hope he doesn't," Rose retorted.

"That is not a very patriotic attitude, my dear."

"It is a practical one. I am sure that Mr. Slidell can do no more than you, Robert. It is time our president appreciated your value to our country."

Several days later, newspapers throughout the country featured bold headlines declaring a breakdown of discussions with the Mexican Government. No one in the Mexican government would acknowledge Mr. Slidell's presence. No member would see him. No one in an official capacity would speak to him. The American people were outraged. "Force the issue!" was the cry of the day.

"I agree," Rose said to her husband as they discussed the matter over their evening meal. "In my opinion, it is time to send American troops into Mexico and force them to discuss this matter with us."

"That would be an act of aggression," Robert replied.

"Call it what you will. Governments are no different from individuals. When one sulks, he must be forced to discuss the issue. How else can the matter ever be resolved?"

"The president has decided to dispatch troops down there under General Zachary Taylor. But he has given him strict orders not to cross the border of the Rio Grande."

"Why must they stop at the Rio Grande?"

"We have no right to advance further, Rose. The Mexicans would be justified in defending their territory and we would be branded as an aggressive nation trying to conquer a smaller neighbor."

"What does it matter, if we accomplish our ends and settle this matter once and for all?"

"You do not understand diplomacy, my dear wife."

"I am able to recognize an affront to our government when I observe it. Fortunately, the majority of the American public agrees with me."

It was only a few days later that the president reported that Mexico had also sent its troops to the border of the Rio Grande, and that the Mexicans had attacked the American forces.

"This is aggression we cannot ignore," Robert declared furiously. "There will be war."

"But Robert, this is what I have been advocating all along," Rose said, astonished by her husband's seeming change of attitude.

"The situation is entirely different. War has been begun by an act by Mexico."

"You are correct, Robert. I do not understand diplomacy. There comes a time when force is the only mediator. It has been evident in this case since the Mexican government ignored Mr. Slidell."

True to Robert's prediction, the following day President Polk claimed that war was imminent, forced upon America by an act of Mexico. On May 13 Congress declared war.

The country grimly mobilized its forces and material wealth and rushed them to the Rio Grande border and beyond as rapidly as possible, to be placed at the disposal of General Taylor.

Parties and receptions were discontinued in the capital while the nation eagerly scanned delayed newspaper reports of the progress of the war.

Rose saw less and less of her husband who was engaged in lengthy conferences at the State Department and with various members of the president's cabinet. In spite of his personal reservations, Rose was happy to note that President Polk continually consulted both Buchanan and Robert on state matters during this critical period. Rose was able to convince her husband on one rare occasion that it would be a welcome change for the men involved to meet at their house for an informal dinner. She had hoped that such a gesture would reduce the tension and misunderstandings that had arisen between the president and the State Department.

One winter evening, the president, vice president Dallas, James Buchanan, and the secretaries of the war and the navy assembled at the Greenhows'. Rose had wished to invite their wives, but the president insisted that it would be more of a business meeting than a social gathering and no woman save Rose would be welcome. Rose, however disappointed, was forced to agree.

It was a very serious business meeting. All during the elaborate dinner which Rose had prepared, the talk was strictly confined to the progress of the war and its effects on other nations of the world. Although the men ate heartily and drank their glasses of Madeira wine lustily, Rose sat silently by. They could have been served mush and hard tack for all the attention the food was getting. She listened attentively as the vast problems of the nation were discussed.

"It is urgent that we assure other nations that we have no territorial ambitions," Buchanan commented, frowning in his concentration.

"It is imperative that we do so, Mr. President," Robert agreed.

"But we do have territorial claims," argued the president.

"Now is no time to flaunt our ambitions before the powers of Europe," Buchanan added hastily. "I recommend that we officially announce that, regardless of the outcome of the war—"

"Which is being waged much to our liking according to present indications," interrupted the president.

"Agreed," replied Buchanan, "but in order to maintain this impetus we must assure neutral nations that we will not acquire California or Mexican territory in any event."

"Why not?" asked President Polk belligerently.

"Because England and France could very well join Mexico in this war," Buchanan dramatically replied.

President Polk turned to face his secretaries of war and the navy. "What do you gentlemen have to say about this?"

The two men looked at each other in a rather nonplused fashion, and William Marcy, the secretary of war, spoke. "I have no thoughts on the possibility of other nations joining the conflict, Mr. President."

"I don't give a damn about that," the president retorted gruffly. "I want your opinions as to our preparedness in the event of such a contingency."

"We cannot align ourselves against all the nations of the world," John Mason, the secretary of the navy, ventured to comment.

"I realize this," President Polk said impatiently. "What I want to know is, has the Mexican war completely drained us of our fighting power?"

"No sir," both men replied almost simultaneously. Mr. Marcy added, "I would say, sir, that our uncommitted strength is still far superior in comparison to what it was during any of our previous conflicts with Britain."

"Then we have our answer." President Polk turned to the rest of the men. "Gentlemen, I won't for one single moment tolerate meddling by any European power on this continent. It is my strong belief that, if forced to, we will meet a war with England or France or all the powers of Christendom if they should choose to wage one."

There was silence in the room. Rose studied the serious expressions of the men sitting around the dining room table. "Do I make myself clear, gentlemen?" the president asked quietly.

"Very clear, Mr. President," Buchanan replied. "I withdraw my suggestion."

"Good, I hope that we can be of one mind in the future," said the president, smiling. "We are destined to be one of the greatest nations this earth has ever seen. We will expand. Before the year is out we will undoubtedly add a twenty-ninth state to the Union. As you know, Iowa has petitioned us. She will be still another state to be carved from that great Louisiana Purchase, which veritably doubled the size of our country. I don't know how we will fare in this present war, but if our initial successes are any indication, I believe we will easily defeat Mexico, and she will be forced to agree to our terms. The land involved will add a great amount of territory to

112

this nation, second only in size to that of the Louisiana Purchase. We will be a nation from one coast to the other under one flag, one government of one united people."

Rose could not refrain from applauding the president's firm statements, and the rest of the men followed her example.

As the applause subsided, Robert said, "If we should win the war, sir, I hope you will make our nation an example to the rest of the world by offering to purchase these territories rather than grabbing them without just compensation."

"I most certainly will, Bob," the president replied. "What, in your opinion, would be a fair amount to pay for this territory?"

"I have given this matter a great deal of thought, sir. I was able to evaluate much of the land involved during my recent visit to Mexico. I believe an offer of fifteen million dollars would not be too excessive and should certainly be considered fair by the Mexican government."

"Particularly if they were thoroughly defeated," added Buchanan.

"Thank you for your suggestion, Bob. Let us start with this amount in mind," the president said as he rose from the table. "Now, if you will excuse me, I believe it is time for me to depart. These harrowing days are leaving me pretty wilted by eveningtime."

The rest of the men rose from the table.

"All that remains is to win the war," Rose uttered as she helped the men on with their coats.

"We will leave that to General Taylor," President Polk replied.

"And I would say it is in good hands, sir," added Secretary Marcy.

The secretary's statement proved correct. General Zachary Taylor distinguished himself by his rapid maneuvers and lightninglike thrusts deep into Mexican territory. Victory upon victory was piled up until the General became a national hero. Before the nation could gear itself for complete mobilization, the most pessimistic person could not help but admit that the United States would soon end the war in complete victory.

Shortly after the beginning of the following year, crowds gathered in the streets to cheer the capture of Mexico City, the adversaries' capital.

The war ended less than twenty months after it began and a treaty of peace was negotiated at Guadalupe Ridalgo. The territory of California and the lands east of it were purchased from the defeated Mexicans for fifteen million dollars. This left only a narrow strip of land west of the Mississippi River still outside the Union.

General Taylor returned to Washington as the man of the hour. He led his troops into Washington and the largest parade that had ever been assembled in that fair city was organized to welcome them home. A national holiday was declared, and, with social affairs once more in vogue, Rose lost no time in staging a reception for the homecoming hero. At first she had planned a party at her house, but the popularity of General Taylor soon made it obvious to Rose that this would be far and above any affair she had ever before hosted. She decided the only celebration befitting the occasion would have to be a formal banquet followed by a truly ostentatious ball. The cost of such an affair was well beyond the means of the Greenhows, but Rose insisted that nothing less would be appropriate to honor the victorious general.

The George Washington Hotel was selected as an appropriate setting. Because it was, in effect, a public affair, President Polk, with the urgings of Buchanan, finally authorized the State Department to underwrite at least part of the expense. It was one of the few times during the staid and proper Polk administration that a frivolous, gay celebration was grudgingly condoned. The banquet was a gourmet's delight, with massive hauls of Rappahannock shellfish noticeably in abundance. Young stuffed roasted pigs were mounted on huge platters for the entrée, and five chefs were hired by the hotel to prepare

114

and serve the banquet from carved mahogany tables heavily covered with thick Irish linen tablecloths especially secured for the occasion.

The desserts were served to the guests at long tables laden with fresh fruits and amply supplied with a display of various types of petit fours, cakes, and truffles.

The men in military uniform accompanied by their fair ladies in long flowing gowns made a picturesque tableau as they danced the innovative waltz that was becoming so popular.

Rose had obtained the services of Pierre Duchante, the famous French designer who was visiting the capital at the time. She had practically bribed him to design a gorgeous, provocative gown for her. She was able to accomplish this without paying his usual exorbitant fee by arranging for him to attend the ball accompanied by Virginia Merriweather, one of the most beautiful debutantes of the season. The result, a long, flowing, green satin gown, attracted the admiration of all the males and the envy of all the females in attendance. Pierre had outdone himself, with an original design of pink ruffles sweeping to the hem of the dress which flowed gracefully on the floor. The dress was topped by an embroidered bodice that amply displayed generous portions of Rose's splendid breasts.

She wore her hair high on her head in a new fashion that would soon sweep the capital as it was copied by all of the wives and mistresses of notable government officials. Robert vowed that his wife had never looked more beautiful.

As she swept into the ballroom the dancing stopped, as did the music. She walked majestically to the side of the ballroom and curtsied low before the president of the United States. Everyone began to applaud, prompted, no doubt, by the striking contrast between Mrs. Polk's plain, almost dowdy evening gown and Rose's gorgeous creation.

As Rose danced her first waltz with General Taylor, the revelers actually cheered. Rose beamed graciously. Tonight she was the belle of the ball. Already the country was beginning to return to normal.

In the days that followed, Rose once again returned to her first love and often visited the Senate. Less than a year later she was thrilled to witness that august body vote to admit Wisconsin into the Union. Thus the thirtieth state, carved from the Northwest territory, was admitted into the United States. Rose recalled the stirring speech the president had delivered privately to some of the government officials at her house and was proud that she was no small part of the men and women who were at the center of this growing nation. Slavery was the only matter which caused great differences of opinion between the north and the south and marred the forging of the great nation. The issues of the day were becoming clear-cut and sides were being clearly formed on this vital question.

Her heart ached as she witnessed old friends taking adamant stands on the issue. She would never forget the stormy sessions in the Senate when erstwhile friends took sides against each other, much to her consternation.

Henry Clay, with his awe-inspiring voice, stood before the Senate one day, swaying its members with his fiery oratory. "I know no South, no North, no East, no West to which I owe any allegiance," he said, casting a derisive look at Senator Calhoun. "I owe allegiance to two sovereignties, and only two: one is to the sovereignty of the Union, and the other is to the sovereignty of the state of Kentucky. My allegiance is to this Union and to my state; but if gentlemen suppose they can exact from me an acknowledgment of allegiance to any ideal of future contemplated confederacy of the South, I here declare that I owe no allegiance to it; nor will I, for one, come under any such allegiance if I can avoid it."

The crowd in the galleries cheered as he finished and the senators themselves began to shout their approval. Such pandemonium arose that the vice president finally declared a recess. Rose rushed downstairs to seek out her friend, John Calhoun. He looked pale and seemed tired and worn as she accompanied him to his office.

116

"I shall rebut him, Rose. He may think that he has effected a compromise between the North and the South, but it is not that easy."

"You must rest, John. You are endangering your health to take so much of the burden upon yourself."

"Someone has got to speak for us. That damn Clay is such an orator. I don't like Clay. He is a bad man, an imposter, a creature of wicked schemes. I won't speak to him, but by God, I love him."

"It is better that you think no more of it, John. You are as white as a ghost. It is not good for you to be living alone. You probably aren't eating right. Why not come and live with us again if only for a short while?"

"Thank you, Rose, but I shall manage. As a matter of fact, I have decided to move back into your aunt's boarding house. I need someone to see that I get a steady diet."

"She will be delighted to have you. You can visit us whenever you are of a mind. In the meantime, rest and forget the burdens that beset you in the Senate."

But they were difficult to forget. The next day, Daniel Webster rose in the Senate, backing Clay on a compromise. He was changing his opinion. He was siding with the North against Rose's and Calhoun's beloved South. Calhoun could stand it no longer. He arose from his seat and stalked down the aisle, coughing as he took the podium.

Looking much older than his years, worn and haggard, he still stood firm and scowled beneath his heavy brow as he spoke. "This great nation has increased from sixteen to thirty states," he said, waving his arms. "Its population now totals seventeen million with two million more persons in the North than the South, but the cry of Union—the glorious Union! can no more prevent *dis*union than the cry of health, health, glorious health! on the part of a physician could save a patient lying dangerously ill."

He started to slump against the podium, braced himself with

117

both hands until his knuckles stood out white, and continued. "The responsibility for saving the Union rests with the North, not with the South. The time has come for an open and manly avowal on all sides as to what must be done. If you who represent the stronger portion, cannot agree to settle these issues on the broad principle of justice and duty, say so; and let the states we both represent agree to separate and part in peace. If you are unwilling we should part in peace, tell us so and we shall know what to do when you reduce the question to submission or resistance." Rose shuddered. This was the first time actual rebellion had been officially mentioned. As Calhoun paused in his speech cheers and applause broke out in the galleries. Rose vigorously joined in. The vice president pounded his gavel for order, which was soon restored, and Calhoun continued.

"If you remain silent, you will compel us to infer by your acts what you intend. In that case, California will become the test question. If you admit her, under all the difficulties that oppose her admission, you compel us to infer that you intend to exclude us from the whole of the acquired territories, with the intention of destroying, irretrievably, the equilibrium between the two sections. We would be blind not to perceive in that case that your real objects are power and aggrandizement, and infatuated not to act accordingly!" His fiery speech had weakened him to such an extent that it was necessary to help him from the podium back to his seat. Shortly afterward the Senate adjourned for the day.

The next week Rose assisted Calhoun in moving into her Aunt Hill's house where he would receive proper care and could rest to his heart's content.

President Polk too was tiring from the exigencies of his office caused by the unfettered antagonism between the North and the South and the administration of the Mexican War. His own health was failing and he decided that he definitely would not seek another term in office.

His enthusiasm for expanding the Union never failed

however, and he sent a message to Spain offering to purchase Cuba for one hundred million dollars. His offer was so soundly refused that he dropped any further mention of it. "We should march in and take the small island for her own good," Rose commented as Robert told her of Spain's reply.

Rose visited Calhoun's office a week later and was disturbed to learn that he had not attended the Senate for two days. Summoning her carriage, she hastened to her Aunt Hill's house to find Calhoun lying in bed. He was coughing and had a fever. She remained with him for a short while, soothing his hot lips with a cool cloth and reminding him, once again, that he must give himself up to complete rest. After consoling him and receiving his assurance that he would remain in bed until he regained his strength, she left.

As she was leaving she met a man coming toward her in the upstairs hallway. It was so dark she did not recognize Henry Clay until he spoke.

"I have heard that Calhoun is ailing. How is he?" said Clay as he stopped beside her.

"He is tired and worn out," said Rose shortly. "He is thoroughly exhausted from fighting for his cause against the likes of you."

"Oh, Rose, I never knew you to hold it against any man for standing up for what he believes is right."

"You are correct, Henry. I must apologize. I just wish that you weren't such a convincing speaker."

He placed his hands on her arms and held her before him. "This is my old wild Rose. You know I have always held you in highest esteem."

She sighed. "I know, Henry. I—"

"You can't know how I have longed to show you how much you really mean to me."

Quickly he drew her to him and pressing his lips to hers kissed her. "My Wild Rose," he murmured tenderly but no less passionately. "Please do not take offense."

Nervously she put her hair in place. "I—I suppose there is

really no harm done as long as it does not go any further."

He laughed. "I can assure you, my dear, that at my age it is not physically possible to go any further." He pecked her lightly on the mouth, then pinching her cheek and patting her soundly on her behind, passed by and went into Calhoun's room.

VIII

The Vice President

As is often the case with returning heroes, General Zachary
Taylor turned his thoughts to a political career. If he chose to
run for elected office, there was little doubt that he would win,
since his name was on nearly everyone's lips. He did choose to
run for the presidency on the platform of the Whigs. Lewis
Cass was selected by the Democratic party as his opponent.
Cass hoped that his nomination against Taylor would give him
national recognition which would lead to a political career at a
later time. He could hope for little more running against the
conquering hero.

General Taylor ran on his war record and received an
overwhelming majority of votes.

"At least he is a slaveholder," Rose commented shortly after
the election when Calhoun was dining with them at their
home.

"He is from the South," Calhoun agreed, "but I'm not
certain we can count on his support. Senator Seward of New
York has been one of his political advisers. Seward leads the
antislavery faction of the Whigs. If this man has any influence
with the new administration we will see more antislavery
legislation."

"Let us hope this is not the case," Robert remarked.
"General Taylor is the first to win the presidency without
having been previously elected to public office. He will have no

political obligations to fulfill. Perhaps he will be a truly independent president."

Calhoun sighed. "I hope this is not wishful thinking."

The southern Democrats and the country at large were not long in learning where their new president stood on the slavery issue. Only weeks after taking office, he firmly announced that California should be brought into the Union as a free state. He thus made it clear that he believed all territories added to the Union should be done so free from slavery. The president actually dispatched troops to New Mexico to prevent any interference from southern leaders with that territory's becoming an antislavery state. Rose was one of the first supporters of the Democratic party to cry "Drive Federal troops out of New Mexico!"

The president warned belligerently, "If any such attempt is made, I will personally take command of the army."

Fortunately for the Greenhows, their own personal affairs were doing much better than their political aspirations. Robert completed his pamphlet, "The Geography and History of the Northwest." Its immediate acceptance as an authority on that subject was most encouraging. So much so that Calhoun urged that the document be expanded to a full-scale book.

"I can help you convert it into a book, Robert," Rose volunteered enthusiastically. "I can edit it for you. I could even assist you with further research."

For the next few months the Greenhows were deeply engrossed in producing the first authorized book on the history of the Northwest territory. Alas, when it was completed, no firm could be found who would agree to publish it. Undaunted, Rose immediately wrote to her British friends, Richard Pakenham, Lady and Sir Henry Bulwer, and Sir John Crampton, all of whom she had known when they served in the British Ministry in Washington.

"It would be greatly appreciated," she wrote, "if you could use your influence in securing a British publisher for this most noteworthy project."

Feeling a certain obligation to this gracious American hostess, her British friends lost no time in procuring a British publisher. Shortly a copy of the book was in Rose's hands. This was truly Robert's greatest achievement. It was her duty to see that it was widely publicized and well received.

On the Fourth of July, she hosted a dinner and fireworks display to celebrate the birth of the nation. Obviously her thinly veiled objective was to promote her husband's new book. Proudly she displayed several tiers of copies of the masterpiece piled prominently in their parlor. She pointed out the historic value of such a volume to all the government officials. Such pleas did not go unheeded by such fine friends as Calhoun and Buchanan. Buchanan, for one, who had returned to the Senate after his stint as secretary of state, was enthusiastic in his support. From the floor of the Senate he extolled the book and its author. "After all, gentlemen," Buchanan expounded, "this loyal staff member in the State Department is making only sixteen hundred dollars a year and he must sell twenty-five hundred copies of his work in order to make himself whole. Mind you," he added quickly, "I have no disposition to do anything for Dr. Greenhow except what is just."

Acceptance of the book was most encouraging, but its British publication was unfortunate. Since it obviously favored American claims to the Oregon territory, it was strongly condemned in British circles. When it was learned who was responsible for its publication in Britain, more than one pointed scowl was aimed at Messrs. Pakenham, Bulwer, and Crampton.

"I really cannot understand the Britons' objections," Robert said. "After all, it only clears up the mistaken and distorted view of North America common to all popular histories used in other countries." Rose did not care one way or the other, just so the book sold; and it did.

Their joy was somewhat dampened by a sudden and prolonged illness which befell Robert. He could eat very little and lost considerable weight. Finally, a continuous series of cramps confined him to bed. The doctors could not determine the reason for his illness which eventually subsided on its own. He was able once again to return to the State Department and resume his work. But the bout with the unexplained malady left him weak and it recurred frequently without warning.

Shortly after the triumphant publication of Robert's book, a new cause developed which demanded Rose's complete attention for many months.

Once again it was Calhoun who, although still in ill health and getting weaker in his battles with the enemies of slavery, never shirked his duty when he felt obliged to intercede.

It was at a reception for the new French ambassador that Calhoun came up to Rose, his arm entwined with that of a tall military stranger. "I wish to present General Narciso Lopez," Calhoun said, smiling as he introduced the dark-haired, distinguishd looking gentleman dressed in full military regalia.

General Lopez bowed low and kissed Rose's hand grandly in the European manner. Rose curtsied slightly, and in return, smiled at this strikingly handsome, debonair, youngish-looking man.

"This is my pleasure, General Lopez," Rose greeted him. "Are you here officially from the Spanish legation?"

"On the contrary, Señora. I presently have no official designation with the Spanish government."

"General Lopez has a most interesting story, Rose," Calhoun explained. "I should like you to hear it."

"It sounds intriguing," replied Rose. "I shall be an apt listener."

"Of course we cannot discuss it presently—too much crowd," the general remarked seriously, his piercing eyes looking directly into Rose's. "Perhaps a more convenient time could be arranged."

"By all means," Rose said graciously. "If the general is available tomorrow evening, would you care to join me at my house for dinner?"

"It would be most enjoyable." General Lopez smiled broadly never taking his eyes from Rose's.

"I trust Mr. Calhoun will be able to attend as well," remarked Rose. "You see, John, Robert has a conference with the British legation tomorrow. He has already advised me it will undoubtedly last well into the night. I am not to expect him for dinner."

"I shall be glad to join you, Rose," said Calhoun.

"Good." Rose smiled. "Shall we say about seven o'clock?"

"I look forward to it, Señora Greenhow," General Lopez replied. "I also anticipate good dining in your house. I have heard what fine cuisines you offer to your guests."

"Thank you, general," replied Rose. "I shall do my best to live up to such a reputation."

General Lopez clicked his heels with military precision, and bowing once again, kissed her hand and abruptly strode away with Calhoun by his side.

Rose liked General Lopez at once. His polished manners fascinated her and his preciseness pleased her fancy. She wondered what his mission could possibly be for Calhoun to imagine that she could be of assistance. Whatever it was, she was sure it would be interesting. Since it obviously could not be discussed freely, it had a quality of intrigue that made the prospect of hearing about it exciting.

Rose was well experienced in preparing small, intimate dinners with little advance warning. However, one day's notice to accomplish the expected culinary masterpieces challenged the prowess of both Rose and her cook. As usual, they rose to the occasion.

General Lopez was glowing in his praise of her unique Chinese water chestnut canapes broiled with crisp bacon and dipped in small dishes of chutney imported from East India. Sautéed almonds accompanied mulled cider which, Rose thought advisable to caution her guests, had been strongly laced with potent apple liquor.

The main course consisted of chilled asparagus tips with

dressing, olive-creamed potatoes, and parmesan oven-fried chicken smothered with julienne green beans with smoky salt and baked apple rings. Each serving was accompanied by generous portions of Madeira wine which elicited General Lopez's particular admiration.

"This wine could only be imported from the south of Spain," he beamed.

"And vintage forty-two," replied Rose. "I am not an authority on wines, but I am told that this was a very good year."

"The best," agreed the general.

The dinner was accompanied by small talk as they leisurely consumed the various delicacies.

"This I miss so much," General Lopez confided. "When one is traveling as much as I, these kinds of luxuries are a rarity."

It was not until after dinner, with the men comfortably seated in the parlor with large black cigars and sipping strong brandy, that the purpose of their meeting was first mentioned.

"I shall let General Lopez explain his mission to you, Rose, since he is thoroughly versed in its many ramifications," Calhoun said by way of introduction, leaning back comfortably and crossing his legs.

"You are familiar with the situation in Cuba?" Lopez plunged directly into his subject.

"I know that it is a possession of your government," replied Rose.

"It is not my government, Señora. I am a citizen of Venezuela. My commission is from the Venezuelan Army."

"I understand," Rose said, although she did not understand at all. "You must forgive my blunder."

"It is no matter. But I'm deeply concerned with the plight of the Cuban people. So much so that I am wanting to take explicit action to change this condition."

"Please explain, General Lopez."

"The situation in Cuba, she is bad, if you do not know."

"I am sure Cuba would be much happier if it were a part of the United States. You must be aware that our President Polk, when he was in office, offered to purchase Cuba from Spain but was soundly rebuffed."

"For good reason, Señora. He had offered one hundred million dollars as the purchase price. The Spaniards receive that much and more from the Cubans each year. They are bleeding the island population dry, and the Cuban people are helpless."

"I was not aware of this situation," Rose commented, frowning.

"Very few people are," replied General Lopez, warming to his subject. "You have heard of the Spanish Inquisition, no doubt?"

"Of course. You don't mean—"

General Lopez nodded. "It is worse. Family fortunes are confiscated. Heads of families are arrested on the slightest provocation, their possessions are stolen in the name of the state. If any object they are severely tortured. Whole families are being executed, including women and children. There is no law. There is no trial. The rights of the people have been abolished. Everything that a person owns is subject to appropriation by local hoodlums in the name of the Spanish government."

"How dreadful. But what can be done?"

"Revolution! The Spanish government in Cuba must be overthrown."

"It is no more than they deserve for such cruel treatment of a colony."

"That is exactly as I have thought, Señora. That is why I have offered my life to come to their assistance."

"How noble of you. But what can I do?"

"I will need the backing of many American citizens. Official sanction from the American government is more than we can hope for."

"To give it would probably lead to war with Spain," Calhoun interrupted.

"But there is nothing to prevent American citizens from joining our cause on their own," General Lopez hurriedly added.

"How can I be of assistance?" Rose asked.

General Lopez smiled as he looked at Calhoun. "Señor Calhoun tells me that if you would agree to use your influence, I could be assured of vast unofficial support because of your position in this great capital."

Rose smiled. "I fear that Senator Calhoun is exaggerating my importance. I do sympathize wholeheartedly with your cause, however. I will willingly do anything that I can to promote it."

"Good!" the two men said simultaneously, both of them leaning forward in their enthusiasm. The rest of the evening was spent in laying plans for the proposed Cuban revolution.

"There is universal feeling in Cuba for inciting a revolution!" Lopez said excitedly. "With only a few more men than I have available, I know the rest of the populace will join us, once we have laid siege to the island."

"How can you be sure?" Rose asked. "Do you know that the people of Cuba will support a revolution?"

"I have spent much time in Cuba, Señora. I have many contacts. So many that the Spanish government has exiled me from the island."

"Then you risk death when you return," Rose commented.

"They will have to capture me first." General Lopez laughed heartily. Then he added, wildly waving his hands in his excitement, "But my life is of no consequence if this oppressive regime can be overthrown."

"We can solicit an unofficial army of American volunteers to reinforce your effort," suggested Rose.

"We will need a competent leader," Calhoun joined in.

"Jefferson Davis will surely join our cause. He distinguished himself in the Mexican war. He would be an ideal leader and can muster a great number of followers if we can succeed in gaining his support."

"He has only recently been married to the beautiful Varina Howell of Natchez," Calhoun commented. "He may not wish to join such an expedition at this time."

"I am sure he will if he is made aware of the situation," Rose replied, her eyes gleaming as she imagined herself leading the efforts of this great humanitarian cause. Then suddenly she announced, "I shall give a reception in General Lopez's honor. We will have speeches. General Lopez can denounce the atrocities that are taking place on the island in the name of the Spanish government. All who hear of the Cubans' plight will join our cause."

"Undoubtedly," urged Calhoun. "The men of the south ought to flock down there in open boats the moment they hear the tocsin."

It was agreed that a reception would be the best means of attracting American support for the downtrodden Cubans. A date for the reception was agreed upon and Rose began to plan the details. The ballroom of the Ambassador Hotel was secured and many of their prominent friends from the south were invited to attend.

As receptions go, the affair was, as usual, a tremendous success. However, there were some who did not share Rose's and Calhoun's enthusiasm. Jefferson Davis flatly rejected their offer to serve as leader of the unofficial American expedition. In an effort to be able to announce the selected leader at the reception, they tried valiantly to secure the best men that would be available. Jointly, Calhoun and Rose approached Robert E. Lee, but he, too, graciously declined the dubious honor. Unabashed, they continued to look for a suitable leader and finally settled for Colonel G. E. White, who had unquestionably distinguished himself by his exploits in the Mexican war.

It was several days before Robert realized what new project Rose had undertaken without his knowledge and he immediately questioned her about it.

"Rose, you don't realize the implications of such a movement."

"You have made me well aware that I do not understand diplomacy. But I can recognize a downtrodden people and their need to be rescued from oppressive masters. I cannot sit idly by without trying to reduce or eliminate their suffering."

"This is treason, Rose!"

"Poppycock. This is merely an unofficial act of a few private citizens to give an oppressed people the same freedom that we experience in our own country."

"I know better than to try to dissuade you, Rose, but mark my words, you are apt to regret it."

"It is too late to change our course now, Robert. But if I could, I would not do so."

"This is madness! There will surely be official repercussions."

"Of course there will be. Spain has a veritable gold mine in her stranglehold, wringing every ounce of gold that she can from these poor people, as she did with her earlier conquests on the mainland of South America. But then there were no sympathetic Americans to come to their rescue."

Robert sadly shook his head. "Will you understand if I do not join you in this activity?"

"Certainly. I understand. I realize your position as an employee of the State Department would render any action unthinkable."

As a result of the reception, volunteers came pouring in to join the crusade to rescue the oppressed Cubans. Rose was elated. Almost every waking hour was devoted to making preparations for the uprising. A secret date was established for the revolutionary force to set sail.

Rose was attending a meeting of some sort nearly every day. Men had to be properly enrolled. Arms had to be secured. Provisions must be supplied. And to support the entire project, money had to be raised. She was active in every phase of the undertaking.

Although the operations were carried out in secret, such a large enterprise could not be conducted without rumors abounding. It was little over one week before the scheduled departure that Robert came home greatly disturbed.

"Spain has officially protested your operation to the president," he announced.

"I was sure that they would when they learned of it," Rose replied calmly.

"You have placed the United States government in a most precarious position. If they ignore this protest, they jeopardize relations with the Spanish government. If they acknowledge it, they must issue a strong condemnation or be branded a party to this proposed mad uprising."

"This is none of the government's business. It is being supported entirely by volunteers and financed by private individuals. There is no need for any government action."

"Rose, you do not understand—"

"I know, dear. I do not understand this sort of diplomacy. Let me tell you what I think of diplomacy. We have engaged a steamer to sail from the harbor of New York with one thousand picked and armed men. Another vessel is due to leave the city of New Orleans with fifteen hundred more men. All of them willing and ready for the perils and honors of the venture. I will not burden you with the date of sailing so you need not be disturbed."

"This will not be accomplished without rejection by our government," Robert said, in some distraction.

Robert conveniently secured an assignment to visit Philadelphia to care for a matter concerning some illegal aliens who had been smuggled into the country. Thus he was not in the vicinity of Washington for the next few days and had no knowledge of what was actually taking place. Rose agreed that going away at this time would be good for his health, since he was beginning to get severe cramps in his stomach again.

The day before the scheduled date of the armada's sailing,

General Lopez came to Rose's house in anguish.

"Señora," he exclaimed excitedly, "your president he has officially denounced our venture."

"I knew he would, General Lopez," said Rose wearily, looking up from a large pile of bandages which she was preparing for her invading troops to use for binding up expected wounds in battle. "I have told you that the Spanish government has already registered a protest."

"Yes, but your president has proclaimed the expedition a criminal enterprise. He warns all Americans against joining us."

"Have you noted any reluctance on the part of our men to continue as planned?"

"None that I am aware of."

"Then ignore the president's proclamation. Send word to as many of your men as you can that all is in readiness and the invasion will depart as originally planned."

"But what of your president, Señora?"

"He does not mean what he says, general. You are aware that his predecessor knew of the plight of those poor Cubans. He tried to solve the problem with money but was unsuccessful. President Taylor is of the same frame of mind."

"Are you sure?"

"I am in a position to know, general. I have definite knowledge that his proclamation is a face-saving gesture. It is merely a matter of diplomacy between governments."

"That is most comforting, Señora. I will be forever grateful to you for your assistance and your assurance in such trying times as these."

"Be at ease, general, our preparations are complete and thorough. My own husband does not know of the exact date of your departure."

"But suppose your president is not exactly face saving. Suppose he tries to forcefully stop us. I am not afraid for myself, Señora, but what if he should suddenly decide to have me arrested? What would happen to all our men without their leader?"

"Have you heard any rumor concerning your arrest or detainment?"

"No, Señora. But he could think of it. The government knows where I am staying."

"There is only one more night for us to worry about, general. And he won't know where you are staying tonight if you should choose to spend it here in my house."

General Lopez was suddenly very much relieved. "I am safe from them here, eh?"

"Completely."

The last night before the invaders set sail their leader was a guest in Rose's house. Ignoring the impropriety of hosting a handsome young South American gentleman in her home while her husband was away on state business, Rose stayed up with General Lopez until the early hours of the morning, reviewing the details of the upcoming venture.

"All the elements of success are with you, General Lopez," Rose said excitedly.

"I am glad, my dear lady. I must admit to you that I am just the littlest bit of nervous."

"There is no reason to be. Every chance has been calculated, and everything which prudence and forethought could suggest has been done to ensure full success."

"You think then that your government is still not aware of the time of our departure?"

"There is no doubt of it. You know yourself that they have done no more than the matter of the proclamation, which was solely demanded for appearance. We have planned well, general. The rest is up to you."

"The first fifteen days are the time of trial, and this I have imparted to all of our men."

"I have a proclamation of my own which I will issue when first I receive word of your success. Do you wish to hear it?"

"It would be most helpful, Señora."

"It might serve as encouragement to your men. I have

133

written an additional copy for you to read to them at the appropriate time."

Rose drew two pieces of paper from the bosom of her bodice, and handing one to General Lopez, unfolded the other and read it to him.

"This heroic project to loose the fetters on an oppressed people invites the moral aid of all true hearts who desire the incorporation of that ocean gem in our sisterhood of states. All who sympathize with a people groaning under the yoke of tyranny, determined to achieve freedom or die in the struggle, offer you their heartfelt thanks. We say to you, God bless you, and may He be always by your side in your endeavors."

Tears welled up in the general's eyes as he placed the paper in his breast pocket next to his heart. "Thank you, dear lady. You will be rewarded for this some day, I am sure."

The next morning Rose herself prepared a hearty breakfast for the general and blew a kiss to him as he left her home.

Even before Robert returned from his mission in Philadelphia, Rose received word of the invasion which she had had such a great part in launching. Apparently the Spanish government had had more knowledge of the proposed revolution than Rose had thought. The invading forces were savagely attacked as they scrambled upon the beach at the Bay of Pigs, and General Lopez himself was killed with many of his followers. The rest scrambled back onto the boats which had brought them. Under heavy fire from shore batteries they managed to escape and returned ingloriously to the United States. Their revolution, which had been so thoroughly planned, had ended in complete disaster.

Rose did not have time to shed more than a few tears for the misadventure to which she had devoted such a great deal of effort, or for the death of its romantic general.

A week later a message arrived at her home from her Aunt Hill's. "Come at once," it advised. "Senator Calhoun is seriously ill."

Calling her carriage, she rushed over to her aunt's house.

134

Robert, who had returned from his trip, was unable to accompany her, since he was again confined to his bed with a severe case of cramps.

Calhoun could hardly speak to her, he was so weak, but he smiled as she came into his room.

"You never did rest as you should have, John," she admonished him cheerily as she wiped his forehead with a cool cloth.

"There wasn't time," he whispered to her. "There was always so much to do for the cause of the South."

His oldest son, John, came into the room carrying a pile of papers. "What do you wish me to do with these manuscripts, Father?" he asked quietly.

"Put them away, son. Read them over carefully. If you can use any of the material, feel free to do so. You can revise them as you see fit."

"You speak as though you will not be needing them again yourself, John," Rose said to him. "Your son had better keep them intact until you get well. Then you can judge for yourself whether they require revision."

Calhoun raised his head slightly from his pillow. "I will not be needing them again, Rose." His head dropped back onto the pillow and he murmured something so low that Rose could not hear.

She leaned close to him and said softly, "What is it, John?"

"Never abandon the cause of the South," he mumbled weakly.

"I never shall."

He smiled. "My Wild Rose." His eyes closed and he sighed. It was his last sigh. His burden of protecting the southern cause from its many attacks was over. At last, he had found peace.

Rose left her aunt's house and aimlessly ordered her driver to travel around the streets of the capital. As she came to the Senate, she stopped him and went inside the great building. Slowly she climbed up to the Senate gallery and listened quietly as the senators spoke. She learned from one of the spectators seated beside her that they had been arguing the burning issue of the day: slavery. Only a few moments ago the senators had been outdoing each other in their declarations for admission of California as an antislavery state. Then the senators from the South followed to argue strongly against admission. All this had ceased as word of Calhoun's death was received.

Now the senators were vying with each other to be recognized by the vice president. All of them to a man voiced words of praise for their departed colleague. Tears rolled uncontrollably down Rose's cheeks as she listened.

Calhoun was buried three days later in a simple government ceremony. The committee on arrangements had allowed her a place with his family for the burial. She stood beside Daniel Webster as both silently watched the hero of the South being lowered into the ground. Then, quietly, almost inaudibly, Daniel Webster said to her, "One of earth's princes hath departed—the purest, best, and greatest man I ever knew."

Nor was this to be the end of tragedy for Rose.

Two months later, President Taylor was taken seriously ill. After several medical consultations, the doctors diagnosed his malady as a severe case of cholera. Two weeks later Rose and the nation were shocked to learn that he had died. The next day Millard Fillmore, who had been Taylor's vice president, became president.

It was only a few days later that Robert was called into President Fillmore's office.

After two or three simple formalities of greeting, President Fillmore looked directly at Robert and spoke seriously. "Bob, with the annexation of Texas there are a lot of land claims that have been left unsettled as a result of the Mexicans' reluctance to discuss them."

"I realize that, sir. I know the state of affairs that many of these claims were in when I previously visited Mexico City."

"With the certainty of California's coming into the Union,

the land claims in that territory are in greater disorder. It is my personal opinion that you are more qualified to handle this complicated situation than anyone else in government."

"I appreciate your confidence, Mr. President."

"I have such confidence that I am assigning you on a full-time basis to the settlement of these Mexican land claims."

"Thank you, sir, but I have several other duties in the State Department—"

"You will have no other duties at the State Department. You are being transferred from there."

"Do you mean—"

"This is a specific assignment that you will be engaged in directly with this administration. I want you to go down to Mexico and straighten out these land claims once and for all."

Robert hesitated. "Under ordinary circumstances, sir, I would be glad to go, but I have been ill of late and I don't know whether I will be up to the hardships of such a long journey at this time."

"I am aware of your illness, Bob, and I regret that duty requires that you undertake such a trip. I must still insist, however, that you start your journey within one week. I can only offer you the compensation of your comforting wife, who is to accompany you on your journey."

"My wife, sir! I—I—this is most unusual. I hardly think she will be any more able to bear up under such a hazardous journey than I."

"I am sorry, Bob, but it is an absolute necessity."

"There is also the matter of our three girls."

"You can do as you wish. You may take your daughters with you or leave them behind. In any event I have issued a special authorization to allow the government to bear the total expense for your entire family's care."

"This is most considerate of you but I—is this not rather sudden, Mr. President? I will have to discuss this with my wife. You can understand that there are many complications in such a move. I don't know—"

"This is an order, Bob. There is no alternative."

"Perhaps I could leave first and if my wife wishes she may follow me at a later date."

"The order applies particularly to your wife, Bob."

"I—I don't understand."

"I think you do. Your wife is a most extraordinary woman."

"She is that, sir."

"Any woman who can bring our government to the brink of a war with a major nation is not to be taken lightly."

"You are referring to the Cuban affair, Mr. President."

"Precisely. The country and my new administration need a cooling off period, Bob, before your good wife devises another of her schemes."

"I beg your pardon, sir, but would you care to tell me if President Taylor was aware of this contemplated action, sir?"

"It was his explicit direction as he lay on his dying bed."

"I see."

Slowly Robert rose from his chair and silently walked out of the president's office. How could he ever tell Rose of this sudden turn of events? He smiled wanly to himself. He would never tell her the entire story. She would probably be delighted to be going to Mexico City with him. She would also undoubtedly be most pleased that his relations with the State Department were finally severed. She could decide what she thought would be best for their girls and they would start for Mexico City.

As President Fillmore himself had said, there was no alternative.

IX

The President

Fall 1851

Rose was delighted to learn that she was to accompany Robert on his trip to Mexico City. She was glad for him, for he was still ailing and she believed a change of climate would be good for his health. As for herself, she had been wanting to travel for some time and this trip, to be fully paid by the government, was ideal. She never learned the true reason for her husband's sudden departure from the capital and from the State Department. On the surface it was a wonderful stroke of good fortune, and there certainly was no reason to look a gift horse in the face.

Her sister, Ellen Cutts, was most cooperative in agreeing to care for her three daughters, since the arduous trip into Mexico was rather trying for anyone, and almost impossible for young children. The thought that she must leave within one week did not deter her in the least. The days passed quickly and there was a great deal to do in a short time. Finally, she was overjoyed to suddenly realize that in less than two days they would be on their way.

The day before they were to leave, Rose ordered her carriage and was driven down to the Senate for one last glimpse at the hub of government power which had meant so much to her during her years in the capital.

The Senate was engaged in a discussion concerning the dispatch of Commodore Perry with a small flotilla of ships to

139

sail to the island of Japan. His express assignment was to open that country's ports to United States trade. The Senate was nearly unanimous in its approval of the voyage and authorization was quickly obtained. There remained only the assignment of a committee to work out necessary details, and the matter was disposed of.

In the next order of business a committee was selected to supervise reorganization of the Post Office system in order to provide cheaper mail rates. Rose smiled as she observed the calm morning session and compared it with the days when fiery senators had almost come to blows debating clearly divergent views on important issues of the day. Then she sighed. She knew that the most important issue—slavery—was far from being solved. She also knew that the northern and southern states were firmly headed in opposite directions on the issue, and there seemed no hope for a peaceful solution to the problem.

With the selection of a committee to oversee the reorganization of the postal system, the Senate adjourned for the noonday break.

She was wending her way slowly down the marble steps from the Senate gallery when she spied Senator Buchanan coming off the Senate floor.

She waved to him cheerily and he immediately came over to her.

"I am glad to see you have honored us with your presence once again," he greeted her. "I was beginning to think that you had deserted us."

"I have been extremely busy the last few days, Jim. Robert and I are getting ready for a trip."

"So I have heard."

"Apparently there is very little that goes on in the capital that the senator does not hear about. You truly surprise me. Pray tell, how did you ever learn about our sudden departure? We have only known about it ourselves for five days."

Senator Buchanan knew the complete story of Rose's forced

140

departure from the capital, but he made no mention of it. He wondered if she was aware of all the facts in her case. Instead he said, "This calls for a celebration. Will you join me for luncheon?"

"I would be delighted."

She took his arm and they went into the Senate Restaurant. As he moved her chair up to the table he placed his hands on her shoulders. "I will miss you, Rose."

She smiled coyly. "It is flattering to hear that one will be missed."

As he sat down opposite her he said seriously, "Your departure from the Washington scene will leave a void for many of us."

"I sincerely hope you refer to more than my dinner parties, which I strive so fervently to make successful."

"You know better than that, my dear."

"Are you aware that with Robert's mission to Mexico City he is ending his duties at State?"

"I know Robert is no longer assigned to that department."

Rose frowned, a strange uncertain look in her eyes. Fortunately the waiter came up to them at that moment and Buchanan added quickly, "This is undoubtedly a promotion for him, Rose. Let us drink to his success. I shall have an old-fashioned whiskey. What will you have?"

"It is rather early in the day for wine."

"Under ordinary circumstances I would agree, but in this case, I must demur. Waiter, bring us a bottle of your best champagne and make my old-fashioned a double."

They had a delightful luncheon and Rose's head was in a gay whirl from three glasses of champagne. When they finished Buchanan suggested they return to his office, for he had several more orders for Robert's book which he wished to give to her.

In his office, he searched in his drawer for the orders and Rose seated herself in a chair before him. "I want you to know how deeply appreciative both Robert and I are for the interest you have shown in his book."

"It is the least I can do. I have long believed that Robert is not receiving sufficient remuneration for his work at State. Perhaps this will change now that he has been transferred."

"I sincerely hope so. Actually, President Fillmore himself has been most considerate in his arrangements for the care of our family while we are on this trip."

"It is no more than you both deserve," Buchanan smiled.

"You also deserve more for your loyalty to our country, Jim."

"You are, no doubt, referring to the editorial in the *Washington Daily Globe* suggesting that I run for president in the next election."

"You would make a good president, Jim. You know the problems that our country faces at home. You are also one of the few persons well-versed in foreign affairs, because of your experience as ambassador to Russia and on the many foreign trade committees."

Buchanan sighed. "I have made myself available both in forty-four and forty-eight, but the Democratic party believed there were other more qualified men, Rose. I am willing to accept their decision."

"But deep down in your heart you believe otherwise."

"I don't know. I'm getting older now."

"You do want to be president, don't you?"

Slowly he shook his head. "I don't know whether I am up to facing these trying times."

"I know that you are. You may rest assured I for one, will do everything in my power to see that you attain this goal."

"Thank you, Rose." He got up and handed her the orders for her husband's book.

"You are more qualified to find a solution to the problem of slavery than any other man in the nation today."

"I'm afraid that I have antagonized many of my own constituents in Pennsylvania with my strong stand on California and other states being admitted to the Union as

142

slave states."

"You have done right, Jim."

"Sometimes I fear I have listened too much to you and your friends, my Wild Rose."

Rose jumped up from her chair to face him squarely. "How can you say that? You know that you are only doing as your own conscience dictates."

"What you say is true, but you must be prepared for setbacks in your cause, Rose. You cannot win every skirmish."

"What do you mean?"

"California will be voted into the Union within a fortnight. A compromise has been agreed upon. She will come in as a free state without slavery."

"Oh, Jim, are you sure?" He did not answer her. "Isn't there anything that we can do?"

"Nothing, Rose. It has been decided. I am sorry."

It hurt him to see the look of dejection that came into her eyes. She seemed so utterly frustrated, defeated. He forced himself to smile as he came around the side of his desk to her. "But this must not spoil the last few moments we will have together in many months."

"I am sorry, Jim. You know how dear the issue of slavery is to my heart. We need all of the support that we can muster. And I was certain that we could count on you."

He took her hand in his and leaned close to her. "You can, Rose. It is just that I believe moderation will solve the problem, for the good of both the North and the South."

His closeness to her disturbed her. She was pleased by his attention but knew that she could not trust herself so near to him. Quickly she withdrew her hand from his and started toward the door. "You will find that moderation will not satisfy either the North or the South, Jim. Now I must be going. I still have much to do. As you are probably aware, we are scheduled to leave the day after tomorrow."

He walked beside her as she went to the open door of his office. Upon reaching the doorway he leaned over quickly and shut it before her. Taking her in his arms he pressed her body to his and drew her face to him. Fervently, deliberately, he kissed her soundly on her lips. For an instant she stiffened against the pressure of his arms, then limply sank against him and slowly raised her arms, pressing his broad shoulders close to her own body. Closing her eyes, she gave herself up completely to him as he savagely pressed his lips to hers, kissing her again and again.

It was ecstasy being in his arms. For a fleeting moment she thought of the wrong she was doing. Her thoughts were muddled. The champagne did not permit her to think clearly, and she was glad for it. She pressed her breasts against his body. He touched one of them ever so lightly then pressed it hard as he bent down and kissed it. He was breathing heavily as he felt for the buttons at the top of her blouse and unloosened them. Wildly, almost mechanically, she drew open the top of her blouse, revealing a good part of her bare breast. He lowered his head and kissed it passionately. She pressed her body even closer to his as she felt him move against her.

Suddenly, quickly she drew her lips from him and forcefully pushed him away. "Jim," she said, her face flushing, "this is madness."

"It is, Rose." Then he took her chin in his hand and kissing her once again tenderly, stepped away.

Quickly she buttoned her tunic and smoothed her disheveled hair.

"Don't forget me, Rose."

"I shan't ever, Jim. But this—this cannot be."

Slowly he opened the door. "As usual, you are correct, my sweet one. But I can always wish and hope."

Rose sighed. "I cannot deny that I enjoyed being so much a part of you. But I—let us say that the champagne tempted me to completely forget myself."

"Yes, that is what it was," Buchanan smiled. "That and the double old-fashioned that I had myself so early in the day."

"I agree, Jim. Except for the fact that I know you have a fair portion of whiskey at this hour every day. I hope that it does not always end as this one has."

"There is only one Rose O'Neal Greenhow."

As he looked deep into her eyes, she suddenly started to laugh. At first she snickered and put her hand to her mouth to conceal her emotion. But she could not help herself, and she began nervously to laugh loud and uncontrollably.

He put his hands on her shoulders and shook her. "My God, Rose, what is so hilarious?"

The shaking seemed to help her gain control. She stopped laughing and looked up at him seriously. "Forgive me, Jim, I— I just could not help myself. You see, I never noticed before that you have one brown eye and one blue eye."

They both laughed and she started out the door. Hastily she looked about her to see if anyone was watching. Assured that no one was, she quietly put her hand to her lips, blew a kiss to him, and departed.

Two days later Rose and Robert started their long, arduous journey to Mexico City. They traveled by train to Selma, Alabama, a most pleasant ride. The scenery was beautiful, the summer flowers just beginning to come into bloom. The first leg of the trip was so enjoyable that they arrived in Selma long before they had anticipated.

"Steam locomotives certainly make traveling a pleasure," Rose commented.

"I'm sure everyone will choose to travel by railroad once they learn of the conveniences."

"Soon, no doubt, rail tracks will crisscross the country north and south and east and west until you will be able to go anywhere you choose by railroad."

"It is unfortunate that this mode of travel is not available clear to Mexico City. It might make the balance of the trip a bit more endurable."

"Oh, Robert, I am sure you are exaggerating. It can't be so bad as you are making it." Rose was in high spirits anticipating her stay in the capital of Mexico, and no mode of travel could dampen her enthusiasm.

However, Robert was not exaggerating. If anything, he had underestimated the trials and tribulations they were to encounter on the rest of their journey.

They boarded one of Ben Holladay's coaches at Selma together with four other passengers. Although the coach was enclosed, it gave them little protection from the dust and dirt of the narrow, swampy road they were forced to pass through. During many portions of the trip, they traveled over land that was best described as field and forest rather than road.

On the third day of their journey it began to rain, and the dry, dusty ruts became soft and thick with layers of mud. In one ravine the four horses were unable to pull the carriage through the mire. The driver and his helper jumped out but could not budge the carriage or the horses. Finally the driver came back to the passengers' cabin and opened the door.

"Them poor beasts ain't got it in 'em to get us out of this ravine," he announced. "And we ain't either. If you folks don't want to stay here overnight, you'd better get out and help us." Four of the male passengers jumped out and Robert started to follow.

Rose detained him. "Robert, you know you've been complaining of not feeling well. Straining to push this coach will only aggravate your cramps. Just rest yourself."

"But they need all the help they can get, Rose."

"If they need more help, I'll volunteer."

So saying, Rose tucked her skirt into the top of her high-buttoned boots and jumped out of the coach, sinking nearly to the top of her boots in the thick mud.

"My God, lady," one of the passengers shouted, "what are you trying to do?"

"The same thing that you are. My husband is ill and can't help, but there's nothing the matter with me." She went back to the rear wheel, and taking her place behind it, grabbed the rim just above the hub where it had sunk into the mire. She was about to heave with all her might when she turned to notice all

146

of the men gaping at her in amazement.

Indignantly she straightened up and putting her hands on her hips said disgustedly, "For Christ's sake, you ninnies. Are you going to stand there and let me try and pull this goddamn box of bolts out of the mud all by myself?"

The spell that seemed to have overcome them was suddenly broken and the men took their places beside the four wheels of the coach and started to heave.

"The coach isn't budging," said one of them, oozing his feet out of the mire with a sucking sound.

"Of course it isn't," Rose shouted, puffing. "All you jackasses are pulling against each other. My God, haven't any of you ever heard of teamwork? You, driver, you ought to know what to do. Now, all of you take your stand and don't move a muscle until I shout heave! Then you all heave as heartily as you can." She was about to take her position when she suddenly stopped and looked up at Robert watching them from within the carriage. "All right, husband of mine, you are not expected to shove this carriage out of here because of your illness, but the least you can do is get the hell out and lighten the load as much as possible."

"I'm sorry, Rose," Robert said sheepishly as he jumped out and sank into the mud with the others. "I never gave it a thought. How inconsiderate of me."

Rose smiled at him and patted him on the shoulder as he sank deeper into the mud. "All set men, ready—HEAVE!" Slowly, surely, the carriage began to move, then suddenly stopped.

Rose sloshed to the front of the carriage where the driver had been pushing against the front wheel. "Driver, haven't you ever been stuck in mud like this before?"

"To be truthful with you, ma'am, I haven't. I've been on the short run between Fort Worth and San Antonio for over two years but I never encountered nothing like this."

"I thought so," said Rose disgustedly. "You've got good roads up there all the way. Now you listen to me and you'll

147

learn something you will never want to forget. When I shout 'heave,' you don't heave at all. You slap those four critters with your whip with one hand and pound their rumps soundly with the reins you hold in your other hand. That way we'll all be pulling together."

"Oh, I see," the driver remarked brightly. "That's a good idea."

"You're damn right it is," Rose remarked dryly. "Now let's all get to our posts and get this coach back on what some politician must have sometime called a road. Let's go, men. Ready—HEAVE!" The men heaved with all their strength as did Rose, who was able to exert nearly as much pressure as any of the men. This time the coach did start to move, and with the urging of the driver who continued energetically to whip the horses, the coach was soon completely free of the mire.

The men cheered Rose lustily as they stood beside the coach they had just freed. "What this route needs is more clever women like you," said one of them respectfully. "Thank you, ma'am."

They brushed off the greater portion of the mud which had been splattered on their clothes and scraped as much of it as they could from their boots. Hopping into the coach, they continued on their journey.

For the balance of their trip a certain camaraderie developed as a result of the incident, and the men talked cheerfully with Rose and listened to her fascinating stories of Washington. She was no longer one woman among seven men, but had become one of them.

The rain stopped and they drove through clearer terrain for the next two days. Before turning south they passed a caravan of covered wagons drawn by oxen whose occupants were going west to settle in California. "We're goin' on to gold country," one of them shouted to them as he passed. "Did you know they've discovered gold in California?"

They changed drivers and horses at the little village of Guanajuato and were within a day's journey of Mexico City

148

when suddenly the carriage stopped with a tremendous jolt. It could go no further. The horses had veered to the side of the road and were stuck in a clump of bushes. Rose, followed by the men in the carriage, got out and went up to the Mexican driver.

"What's the trouble, driver?" asked Rose.

The new driver merely shrugged his shoulders. He could not speak a word of English. Robert then came to the rescue, since he spoke Spanish fluently.

After a lengthy discussion with the driver he turned to the rest to explain. "The two horses on the left side were frightened by a bevy of grouse which flew up in front of them. They will not go a step further. The other two horses, knowing the trail lies ahead, will not go backward and the driver is unable to get them to pull together no matter how hard he tries."

"Tell him to force the horses who won't budge," Rose said simply.

Acting as interpreter, Robert talked to the driver again. Presently he turned to Rose. "He contends that he has tried everything. Two horses will not go forward and the other two will not budge backward."

"This is ridiculous. We are scheduled to arrive in Mexico City before nightfall. We will never make it if we don't soon continue on our way."

"I have told the driver this. He merely shrugs his shoulders and asks 'What can I do?'"

"Tell him to let me have the reins. I'll get them out of there."

But when Robert conveyed this suggestion to the driver, he objected vociferously. No woman was going to attempt to drive his carriage. Whereupon the rest of the men added their voices to the argument. They told Robert to advise the driver that Rose was a competent horsewoman and that they insisted she at least be given a chance to make the horses move. The men shouted to the driver although they knew he could not

149

understand them, to emphasize their desire that he give Rose the reins.

Finally the driver relinquished his seat and jumped down, after he had Robert's assurance that he would be responsible if anything drastic happened to the carriage or any of its occupants.

Rose jumped up onto the driver's seat, and grabbing the whip in one hand, pulled hard on the reins with the other. She laid the whip heavily on the two horses who had refused to back up while pulling back as hard as she could on the reins. The two rebellious horses finally gave in and the coach began to move. As the horses started to back up she lightened her whip, still straining with all her might to pull back on the reins. Slowly, gradually, the coach backed away from the brush and turned out once again onto the road. The men, standing beside the coach, threw their hats into the air and lustily cheered Rose. She had added four more men to her large group of ardent admirers.

The rest of the journey was uneventful, except for the incessant swaying and jolting of the carriage. They drove into Mexico City before nightfall, as scheduled.

One of the first bits of news they received was that California had been admitted as the thirty-first state to join the United States of America. With the compromise of 1850, California became, as Buchanan had predicted, a free state.

Rose's stay in Mexico City proved well worth the grueling trip which they had experienced on their way down. For the next few months a whole new world opened for her. They settled in a lovely house on the Calle de Palmas y Plateros, the main street of the city, conveniently located near the many famous buildings. The main streets were beautiful, with marigolds, daisies and white roses profusely in abundance along the edges of the wide avenues. Robert studiously delved into archives, tracing origins of Mexican and Spanish land grants to determine rightful owners. Rose would often drag Robert away from his tedious work to accompany her as she

150

visited the great cathedrals, the Botanic Garden, the Museum and the Alameda. Disregarding Mexican tradition and customs, she freely strolled through the streets of the city where few Mexican ladies were ever seen.

She thrilled to the hustle and bustle of the marketplace, and on many mornings she would rise at dawn to hurry to the market and watch the Mexicans coming to shore in their light canoes, laden with fresh fruits and vegetables, flowers and maize and meats. She tasted new Mexican delicacies such as figs and passion fruits and noted how the Mexicans concocted new and exotic dishes using these ingredients. She insisted that they visit the cock fights and the bull ring but was disgusted at the inhuman treatment of the animals.

She soon learned that the fashionable people of the city promenaded in their fine coaches each evening. She delighted in joining them at six o'clock, slowly wending her way through the picturesque Paseo. She marveled at the beautifully painted coaches imported from France and sighed with compassion as they passed bedraggled mules being driven by dirty peons in rebozos. The minority of the rich were tremendously wealthy, while the majority of the Mexicans lived in abject poverty and dirt.

As usual, the ambitious Rose chose to throw her lot in with the fashionable socialites. She quickly made friends with Frances Erskine Inglis, the Scottish wife of Don Calderon de la Barch, the Spanish minister to Mexico. She freely talked of her associations with Dolly Madison, Jefferson, Calhoun, and the other great American leaders whom she knew. With Frances as her sponsor, she soon became a welcome guest at local parties and receptions, Mexican masked balls and diplomatic dinners. She particularly delighted in welcoming the French and British visitors and began her usual routine of entertaining them with delightful dinner parties in her new home. In return she was constantly being invited to their grand affairs. It was at a reception for the newly appointed ambassador of the French legation that M. de Joquet, the secretary to the legation, introduced her to Jose Y. Limantour.

At first she did not like him, thinking him arrogant and bold. But what little she heard of his story so intrigued her that she invited him to her home to meet her husband and tell his story to him.

So it was that less than two months after their trip from Washington, where they had presumably left intrigue and conspiracy behind them, Rose became enmeshed in a grander scheme than ever before.

As Jose Limantour arrived at their house, Rose introduced him to her husband. "This is the man I was telling you about, Robert. Mr. Limantour, this is my husband, Dr. Greenhow. As I told you, my husband is one of the foremost authorities on boundaries in the United States."

Limantour bowed grandly and smiled smoothly, almost disdainfully, as he remarked, "I have heard of you, Dr. Greenhow. You see, your reputation precedes you."

"I hope the information you received was complimentary, Mr. Limantour."

"I assure you it was. That is why I have made such a great effort to meet you when I learned that you were in Mexico City. But you can just call me Jose. All my friends do so, and believe me, I will show you it is to your advantage to consider me your friend."

"It sounds intriguing," Robert said, noncommittally.

"Oh, it is," Rose hastened to explain. "Jose told me only a little of his venture but it was sufficient to make me believe that you should know about it."

Rose had concocted an exceptionally fine dinner for the occasion, consisting of local delicacies. Candied chestnuts, passion fruits, and figs dipped in a tangy fruit sauce were served in earthenware bowls. The main courses of wild duck cooked on stone and Jambalaya with buttermilk cornbread were individually served by a sharp-faced young Mexican boy in a gold tasseled hat and richly embroidered jacket. All of these were washed down with generous portions of a potent native

152

drink called pulque.

Rose was extremely disappointed when Jose made no mention of the food but plunged directly into his own personal mission—as any good salesman would undoubtedly do, she thought, comforting herself.

"Your good wife tells me that you are familiar with land grants in California."

"They have been assigned to me to explore here in Mexico, so as to determine their rightful claimants. This is my second visit on this mission. I have had an opportunity to investigate nearly all of the questionable claims."

"Good. Then perhaps you can be of help to me and I can be of help to you."

"How so, Jose?"

"Let me explain. I have lived in Mexico for twenty years. I am not too educated, and I am sure that you, Bob, who speak fluent Spanish, have noticed that my Spanish is not too good."

"I have observed that you prefer to speak in English."

"Aha, you notice such things. But I am a good businessman."

"What is your business?" Robert asked.

"I am in business for myself. I am a salesman. But I modestly say to you that I am a good salesman."

"What do you sell?" asked Rose.

"Arms! This is why I have stayed in Mexico for so many years. As you know the Mexicans are happy to oblige any interested parties by starting a revolution upon the slightest provocation."

"They are noted for this," agreed Robert.

"But they would get nowhere without sufficient arms. I see to it that they are kept well supplied."

"A merchant of death," Rose remarked, without smiling.

"Do not judge harshly, my dear Rose. They provide the impetus for revolutions themselves. These people are only happy when they are fighting," Jose carelessly shrugged his shoulders. "I merely oblige them. I am a government contractor. And as a result of my business I have considerable influence with both the French and Mexican officials."

"Monsieur Joquet, the secretary of the French legation, introduced Jose to me," explained Rose to Robert as she listened intently to Jose's story and watched Robert's reaction.

"But I am getting ahead of my story. My business frequently takes me to the territory of California so I finally decided to settle there—a branch office you might say. About ten years ago I selected the village of Yerba Buena as a central location."

"That has recently been incorporated into the city of San Francisco."

"Yes. Three years ago, as a matter of fact. But when I first located my business it was nothing but fields and scrub pines. It was there I met Eugene Duflot de Mofras. Are you familiar with that name?"

"I know the French author of that name," Robert volunteered.

"That is the one. He was traveling in California exploring the coast for Louis Philippe."

"And you became friendly with him?" Rose asked with interest.

"Very. We were both far from home and spent many evenings together, drinking and talking."

"His explorations prompted French interest in California for a while," said Robert.

"You are very knowledgeable, my dear Bob. Eugene said that this region would become the commercial center of the future. He predicted that there was a golden opportunity. He told me I should buy as much land at Yerba Buena as I possibly could."

"And did you?" asked Rose excitedly.

Again Jose shrugged his shoulders. "I bought a little. It was not a very large amount. I was not making much money at the time."

"Oh, what a shame," Rose exclaimed. "You could have been worth a fortune by now if—"

"Ah, but wait," Jose interrupted, his eyes widening. "Two years later I had certain business with Manuel Micheltorena." Jose turned to Robert. "You know him?"

"He was the governor of the California territory."

Jose beamed broadly. "I cannot catch you, Bob. You do know your history!"

Robert smiled. "It has been my life's work."

"Your business with the governor—of course it was the sale of arms," Rose interjected.

"Precisely. And I am not ashamed of it, my dear lady. I met with him in Los Angeles. I sold him a vast quantity of arms. I offered him a good price. Then I learned that the good governor required many more arms than he was able to pay for. He offered me four thousand dollars in cash, which was less than a third of the value of the arms. He said that he would pay me the balance within one year."

"Did you accept his offer?" Robert asked.

"Not exactly. You must know that such transactions, of necessity, are on a strictly cash basis. Who knows? In one year my customer may be dead. Or he may lose his revolution and I would not be able to collect one peso that was rightfully due me."

"It is the same with the political debts that are encountered before an American election," Rose commented dryly.

"Yes," replied Jose. "That is when I suddenly remembered what Eugene de Mofras had once said to me. Here was such a golden opportunity resting before my eyes. It could truly be a windfall. So I told the governor, 'I will take your four thousand dollars cash. For the balance due me perhaps we can work out a transaction that will be mutually agreeable.' Since he seemed interested I said to him as follows: 'Governor, you have much land that is practically worthless and I have many arms that you wish to purchase. Why not grant me some of this land in return for the balance due me on my arms and we will consider the deal completed.'"

"You accepted a grant?" Robert asked, beginning to share

Rose's enthusiasm.

"He granted me title to all of Yerba Buena, Alcatraz, the Parallones, and Punta del Tiburona."

Robert jumped up from his chair and stared wildly at Jose. "What did you say?"

"You heard correct, sir. I repeat, he granted me title to Yerba Buena, Alcatraz, the Parallones, and Punta del Tiburona."

Rose watched her husband in astonishment. Robert was not one to become unduly excited without reason. "Is that a large grant of land?" she asked innocently.

"That is more than the entire present city of San Francisco." Robert turned to Jose, leaned over his chair and looked directly into his eyes. "Do you understand the magnitude of your claims?"

"Of course I do," Limantour replied calmly.

"My God, man, I don't think you realize what you are saying. You can't—you couldn't possibly—else you would not be sitting before me so calmly."

"But I do, Bob. I have held the title to this land for these many years."

Robert sat down again and stared unbelieving at his guest. Finally he started to talk, then stopped, and cleared his throat before continuing. "Do you have written proof of your claim, Jose?"

"I have the land grants themselves as proof. I do not have them with me, they are too priceless."

"Would you be willing to show them to me?"

"Of course."

"Would you permit me to study them? To investigate them?"

"Most certainly."

"Governor Micheltorena is still alive. Is he willing to corroborate your story?"

"He is and he has."

There was nearly a full glass of pulque sitting at Robert's

156

place. Frantically he grabbed it and swallowed it down in one long gulp. "This is the most astounding story I have ever heard in my thirty years of searching government land grants."

Jose Limantour beamed. "I need assistance in verifying my land claims. Will you help me?"

"I—I—will do anything I can," Robert stammered.

"Good, I was hoping that I could count on you."

"I shall have to study the original grant deeds most thoroughly," Robert said.

"Of course. I have them in a safe place. I can make them available to you at any time."

"Do you wish me to inspect them in your home?"

"I can bring them here if you so desire."

"How soon?"

"Tomorrow evening?" Robert nodded absentmindedly, as if he were in a trance. "I shall bring them over after the dinner hour. I cannot impose on your wife's most generous hospitality so soon again."

"It was a pleasure having you, Jose," Rose hurriedly volunteered.

"Now I must be going," Limantour said rising. "I can assure you that any assistance you provide me will be well repaid."

"That will not be necessary."

"I expect no one to perform any service for me for nothing."

As Robert rose, he asked casually, "Jose, tell me, have you succeeded in having any validation to your claim recorded?"

"The official seal of the French legation is clearly in evidence on every one of my documents."

"The possibilities of your grants are most interesting, Jose," Robert said as he and Rose accompanied him to the door. "If your claim can be substantiated and bears up under any challenges in the courts you will probably become one of the wealthiest gentlemen in America, if not *the* wealthiest."

"I realize that, sir. And if you will assist me in substantiating my claims, I assure you your reward will also be substantial."

Robert smiled. "We can discuss that after I have had an

opportunity to study your papers, sir."

"Very good. And now may I bid you a pleasant goodnight. And I wish to thank your lovely wife, Rose, for a most magnificent dinner."

He left, and Robert stood by the door for a long moment before he finally closed it.

"I have never seen you so excited, Robert. Pray tell, what are you thinking?"

"I am dumbfounded by what this man has told me."

"Is it possible that he owns rights to as much land as he claims?"

"I can only say that his is probably the largest land grant I have ever had the opportunity to investigate."

"Do you believe that his claims are genuine?"

"I can tell you more when I have studied his documents. It will take days of research to validate his claims, Rose."

"Do you intend to do so?"

"I do. This is of such great importance I believe I shall acquaint President Fillmore with this man's claims—after I have inspected his papers."

Robert's decision to contact the president concerning Limantour's claims was not delayed very long. He spent the next few days studying Limantour's many documents. He poured over his claims and maps for hours. He secured verification from Monsieur de Joquet, the secretary of the French legation, as well as from Governor Micheltorena. Everything seemed to be in order, and indeed, Jose Limantour's claims appeared to be true, legal documents.

Robert immediately wrote a factual letter to the president, briefly explaining Limantour's vast claims and requesting a decision as to whether or not he should investigate the matter further. He knew it would be well over a month before he would receive a reply.

During this time, he became more and more interested in Limantour and his huge claims.

"I shall complete my research in Mexico within the next

month or so," he said to Rose one evening while they sat in their parlor. "I am sufficiently convinced of the authenticity of Limantour's claims. So much so that I believe they should be explored further in San Francisco."

"Robert, are you suggesting a visit to San Francisco?"

"I am thinking very seriously about it. Since it has become a state there are many claims such as Limantour's—of course on a much smaller scale. Would you care to accompany me to San Francisco?"

"Oh, Robert, I would be delighted."

"Then let us think seriously about going. I have even thought of opening an office to help settle these many claims."

"It is a natural conclusion, Robert. You are the foremost authority on boundaries in the country. You should be where so many of the claims are being contested."

It was unusual for Robert to share Rose's enthusiasm for one of her projects, so Rose lost no time in becoming thoroughly acquainted with this man who had suddenly come into their lives. A few days later, while she was dining with Limantour at the French legation, she told him they were seriously considering going to San Francisco to assist him in verifying his claims.

"I was hoping that you would make such a decision, my Rose, and I have been preparing a little surprise for you when this occurs." He drew forth a small map from his waistcoat pocket and laid it out before her. There was a small area marked on it in red pencil. "This is the Point Lobos area. It is choice land overlooking the Pacific ocean. If your husband will act as my representative, I shall grant you two square leagues of this area."

After thanking Limantour profusely for his generous offer, Rose hastily bid him goodbye. She rushed home to advise her husband of Limantour's proposal. They immediately agreed that they should definitely go to San Francisco and set up an office to take charge of Limantour's land claims.

Three weeks later, an urgent letter was received from

President Fillmore. The government was aware of Jose Limantour's claims and the president hoped that Robert could complete his business in Mexico City at an early date. The president advised further that he would authorize payment for their expenses to proceed to San Francisco and explore the outstandingly large claims of one Jose Limantour.

So it was that as fall arrived in Mexico City, Rose and Robert set out for San Francisco with Jose Limantour agreeing to follow them a short time later.

X

The Agent

Summer 1852

A single word had turned San Francisco into a thriving, bustling metropolis—GOLD. With the discovery of that ageless commodity in great quantities the 49ers stampeded the countryside in search of riches. By the time Rose and her husband arrived, the city had suddenly grown to a population of fifty thousand. There was an overabundance of men—who had not only come from every state in the Union but from many countries in Europe. There were also many coolies, all seeking a better life than they had experienced in their native China.

The trip from Mexico was an easy one compared to their journey southward to the Mexican capital. There was a well-beaten road through the Mexican country to California. They arrived in the United States tanned and in good spirits. They continued their journey from San Diego to San Francisco traveling along El Camino Real, where the good Franciscan monks had conveniently established a mission at the end of each day's journey.

San Francisco was exactly as Rose had imagined it. Bursting with new energy, wild with miners and shopkeepers exchanging gold dust for merchandise in a devil-may-care atmosphere. It was truly the Wild West. The keenly observant Rose was soon to learn that values were established more by priorities than by any civilized control by the government, and life itself was sometimes placed very low on the scale.

They arrived at midday and immediately went to a cafe, where they anticipated having their first good meal after many days of traveling.

The waiter who served them was a middle-aged man with graying hair and a pleasant, dignified smile. He handed them a menu soiled and slightly torn, with the prices scribbled in bold pencil and showing signs of such frequent revisions that it was difficult to read.

Rose gasped as she was able to decipher one of the items. "One dollar for one egg?" she exclaimed.

"Yes, ma'am," the waiter explained patiently. "Chickens are pretty scarce hereabouts and eggs are almost unobtainable."

"But where are your dinners listed?"

"We don't have dinners, ma'am. Everything is à la carte."

"This will take a bit of getting used to," Rose fumed disapprovingly, scanning the menu closely. Then she looked up at her waiter. "Are you the owner of this cafe?"

"No, ma'am, I just work here."

"Oh, I thought that—well—"

"You thought I looked as if I were a—a professional man."

"I didn't mean to imply—"

"That's all right, ma'am. Actually you are correct. I am a lawyer by profession."

"You are?" exclaimed Robert eagerly, jumping up from his chair. "So am I. I'm Robert Greenhow out of the District of Columbia."

"My name is Edward Jenkins Pringle. I'm pleased to meet you." The two men shook hands.

"But what are you doing here in this cafe?" asked Robert as he sat down again.

"Waiting on tables?" Ed smiled and shrugged his shoulders. "It's very simple. I like to eat. I came out here from New York, where I was practicing law. Originally I am from Charleston, South Carolina. I wanted to improve my fortunes the same as thousands of other men. I couldn't find a claim to stake and

162

finally had to give it up. So I moved to San Francisco."

"But couldn't you practice your profession, counselor?"

"Oh, I plan to eventually, but it isn't so easy. There's not too much call for lawyers. You see, many of the men take the law into their own hands and settle their differences out of court."

"How uncivilized," Rose commented disdainfully.

"Exactly the way I feel, ma'am. I'm sure it will settle down to law and order eventually, but we are moving ahead too rapidly. The miners are most impatient. They want justice on the spot. The best man with a Derringer is the one who wins."

"Exciting, but rather unnerving," remarked Rose.

Ed smiled good-naturedly. "You folks are new here, aren't you?"

"Yes, we've just come up from Mexico City where I have been investigating and verifying land claims."

"You should do well here. Land claims are the greatest topic of discussion these days next to gold. Do you plan to stay?"

"Yes, for a while. I thought I would establish an office and help settle some of these questionable claims. Perhaps we can work together."

"I'd be glad for that. You can find me here every day. I've been in San Francisco over a year now. Perhaps I can help you get settled."

"Do you know of any houses that are for hire?" Rose asked quickly.

"Well, there's one down on Market Street that I hear is going to be vacant in a week. The owner wants one hundred and twenty-five dollars a month for it in advance."

"One hundred twenty-five?" Rose exclaimed in despair. "We don't need a mansion, Mr. Pringle."

"This is not a mansion. It is a parlor and two bedrooms in a brick office building over a drygoods store."

"We'll have to do better than that," Rose said, shaking her head. "But now we had best have something to eat and be on our way."

Hastily they each ordered a French dipped beef sandwich,

which proved to be one skimpy slice of beef tucked into a stale sourdough roll and dipped in a watery, greasy gravy. A cup of coffee was surprisingly good, and throwing caution to the wind, they ordered two pieces of apple pie as well. Their bill was eight dollars. "More than we have spent for food during the last week," Rose commented as they paid Ed and rose to go.

They left after Robert promised to get in touch with Ed again when they were settled.

They spent their first night in a crowded hotel whose first floor had been converted into a dance hall. A fiddler and piano player played incessantly, and the cheering and shouting of the revelers continued throughout the night. Neither of them got much sleep, in spite of their exhaustion from being on the road for many weeks.

Three days later Rose located a wooden cottage at eight and nine Montgomery block and suggested to Robert that he could open his office in their parlor. He had a fancy wooden sign made and placed it on the front of their house. He then took out a small advertisement in the *San Francisco Evening Bulletin* announcing that he was an authority on settling land claims. Almost immediately their parlor became a meeting place for miners, businessmen and local politicians.

Business became so brisk that before the month was out Robert had contacted Ed Pringle, who agreed to work with him on a part-time basis until their business warranted his joining Robert as a full-time partner.

However, it developed that there was another expense that was to be added to their budget before Ed became a member of the firm.

As Ed had mentioned, the men were in the habit of taking business matters and the law into their own hands. Whenever more than one man visited Robert's office, there followed a loud discussion. The men would argue with each other as to where one man's claim ended and the other's began. They would become boisterous and swear at each other incessantly.

164

At first Rose took to bringing in cookies and punch in the hopes that her presence would help maintain a certain bit of calm. It soon became apparent that this did not help the situation, for the men ignored her completely. She decided she would have no part of their business and left it entirely to Robert.

This continued for several more weeks until one day it came to a decisive head. Four men were visiting the office. Three of them had one land claim which they insisted had been granted to them by Spanish authority. The fourth man claimed the same piece of land, insisting his grant was authorized by the Mexican government.

Sitting in the kitchen, Rose could hear them swearing at each other.

"You damned swindler, you are trying to steal my territory from me," one of them shouted, with a decidedly French accent.

Whereupon another man shouted back, "We ain't the swindlers. This is our land. It has been rightfully granted to us. We have been living on it!"

"I know you have, you goddamned poachers. That don't make the land yours."

She could hear Robert's voice shouting above them, trying to quiet them. "Please, gentlemen. This will get us nowhere. If you will keep calm I shall investigate each of these claims and tell you who is the rightful owner."

"This land was deeded to Roger Morton," said one of the men, evidently the leader. "That's me! Here's a sworn copy of my claim. Look it over!"

"That's right," shouted another. "Read it carefully and you will see that this land was legally granted to Roger Morton. I'll vouch that this is him. I been working with him for nearly six months now."

"You're a liar," shouted the Frenchman.

"Careful how you say that, you damn Frenchman," countered one of the others. "You know you're just trying to get something for nothing."

"You're a cheat!" screamed still another.

"Who's a cheat?" hollered the Frenchman.

"You are!" shouted all three of the other men in unison.

Rose put her hands to her ears to blot out the unpleasant argument. Still, above the din, she distinctly heard the shot that was fired. Rushing into the parlor she found one of the men lying on the floor clutching his chest.

Robert was leaning over him. "Get a doctor," he said excitedly.

"Bullshit," said one of the men putting his gun into his holster. "He ain't worth the trouble."

"You can't let the man bleed to death!" Robert shouted. Rose gasped as she saw red blood spreading over her carpet. Frantically she rushed out the door and attempted to hail a carriage. Two or three passed her by before one finally stopped.

"A man's been shot in my house," she exclaimed frantically to the man inside the carriage.

"What, again?" the man said casually as he drew to the side of the road.

"He's inside bleeding profusely," Rose explained. "Won't you please take him to the hospital?"

As the man got out and hurried up the walk, he noticed Robert's sign. "Land claim specialist, eh?" he said sardonically. "Is that your husband?"

"Yes, it is."

"Then he's in the kind of business you got to expect this sort of thing, lady."

They went inside. Robert was trying to stop the flow of blood by tying a large rag around the wounded man's body. The other three men were standing together talking among themselves.

The visitor turned to Rose, who was wiping a tear from her eyes with her handkerchief. "Greenhow," he said looking at her in astonishment. "My God, you're Rose Greenhow."

"Yes," she replied simply.

"I met you years ago in Washington, D.C. I'm William M.

Gwin—formerly Senator Gwin." He held out his hand, but Rose, looking at the man lying prone on the floor, did not notice him. "You shouldn't have to contend with this sort of thing. Here's my card, Mrs. Greenhow. Please drop in when you are down that way." He handed the frightened Rose his card and went over to the wounded man. "Here, you men. Help me put this man in my carriage. He seems to be hurt badly."

One of the men went over and helped Senator Gwin and Robert pick up the man and carry him out to the waiting carriage.

The other two remained where they had been standing. "I guess he won't argue with us about what is rightfully ours again," said one of them.

The other laughed and poked his friend in the ribs. "That's right, Roger, goddamned Frenchmen is all alike. They'd steal you blind if you'd let 'em."

Rose looked at both of them loathingly. "You horrible brutes," she spat, "you can speak so of a poor man who may be dying by your own bullet."

"'Tweren't my bullet, lady," said Roger. "'Twas that other guy that plugged him."

The other man looked at him in astonishment. "How can you say that, Roger? You know damned well that you—"

"Shut up!"

Rose went into the kitchen for a basin of water and a cloth. Quickly returning, she started to wipe up the blood. Presently Robert returned from outdoors with their crony. "I could have verified one of your claims, men. There was no need to—"

Roger snorted savagely. "It's settled now, ain't it, Greenhow? The land belongs to us."

"It hasn't been settled to my satisfaction, gentlemen."

Once again Roger drew his gun from its holster and rested it casually across his arm. "I'd say it was settled, Greenhow."

There was silence in the room as both men stared unflinchingly at each other.

Robert, who had bent over to help Rose, slowly got to his

feet and walked over to the men. "Gentlemen, I represent law and order in this city. I told you I will investigate your claim and that of the Frenchman. When I have had the opportunity to determine who is rightfully entitled to the land, I shall let you know."

The man with the gun slowly raised it. "How soon will that be?"

"It shouldn't take more than a few days. If you will come back Monday I should have an answer for you."

"OK," said Roger repeating the phrase so familiar to Rose. Casually he put his gun back in his holster. "We'll be back Monday and your decision better be a good one for us, Greenhow."

"I shall tell you who, in my opinion, rightfully owns the land," Robert said, firmly facing all three of them. "You have come to me to determine the legal owner of this claim. That is the information I will have for you. If it does not suit you, you may take the matter to the courts. But I assure you that you can rely on my judgment as being fair."

The three men looked at each other and then one of them said, "That's what we come here for in the first place."

"Yeah, that's right. Come on let's go."

As they started out the door, Roger turned back and said, "I ain't much for this law business. I suppose it's all right if there's somebody honest working on it. In that case, you'll just be proving that that land is rightfully mine."

"That is what you have asked me to verify. Now, if you will excuse me, I shall assist my wife in cleaning up this mess. Good day, gentlemen."

They left. Robert went over to Rose and silently bent down to help her clean the carpet.

"That poor man," Rose murmured.

"He seemed to be in some pain when we put him in the carriage but the flow of blood has subsided. I don't believe it is fatal."

"You must report this to the police."

"I suggested that to Senator Gwin but he advised against it."

Rose stared at him in disbelief. "In heaven's name, why not?"

"First, one of the men might try to take his revenge out on me or even you. Secondly, the courts are not well organized and are poorly staffed. If charges were pressed it would be months before a trial could be held."

"But they attempted to murder this man."

"I'm sorry, Rose, but I can readily understand why any action would be ill-advised."

"I was proud of you the way you stood up to those men without a gun."

"I hope I didn't look as frightened as I felt. This is such a beastly business. I'm sorry this had to happen in our home."

"You must realize that I cannot tolerate such lawlessness in our house, Robert."

"Senator Gwin was most emphatic on that point. I shall move the business out of the house as soon as I find a place."

"I shall find you an establishment, Robert."

The next day Rose located a room for Robert. It was on the second floor of a building at 145 Montgomery Street, not far from their home but far enough away so that Rose did not have any more to do with Robert's business or his clients.

Only a few days later Robert came home to advise Rose that there were other lawyers within a block of him who were investigating land claims as well.

"Arguments are a daily occurrence in one or the other of these places."

"How disgusting."

"There was a fist fight today in the establishment next to mine. No one was seriously hurt."

"This should be reported to the president. A commission must be appointed to assist these men in peacefully settling their claims."

"It is too early to report this matter to the president. The rival claims may subside after this first—"

"Then I shall write to President Fillmore and acquaint him with the situation."

"No—no, Rose, don't you write."

"Why not?"

"I shall write to the president and acquaint him with the situation."

"At once?"

"Immediately. I have completed my investigation of the men who quarreled at our house. The claim was rightfully Roger Morton's. I have taken my report to him. I felt you would prefer that rather than have him come to our house."

"That was thoughtful of you, Robert, and I thank you. Have you heard any more about that poor Frenchman?"

Robert smiled. "He is out of the hospital. He was at Morton's office when I visited him. It seems that the Frenchman's claim is also valid but it is the property adjoining Morton's. He discovered his mistake before I could report to him. By the time I got there they had settled their differences and the men are all working both claims together."

Rose shook her head. "And a man could have lost his life over the matter."

Shortly afterward Rose made it a point to call upon Senator Gwin. She had learned that he was active in establishing a Democratic party in the new state. This field of operation was much more to Rose's liking.

Gwin was not in his office when she visited him. She left word with a young man that she would return the same time the next day. When she did so, she was happy to note that Senator Gwin was expecting her.

"Come in, Mrs. Greenhow," he greeted cheerfully. "I am delighted to see you under much more auspicious conditions."

"I wish to thank you for helping us the other day."

"I was happy I could be of assistance."

"I must apologize. I fear I was not very civil when you appeared on the scene. I was frantic."

"Well you should be. I told your husband he should never

170

have opened a claim advisory office in his home. It is too dangerous."

"He has since moved to another location."

"I am glad to hear that." He beamed at her as he pressed his hands against his desk. "This is a most unexpected pleasure. And an honor, I might add. The famous Mrs. Greenhow sitting right in my office. Do you plan to be here long?"

"Oh, yes. My husband will be working on land claims for quite some time. We haven't spoken about our future plans, but he is exceedingly busy now and I am sure that this will keep him occupied for some time to come."

"Delightful. Then why don't you become active in our Democratic party that we are forming? We could use an astute woman with your tremendous talents."

"You're very flattering, senator. I think that it is only fair to advise you at the outset that I worked closely with Senator Buchanan back in Washington."

Senator Gwin frowned. "You don't have to tell me, Mrs. Greenhow. I am well aware of your political activities."

"I know that although you and he were on most cordial terms at one time, you have drifted apart of late."

"Very true, Mrs. Greenhow. But I assure you that there were no great differences of opinion that could not be compromised."

"I am pleased to hear that. Then perhaps I can be of help to your new organization."

"Very good! It is my personal belief that California is destined for political greatness."

"This is my opinion as well, senator."

"The new Republican party is also very active here. We need to organize against them thoroughly and quickly. To bring you up to date, Jessie Fremont is working most energetically to establish a Republican stronghold. Do you know her?"

"I do, senator," said Rose, her lips tightening.

"Between you and me, I think she's doing it to promote her husband, General John C. Fremont, for the presidency."

"That is mighty interesting, senator. Has the general expressed any opinion on the matter?"

"Oh, he denies it emphatically. You know he has purchased a claim in the Mariposa in the Sierra foothills and he has some men exploring the area trying to track down that elusive maiden's glory—gold. He tells everyone that this is where his interest lies. He confesses himself utterly unsuited for the part he had been appointed to play upon the world's great stage."

"An opinion in which I most heartily agree."

"Them's my sentiments exactly. Mrs. Greenhow, we should get along just fine."

"I look forward to the opportunity."

"By the way, my wife and I are hosting a little dinner party at my home in South Park this weekend. Why don't you and your husband join us for a social get-together? It will give you an opportunity to meet some of the fine upstanding citizens of our community."

"We would be delighted to attend."

"We won't dine until eight but why don't you plan on joining us about three o'clock in the afternoon? It will give me plenty of time to introduce you and your husband around."

"That is very gracious of you, senator."

"It's my pleasure, ma'am. And now that we've gotten to know each other, why don't you call me just plain Bill."

"Thank you, Bill, I'll do that. Providing, of course, you call me just plain Rose."

Bill Gwin laughed heartily. "Rose, it is then. And I have heard it mentioned in Washington that some of your friends fondly call you their Wild Rose."

Rose's eyes twinkled and she graciously smiled at him. "You bring back pleasant memories, Bill."

"Ah, yes." He looked away as if relishing the days gone by when he was part of the bustling Washington scene. Quickly he turned to Rose with his usual beaming smile. "Then we can

172

look forward to seeing you next Saturday afternoon?"

"I assure you we would not miss it."

Rose left Senator Gwin's office in a gayer mood than she had experienced since coming to San Francisco. This was the sort of life she was accustomed to. She was on ground where she need not bow to any man or woman. As she got into her carriage, her eyes narrowed and her chin jutted out in a firm, defensive manner. "So Jessie Benton Fremont believes her husband should be president of the United States! I might have other ideas on the matter. Let us see who wins this foray!"

Senator Gwin and his wife lived in a beautiful mansion atop a hillside overlooking much of the city below. As Rose and her husband rode through the grilled iron archway in front of the high, pillared house, they were met by a black servant, who took the reins of their horse and drove them to the entrance of the mansion.

They were met by Senator Gwin standing on the wide veranda.

"So glad you folks came early," he said. "I particularly want you to meet my wife." He ushered them into a spacious room in the front of the house, where a formally dressed orchestra was playing a lively mazurka. A large crystal chandelier hung low in the center of the room, and ceiling-high mirrors were spaced between narrow mahogany panels along the inside walls. All in all, the magnificent room more resembled the ballroom of the National Hotel in Washington than a room in a private house. When Rose mentioned the resemblance, Senator Gwin laughed heartily. "I had the architects research the plans of that hotel before designing this house. I wanted my old friends from the East to feel right at home."

The senator introduced the Greenhows to his wife, a very charming woman several years younger than himself. He then personally escorted them around the room and into the luxurious gardens outside, introducing them to important businessmen, lawyers, and politicians of the city.

"There don't seem to be many leaders of this thriving city

173

whom you do not consider your friends, Bill," Rose commented.

"That's the way I want it, Rose. Reminds you of the Washington scene, doesn't it?" The senator jovially poked Rose in the ribs.

"It surely does. It almost makes me homesick for the capital," she commented.

"Well, you won't be homesick for long. You will fit in dandy with these people out here," Gwin remarked.

"I surely hope so," replied Rose.

"You put your lot in with us, Rose. Between your husband's associations with claim holders, jumpers, and swindlers, and my merchants, bankers, and industrial friends, you'll get to know the vast majority of people in this booming metropolis."

They laughed at his feeble attempt at humor as he suddenly became serious. "That reminds me. I have it on good authority that Jose Limantour will be visiting us before the end of the year. Do you know him?" Without waiting for an answer, he continued. "You ought to get to meet him, Bob, he is one of the biggest claim holders in the state."

Robert smiled. "Mr. Limantour is our client."

"As a matter of fact, it was our interest in his claims that prompted us to visit San Francisco," Rose added.

"Is that a fact?" Senator Gwin seemed surprised. The information greatly impressed him. "When he arrives I should like to meet him."

"I will be glad to introduce you, senator," Robert replied.

"Will you? It might prove advantageous to us all," Senator Gwin replied, narrowing his eyes and looking away for a moment as if he were thinking of something else. Quickly he turned his attention to them. "If you will excuse me, you folks mingle with my guests for a while. I've got to be sure the others are enjoying themselves."

As he left Rose remarked to her husband, "Something seems to have struck a concordant note with our friend, the senator."

174

"My guess is it stems from the mention of our acquaintance with Jose Limantour."

Both Rose and her husband enjoyed their evening at the Gwins'. For Rose, particularly, it was the first opportunity she had in San Francisco to become a part of the kind of social life which had always comprised so much of her very existence. Several times during the evening they noticed Senator Gwin talking seriously to some of his friends, and, during the course of the conversation, glancing at the Greenhows.

They were taking their leave of Mrs. Gwin when the senator came up to them. "Sorry, I wasn't able to get back with you people. The evening passed so quickly."

"It usually does when you are enjoying yourself," Rose smiled.

As the men shook hands Gwin said, "By the way, Bob, if you are handling Limantour's claims you must be fairly certain that they are valid."

"I verified them as much as I could in Mexico City," Robert replied. "My research thus far in San Francisco bears out my original findings."

"My God, they are extensive holdings!"

"The largest, I believe."

"I have some influential friends who have expressed an interest in them," said the senator hastily. "Perhaps we could form a combine to promote them. When he arrives, do you suppose we could arrange a meeting to discuss the possibilities?"

"I see no reason why not," Robert replied.

"Good." Senator Gwin smiled with satisfaction. "Let me know when he gets here."

"I most certainly will."

As a result of Senator Gwin's party and her continued association with him, Rose's social life expanded considerably. She became active in Democratic circles, staging many soirees and fund-raising events on the party's behalf. Once again she was becoming so busy that she was not aware of Robert's

175

activities. His business, however, was growing tremendously. He was so deluged with requests to verify land claims, and so busy separating the genuine ones from the fake, that he brought Ed Pringle into his law firm as a full partner.

Shortly before the Christmas holidays, he received a letter from Limantour advising that he was immediately leaving for San Francisco, and would like to meet with Robert upon his arrival.

"I suppose Limantour wants to see you about his claims," Pringle remarked when he read the letter.

"Ed, we've both been so busy since you joined me I haven't had time to tell you. Limantour is one of our clients."

Ed jumped up from his chair. "My God, you mean we are representing his holdings?"

"We surely are. And I'd better spend more time investigating them before he arrives."

"I should say so. He claims title to Yerba Buena, Alcatraz—"

"The Parallones, and Punta del Tiburona. I am sure you will understand if I request that you undertake responsibility for our other business while I conduct a further search in the archives on Limantour's claims."

"By all means. The Limantour claim alone could finance our business."

"Not exactly. He hasn't received clear title as yet. His personal business is not too extensive. So far I haven't received any fee other than a grant of some property in Point Lobos."

"Which cannot be clearly held until Limantour's claims have been verified."

"Exactly."

"Get busy, man."

Robert devoted the next few days exclusively to exploring Limantour's claims. His further research made him more secure in believing that Limantour's claims were valid.

By the time Limantour arrived, Robert felt quite confident in assuring him that his claims would be upheld in court.

"In court?" Limantour exclaimed. "Why do I have to ask the courts to rule on what is rightfully mine?"

"Because there are many people who can't believe any one person can lay claim to such a vast quantity of land; particularly since it lies within the boundaries of San Francisco."

"Dragging this into the courts is going to cost a lot of money."

"I realize this, but there is no other way. I believe I have a solution where this is concerned."

"Just so it does not jeopardize my claims."

"I assure you, it won't. You must be aware that the means to protect such vast holdings are generally beyond the financial capabilities of the average man."

"I cannot afford to go to court to substantiate my claims if that is what you mean. I do not have the money."

"There is a group of men who might be willing to form a combine to finance your litigation in return for a partnership to promote your lands."

Limantour sighed. "Deep down I knew in my heart that my claims would go beyond my own personal capabilities."

"That is why you need influential men to come to your assistance, Jose."

"When can I meet them?"

"They have already asked me to advise them when you arrive. I am sure they will meet with you promptly."

Robert arranged a meeting with Senator Gwin and several other prominent men. Limantour readily agreed to form a corporation with them to promote his holdings. In return, they would provide the necessary capital to finance any court battles that might arise as a result of his claims. It was further agreed that, although all necessary legal funds would immediately be provided, there would be no need to form a corporation until after Limantour had received clear title.

In high spirits everyone concerned entered the Christmas

season with anticipation of great riches. Rose and Robert were invited to a Christmas party at the spacious home of Judge Matthew Hall McAllister, the first U.S. circuit judge in California, whose father had rendered decisions on many land claims. Jose Limantour was also among the honored guests. The guest list included most of the leaders of San Francisco, for Mrs. McAllister was the recognized matron in that city's society.

Their home was actually a castle, brought over piece by piece from Central Europe and erected as an exact replica of the original building, with tall minarets, square towers, and a running brook representing the original moat. The ballroom was dimly lit with large red and green beeswax candles, and two orchestras took turns playing, so that there was continuous dancing. Rose had never seen her husband enjoy himself more. She danced the Virginia Reel with him, and when he finally tired, she coaxed Jose Limantour to join her on the dance floor for a lively Old Tucker followed by the racing Fox and Geese, which left the participants breathless but in a gay, holiday spirit.

Afterwards, they assembled in the conservatory where they played charades and blindman's buff. At midnight Mrs. McAllister sang for them, accompanied by the thunderous strains of a huge pipe organ. Mrs. McAllister then invited her guests to join her in singing Christmas carols.

It was well after midnight when a huge buffet was set up on a balcony surrounding the dance floor. Gaily painted Italian ceramic tureens brimmed with *fricassee de canard*, its vinegary sauce wafting down to the ballroom below. Huge copper pots were filled with *risottos con vegetale* and *oeufs chimay*, and everyone was invited to dip in. Large platters of simmering *gnocchi* and Moroccan *bastila* were set out with the hors d'oeuvres and platters of mixed cheeses cut into fancy designs and squares.

In the center of a large table was a steaming tureen of spicy Welsh rarebit with trays of warm, toasted sourdough bread iled beside it. Ham salad fruit boats and dishes of sole wrapped around spinach alternated with other exotic dishes. One table was laden with three- and four-layered white and chocolate cakes, vying with *gateau au chocolat* and buttermilk pie to tempt the guests' palates. Rose and Robert ate heartily after the evening's strenuous activities, but she confided to him that she missed her favorite Rappahannock shellfish. Although she did confess that the buffet was a considerable step forward from their first meal in San Francisco.

Among the many guests, Jessie and General Fremont were in attendance, and Rose took particular pains to avoid them the entire evening. But she could not avoid a discussion concerning them, when Senator Gwin came up to her while she sat out one of the dances.

"Have you heard that gold has been discovered on General Fremont's Mariposa ranch?" he inquired.

"I had not," Rose replied stoically.

"They have had the gold assayed and the samples have proven to be of high gold content. Jessie and the general are planning a trip to Europe to raise money to develop a mine on their ranch."

"No shareholder will reap any reward as a partner to the Fremonts."

Senator Gwin scratched his temple and shook his head. "They sure are convincing. They claim the assayist has reported that if their vein holds up as those first samples indicate, they will be taking out hundred-pound bags of gold when the mine gets in operation."

"That is the dream of every speculator."

"They have already started bringing out gold. That rare emerald that Jessie is wearing is sure going to convince a lot of people."

"It might be a boon to our plans. With the general so preoccupied, he will no longer be thinking of the presidency. This, of course, will make it much easier for James Buchanan to convince our party that he can readily capture the office."

179

"Very true," agreed the senator. Then, half to himself he added, "The general might be a likely candidate for the board of directors of the bank we are forming. Since we have some of the same directors, we're going to name it after that successful transportation company, Wells Fargo. Let us hope that our venture does anywhere near as well." Senator Gwin coughed as he noticed Rose's disapproving look. He shrugged his shoulders. "I'm sorry, Rose, but his money is as good as anyone else's, and if he has discovered a gold mine—" He was saved from further explanation as Robert came up to them. Throwing his arm around Robert's shoulder, the senator quickly changed the subject. "I guess your work will be lightened when the government steps in to settle these land claims."

"I hadn't heard that the government was stepping into this mad foray."

"Judge McAllister advised me that President Fillmore is considering appointing a land commission."

"Well, that is good news," Robert remarked.

"I am glad to hear the president has heeded Robert's warnings."

"Oh, so you had a hand in this, Bob?"

"I reported the daily altercations that were taking place and suggested that the government take drastic action since the situation is so volatile."

"Such a move by the government would certainly facilitate Limantour's claims," remarked Senator Gwin.

"We can only hope for the best," Rose commented.

But it was several months before they heard any more about the land commission. During this time, Robert's business was continually expanding.

Strong factions were being formed on each side to refute or defend Limantour's claims. It became apparent that a land commission or the courts or both would be required to finally settle them, but Robert continued to assure Limantour that his backers stood ready to pay all the costs involved in litigation.

It was late the following summer that Rose came to Robert to announce that she would like to return to the East.

"But Rose," he exclaimed, "I can't go East now. I cannot spare the time."

"I must go back, Robert. I haven't seen our girls in a year. They will forget their mother if I don't see them soon."

"I miss them too, darling, but with winter coming on and the assurance that President Fillmore is appointing a land commission, the timing is most inconvenient."

"There is no reason why I could not go back. It is imperative that I return, Robert. And I wish to be back there before the snows set in."

"What is so pressing that cannot wait until a more opportune time when I can join you?"

"Well, for one thing, I won't be able to bear traveling later this year."

"Why not?"

"Can't you guess?" As Robert looked at her with such a completely blank expression, she frowned. "Men are so silly about such things. We are going to have another baby, sweetheart."

"We are?" He rushed to her and grabbing her around the waist lifted her off her feet and swung her around. "Wonderful, darling. I am silly about such things. I never thought."

"I haven't known for very long, Robert. I'm glad you are happy about it."

"Am I!" He pressed her to him and kissed her passionately.

"Put me down, you ninny." Rose smiled, squirming away from him.

"I forgot. I must be careful, mustn't I? But how will you ever be able to make that trip back East?"

"Haven't you learned by now that a pregnant woman can stand a great deal of physical effort? It really is better for her to remain active."

"Well, if you prefer to return East to have your baby, by all means go."

"Then I shall plan on it. Do you want a boy or a girl, Robert?"

"I'll settle for either, Rose, my darling. I have only one request to make."

"What is that?"

"If it is a girl, I want to name her Rose."

Rose pursed her lips and thought for a moment. Then she smiled and said, "Yes, that would be nice, wouldn't it?"

"I'm glad that is settled."

"There is another reason for my wanting to go back at this time, Robert."

"Oh?"

"I wish to encourage your appointment to the land commission."

Robert frowned. "Rose, please do not go to President Fillmore about this, will you?"

"Why not?"

"Because, Rose, I—if the president learns that I want to be on the land commission, he might—" Suddenly he walked away from her and waved his hands impatiently in the air. "Damn it, Rose, can't you trust my judgment for once without my having to give you a reason?"

"Why, of course, darling. You do want to be a member of the commission, don't you?"

"Of course, I do, but I urge you not to bring this matter to the attention of President Fillmore."

"I promise, dear. You know there are many other influential men in Washington besides the president. And I know them all. I had not planned to see the president in the first place."

"Good."

"I'll keep you posted on developments, my darling husband, both with the government and the home front."

Two days before Rose left she called on Senator Gwin.

"I'm leaving for Washington the day after tomorrow and

182

dropped by to bid you farewell."

"We'll miss you, Rose. I understand your husband will be staying here."

"Yes, he is so involved in land claims that he really cannot spare time to be away."

"Perhaps you can expedite the formation of the land commission back there. That would certainly ease his burden."

"I shall make every effort to do so. With regards to him, I am wondering if you would consider doing me a favor?"

"Of course. Just name it."

"Since you are well aware of Robert's activities in San Francisco, you can appreciate that he should wish to become a member of this commission."

"I can think of no one more qualified."

"Would you be kind enough to put that thought in a letter that I may take back to Washington with me?"

"I would be glad to. Wait a moment and I shall write it immediately." He reached in a drawer, brought out a sheet of paper and picking up a pen from his desk asked, "Who do I address this letter to?"

"No one in particular. I have not as yet decided where it will do the most good."

Hastily, and in a bold hand, the senator scrawled a brief letter, and after blotting it and reading it, passed it on to Rose. "How does that read?"

"Better than I could have hoped for," Rose remarked as she hastily glanced over it. "Personally, I believe I would give this man the appointment on the strength of this letter alone."

She rose to go and Senator Gwin accompanied her to the door. "Hurry back, Rose," he smiled. Leaning close to her he kissed her lightly on the cheek. "Gad, San Francisco won't be the same without you."

"Thank you. But don't worry, I shall return before you can forget me."

"I hope so."

Waving gaily, she left his office.

Two days later, Robert accompanied her to the coach stop where she was to begin her long journey to Washington. "The trip shouldn't be too difficult," she said to Robert, "since railroads have been extended to the Great Lakes. I'll only travel to Toledo, Ohio, by coach and then I can ride the railroad through to Washington." Rose lingered for a long moment in her husband's arms. Then, kissing him fondly, she boarded the coach and was on her way.

It was when she changed coaches at St. Louis that eight more men got on the coach with her. They were delegates from Missouri, headed for Baltimore to attend the Democratic convention.

When they learned that she was returning from California to her home in Washington, they immediately struck up a conversation. Three of the men remembered having heard her name mentioned in political circles in their home towns. They were not too far along the way before she had convinced them that James Buchanan was the best man to lead their party to victory in the fall elections.

"Some of us have been pledged to vote for him," one of them said. "But after listening to you, I think you can be assured that we'll all cast our votes for him after the first ballot."

One of the other men leaned close to her to get her attention and said, "If you have been out West for very long, you may not have heard that slave trading has been abolished in Washington."

"No, I hadn't heard," Rose remarked, surprised.

"Yep," replied the stranger, waving his coonskin cap importantly. "They passed a resolution nearly a year ago. Of course slavery is still permitted."

"Thank heavens for that compromise," Rose sighed.

"If you've come from California you might be interested to know that President Fillmore has appointed a land commission for that state."

"He hadn't appointed it when I left San Francisco," Rose

replied, trying to appear calm.

"Well, he has now. Three commissioners. It came over the telegraph last week. You know, we got a telegraph right to St. Louis now."

"Yes, I believe I had heard of that," Rose replied absently. "So, the president has finally appointed his land commission," she said aloud, then added, to herself, *before I have had an opportunity to plead Robert's case.* She threw back her head defiantly and with set lips smiled stubbornly to herself. It didn't matter. There was always room for one more!

XI

Espionage

Rose didn't realize how much she had missed Washington until she returned. She breathed the air lustily and stretched her arms wide. It was like returning to civilization after being imprisoned in—well, being *confined* to Mexico City or San Franciso. She hurried to her sister's house, and tears rolled down her cheeks as her three daughters swarmed about her, welcoming her home.

"We've missed you so much, Mummy," Gertrude cried, hugging her tightly.

"I have missed you all ever so much," said Rose wiping her cheeks, first with the back of her hand, then with her handkerchief.

Leila hardly knew her mother and stood back clinging to Aunt Ellen's skirts. "I tried to explain to Leila that Mummy was coming home, but she didn't seem to understand," Ellen said.

"Ellen, I don't know how I can ever thank you for all you have done for our family."

"It was a pleasure, and the girls have been so good," replied Ellen.

"Well, girls," Rose said brightly, "we must be starting for home. Putting our house in order will take some doing."

"Oh, Mums, I can't go today," Florence said quietly.

"Can't go home?" Rose said, astonished. "Pray tell,

186

why not?"

"Well you see, I—please understand, but tomorrow night there is a grand ball at the armory. The men are scheduled to depart on their annual maneuvers the first of June and this is their final celebration before they leave."

"I understand, dear, but what has this to do with you?"

"I have been invited to the ball!"

Rose gasped. "You mean—Ellen, do you permit Florence to attend such social functions?"

Ellen smiled. "Do you remember our first ball, Rose? I know we were a little older. . . ."

"Aunt Ellen has bought me a new evening dress just for the occasion. Let me show it to you." Florence rushed out of the room leaving her mother speechless.

"She's been counting on this for so long, Rose," Ellen said quietly.

Rose sighed. "I suppose I will be confronted with many surprises."

"Very much has happened while you were away. For one thing, your girls are growing up."

Florence ran back into the room carrying a long white taffeta dress with a wide yellow satin ribbon drawing it in at the waist. She held it up before her. "Isn't it adorable?"

"It's the most beautiful dress I believe I have ever seen, darling."

"Can I wear it to the ball tomorrow night?" Florence asked anxiously, then added, "Can I go, please Mums?"

"The dance will be well-chaperoned, Rose. Our daughter, Addie, is also going. Young Edward Everett has invited Florence. He's the eldest son of our secretary of state."

Rose slowly shook her head. "We have gone full circle, haven't we? Our daughters are starting second time around in our footsteps."

"This is life, Rose. It does go on."

"May I please go to the dance, Mums?" Florence asked her mother plaintively.

"I told her she could go," Ellen said, half-apologetically. "We had no way of knowing when you would arrive."

"Of course, dear, if Aunt Ellen thinks it will be all right," Rose said, smiling.

Florence ran over and threw her arms around her mother. "Thank you, Mums."

"But that is no reason for you not to come home with me. I will send instructions to Mr. Everett to call for you at our house."

"Oh, will you Mums?"

"Now we had better pack your things and get home. There's so much to do after all these months."

"The girls have a few things packed, Rose. We can bring the rest of their clothing over in a day or two," Ellen suggested.

"That might be better." Rose went to Ellen and hugged her tightly. "Thank you again, Ellen."

There were tears in Ellen's eye as she fondly kissed the three girls goodbye.

Vying with each other to get closest to their mother, the girls left their Aunt Ellen's arm and arm with Rose. Rose's faithful slave, Randy, accompanied them back to their home. They spent the rest of the day unpacking and airing out the house which had become musty from having been shuttered and closed for so long.

The following day Rose had her horse and carriage delivered to their home from the livery where it had been stored and she drove over to the Senate. The Senate was not in session, in preparation for the Democratic convention, but she found Senator Buchanan in his office. He was conducting a meeting with several other men, but when she sent word to him he rushed out to greet her.

"Rose, what a pleasant surprise!" he said taking both her hands in his. "When did you get back?"

"Yesterday. You can see I wasted no time in renewing old acquaintances!"

"I'm delighted that you did. I'm sorry I'm tied up right now.

The convention, you know. We're meeting for luncheon as well. Could I see you later in the afternoon?"

"Why not join me for dinner at my house this evening?"

"That would be a pleasure," he said hurriedly, then added, "Those men must think I've lost my good senses. I begged to be excused, telling them an emergency had arisen." He pressed her hands firmly and disappeared into his office.

Rose returned to her house but not before stopping at her old market, where she and Randy stocked up on provisions.

She hummed gaily to herself as she began to prepare dinner. "Girls," she said cheerfully, "has Aunt Ellen taught you any of the secrets of fine cooking?"

"Oh, yes, Mums," they answered proudly in unison.

"Well then, you may help me prepare dinner for this evening. Mr. Buchanan will be joining us."

"Mums, do I have to?" wailed Florence. "I was about to start to get ready for the ball."

Rose smiled and sighed as she remembered how excitedly she had prepared for her first formal affair. "You may as well go upstairs. I'm sure you will be no help to us here in the kitchen." Florence squealed with delight, and disappeared quickly into the hall. Gertrude and Leila joined their mother preparing the dinner. Rose told Randy it would not be necessary for him to assist since the girls would be helping. Deprived of his normal duties, for he had become a most proficient cook under Rose's tutelage, Randy merely sat in the corner of the kitchen and pouted. Finally Rose could stand it no longer and told him he could work with them. He jumped up and joined them.

The girls winced as they watched Randy and their mother drop four wiggling lobsters and several live soft shell crabs into boiling water. "The best shellfish, from the waters of the Rappahannock," she told them, ignoring their squeamish outbursts. They helped her prepare baked flounder fillets and a salmon mousse with creole sauce. For a side dish, she showed them how to fix a batter and mix it into a concoction of beans,

189

carrots, onions, and potatoes with tempura.

She set bottles of Madeira wine and champagne in buckets as the girls chopped ice and packed it around the bottles. When all was in readiness, she patted her girls and said, "Suppose you go upstairs and get ready."

"Aunt Ellen helps me," said Leila shyly.

"Of course, I shall help you, dear. Now both of you scoot upstairs." As they started to go, she called after them, "And don't either of you bother your sister."

Shortly afterward, she went upstairs herself. After looking in on the girls and helping Leila tie a wide, brightly colored bow in her hair, she spent considerable time meticulously dressing herself for the occasion.

She had hardly finished her preparation and checked dinner once again, when the doorbell sounded.

It was Senator Buchanan. He was immaculately dressed in a ruffled shirt, stiffly starched in front, a white wing collar, a long tailored formal black coat and a waistcoat beneath, with a thick gold watch chain dangling from its pockets.

"You look absolutely ravishing, my dear," he said as she led him into the parlor.

"Thank you, senator." She curtsied and smiled at him coyly.

As Buchanan looked about the room he inquired, "Isn't Bob home?"

"Robert did not come East with me, Jim. He's been so terribly busy he could not spare the time."

The girls, who had been shyly watching from behind the drapes, suddenly bounced into the room and stood beside their mother. Buchanan came over to them.

"Gertrude and Leila. My goodness, how you have grown." He put an arm around each of them.

"The girls helped prepare our meal this evening."

"And where is Florence? I imagine she has become quite a young lady since last I saw her."

"I fear we will not see much of Florence this evening. She is

190

preparing for the hundred-thirteenth division grand ball tonight."

"My niece, Harriet Lane, is also attending the ball. It is to be a memorable occasion."

Rose opened a bottle of champagne and poured two glasses. "You look tired this evening, Jim."

"I have never attended so many meetings in my entire life."

"The convention?"

"Yes. They want me to try for the nomination again."

"I rode back with some of the delegates from Missouri. I firmly convinced them that you are the only man who can capture the presidency for the Democratic party."

"Thank you, Rose."

They touched glasses and sipped their drink. Her daughters eagerly watched them. Feeling slightly uncomfortable under their close scrutiny Rose said, "Girls, dinner is ready by now I am sure. Why don't you set it on the table for us?"

"All right," said Gertrude reluctantly. She took Leila's hand and they scampered out of the parlor.

"Are you confident the convention will nominate you early in the session, Jim?"

"I don't know. Lewis Cass is also being placed in nomination."

"Mr. Cass apparently wishes to be our perennial flag bearer. But he has had his day. After his overwhelming defeat by General Taylor in the last election I should imagine he would hesitate to seek the convention's full-hearted support again."

"His record as secretary of war has been excellent. He has some powerful men on his side with Bill Marcy and Jim Guthrie advocating his nomination. They have joined forces with the North to offer a unified stand against my plea on behalf of slavery."

"That will win you the nomination, Jim. Work hard for it this time."

"I can't work any harder than I am. Rose, why don't you come to the convention?"

"I would like to. Actually, I've followed many conventions closely but I have never attended one."

"Then why not plan on it? The railroad is running special sections up to Baltimore and I can assure you a room at our headquarters."

"If Ellen will be willing to care for the girls again on such short notice. The convention begins next week."

"It will be a hectic time, as you can imagine. There are so many details to be attended to. You are experienced in such matters. It would bolster my own morale to know that I have someone up there who I can count on regardless of what happens. And, as you know, anything can."

"If I can make arrangements, I'll plan on going."

"It's settled then. Knowing you, you will be able to make necessary arrangements. My group will be leaving Friday night to complete preconvention tasks over the weekend. I'll have tickets and reservations sent over to you. I shall welcome your encouragement when the infighting gets rough."

At that moment Gertrude and Leila came in and proudly announced that dinner was ready. As Rose and Buchanan started toward the dining room, the door gong sounded. Rose answered the door to see young Edward Everett standing nervously in the doorway.

"Good evening," he smiled. "I am looking for Miss Florence Greenhow. Can you tell me—"

"You must be Edward Everett. Come in, please. I am Florence's mother."

"Thank you. Pleased to meet you," he said ceremoniously.

Rose called to her daughter. "Mr. Everett is here for you."

A faraway voice came floating down. "Thank you, Mums, I'll be right down."

"Which means anytime within the next half-hour," Rose advised. "Won't you join us in the parlor?"

Everett followed her into the parlor, whereupon the two girls came running out of the dining room, smiling at the latest visitor. As they sat down, Rose started to introduce them, when he volunteered, "Oh, I met your daughters when I visited Mrs. Cutts."

"And Mr. Buchanan?"

"We are old friends," said Buchanan, "but it is good to see you again." They shook hands.

Almost immediately Florence came downstairs. Rose gasped at the beauty of her oldest daughter as she slowly, majestically descended. Her striking appearance was not lost on either her escort or Buchanan, who both rose as she entered the parlor.

"Your dress becomes you, my dear," Buchanan said, taking her hand.

"Thank you, Mr. Buchanan," Florence said, her face radiant.

"I agree," said Everett enthusiastically.

"You do look lovely, dear," Rose said proudly. "But what about dinner? We were just about to sit down."

"I'm really not hungry, Mums."

"Besides there will be refreshments at the ball, Mrs. Greenhow," Everett reminded her.

"Shall we go, Edward? I don't want to miss one single dance, you know."

As Buchanan watched them go, he said, "She is the picture of her mother."

"I hope none of the dinner has gotten cold," Rose remarked as they went into the dining room and sat down. Gertrude proudly poured the Madeira.

The meal, as usual, was excellent, and Buchanan lavishly praised the girls for their part in preparing it.

After dinner, the girls volunteered to help Randy clear the table while Rose and Buchanan retired to the parlor. As Buchanan seated himself comfortably and lit up a dark Havana, he said, "California is exciting territory, isn't it?"

"It is, indeed. Between the rugged miners who stop at nothing in their search for gold and the quarrels over land claims, a very low price is placed on life."

"We have been hearing stories of bloodshed over land grabs

and fraud."

"A man was shot in our parlor where Robert had his office."

"My God, that must have been a harrowing experience."

"It was. I insisted that Robert move his office out of our house. He has been engaged in nothing but land claim disputes since we arrived in San Francisco. I finally convinced him that the matter should be reported to President Fillmore!"

"Then he will welcome the appointment of the land commission for California."

"He most assuredly will. As one of the most authoritative men on the subject he would be a competent addition to the commission."

"You may not have heard, but the president has just appointed the commission."

"I have heard. I sincerely hope that it is not too late to have Robert added to the commission. You will agree that he is most qualified."

"I realize this, Rose. However, you know it is my policy not to intercede in any of the president's appointments."

"I am sure an exception can be made for old friends."

Buchanan puffed heavily on his cigar. "Rose, only this month I refused to recommend my own niece's husband for an appointment as naval officer at San Francisco because I have vowed not to interfere in any California appointments."

"I was counting on your assistance, Jim. Robert should be on that commission. He knows more about land claims and territorial boundaries than any other man in the country."

"You are making it difficult, Rose. I also recently refused to recommend the son of a near and dear friend for an Indian agency in California on the earnest appeal of his mother. It is a matter of principle."

"Oh, poppycock, Jim. You know principles in politics exist to be broken." She reached into the bosom of her dress and drawing out an envelope handed it to him. "Here is a letter from Senator William Gwin urging that Robert be appointed to the commission. Read for yourself how highly Robert is recommended."

Taking the letter Buchanan placed it in his pocket. "I shall read it later, Rose. But it isn't necessary. I well know Robert's excellent qualifications. It is just that—"

"Just what, Jim?"

"Damn it, in the first place the commission has already been appointed. Notwithstanding that, you know my beliefs about the flagrant abuse of patronage."

"Patronage is the basis of all successful campaigns in our democracy."

"What can I do?"

"Intercede on Robert's behalf."

"What is my justification? If I agreed to do so, there are no vacancies on the commission."

"Establish one. Enlarge the commission."

"That will take an act of Congress."

"You know something can be done."

"You are a persistent woman, Rose Greenhow!"

"Would you have me any other way?"

He was scowling as he looked at her, finally turning away from her steady, burning gaze. "I have seen you in action before, my Wild Rose, but I have never before been the victim of your relentlessness."

"I only persevere in what I believe to be right, Jim."

They were silent for a moment. The girls gaily laughing in the kitchen and dishes rattling were the only sounds that could be heard. She leaned back on the sofa beside him, her arm stretched along its back nearly touching him. Finally, he moved heavily and faced her squarely. "You know full well that nothing can be done concerning the commission. It is unfortunate that you did not bring this to my attention before the commission was appointed. That is your error."

"I had no way of knowing the president was about to make a decision. He has been dawdling on the matter for months while the situation in California grew progressively worse."

"What may be said in your behalf is that there is a

195

distinction between the cases I have mentioned and the appointment of land commissioners. Be it so; I am willing to look for almost any distinction which will enable me to make the attempt to serve you; but I cannot suggest to the president that he remove three commissioners whom he has just appointed. I doubt very much whether he will do it, but I have other means of approach in mind. Robert could be appointed as associate law agent of the commission."

Rose's eyes sparkled. "Oh, Jim, would you suggest this?"

"I shall recommend his selection to the president immediately while the commission is still fresh in his mind. I am certain he will accept my recommendation."

"Sufficiently certain for me to so advise Robert?"

"Absolutely. The president owes me a favor or two. Such are the shortcomings of the patronage system. One always returns to collect for the favors bestowed."

"Thank you, Jim. I am deeply indebted to you."

"Remember that, dear lady. I may have cause to collect my due some day." He drew his gold watch from his waistcoat and whistled softly as he noted the time. "I must be going, my dear. I have a meeting scheduled for six o'clock tomorrow morning." He sighed. "Sometimes I wonder if it is worth it."

She fetched his coat and smiled as she helped him put it on. "You know you couldn't possibly do without this sort of life. The glory and the fulfillment of one's ambitions more than compensate for the tiring sessions and boring speeches."

"And the opportunity to know such a vivacious woman as yourself." He chucked her under the chin. Shouting goodbye to the girls and thanking them again for the wonderful dinner that they had helped prepare, he left.

Before going to bed, Rose wrote a short letter to Robert telling him he could expect an appointment as associate law agent to the land commission.

The following day she visited her sister to see if the girls could stay again for a few days while she attended the Democratic convention.

Ellen assured her she not only did not mind but would be glad to have them back with her, she had missed them so about the house.

Pandemonium reigned at the convention. Crowds were everywhere and the Lord Baltimore Hotel, where the convention was being held, was so jammed with delegates that it was difficult to wend one's way through the lobby. Every room was occupied, many of them containing twice the number of occupants originally intended. In spite of this, Buchanan had secured a private room for Rose on the third floor not far from his own campaign suite. In spite of their proximity, she saw very little of him.

The first evening, she supervised preparations for the reception to the delegates. It was a gala affair with a buffet dinner followed by a cotillion in the main ballroom. As the orchestra played gay waltzes of the day, Rose made a striking figure as unofficial hostess to the conventioneers. Her hair was wound around her head in braids, coronet fashion, a new hair style which she had the satisfaction of noting several other ladies copying in the days that followed. Her rosetted slippers, short white gloves, and black folding fan accentuated her shimmering black, wide-hooped gown topped by the popular bertha neck. She smiled with satisfaction noting the envious glances of many of the woman as she danced with such prominent southern delegates as Pierre G. T. Beauregard, Jefferson Davis, and Clement C. Clay of Alabama.

While the delegates and their wives or lady friends danced and ate, a small group of men marched outside the hotel carrying crudely drawn placards bearing such slogans as "Remember Uncle Tom's Cabin" and "Help poor Uncle Tom."

Once during the evening while she danced with Buchanan, one of the men managed to slip into the ballroom and shouted above the din and music, "Ask Buchanan what he's going to do about the poor old Uncle Toms!" The man was quickly seized by guards and ejected from the hotel.

"What in heaven's name is that man talking about? Who is

197

Uncle Tom?" Rose asked Buchanan.

"It is a book by Harriet Beecher Stowe that has just been published."

"Derogatory to slavery, I surmise."

"Extremely so."

"What harm can one more book possibly do?"

"It is sweeping the northern states, Rose. In three months, over half a million copies have been sold and the publisher cannot keep up with the demand for more."

"I shall have to read it so I can be explicit in my denunciation of such bigoted trash."

After the delegates were duly sworn in and their credentials accredited, the convention began to get down to the business of selecting the man who was to lead their campaign as their nominee for president. Both Buchanan's and Cass's names were placed in nomination. However, after two grueling days, it became apparent that neither man could claim a clear majority. The few moments when she saw Buchanan each day, Rose noticed that he was becoming more irritated and nervous.

"What is troubling you, Jim?" she asked when they were sitting eating pigeon pie in the hotel dining room late one evening. "You've been in many political battles before. There certainly is nothing unusual about this one."

"But there is, Rose. Cass has a lot of sharp politicians running his campaign. They're pulling many new stunts that seem to be gaining a great bit of support from the delegates. If I could only know what they were up to I might be in a better position to counter them."

"It is clearly a matter of being informed of Cass's moves before he makes them."

"That is the answer to the problem. But it is not so easily accomplished."

"I think it can be. I have an idea that might help. Meet me at your headquarters tomorrow morning before the convention opens. I suggest about eight o'clock. I may have some information for you." She got up quickly from her chair.

"Now I have some business to attend to."

Early the following morning Rose met Buchanan in his campaign suite. Briefly, but precisely, she outlined in detail the plans for the proposed Cass campaign for the day.

"But how do you know this is what they plan to do?"

"Trust me, Jim. I know I am right."

As the day progressed, the strategy of the Cass followers developed exactly as Rose had predicted. Roll call after roll call was tabulated and Cass's votes gradually increased until the delegates were equally divided. By the thirtieth ballot it was obvious that Buchanan and Cass were hopelessly deadlocked. When the convention adjourned late that night, both factions were agreed that neither one of them could win.

The next morning when Rose met Buchanan, she came directly to the point. "Who is Franklin Pierce?"

"He was president of the New Hampshire constitutional convention. He has been both a congressman and a senator. Why do you ask?"

"Because if the Cass people cannot overtake you in the next four ballots, they are going to place his name in nomination."

Buchanan looked at her aghast. "Rose, can you be sure?"

"I am certain."

"If this is the case, it could be the beginning of the end. He is a northerner but he has always advocated the extension of slavery in the new states. He is acceptable to both the northern and southern Democrats. How did you get this information?"

"Do you really want to know?"

"It is imperative that I know whether or not I can rely on what you tell me."

"One of the men with whom I rode out from St. Louis by the name of Morrison was a pledged delegate for Cass. I convinced him that, after he was released from his obligation to Cass on the first ballot, he should swing his vote to you. He did!"

"A very fine campaigner, Rose. I'm lucky to have you on my side. But I don't understand—"

"When you told me how important it was to know what Cass

was planning, I went to Morrison and suggested that he swing his vote back to Cass."

"Another deserter from my thinning ranks."

"Will you forgive me, Jim? Especially when I tell you by so doing, Morrison was able to attend the strategy meetings of the Cass organization? It has placed him in a position to know their daily plans."

"Rose, this is espionage within our own party."

"Together with the secret deals that are being made behind both Cass's and your own doors. I told Morrison if he really wished to help your cause, he should report Cass's plans to me each morning. He has faithfully done so."

Suddenly Buchanan jumped up. "I must see Franklin Pierce immediately." Squeezing her hands, he hastily left.

Again the convention the next day progressed as Rose had predicted. Cass could not pick up more delegates and neither could Buchanan. On the thirty-fifth ballot, Pierce's name was entered into nomination. By the forty-ninth ballot, enough delegates had swung from both groups to nominate Pierce, the dark horse, as their candidate for president.

When she saw Buchanan late that night in the lobby of the hotel, he seemed haggard and worn.

"Where in the world have you been?" she asked him.

"Among other things, congratulating our candidate for the presidency."

They sat down beside each other on a heavily stuffed sofa. "Pierce probably planned to enter the race as a dark horse from the beginning," Rose said bitterly. "I shall not lift a finger to help him in his entire campaign."

"Don't hold any ill feelings, Rose. It is politics."

"I don't care. He could have thrown his strength to you anytime after he was nominated and you would have won."

"It was obvious I could not win. Don't worry, Rose. I will be taken care of. I have seen to that."

"I shall never forgive him."

"It's all over now."

"It's been a hard week, hasn't it?"

"It has, Rose. And you are the only one to know how I truly feel. I almost want to cry."

"I know. It's a bitter pill to swallow after all the work you have done."

"Not only this time but in two previous conventions."

"There will be other conventions."

"No, Rose, not for me. I don't think I will ever run for senator again. I'm just going to retire and enjoy watching the circus from the sidelines."

"You will never do that, Jim. No man, least of all you, should pass his time ingloriously in ease and retirement."

"Ingloriously, you say? At this moment I find that a life of idleness, or rather a life in which I can just enjoy myself as I please, would be exceedingly agreeable. I no longer indulge in any ambitious aspirations. I would not if I could, have avoided being a candidate for the presidency. That is now past and gone and my defeat cost me not a single pang. Instead I felt it more on account of my friends than on my own account. It is a delightful privilege for one to have it in his power to bestow favors upon those to whom he feels himself indebted for acts of kindness. The power of patronage of the government will now be wielded by the men of a younger generation; and it is the true policy of the old fogies to retire gracefully from the political arena before they are driven from the lists. Benton and Cass will, I have no doubt, hold on to the last."

"A beautiful speech, Mr. Buchanan. Spoken, no doubt, in the throes of utter defeat. But if I know you, you will feel differently tomorrow."

"I am going over to the tavern and get uproariously drunk!"

"That is just what your enemies want you to do so that you will make a public spectacle of yourself."

"Will you join me?"

"You know ladies are not permitted. But if they were, I would not go. You are your own master, Jim. You may do as you please, but you are extremely tired and most discouraged.

201

If I were you, I would go up to my room. You have plenty of liquor in your suite. Take three or four good stiff drinks of corn whiskey, then go to bed and forget this cruel world and the curious meanderings of its people."

Sorrowfully he leaned his head on his chin for a moment, staring wearily at her. Then slowly he got up. "As usual, you are right. I shall do just that. Good night, Rose."

"Good night, Jim. Sweet sleep and pleasant dreams."

"God, I sure could stand some."

When Rose returned to Washington, she learned that President Fillmore had appointed Robert an associate law agent to the California Land Commission.

Buchanan plunged diligently into touring the eastern states, helping to set up campaign organizations for Pierce's election campaign.

Rose had not seen him for over a month when he called on her early one afternoon without any advance warning.

"Jim, what a pleasant surprise," she greeted him. "Come in and sit down. I didn't know you were in Washington."

"I just returned late last night."

"But why are you working so hard to elect Pierce? He has never been a close friend of yours."

"I think he has a good chance of winning, Rose. I'm not too proud to accept second best."

"What do you mean?"

"If Pierce is elected, he has promised me I will go to London as minister for the United States."

"What an honorable assignment. Robert often has said it is the most important appointment overseas."

"It is what I have agreed to accept." He looked at her silently for a long interval. "I relish the appointment, but if I go I will miss you, Rose."

"Our paths will cross again, Jim. It is destined. Until they do, we must keep in contact with each other."

"Yes, we can write, can't we?"

"Of course. I will advise you what is happening in

202

Washington and you can tell me what it is like in London. I would like to go there, sometime."

"You will, Rose. I know you, and if you want to, you will go."

As the election drew near, Rose began to stay at home more than she ever had before. True to her promise, she did nothing to help Pierce in his campaign. She was happy to use her expected baby as an excuse. Buchanan, on the other hand, was rarely in Washington; he was continually crisscrossing between the eastern and midwest states on behalf of Pierce.

With the advent of the telegraph, which now stretched to St. Louis, the results of the election were known in Washington within two days. Franklin Pierce had been overwhelmingly elected, receiving more than five times the number of electoral votes his Whig opponent, Winfield Scott, received.

Shortly after the holiday season, Rose gave birth to her fourth daughter. In accordance with her husband's wishes, she named the baby Rose. With her daughter's birth, Rose was free to become more active in Washington society. But she did not. She spent considerable time at home, getting to better know her daughters and seeing to their proper education. She rarely visited the Senate and watched the preparation for the inauguration of the new president from afar, taking no active part in it.

Just before Pierce's inauguration, his only surviving son was killed in a train wreck. Mrs. Pierce was heartbroken and the tragedy cast a pall over the inaugural ceremonies. Rose sent a sympathetic letter of condolence to President Pierce and his wife. However, she did not attend the inauguration or the ball that followed.

That summer, Rose frequently took her girls away with her and visited many of the southern plantation owners whom she knew. She would be away from Washington for weeks on end, visiting the Jefferson Davises, the Robert E. Lees, and the Alexander H. Stevenses. She wanted to be sure that her girls would grow up knowing the true southern traditions that she herself had loved so dearly.

As Buchanan had predicted, he was appointed minister to England and sailed to London shortly after the new administration took office. Rose and he constantly wrote to each other, and Rose's daughters enjoyed hearing about the gay times that Buchanan's niece, Harriet Lane, was experiencing when she visited her uncle. Florence and Gertrude giggled excitedly as they read of Harriet dining with Queen Victoria and her Prince Consort Albert. Harriet admitted that she was struck with awe when the aristocratic Lady Windsor joined them.

Buchanan kept his Wild Rose informed more on political matters, telling her how proud she would be of his initiative in promoting the Ostend Manifesto, which suggested that Spain sell Cuba to the United States. If Spain did not agree, the manifesto continued, the island should be taken by force and brought into the Union as another slave state. He knew such a project was dear to Rose's heart. It would surely help protect the institution of slavery. But the manifesto was generally ignored. Soon it was forgotten. Buchanan begged Rose to continue to keep him closely informed on all matters of interest in the capital and on her many travels, for he often utilized incidents she related to him to brighten up his conversations at many staid British dinners and social occasions.

As the months passed, Rose continued to write to her many friends as well as to her husband. For a while she considered writing a book but delayed the project indefinitely, since her letter-writing, child-rearing, and occasional visits to her many southern friends did not allow her sufficient time.

She was disturbed to receive a letter from Robert in February advising her of a rather nasty accident that had befallen him. He was walking down Pacific Street when he crossed over some wooden planks that had been temporarily placed over a six-foot-deep ditch which had been dug for new construction. It had been raining and he had slipped on the planks and fallen to the bottom of the ditch. He advised her that he seemed to be none the worse for the experience, with the exception of his leg, which hurt quite a bit. He assured her it would be better in a short while, so she should have no cause to worry.

Six weeks later a telegram was hand-carried directly to her home. It was the first telegram she had ever received. The boy who brought it told her it had been sent from California and was telegraphed from St. Louis that very morning.

She gazed at the yellow envelope a long time before opening it, thrilled by this latest example of the many marvelous inventions that were developing as the nation grew.

She carefully opened the envelope, deciding to save it as a memento of the country's progress. The brief message printed in bold letters stunned her:

HUSBAND ROBERT DIED MARCH 17 FROM ACCI-
DENT STOP LETTER FOLLOWS   PRINGLE

XII

Mourning

Rose did not immediately return to California. She was deeply grieved that she had not seen her husband for so many months. She often wept when she thought that now he would never see his young Rose. It was some consolation that Robert and she had had nineteen years of a happy marriage. She did not go out for many weeks. She donned heavy mourning and for a short time refused to see any of her friends. Her sister, Ellen, visited her often, begging her not to abandon her normal way of life.

"You must begin to plan your future, Rose," her sister admonished her.

"What plans can I make? I was going to return to California as soon as traveling was bearable."

"Then go, Rose. If you wish, I shall take care of your girls again."

"But Rose isn't a year old. She is still a baby."

"I have cared for babies before."

"There are so many things left unsettled in California. Ed Pringle has written advising that he is maintaining our establishment. He asks if I wish for him to continue. How should I know? How can I know until I have been there and assessed the situation?"

"You can't, Rose. But it is not natural for anyone to become a recluse, least of all you, who have always been so active."

206

"Perhaps it would be better if I went back."

"It would be. You have always been able to bounce back. This horrible accident—it is the Lord's will, but you are the first to say that living must go on." Ellen paused and watched her sister staring listlessly ahead of her without seeing. "Will you go back to California?"

"I'll have to think about it."

"At least get out of your house, Rose. I have looked forward to your accounts of the administration balls and receptions. Have you been to a session of the Senate recently?"

"No."

"Why don't you go, Rose?"

"Yes. I'll—I'll have to think about it."

Rose continued to think about it. It was a new life that she was contemplating. Robert had never interfered with anything she wished to do. She always knew that she could count on his support. This was probably her greatest loss. He would not be there supporting her every move—her every whim, regardless of how fanciful or illogical he might think it.

Several weeks went by and when Ellen had not seen her sister or heard through the Washington grapevine of her attending any of the social functions that accompanied the winding down of the spring session of Congress, she took it upon herself to visit her sister again. She found Rose sitting in the parlor of her home with the curtains drawn, knitting a sweater for one of her daughters.

Impatiently Ellen strode over to the curtains, drew them, and threw the windows wide open, saying, "This is ridiculous! You are acting as if it is the end of your life on earth. No one had more respect for dear Robert than I. He was a man of great industry and very varied attainments. He was universally respected among his acquaintances, of singular purity, uprightness, and singleness of character and purpose. But he is gone! He would be the first to encourage you to pick up the strands of life and be more active than you have ever been before."

207

"I know, Ellen. What you say is true."

"When are you going to start doing something about it?"

"It's just so hard to—well, there are things around the house that I must do."

"What? Good heavens, Rose. That sweater you are knitting. Why are you working so industriously on that now?"

"Gertrude sorely needs a sweater. She has outgrown her others."

"But summer is just around the corner. She won't need that sweater for six months. The full bloom of summer will soon be upon us. And here you sit knitting a heavy sweater for next winter!"

Slowly Rose put her knitting down in the middle of a row and looked directly at her sister as if seeing her for the first time.

"I am being rather ridiculous, aren't I?"

"You are driving yourself to insanity."

"I—I must force myself to become active again."

"You must. You need not think about it any longer. Rose, you have lost all contact with the outside world. I'll wager that you are not aware that Congress has passed a bill authorizing thirty thousand dollars for a camel corps to cross the barren western lands and deliver passengers and mail to Los Angeles."

"They have?"

"The camels have actually been purchased, according to the *Washington Morning Chronicle*."

"Why, that is ridiculous."

"Isn't it though? Can you imagine camels parading through the streets of the city of Los Angeles?" Ellen laughed heartily and suddenly Rose joined her.

Slowly she got up, and leaning her head on her sister's shoulder, began to cry.

"It's been so hard knowing that he would not be there for me."

"I know it has, Rose."

Rose sighed and dried her eyes. "I shall return to California, Ellen. If you will attend to the girls."

"I will be delighted. You can take a train clear to Chicago now."

"Oh, but that is only a third of the way across the continent. I could never stand the incessant swaying and jolting of those stages day in and day out again."

"But you said you were going back."

"I shall go by way of the isthmus."

"Panama?"

"Yes."

Finally, after months of inactivity, Rose began to prepare for her trip to California. Although her girls were sorry to see her go, for they had gotten to know their mother for the first time since growing older, they looked upon their Aunt Ellen as their second mother. Florence was attending the gay parties of the Pierce administration and Leila and Gertrude were deeply involved in their school activities. Rose had taken her first steps and would not be a baby much longer.

They all went with her on the train to Norfolk and gaily waved her off on her ocean voyage. The sea breezes had their magic effect on Rose as the ship sailed along the coast of America. Although she was still dressed in deep black mourning and her heart was heavy, she mingled freely with the other passengers. Soon she was entertaining them as of old with stories of the Washington scene. She reminisced about her glorious days as a young girl with Dolly Madison, Clay, Calhoun, and Webster. She told them intimate stories of the presidents and their wives—many they would never read in history books.

As they sailed past Cuba, she related her exciting adventure with General Lopez and how she had upset the entire United States government by backing an attempted revolution in that oppressed country.

Several of her fellow passengers were on their way to California for the first time, to start new businesses in the land of golden opportunity. She regaled them with stories of her experiences in California shortly after gold was discovered.

The harbor where they finally docked, a short distance from Portobello, was beautiful. The lush foliage grew almost to the water's edge making the port a tropical paradise. Mr. Aspinall was building his railroad across the isthmus, but Rose learned to her chagrin that, so far, only twenty-five miles of rail had been laid. Having no other choice, she boarded the antiquated train with the other passengers and they started off. The eleven passenger cars chugged majestically along, proving that man could overcome nature's thickly vined forests, marshy soil, and sand-swept plains.

At Barbacoas, Rose and her fellow passengers boarded boats which were to take them along the Chagres River. Actually, it took them longer to transfer their baggage to mules and hop aboard the boats than their entire trip on the railroad had taken. The current was strong and the small canopied boats tipped precariously as the natives heaved vigorously against the stream. The men sang lustily, poling along, occasionally stopping to drive inquisitive monkeys and parrots away with pistol shots.

At nightfall they came to the end of their boat journey. They disembarked and prepared to spend the night in the local tavern before going on early in the morning.

As Rose and the others huddled together before a dilapidated wooden hut beside the dock, she asked, "But where are we going to spend the night?"

"In the tavern, Señora."

"But where is the tavern?"

One of the oarsmen pointed to the forlorn hut, shrugged his shoulders, and smiled.

"That building does not look as if it can support *itself* through the night," a passenger remarked.

"Let us go in and investigate," Rose said hopefully. "It might not be so bad inside."

However, the accommodations proved to be even worse than they appeared from outside. They entered the tavern and their eyes widened as they beheld a large, square room with a solid oak bar at one end and tables and chairs spaced close together before it. It was an unimaginably filthy room. One area was cleared.

"Obviously for the benefit of dancers," Rose commented as a wizened old man with a rough, weatherbeaten face came up to them smiling and nervously wringing his hands.

"Oh, no, Señora," he replied in broken English. "That is for the sleeping accommodations."

"But I see no beds," one of the other ladies gasped.

"We are prepared for that, Señora," said the tavernkeeper, still smiling, and adding that his name was Pele. Walking to the rear of the building Pele pointed to several sets of wide planks that were hinged against the wall. Carefully he removed the crudely fashioned hooks, and one slat fell to a horizontal position revealing a thin stuffed mattress. Two legs at each end dropped, one end resting on the floor. As he removed the hinges from the slats above it, they too automatically fell into position and two more legs fell into place, one end resting unceremoniously on the first row of slats.

"But our party consists of both men and women," wailed another of the female passengers.

"We have also taken that into account, Señora." The wizened Pele smiled graciously. "If the gentlemen will help, we have these barriers that can be moved into place." He pointed to three partitions that were nailed together to a height of ten feet from the floor and were self-supporting.

"If we are to have any privacy, we had better start moving these partitions," commented Rose, as she strode over and grabbed a side. The rest of the party helped move them into place, one in the center of the room separating the ladies from the gentlemen, and two together to separate their sleeping quarters from the rest of the large room.

"This is not what I consider privacy," remarked another of the ladies, younger than the rest. "I shall not sleep in these miserable quarters."

"You'll sleep here or not at all," suggested Rose crossly.

Then she turned to the proprietor and asked in mock-seriousness, "Which side do you designate for the ladies?"

"We leave that entirely to our guests," he smiled benevolently. His eternal smile was beginning to get on Rose's nerves.

"I don't suppose you serve meals at your tavern," she said, not bothering to make it a question.

"Oh, we offer a spread of meats and vegetables which our guests can partake of for free," Pele replied grandly. "That is, all guests who purchase our fine domestic brandy."

"I would prefer to buy the meat and vegetables," suggested one of the women.

"Oh no, Señora. That is not the policy." Whereupon both men and women walked over to the long bar and ordered brandy.

Some of the women gave their brandy to their traveling companions, but Rose drank hers. She had a feeling that she would welcome its sustenance before they again saw daylight and started on their way.

They hastily placed meats and vegetables on small tin plates and hungrily pitched in to eat. They were rather disturbed to learn when they went back for second helpings that this luxury was reserved for those customers who purchased at least one additional brandy.

"There is one consolation," Rose said laconically, "the coach should arrive early tomorrow morning to take us out of here."

"But there is no coach, Señora. There is no road."

All members of the party stopped eating and looked aghast at Pele. "No coach? No road?"

"But I was led to believe that there was an Indian path across the isthmus," said Rose.

"There is, Señora. It is a historical monument to the Spanish conquistadors who used it to bring their treasures to the coast for shipment to Spain."

"Well then—"

"It was only paving stones and they have been dislodged and upended by the passage of time and beasts. It is now only fit for mules."

"Mules?" said one.

"My God!" exclaimed another.

The young woman who had vowed that she would not sleep with such little privacy changed her mind. "I think I shall attempt to sleep. It appears that the most adventurous part of our journey lies ahead."

As they began to bed down for the night, it became apparent that there were not enough tiered bunks to accommodate their party. This was called to Pele's attention, but he merely shrugged his shoulders and spread his hands wide, pointing to the floor.

It was early in the evening, but they were all tired, except for a few of the men who remained at the bar drinking the fine domestic brandy. Most of them got into bunks or spread out on the floor and tried to rest as comfortably as they could. There seemed to be a particularly large amount of noise, which they blamed on the few men left at the bar. Rose shouted, "Please take into consideration those of us attempting to rest, and be quieter."

"But we are not making any noise, ma'am," replied one of the men.

"It is coming from the other building down the road," Pele chimed in.

"Other building?" Rose jumped out of her bunk and poked her head around the partition. "We didn't see any other building when we arrived."

"We keep it out of sight," said Pele with his incessant smile.

"I wonder if the accommodations are any better than this one?" mused Rose. "If we had known we had a choice, we would have—"

"Oh, no, Señora," Pele hastily replied in horror. "That is not for ladies. It is only for the sports of the village of Gorgona."

213

"Do you mean—?"

"Yes, Señora."

Rose turned to the other women. "It is a bordello! We had best be satisfied with what we have."

Hours later, Rose managed to doze off into a fitful slumber. She was occasionally jarred into wakefulness by a squeaking violin and the sharp click of castanets from "down the road." Early the following morning, while it was still dark, she was startled by a loud commotion outside her window. Sleepily jumping up, she furtively peeked out the window. In the darkness she could faintly make out animals being pulled toward the building by shouting men. As her befuddled brain finally wakened, she groaned to herself, "It is the damn pack train arriving with our baggage and the donkeys for our trip across the isthmus. Why could they not have followed closer to our boat to arrive before we retired?"

None of the ladies, who by this time were sitting up startled in their bunks, could offer her an appropriate explanation. However, one of the men, from beyond the dividers, remarked sleepily, "If they have been traveling at this hour, they will be in poor shape to carry us in the morning."

It was impossible for Rose to sleep anymore, so she got up and lit one of the lanterns which hung from the rafters above. Quietly she put on her shoes, the only part of her attire which she had removed, and stealthily slipped out of her makeshift bedroom. Much to her surprise, Pele had placed a large tub of water and some small bars of strong soap on one of the tables. Finding a basin nearby, she dipped out a small bit of water and gave her hands, arms, and face a perfunctory cleansing of the previous day's layers of dirt and grime.

As the first rays of the sun began to filter through the lush foliage, the rest of the passengers began to stir. Worn and tired, they struggled wearily into the large room. Pele was just entering, with his usual indomitable smile, bearing two huge platters. "A special treat for the Yankees," he beamed. "Tortillas and flapjacks."

214

The tortillas were soggy and the flapjacks were pitifully heavy but the travelers ate them with gusto. They had barely finished when the mule boss came in to announce that the caravan was ready to start. Each mounted a mule and they were promptly on their way. It was a most precarious journey. Rose's mule stumbled over sharp rocks and slid down hills, throwing up dust and stones. She smiled sardonically to herself as she recalled telling her sister she would not undertake the overland route to California because of the swaying and incessant jerking of the stage.

After skidding down inclines and splashing through shallow streams where they were thoroughly spattered with mud and water, they finally arrived at the level plains leading into the city of Panama. They had reached the shores of the Pacific ocean. Completely exhausted, the entire caravan ate heartily of a mutton stew provided for them at the inn, and immediately went to bed.

The next day they boarded a ship to take them to the port of San Francisco. Although they sailed over three thousand miles, Rose enjoyed every bit of the trip. She formed many friendships that were to continue beyond her arrival in San Francisco. She was a welcome guest at the captain's table, once again regaling the travelers with tales of her exciting experiences in the nation's capital.

Six weeks later she finally set foot on American soil at the port of San Francisco. She spied Ed Pringle waiting at the dock for her, and as she ran to meet him, she began to cry uncontrollably.

"Forgive me, Ed," she sobbed on his shoulder. "It's just that—there are so many sad memories."

"I understand, Rose. I would invite you to stay at my house, but it is against my bachelor mode of living."

"It doesn't matter, Ed. I have written the Oriental Hotel to expect me."

As Rose had anticipated she was kept extremely busy after her arrival in San Francisco. After the first shock of visiting the many places she and Robert had gone together, she became fully resigned to the fact that it was over and her life must go on. There was so much to be done that there was little time to dwell in the past.

"You haven't changed a bit," Ed told her as she met with him in their office a few days later.

"I am glad to hear that, Ed. Sometimes I feel as if I have aged twenty years."

"If anything, it strikes me that you actually seem younger."

Rose patted his cheek. "You dear man. Thank heavens for your natural instincts, which prompt you to say the proper words to a bereaved widow."

Ed smiled. "Whenever you feel up to it, there are many business matters I must discuss with you."

"The sooner we cope with them the better."

"Are you prepared to make any decisions yet, Rose?"

"Making decisions has always made me feel better. Why don't we start?"

"Very well, then. Our business has grown substantially. It would be unfortunate if we had to dissolve it."

"Then why don't we continue? May we retain the same name?"

"It is agreeable to me."

"I believe that Robert advised me that all expenses were paid monthly before you and he divided the balance of the money equally."

"That is correct."

"Let us continue with this arrangement. However, since I will not be able to assist you, I suggest that you receive seventy-five percent of the proceeds after expenses."

"That seems more than fair."

"This would enable you to hire someone to assist you."

"I have had someone assisting me occasionally. I entered his recompense as an expense to the business."

"Under this arrangement I will be able to review Robert's papers at my leisure."

"Yes. He was working on a book, which is unfinished."

"I should like to complete that, or I might need help."

"It is going to be unpleasant for you to discuss this, Rose, but I feel very strongly that Robert's death was caused by the negligence of the city."

Rose's eyes blinked as she returned Ed's steady gaze. "What are you proposing?"

"I suggest that we file suit for damages against the city."

"Will you handle the case?"

"Of course. It will be an ordeal for you."

"I will have to do it for my daughters' sakes."

"Then I will commence proceedings. Jose Limantour's claims are scheduled to come before the land commission within a couple of weeks. I will be assisting him in his defense, although my other work has forced me to secure James H. Wilson to act as his private council at the hearings. Wilson is a very competent attorney."

"Is Jose in the city?"

"No. He is scheduled to arrive within a week. I was planning to visit San Jose, the state capital, to further explore background data on his claims. But if you wish me to stay in San Francisco, I can cancel my trip."

"Please go. I am personally interested in seeing Limantour's claims settled."

"Robert told me of your Point Lobos claim."

"Which of course is valueless until Limantour's claims are verified."

"Then I shall leave for San Jose day after tomorrow as scheduled."

The following day Rose visited Senator Gwin. He was in his private office with a visitor but when he learned that Rose was there, he immediately came out to see her.

"Rose, so glad to see you," he greeted cheerfully. "I hadn't heard that you were back."

"I arrived a few days ago but I have been so busy."

"Please come into my office."

217

"I was about to leave, Bill. Your young man said—"

"I have an old friend visiting me. I should like you to meet him."

As they entered Senator Gwin's office, a tall, extremely good-looking man in military uniform jumped up smiling.

"Rose, I want you to meet Colonel Erasmus D. Keyes. You certainly must have heard of Rose Greenhow, colonel."

Colonel Keyes bowed graciously. "I have heard Mrs. Greenhow's name mentioned on many occasions while I served back East as aide-de-camp to General Scott. However, I have never had the distinct pleasure of meeting the lady."

"I know General Scott well, but, you are correct, sir, I have not had the pleasure of your acquaintance."

As they sat down, Senator Gwin said without his usual smile, "I was extremely sorry to learn of your husband's sudden death."

"Thank you for your condolences, Bill. It was a great shock."

"And a great loss to our community," Senator Gwin replied. "The colonel and I have just been discussing the great advances that have taken place in our city. It is unfortunate that such progress must be accompanied by so much construction and inconvenience to its citizens."

"That is still no excuse for negligence, Bill. I am holding the city responsible for Robert's untimely death."

"Well, you should. But he would be the first to warn you against dwelling on this unfortunate experience. I hope that you will join us again in our social endeavors."

"I have confined my activities strictly to business since my arrival."

"Then this situation has continued long enough. Mrs. Gwin and I are staging a polka cotillion this Saturday and we shall be honored if you will join us."

"It is embarrassing for a widow to attend a cotillion of matched couples alone."

"I believe I could rectify that, ma'am," volunteered Colonel

Keyes. "That is, if you would not consider it too bold of me to suggest that I accompany you."

"But, sir, would it be appropriate?"

Colonel Keyes nodded and a faint reminiscent smile crossed his face. "Unfortunately I, too, lost my beloved only last year. I know all too well the severe adjustment which you are undergoing."

"We would be delighted to have you, Rose," coaxed Senator Gwin. "My wife will be extremely disappointed, when I tell her you have returned, to learn of your refusal."

"I would consider it an honor if you would join me, Mrs. Greenhow," Colonel Keyes hastily added.

"It is most considerate of you," Rose replied. "I—I don't know whether I am ready to—"

"The good senator had just extended a similar invitation to me and I declined his gracious offer for the same reason. I suddenly find that circumstances alter cases."

Rose laughed, feeling suddenly lighter. "I shall be glad to join you, Colonel Keyes. I trust that I can refrain from being too boring."

"I can assure you, colonel, if Rose accompanies you to our cotillion, you will never have a boring moment."

Colonel Keyes laughed. "I have heard this sentiment expressed before concerning Mrs. Greenhow."

"My friends call me Rose."

"Rose it is, then," said Colonel Keyes. "Then I may have the pleasure of your company at the cotillion?"

"I shall be delighted. I am staying at the Oriental Hotel on Market Street."

"Come for supper," volunteered Senator Gwin. "I would say about five o'clock."

"I look forward to it, Bill." Rose got up from her chair. "And now I must beg my leave of you. There are so many things a widow must do which previously were shared by two."

Colonel Keyes rose. "I understand and sympathize with you, madam." He took her hand and pressed it. "I shall call for

219

you at four o'clock Saturday, then."

Rose went to the cotillion with Colonel Keyes and was almost ashamed of herself for having such an enjoyable time. The colonel was a fine dancer and proved to be an excellent partner. She met many of her old acquaintances and was delighted to see one couple who had accompanied her on her recent trip across the isthmus. They laughed heartily over their harrying experiences. "For such a brief fifty miles, I marvel that they have incorporated every known obstacle to travel," Rose said.

She saw a great deal of Colonel Keyes in the weeks that followed. She chided him about his staid Massachusetts upbringing. "But I warn you I shall never stop trying to influence you until you see the problems that confront this nation in their proper perspective."

"You mean through the rose-colored glasses of our southern compatriots?"

"I do, sir. Including you northerners' self-righteous view on the issue of slavery."

"You sound as if you are willing to fight for your cause."

"Willing and able, colonel."

"Well, let us not permit it to come between our fine friendship."

"It will never separate me from such a gallant man of worldly wisdom by *my* doing."

"Thank you, Rose. But you know, once alerted, a good soldier always remains on constant guard."

She took him out to Point Lobos and showed him the acreage that Jose Limantour had granted her. They discussed Jose's claims and she was surprised to learn how familiar he was with them.

"Everyone in San Francisco knows of Limantour's great claims," Colonel Keyes told her. "But this is the first I have known anyone directly involved in them."

"It is the only payment my husband received for representing him these many months."

"Do you think his claims will be verified?"

"Robert investigated them in Mexico City and again in San Francisco. As far as he could determine they were authentic. There *are* many persons coming to the fore claiming that they are fraudulent. But I can't believe that my husband could have erred in his investigations."

"I am sure Limantour's claims will be upheld by the new land commission."

"I hope so. It is so beautiful here."

They watched silently for a few moments as the sea lions scampered up and down the rocks not far offshore. As a breeze came up, she shivered and he put his arm about her waist. "It is the kind of paradise that every romantic dreams of."

"If it is ever mine, I shall build a house on this very point. The side facing the sea shall contain nothing but windows."

"So that you can watch the setting sun and marvel at God's crimson paintings as they spread across the sky at dusk."

"My, you are a romantic, colonel."

"I have come down to the sea many evenings at dusk. It fascinates me."

"When I have built my house, I shall invite you over to witness God's handiwork."

"Will you, Rose?" He looked deep into her eyes, then slowly drew her to him and kissed her gently. Her body tingled as she reacted to the first kiss she had had from a man since she had rested in Robert's arms and bade him farewell so many months ago.

Slowly she turned to the man beside her and, slipping her arms about his neck, drew him to her and kissed him passionately. He returned her kiss with equal passion and for a long moment they stood against each other in the lonely wilderness. He kissed her more passionately and then released her. She pulled him back close to her. It was so good to feel his strong body against her. He held her face in his hands and drawing her to him kissed her again. Slowly he released his hold on her and turned toward the sea.

"I suppose we had best be returning to civilization."

"It is getting chilly, but I hate to leave."

"I agree. Henceforth the sea will have a different meaning for me, Rose."

"It will for me, too."

Colonel Keyes accompanied Rose to Limantour's hearing before the land commission.

Limantour laid out his papers before the commission. "Here are the boundaries outlining my property," he said importantly.

One of the commissioners rubbed his chin. "I note that your claim includes Goat Island and Cedros."

"You are correct, sir. This is in addition to the other land in San Francisco."

"These claims are most extensive."

"They are, sir. They have been thoroughly investigated by Dr. Greenhow, my most noteworthy counselor, who has determined them to be authentic."

"Very well, Mr. Limantour," said another of the commissioners, "We shall take this under advisement."

"Under advisement? You can plainly see for yourself the boundaries of my grant."

"But there are many others who have laid claim to parts of your lands. We must hear them out as well as yourself."

"I can't see why. I have laid my claims before you. I have shown you the authentication by the French legation and sworn statements from the governor. What need is there for any further proof?"

"We have to investigate all claimants," replied one of the commissioners. "You must agree that is only fair."

"I do not agree, sir. There can be only one true claimant. I have presented my claims herewith. Do they not seem to be in order?"

"They do, sir."

"Then I fail to understand why you cannot give me full authorization. I realize my claim is vast, but I have been waiting for many months—years, in fact. I had hoped that your commission would relieve me of any further delay."

"We shall explore your claims thoroughly, as well as the others, Mr. Limantour, and we will advise you of our decision in due time."

Jose Limantour jumped up from his chair. "In due time? What has your commission been appointed for?"

"To settle conflicting land claims."

"Well, you can see with your own eyes what I have placed before you. It is a clear, open-and-shut case. Your own attorney to the commission, Dr. Greenhow, has verified my claims. Is not that sufficient evidence?"

"Anyone can make a mistake, Mr. Limantour. I trust you will understand that—"

"I don't understand anything, commissioner. I came into this room today feeling that finally justice was about to be served. Now I find that I am confronted with the same doubts and questioning I have received in the past. It is imperative that I have a decision now! I can't wait any longer."

"You must wait until we have thoroughly examined every claim that has been brought forward for the same lands that your properties cover."

"But that could take years!"

"We shall move on the matter as rapidly as possible. We advise you strongly to be patient."

"I've been patient as long as I can. I need an uncontested claim to my properties and your commission is the group assigned by the president of the United States to give it to me. I want it now!"

"The president has instructed us to issue claims to the rightful owners. That is what we shall do."

"Are you calling me a liar?"

"This is getting us nowhere, Mr. Limantour. You have had your opportunity to present your side. There is nothing more that can be done at this time. The matter is concluded. We hope you can see our position."

"No, I can't see your position."

Another of the commissioners rose. "That will be all, Mr. Limantour. May we bid you good day?"

"But you don't understand what this means to me."

"It means a great deal to everyone concerned, Mr. Limantour. Now, good day, sir."

Angrily Limantour grabbed his papers and started to leave the room. As he neared the door, he turned to the commissioners and shouted, "I better be hearing from you within the next two months or I—I'll sue you."

"Good day, Mr. Limantour."

Muttering under his breath, Limantour stormed out of the room.

Rose and Colonel Keyes lunched together after the commissioners' session.

"Limantour's claims do seem to be in order, Rose. Forgive me, but I cannot like the man."

"He behaved abominably in the commissioners' office today. I shall tell him so."

"He did not gain any friends on the commission—that is for sure."

When Rose arrived home that afternoon she was delighted to find a letter from Buchanan. He told her in detail of events in London:

"I have received an honorary degree from Oxford, for which I am exceedingly grateful. My niece, Harriet, and myself had the pleasure of a private audience with the emperor and empress of France when they visited London. In the case of Louis Napoleon, fact is stranger than fiction. Whilst in London as an exile, he was never appreciated to be a man of talent. Now, he is the foremost man of all Europe, and at the present moment possesses more extensive and real influence than ever did his great uncle. I cannot understand the failings and the unpredictableness of the common people." Later on in the letter he told her, "Harriet and I dined with the archbishop of Canterbury and Harriet Beecher Stowe's *Uncle Tom's Cabin* was discussed. You would be proud of the way I condemned the thesis upon which the book was based. I care not that the book has already sold over two million copies, it is obviously an author's efforts to take advantage of a volatile situation."

It was good to hear from her old friend. She was surprised that he made no mention of Robert, although he had sent her his condolences earlier when he had learned of his death. It was a rather impersonal letter, dealing mainly as it did with the political issues of the day. She wondered if he thought of her in his busy says of turmoil at the court of St. James. At least, he ended his letter sending his love to Gertrude and Florence.

It was not long afterward that she received a letter from her oldest daughter, Florence. Florence had kept up her correspondence with Buchanan's niece, Harriet. She relayed the information that Harriet had told her of having a long talk with the Empress Eugenie, who was striking and graceful in green silk flounced with white lace, a matching mantle and a white crepe bonnet with feathers. But her description of the emperor was far from complimentary. She quoted from Harriet's letter: "He is extremely short, with weak shanks, and is not very imposing in appearance." Florence then called her mother's attention to a letter she enclosed.

It was from a Captain Treadwell W. Moore and respectfully requested his permission to marry her daughter! Rose was shocked. Florence had not mentioned Captain Moore before, and suddenly Rose was confronted with a fact that seemed almost accomplished. How long had her daughter known this man? What was his age? Where was he from? Were his parents active in Washington? She decided it was time she had a serious discussion with her oldest daughter. A discussion that could not take place three thousand miles from each other.

She immediately went to Ed Pringle to determine the status of her suit against the city.

"They admit that their construction men were negligent in their duty in not adequately protecting the excavation where Robert fell. They have already offered us ten thousand dollars, but I believe we can settle for much more if we prolong the negotiations."

"Please settle for the amount they have stipulated at once."

"This is not advisable, Rose."

"I must. Some matters have arisen in Washington that make it imperative that I return. I would prefer to have this distasteful matter settled before I leave."

Ed frowned, then shrugged his shoulders. "I shall initiate a settlement immediately."

That evening she wrote a hurried letter to her daughter advising that she was returning to Washington and asking her not to take any action with regard to Captain Moore. "At least not until I have an opportunity to meet the gentleman," she ended her letter.

She then called on Colonel Keyes asking him if he could secure any information on the gentleman in question.

"I am sure that I can if you wish to know more about him."

"I wish so very much. He has requested my daughter's hand in marriage."

"I shall start an investigation immediately."

Two weeks later, Ed Pringle handed her a draft for ten thousand dollars from the comptroller of the city of San Francisco. The draft was accompanied by a letter addressed to the board of aldermen to be signed by Rose, advising that she did not hold them further accountable for the unfortunate accident which had resulted in the death of her husband.

She signed the letter and promptly made arrangements to return to Washington by the overland route. The railroad had been extended to St. Louis by now. "At least the jolting and bumping of the miserable coach ride has been reduced by half," she told Colonel Keyes as he dined with her at the hotel the night before she went.

Early the following morning when he came to take her to the coach station, Colonel Keyes advised her that he had secured some information on Captain Moore. "Treadwell Moore is twenty-three years old and plans to make a career of the army.

226

He comes from a small town not far from Portsmouth, Ohio, by the name of Friendship. His father runs a general store, including dry goods, and he is mayor of the town. It is not far from the Kentucky border so, who knows, he may even have southern leanings. A dossier on him is on file at the Presidio, for he has requested a transfer to that San Francisco installation."

"Which indicates that he and supposedly my daughter wish to come West to live—after they have married."

"It would seem so."

She placed her hand affectionately on his arm. "I do sincerely appreciate your getting this information for me."

"It was the least I could do, particularly since it is the first opportunity I have had to be of assistance to you."

"Thank you, colonel."

"Do you wish me to follow this up at the Presidio to see if anything can be done to expedite or grant the young man's request?"

"Please do nothing yet. Wait until I have had an opportunity to meet the gentleman—and appraise him."

"Very well." He patted her hand gently. "I shall miss you, Rose."

"I shall miss you, colonel. You have brightened my San Francisco visit considerably."

There was an awkward pause as the two of them stood beside each other by the stage coach.

The driver mounted the coach, shouting that the Eastbound express was departing. Rose turned to the colonel, and fondly brushing his military lapel, said softly, "Goodbye, dear!" Then, reaching up on her toes, she lightly brushed his cheek, smiling as she kissed him.

"Hurry back," he shouted to her as the coach started off. She watched him waving to her until they turned a corner and disappeared from view in a cloud of dust.

XIII

Noon

The railroad station in Washington, D.C. was one of the largest privately owned buildings in the capital. With the railroads linking every state east of the Mississippi, trains were arriving at the huge, high-ceilinged building every hour of the day and night. Its main waiting room was constantly crowded with incoming and departing passengers, except for the few hours around midnight.

Rose arrived late in the evening, and although she had wired ahead the scheduled arrival of her train from Chicago, she hardly expected anyone there to meet her. To her surprise she spotted all four of her daughters waiting for her at the passenger exit even before she disembarked from the train. She was not remiss in noting that they were accompanied by a tall, handsome young man in military uniform. Gertrude was carrying Rose.

Her daughters rushed to meet her and amidst exclamations and joyful greetings, Florence introduced her to Captain Treadwell Moore.

"So this is the man who is taking my oldest daughter from me," she smiled as he efficiently took her two bags and they started out of the terminal.

"Oh, Mums," Florence said impetuously, "we have so much to tell you. I'm so glad you came home."

"They're going to California," Leila announced.

228

"Oh Leila, now you've spoiled it. I wish you'd let me tell Mother in due time."

"Leila has spoiled nothing," Rose remarked as they got into their waiting carriage. "I know Captain Moore has requested a transfer to the Presidio in San Francisco."

"Mother, how could you ever—? I should know better than to try and keep a secret from you. Not that it was a secret, really. We just decided that as long as you were coming home we would wait until you got here to—"

"I understand, dear," Rose said as she glanced at her baby daughter. Through all of the homecoming commotion young Rose had been sleeping peacefully in Gertrude's arms. "My, how she has grown."

"She walks now, Mum," Gertrude volunteered. "She talks, too. She has given me a new nickname. She can't say Gertrude so she calls me Trude. I like that. I tell my friends to call me Trude."

Their home was not far from the station. As they arrived, Captain Moore volunteered to put the carriage away in the stable as the rest went into the house. No sooner was he out of earshot than Florence grabbed her mother's arm. "Isn't he divine, Mums?"

"He seems very nice." Rose was actually well-taken with the young man. He was most attentive to Florence and at the same time very considerate of the other girls and polite to Rose. "Of course he would be on his best behavior on the occasion of our first meeting."

"Oh, but he is so kind and gentle. Wait until you get to know him."

"If he is kind and gentle, he has certainly chosen the wrong profession."

"But Mums, fighters are only required in times of war. There isn't a chance of war in America for many years to come."

"I can see that you do not follow the opposing views that are so vehemently expressed on the floor of the Senate these days."

"What do you mean?"

"Never mind. Come help me put Rose to bed."

As they started to go upstairs Captain Moore knocked and came into the house.

"Make yourself comfortable, Moore, while I help Mums put my sister to bed," Florence shouted down to him.

Florence had one subject in mind this evening.

"You do approve of him don't you Mums? I couldn't bear it if you didn't."

"My first reaction is most favorable. Now, what are your plans?"

"We stopped making plans after we received your letter. I had thought you would accept our marriage as a matter of fact. Then, when we received your letter, well—it came as sort of a shock. We decided not to do anything further until you arrived."

"That was very considerate of you. But the captain has already requested a transfer to the Presidio."

"That was quite a while before we received your letter, Mums," Florence hurriedly explained.

"I appreciate your waiting until I got here."

"We will have your permission to marry, won't we?"

"I do not anticipate any problem. The background information I have received on Captain Moore has been most complimentary."

"Mother!" Florence gasped. "How could you possibly know anything about his background?"

"When a young officer requests a transfer to an army post, that post receives a complete dossier on him."

"You have seen it?"

"No. But I have an accurate account of what is in it."

"Mother, you would make an intriguing spy."

"Thank you, dear. Now, when do you wish to be married?"

"Oh, I wish it were tomorrow."

"I'm sure you do, Florence. That is discernible from the

admiration in your eyes when you look at the young man."

"I didn't realize I was that obvious."

"All girls throw discretion completely to the winds when they fall in love," Rose said hastily. "It's time we went downstairs. We've been keeping your captain waiting far too long." They kissed Rose and the others goodnight and joined Captain Moore. The three sat up into the early morning hours getting further acquainted and discussing the young couple's plans.

"Florence advises me that you have not decided on a date for your wedding."

Captain Moore smiled impishly. 'Well, after your letter, ma'am, we thought it best to wait until you arrived. Then, too, a lot depends on my application to the Presidio."

"You haven't heard from them?"

"No ma'am.'

"Are there any difficulties that you know of?"

"There has to be a vacancy in the table of organization," explained Florence importantly.

"But surely there are openings at the Presidio. It is one of the largest posts in the country."

"Oh, yes ma'am. I have applied for quartermaster, which I know to be vacant. But there is—"

"There's so much red tape involved," Florence broke in. "It's most discouraging having to wait and wait for an appointment that we both know Moore can handle most efficiently."

"Let me see what I can do."

"Will you, Mums?"

"I can promise you nothing but I shall certainly try. Who is your commanding officer, captain?"

"Colonel Charles P. Stone."

"I have met the gentleman. Then you are stationed at Fort Washington?"

"Yes, ma'am."

"At times a little feminine prodding can work wonders. Now

it would behoove us all to get some sleep."

Florence and Captain Moore were radiant as he rose to go. Hand in hand they slowly walked to the door. He thanked Rose for offering to help them and slyly pressed Florence's hand as he bid her goodnight and left.

Rose and her mother slowly walked up the stairs together.

"I do hope you can help us, Mums. We have been waiting for so long."

"Waiting seems so much longer when you are young." Rose patted her daughter's cheek and kissed her goodnight.

As exhausted as she was, Rose wrote two letters in the early hours of the morning before she retired. The first was to Colonel Keyes requesting his assistance in expediting Captain Moore's transfer to the Presidio. The other was to Buchanan asking him to intercede with the proper army personnel to secure Captain Moore's appointment as quartermaster at the San Francisco Presidio.

Late the next morning after a light breakfast Rose instructed Randy to hitch up their carriage and drive her to Fort Washington. Colonel Stone was delighted to see her and immediately ushered her into his office.

"I know you are busy, colonel, and I won't take but a moment of your time."

"I consider it an honor to have you visit us, Mrs. Greenhow."

"You are familiar with Captain Treadwell Moore?"

"I am his commanding officer."

"Would you be frank with me, colonel, and give me your personal opinion of the gentleman? He is planning to marry my daughter."

"Oh, yes, he did tell me about that. But then there seemed to be a delay."

Rose's lips grew firm. "They very considerately waited for me to return from San Francisco."

"Ah, yes. Well, I tell you, Mrs. Greenhow, if I had a daughter of marriageable age, I would be happy to see her marry Captain Moore. He is a sincere, courageous soldier. He's frank, he's honest and industrious. I have no doubt, when giving him an assignment, that it will be carried out properly and expeditiously. Does that set your mind at ease?"

"It does Colonel Stone, I appreciate your candor. It sounds as if he comes from a right respectable family."

"He definitely does. He speaks of his family often. I gather that they are quite wealthy. His parents are among the leaders of their community."

Rose's brow arched and a faint smile crossed her lips as she stood up. "I shall not detain you longer." She was cheerful as he accompanied her out of the room. "I trust I shall see you at the wedding."

"You may count on that, Mrs. Greenhow."

"Oh, and colonel, I hope that we can keep my visit to you confidential."

"I assure you, ma'am, no one will hear of it from me."

"Thank you, Colonel Stone."

Rose got into her carriage and instructed Randy to drive her directly to the post office. She personally posted the two letters she had written earlier in the day and then promptly returned home.

As she lunched with her daughters that noon, Florence's impending wedding was the main topic of discussion.

"We shall announce the betrothal and set the date for the wedding at once," Rose announced.

"This is exciting," Gertrude giggled.

"Can we be married next month, Mums?" excitedly asked Florence.

"Next month! My dear child, there are many arrangements to be made; we must allow necessary time for the mails to deliver our invitations and receive replies. I would suggest the first of October."

"Oh, Mums," Florence said, crestfallen. "Such a long time!"

"Fall is a beautiful time for a wedding. There are so many

matters to be attended to. Before the date arrives you will wish that you had selected a later date."

"Yes, Mums," Florence sighed. "I am sure you know best."

"Besides, there are other matters to take into consideration. I find that it will be necessary for us to reduce our living expenses. We must, therefore, seek a more modest home in which to live." As the three girls looked at her in amazement, she quickly continued. "It has become necessary for us to conserve our meager assets. We can live very comfortably in a smaller house. Scheduling the wedding in the fall will allow us sufficient time to sell this house and be well settled in another before the wedding."

"Do you plan to sell our home immediately, Mums?" Gertrude asked in a thin, startled voice.

"I shall place an advertisement in the *Washington Daily Globe* at once. Now, please, girls, this is not a great catastrophe. I assure you you will continue to live in a cozy home that will be acceptable to all of us."

Rose herself was not prepared for the quick turn of events when she advertised the sale of their home. Within a month one of the first couples who looked at it had decided they were delighted with the grand house and its convenience to the central part of Washington. They not only agreed to buy it, but requested that they be permitted to occupy it immediately. Rose was forced to seek temporary quarters.

"There is no alternative," she told the girls. "I have secured rooms at Brown's Hotel until we find another home."

Although living in cramped quarters was an old matter for Rose, her daughters were extremely unhappy with the sudden move.

She was discussing her predicament with Jefferson Davis, the secretary of war, whom she happened to meet at a session of the Senate where he had been called to testify on the budget for the army.

"My daughters don't take very well to hotel living," she lamented.

"What do you plan to do?"

"I shall purchase another home as soon as I find one that is satisfactory. I never dreamed that our old house would be sold so readily."

"I think I might be able to help you. General Burnside has just been assigned to Fort Bragg, North Carolina, and he wishes to sell his own home before he leaves. It's located on Sixteenth Street."

"We are looking for a fairly small home, sir."

"This should meet your requirements. When you have some free time I would be glad to arrange an appointment for you to see the house."

"I am available at once. If it is to our liking, the sooner we move into a house, the better."

Davis drove Rose in his carriage to General Burnside's house at 398 Sixteenth Street. It was exactly what she had been looking for, and that very day she made arrangements to purchase it.

Within three weeks, she and the girls moved into their new home. Her daughters were delighted to be living in a house once again. Rose laughed at their civilized outlook on life.

"You should have to live in San Francisco with cardboard-stiffened muslin walls, or perhaps spend a night in a strange tavern in the wilds of the Isthmus of Panama!" she told them.

Rose was beginning to adjust to her widowed life at long last. She enjoyed attending promenade concerts with Joseph Lane of Oregon. He was the official delegate from that territory to the United States government. Delegate Lane was his own best admirer, but Rose enjoyed listening to his many exploits.

While they were sitting out a dance number he seemed to feel that it was his duty to entertain his lively guest by talking incessantly.

"Did you know that this week marks the tenth anniversary of my trek into the wilds of Oregon?"

"I wasn't aware of that, Joe."

"You weren't? Well, goddamn, I'll have you know that for

235

five weary and desolate months I led a little band of brave frontiersmen amid the gorges, defiles, and snows of the Rocky mountains."

"That must have been exciting."

"Exciting and dangerous. I finally reached my goal on one of the coldest March days Oregon has ever witnessed. Yep. Oregon appreciated what I did for them. That's why they made me their first territorial governor."

"No!"

"Yep. I was granted that great honor because of my meritorious trek on Oregon's behalf. You know what President Pierce says of that bold venture? He compares it to Napoleon crossing the Alps. That's what he thinks of my achievement! There's a lot of other folks think the same way. That's why they voted me their territorial delegate here in Washington. They know I will watch out for their interests."

Rose smiled. She was content to look about the ballroom and see the vast majority of women wearing their hair in a knot on top of their heads. The very fashion that she had introduced into Washington society. It had come to be known as the Greenhow hairstyle.

Riding home that evening, Delegate Lane suddenly asked Rose, "How far can you trace your genealogy?"

"Good heavens, I really haven't given the matter much thought. I don't—"

"I can trace mine clear back to the Crusades."

"You can?"

"I sure can. I'm right proud of my family tree."

"I'd like to see your table of ancestors, sometime."

Lane brightened noticeably. "Would you really? I'll bring a copy over to you next time we meet. I got several copies. You can keep it, if you want."

"I'd like that."

As they arrived at Rose's home, Lane helped her out of his carriage and escorted her to the front door of her house. He gave every indication that he planned to go into the house with her.

"Thank you, Joe, for a most entertaining evening."

"But can't I come in?"

"It's late, you know."

"It's never too late for friends who have so much in common."

He stood arrogantly by her side, waiting for her to relent. Presently she patted him on the cheek. "I'm extremely tired, Joe. Perhaps we could continue our discussions the next time we meet."

"Well, if you insist."

"I do!" She reached up to his face and kissed him gently on the cheek.

"That ain't no way for friends to treat each other." He grabbed her in his strong arms and bending her backward drew her close to him and kissed her soundly. As he released her, he beamed with satisfaction. "Ain't going to leave no unfinished business with old Joe Lane. Don't you ever forget that."

"I won't, Joe. Until next time, then." She pressed her body against him and kissed him passionately.

He waved gallantly to her and swaggered down the walk to his carriage.

It was still two months before Florence's wedding, when they were surprised to have Captain Moore hurriedly visit them at noon, on a hot, humid summer day.

"I have received my appointment as quartermaster," he shouted, perspiration standing out on his forehead from his hurried trip to their home.

"How wonderful!" Florence squealed and then threw her arms around her mother's neck. "Oh, Mums, thank you so much for helping us."

"I am to report to the Presidio the first of next month."

"Next month?" wailed Florence. "But that is before our wedding!"

"We will have to reschedule your wedding," Rose said quickly. "It must be before the end of this month."

"But, Mums, the arrangements have been made. We have already invited our families and friends."

"You must be wedded before the end of this month, daughter. Unless, of course, you wish Captain Moore to journey to the Presidio alone."

Abruptly the plans for the wedding were changed. Florence wished to have a military wedding, and the reception was to be held in the officers' reception room at Fort Washington. This now posed a problem, for a military conference was scheduled to be held in the reception room at the same time. The conflict was quickly resolved when Rose paid another visit to Colonel Stone. After subtly reminding him of her close friendship with Lieutenant-General Winfield Scott, commander in chief of the army, and complimenting the colonel on his daring exploits in the Mexican-American war, which had been related to her by the good general, Colonel Stone finally agreed to reschedule his military conference.

With Rose officiating as hostess, the wedding was a memorable occasion. The room was gaily decorated with the regiment colors, interspersed with chrysanthemums and other fall flowers. In spite of the hurried preparations, Rose had managed to muster an outstanding reception, with platters of prairie hen, wild turkey, and reed birds, served along with the terrapin, oysters, and lobsters from her beloved Rappahannock. The delectable cuisine was topped off by a cherry cobbler and a four-tiered wedding cake for dessert. During all the festivities, champagne flowed freely.

Florence was beautiful in her wedding dress, and Rose was the height of fashion in her flowing, many-tiered pale pink gown. She had insisted her dressmaker design a dress specifically to her requirements, so that she could utilize it at other Washington affairs. Then she drove the poor woman almost to distraction, making her work exclusively on her creation so that it would be ready for the earlier wedding date. The neckline was cut daringly low, generously exposing a good portion of her splendid breasts. It was truly breathtaking, and

Rose had the satisfaction of seeing many similarly designed dresses at other state functions in the ensuing season. It came to be known as the Greenhow dress.

In addition to the O'Neal and Greenhow clans, the groom's family had journeyed east from Ohio to attend the wedding. Rose was delighted with both of Moore's parents. Moore was the spitting image of his father, a tall, well-built man with a free and easy manner that made him easy to talk to. The elder Moore had the air and confidence of a good businessman, but it was obvious that his mother was a very strong-willed woman and held no small amount of sway over her successful husband. This pleased Rose no end. They, in turn, were appropriately impressed with the leaders of the country who were also in attendance. President Franklin Pierce and his wife, Jane Means Appleton Pierce, headed the distinguished list, followed by Vice President William King, Secretary of War Jefferson Davis, Secretary of State William Marcy, Lieutenant-General Winfield Scott, and all of their wives, as well as many of the prominent senators and representatives from both the northern and southern states.

As Rose watched her daughter walk out of the hall on the arm of her husband beneath the traditional arch of drawn swords of the men of his company, Rose conceded that it had all been worthwhile.

The next day she saw them off on the first leg of their trip to the Presidio in San Francisco.

The following week, Rose attended a polka cotillion accompanied by Senator Henry Wilson from Massachusetts. She had been seen at many of the social functions in Washington with him and their names had been linked on several occasions. He was a most unlikely partner for Rose, being strongly antislavery, but his affiliation did not deter her in the least. In fact, she looked upon her association with him as a challenge.

"You and your staid and proper attitude toward slavery," she chided him. "When you know that the plight of young children working in the sweatshops of your own state are far worse than slavery."

"I am trying desperately to do something about this unfortunate circumstance, Rose."

"That is the talk of a politician. I shall believe you when I have noted any accomplishment."

"But must we talk of our transgressions this evening? We are here to enjoy ourselves."

"You are correct, Henry. I do not mean to be harsh. It is just that the matter of slavery is close to my heart and it depresses me to see those I hold dear speaking out so strongly against it."

"I am flattered that you hold the senator from Massachusetts dear to you."

"I truly consider you one of my dearest friends, Henry." As he placed his hand on her lap and smiled lovingly at her, she rose hastily. "Come, the music has started. I just love to dance the polka, don't you?"

"Yes, I enjoy the polka when I am dancing with someone I hold dear to *me*."

Gaily, she slapped his cheek lightly with her fan as they joined the group of dancers.

Riding home that evening Henry became serious when Rose casually mentioned Delegate Lane in her conversation.

"Rose, may I caution you as a friend against the territorial delegate from Oregon?"

"Whatever are you referring to, Henry?"

"I know that he has been seen with you on many occasions. He is not a suitable companion for you."

"Why, Henry, I do believe you are jealous."

"Jealous? Yes, perhaps. But it is of you I am thinking. You surely have heard the stories of his drunk and disorderly behavior right here in the capital."

"He has always acted as a gentleman when he was with me."

"He does not have very high standards, Rose."

"He has changed his opinion considerably on his stand against slavery."

"That is probably, no doubt, to put himself in your good graces. I have heard on good authority that he enriched himself in the war at the expense of others."

She looked at him closely for a moment before she spoke. "Why are you telling me this?"

Henry's face became flushed in his denunciation. "I want you to see him for the man he is. Not the one he takes pains for you to know when he is with you. He has been accused of cheating the Indians in his own territory."

"These accusations—"

"They are more than accusations, Rose. Are you aware that he is married to a poor, illiterate wife who has borne him ten children?"

"You are married, Henry."

"I know. I am devoted to my wife, Harriet. But New England is so far away. When I am with you—" He turned toward her and laid his free hand on her lap. "Nothing else matters," he said softly. "Absolutely nothing, when I am with you."

They were approaching Rose's house and he quickly drew his carriage to the side of the road and bridled his horse. He helped her out of the carriage and accompanied her to the door.

As he stood beside her, he smiled almost apologetically. "I am sorry if I have behaved like a boor. I did not mean to be so serious. It is just that—believe me, Rose, it is only your best interest that I have at heart."

"I believe you, Henry." She touched his arm lightly and then added, "Will you come in?"

They entered the house and he took off his coat and unloosened his stiff collar and tie as she mixed them a Queen Charlotte Cocktail.

"Have you ever had a Queen Charlotte Cocktail, Henry?"

"I never have. I have heard about them and have been cautioned that they are extremely strong."

She brought him his cocktail and sat down beside him on the sofa as they drank.

"It is superb!" he exclaimed.

"I thought you would like it."

She placed her arm on the back of the sofa touching his shoulder. "Although this is an inopportune time, I rarely am able to see you privately to discuss matters of state."

He gulped the rest of his Queen Charlotte Cocktail down. "Oh, Rose, not at this hour."

As she poured them another cocktail she said, "I think it most inappropriate of you to have voted against the Ostend Manifesto. Do you realize how hard Mr. Buchanan and President Pierce himself worked to try and put that plan into effect?"

"It is not practical to suggest adding Cuba to our country when Spain has twice rejected such overtures."

"But you publicly backed the president in his attempt to purchase Alaska from Russia and to annex Hawaii."

"But the circumstances were entirely different. Cuba was to be brought into the Union as a slave state."

"On the contrary, it was to be decided by the majority of the voters. The same situation confronts the settlers in the Kansas Territory. The president advocates the passage of the Kansas-Nebraska act. How do you plan to vote on this legislation?"

"You forget that I am antislavery, in spite of everything you say or do."

"This is not a matter of personal opinions, Henry. It merely repeals the Missouri Compromise of 1820. It gives the settlers the right to vote their own preferences for or against slavery."

"To give them this right is only passing the burden of decision on to them. It will undoubtedly lead to bloodshed between opposing factions within the territory in the days to come."

"Do you believe in denying the settlers their franchised right to vote their opinions?"

"Of course not."

"That is what you are doing if you vote against the president's Kansas-Nebraska act."

Henry sighed. "I repeat, I haven't completely made up

my mind."

"A vote for this act is actually a vote for democracy, Henry."

"I'll see."

"Our country needs fair-minded legislatures during these trying times. We need all the help that we can get."

"You mean the South needs all the help it can muster."

"Our country needs it, Henry. Yours and mine." She moved closer to him.

Her low-cut gown exposed the upper portion of her fully developed breasts. He sighed. "You are a beautiful woman, Rose O'Neal Greenhow. You truly are my Wild Rose."

"I try to be considerate of those I hold close to my heart."

"That is the duty of every woman. It's just that—"

"Just what, Henry?"

"Oh, the hell with it." He took her in his arms and kissed her. The pleasure of being beside him thrilled her. She leaned against the back of the sofa, resting contentedly in his arms.

He gently stroked her hair which had been held in a knot on the back of her head. Gradually it fell down below her shoulders and he ran his hands gently through her dark tresses. He drew her to him and kissed her cheek, her forehead, then, passionately, her lips.

Deftly he lowered his hand to her partially exposed breast and pressed it hard against her body. His hand slipped beneath the low-cut dress and found her exquisitely firm breast. Her cheeks were flaming. She watched as he slowly undid the little pearl buttons, letting the shoulders of her dress slide down her arms. She was becoming excited. With a simple movement of her shoulders, she dropped the top of her dress from about her. He slipped her chemise over her shoulders, letting it rest in a rumpled mass at her waist. He reached behind her and unbuttoned her camisole. He kissed her bare shoulders. Then, lowering his head, he fervently kissed her lovely breast, holding her other tightly in his hand and pressing it against her bare body.

He drew away from her ever so slightly as he turned her toward him and put her breast in his mouth, running his tongue around the tip. He unloosened the sash about her waist and dragged her dress down. With a slight movement on her part it slipped away from her and fell to the floor. Almost savagely, with one skillful stroke, he drew her petticoats off, throwing them carelessly away. She helped him take off her chemise. His hand shook as he drew her pantalettes off and threw them on the floor. He ran both his hands over her back, then over the front of her. She closed her eyes and gave herself up completely to him. His passion raised to fever pitch, he pressed her onto the bed of the couch until her body lay prone before him, her head resting on the arm. Slowly but firmly he drew one of her legs apart until her foot dropped and rested on the floor. He leaned over her.

She was breathing heavily now, feeling his warm body as he pressed it against her own. Whatever he wished to do to her, she was his. He fumbled nervously with his pants, then suddenly he stopped, and quickly pressed his whole body to her. He pushed heavily against her, and lying rigidly motionless, pressed his body as hard as he could against her soft, warm flesh.

He lay steadily against her, not moving, breathing heavily as he gradually released his hold on her bare breasts. He did not move for a long time. She did not speak as her own passion subsided, her breathing once again becoming normal.

Slowly he turned away from her and dropped one of his feet on the floor to avoid falling. A low, guttural growl escaped him. He had completely spent himself before any part of his naked body had touched her. Quietly he fondled her breast, and kneeling on the floor beside her, gently kissed it. Then he cupped both her breasts in his hands and once again kissed her cheeks, her lips, her hair, and both of her breasts.

He sighed and gradually stood up, straightening his disheveled clothing. She reached over from the couch and silently picked up her undergarments. Rising to a sitting position, she unceremoniously slipped them back on.

Neither of them spoke until she was putting on her dress and retying the sash about her waist.

"I am sorry, Rose," he mumbled guiltily. "I regret that you have not been fulfilled." Then he sighed a long, low whistle. "God, it's terrible to begin to get old."

She smiled and gently touched his arms as he sat down once again beside her. "It was wonderful, Henry. I have been deprived of any man for so long. It was bliss being in your arms."

As he leaned his head on the back of the sofa, she said softly, "Do you want a drink?"

"I don't want anything. Do you mind if I just sit here for a short while and relax?"

"I want to do the same." She nestled against him and he put his arm about her shoulders. They both drifted off into a quiet, peaceful half-sleep. Presently he raised his head and said, "My God, it is almost dawn! I must be going!"

Hurriedly he buttoned his collar and straightened his tie. "Jesus, it is a terrible price to pay," he said, as she helped him put on his coat. "But I will vote for the Kansas-Nebraska bill!"

"Thank you, Henry. But do you think I gave myself to you just to achieve that?"

He looked at her. "I hope not, my Wild Rose. God, I hope not."

He left, turning to wave to her as she watched him go.

Rose once again began attending Senate sessions. She was pleased to see them quickly ratify President Pierce's Gadsden Purchase, which secured the southern parts of Arizona and New Mexico. The purchase from Mexico was approved with little haggling over the price of ten million dollars.

The Senate and the gallery joined in enthusiastic applause when Vice President King introduced a report from Commodore Matthew C. Perry advising that he had signed a treaty with Japan that opened its ports to American shippers.

245

America was still on the move and ever expanding.

Rose continued to attend soirees, promenade concerts, and polka cotillions, accompanied by either Delegate Lane or Senator Wilson. She was inwardly delighted to note Senator Wilson's sullen glare and obvious discontent whenever Delegate Lane was her partner. As partners were exchanged, he could not wait to be matched up with her.

"You do not heed my warnings about that man, Rose."

"I am sorry, Henry. I find his company amusing."

"The likes of him is not good for your reputation."

"I am perfectly capable of deciding that for myself. You do not own me, you know."

"I am only looking out for your best interests."

"I shall thank you not to do so. For some reason you are childishly jealous of Delegate Lane. I do not find this sufficient reason to refrain from seeing him."

She actually felt sorry for Senator Wilson as she saw him pouting dejectedly in a corner of the ballroom for the rest of the evening.

Slavery was becoming the major issue in the Senate and the northern and southern factions were drawing further apart with every session. It became evident that there could be no amicable solution to the burning issue. She was delighted to witness the passage of the Kansas-Nebraska act by a small majority. She waved to Senator Wilson when the vote was finally tallied and threw a kiss to him.

Some time later she was chagrined to hear the senators debating the results of the act. Actual warfare had broken out between opposing forces, and she sorrowfully listened to them as they referred to the tense situation in "Bloody Kansas."

Florence wrote to her often, excitedly describing her new life in San Francisco. She was happy, she loved military life, she loved San Francisco, and she wondered when Rose would be coming out to visit them.

Rose became very concerned about Gertrude. She would be ill for several days but no doctor could diagnose her ailments.

After feeling so miserable she would finally be forced to take to bed. Eventually, she would throw her malady off and return to school, assuming her normal routine. Unfortunately, her ailment would return without warning, and no medicine seemed to counteract its debilitating effects. Rose took her to Baltimore where she heard a noted physician had worked wonders with diseases that other doctors had previously been unable to diagnose. After thoroughly examining Gertrude, the doctor could only shake his head, unable to offer any suggested cure.

Rose returned to Washington and did her best to make Gertrude's life a happy one, for she had begun to lose weight and coughed considerably. Rose was quite frightened for her.

She was surprised to receive a letter from Buchanan in November of 1855, advising her of a possible change in his status.

"It is long since I have enjoyed the pleasure of writing to you; but you need not be assured that my sincere friendship and regard for you still continue undiminished, and I feel the most perfect confidence that you still think kindly of your old friend. I had hoped to meet you at Washington, but the existing relations between the two countries rendered it improper for me to abandon my post. I shall leave as soon as duty may permit, because I am heartily tired of my position."

Over a noonday luncheon a few days later, she was discussing Buchanan's sudden change of heart with John Slidell, who was visiting Washington from California, where he was the political leader of the Southwest.

"I know Buchanan wishes to return to America," Slidell advised her. "I have been urging him to run for the presidency next year."

"Again?"

"That is precisely what Buchanan wrote. He told me he would hesitate to take it. He said that before many years the abolitionists will bring war upon the land. He thinks it may come during the next presidential term."

247

Rose's eyes took on a dreamy, faraway look. "No man will be more capable of dealing with the situation than Mr. Buchanan, as president."

"That is exactly the way I feel."

"I shall do my best to see that he attains that goal."

"So will I."

She leaned her elbow on the table and cupped her hand in her chin. For the next few moments she was a most inattentive luncheon companion, obviously distracted by faraway thoughts. This was not at all like Rose.

XIV

Night

Early in May of 1856 Rose went to New York to see about investing a portion of her savings. It was not coincidental that she arrived in the city only a few days before Buchanan was scheduled to return from London after completing his mission at the U.S. Embassy.

After settling in the Vanderbilt Hotel, she went directly to S. Morgan and Company, where her good friend, Senator Seward of New York, had given her a letter of introduction to the prominent son of the firm's owner, John Pierpont Morgan.

"It is always a pleasure to welcome so distinguished a person to the city of New York," J. P. Morgan said, greeting her grandly as he ushered her into his private office.

"You flatter me, Mr. Morgan."

"I am sincere, Mrs. Greenhow. I cannot express my delight at the prospect of meeting you. I hope that I can be of service during your stay in our fair city."

"Thank you, sir. I trust you will not be disappointed when you learn of my mission. Senator Seward has no doubt explained that I wish to invest in one or two of your local enterprises, but I fear my paltry sum will seem rather infinitesimal when compared to the vast millions that you are in the habit of dealing in."

"Mrs. Greenhow, there is no such thing as a paltry sum. In our country's great expansion small amounts of money can readily bring vast sums in return."

"It is encouraging to hear you say that."

"These sums can be realized only when invested wisely and properly."

"That is why I have come to you."

"How much do you intend to invest?"

"I can spare nine thousand dollars from funds I have received as a result of my late husband's death and the recent sale of my house."

"I would say that is sufficient to start you on a satisfactory program. If I were you, I would put some of this money in a stock that pays consistent dividends. Then I have another investment that would realize a much tidier sum, but is of a more speculative nature."

"I am afraid I do not understand money matters too clearly, Mr. Morgan."

"Let me be more specific. We are constructing an office down on Wall Street to house our New York operations. There is a second building planned adjacent to ours. We are handling the financing of that building and I would recommend that you buy into that combine. You can never go wrong putting your money into a landed enterprise."

"I shall rely completely on your judgment, sir."

"Thank you. For an investment that will bring you continuing dividends, I suggest that you purchase a like amount of stock in the New York Central Railroad, which is being greatly expanded."

"I have ridden on that railroad many times in my travels."

"It is an excellent investment, Mrs. Greenhow. I myself have a great many shares of its stock and have already begun to receive dividends."

"How can we arrange this transaction?"

"If you will issue me a draft on your bank for the total amount of money you wish to invest, I will take care of all particulars."

"I do not presently have a draft with me."

Morgan broke out in a very patronizing but gracious smile as he handed a note to her. "We have forms printed for such contingencies. Just fill in the name and address of your bank and the proper amount you wish to assign to your account with us."

Rose filled in the paper and signed it. Hesitating, she finally handed it back to him. "It is a little frightening to realize how simple it is to dispose of one's precious funds. I certainly hope I may eventually receive more than this in return. Insignificant as it may seem to you, it is my widow's mite."

"I shall treat it as if it were my own. I would like to show you the parcel on Wall Street that I am recommending to you. I am tied up today and I have a meeting tomorrow, but the next day—would you be free to accompany me to Wall Street and see the plans for this new venture?"

"I will only be available in the morning. You see I am meeting the next president of the United States in the afternoon."

"I beg your pardon?"

Rose smiled bewitchingly. "Mr. James Buchanan is scheduled to arrive by boat from London tomorrow afternoon."

"And you believe he will be running for the presidency?"

"I am quite certain he will, Mr. Morgan."

"Well! We cannot let such a memorable occasion go unrecognized. If I am not interfering, I should like to place my coach at your disposal and would consider it an honor to accompany you to the dock to meet the good gentleman upon his arrival."

"I am sure Mr. Buchanan will be delighted."

"Do you have any objections to my acquainting the *New York Herald* with this striking bit of news?"

"None whatsoever, sir."

So it was that two days later Mr. Morgan spent the day with Rose. In the morning he took her to the site of the new office building that was to be constructed. At present it consisted of several dilapidated wooden frame buildings that were being

251

torn down. Rose was not too impressed with the project, but soon shared Morgan's enthusiasm as he showed her the plans and the architect's drawings of the eight-story building that was scheduled to rise on the site.

After a sumptuous luncheon at Delmonico's, they drove down to the dock at the mouth of the Hudson River to await Buchanan's arrival. As the vessel drew into port, they were joined by James Gordon Bennett, managing editor of the *New York Herald*, who had come to welcome Mr. Buchanan and discuss his future political plans.

They impatiently waited over two hours after the ship had docked before passengers were permitted to disembark.

Buchanan grinned broadly as he spotted Rose while he was going through customs. He waved enthusiastically to her, then quickly tipped his hat with dignity as he recognized at least one of her companions.

Finally released from customs after a cursory inspection of his luggage, he came over to them. "Rose," he said, his eyes shining, "it's good to see you." He bowed and kissed her hand.

"It's good to see you, Jim, after such a long time. You know Mr. Morgan, I believe."

"Yes, we have met in London. How do you do, J. P.? Am I to assume that Rose has succeeded in winning one of the staunchest supporters of the new Republican party to our cause?"

"I'm afraid I cannot claim that conquest. Mr. Morgan has been graciously helping me with my investments. Have you met Mr. Bennett of the *New York Herald?*"

"I met you at the last Democratic convention, Mr. Buchanan." Bennett smiled. "I don't know if you recall it."

"I most certainly do," said Buchanan cheerfully. "I am quite flattered at this notable reception upon my home-coming!"

"We thought the occasion called for a celebration, Mr. Buchanan," said Morgan, as they loaded Buchanan's baggage into his carriage. "I have reserved a table for us at Delmonico's for dinner this evening, with your permission."

"I shall be delighted, if I may first secure accommodations at some hotel."

"I took the liberty of registering you at the Vanderbilt where I am staying, Jim," Rose hastily volunteered.

They drove to the Vanderbilt Hotel and Buchanan made arrangements for his luggage to be forwarded to his Washington address and two of his bags delivered to his room.

The three distinguished men and Rose then drove over to Delmonico's, where they were graciously escorted by the maître d' to Mr. Morgan's private dining room.

It was a gay evening, and as could be expected, they were hardly finished with their main course of quail and lobster washed down with a vintage Chardonnay wine imported from France, before the conversation turned to politics.

"Is it true, Mr. Buchanan, that your name will be placed in nomination for the presidency next month at the Democratic convention?" asked Mr. Bennett.

"I have not fully decided," replied Buchanan. "I have received most disturbing reports in London of the bitter debates that are constantly flaring up in the Senate."

"You refer to the slavery issue, which is forcing a southern coalition of legislatures to take issue with our northern representatives."

"I am, sir. It has spawned unreconcilable differences. I greatly admire our first president, who fathered this country, but I have no desire to preside over it should it become twins."

The three men laughed, but Rose hurried interrupted. "You are being too modest, Jim. It will take a man of your stature to force both factions to resolve these issues so they will not become twins."

"But, Mrs. Greenhow, don't Mr. Buchanan's pro-slavery opinions stand in the way of his support by our northern sympathizers?"

"I am from the North, Mr. Bennett. Personally I disapprove of slavery." Mr. Morgan cleared his throat before speaking.

"Mr. Buchanan, you were known to be one of the originators of the Ostend Manifesto which advocated bringing Cuba into the Union by force, if necessary, and as a slave state."

"Mr. Buchanan is against slavery the same as he is against the sweatshops and the dreadful child labor conditions right here in your own city, Mr. Morgan," Rose explained. "Laws are required to persecute any who violate the rights of all three groups."

"I see." Morgan and Bennett exchanged hasty glances which said without speaking: So this is where Mr. Buchanan's pro-slavery opinions originate.

"Do you think your stand is more acceptable to the Democratic party than that of Stephen A. Douglas?" asked Bennett.

"Douglas is a blind abolitionist, sir," Rose said, bitterly making it plain by her inflection where that gentleman stood with her.

"I believe that the differences between the two factions can be solved by compromise on both sides," Buchanan said. "I think that the majority of the Democratic party are of the same opinion."

"Then you do not anticipate any great opposition from Douglas at the convention?" asked Morgan.

"I do not sir."

"Perhaps you are correct, Mr. Buchanan," said Bennett. "In any event, he will undoubtedly have his mind on other matters, what with his romance with young Miss Rose Adele Cutts."

Suddenly Rose stiffened in her chair. "Addie Cutts is my niece, Mr. Bennett. There is no serious intention on her part in connection with that addlepated Douglas bigot. I admit that they have been seen together on occasion, but I can assure you that my niece has better sense than to become romantically involved with that dirty old man—who is of sufficient age to be her father."

"I am sorry, Mrs. Greenhow," Bennett said quietly.

"Apparently you have not heard."

"Heard?"

"Miss Cutts's engagement to Mr. Douglas was announced yesterday."

Rose's face suddenly became flushed. "Are you sure, Mr. Bennett?"

"It came into our editorial office by telegraph from Washington. We have confirmed it by reply telegram."

There was silence in the little dining room for a moment, interrupted only by Rose's heavy breathing. Gradually the color left her face, and she became pale.

Bennett, who was sitting beside her, leaned over and gently touched her arm. "Are you all right, Mrs. Greenhow?"

"Of course, I am all right." The hard glint in her eye gradually softened and she quite promptly became calm. She smiled pleasantly. "Obviously, I was not aware of the seriousness of my niece's infatuation. I would appreciate you gentlemen not mentioning to anyone my comments or my reaction to her proposed marriage to that—that dirty little bastard!"

Morgan nodded uncomfortably. "We understand, Mrs. Greenhow."

Buchanan, in an effort to make light of the awkward situation, said hurriedly, "If you were not aware of this impending announcement it is one of the few instances which I can recall when you were not completely informed. I tell you, gentlemen, I have relied heavily on information with which Mrs. Greenhow kept me so aptly informed during my long stay in London."

"Is that a fact?" asked Bennett, relieved to continue the conversation in a lighter vein.

"I should say so. On many occasions I utilized anecdotes written to me by Mrs. Greenhow to enliven a sedate and formal British banquet."

"Then, Mrs. Greenhow, perhaps you would consider writing some of your observations in the capital for me to be included

255

in our daily news."

"I fear it would not be appreciated if it were known to come from me, Mr. Bennett. Your readers might misunderstand my motives."

"I can rectify that. We can print your assertions as coming from a reader. Or better still, why don't we attribute your letters of any social comments which you choose to write about as coming from—Veritas?"

"This could have interesting possibilities," Rose said, starting to warm to the idea.

"Will you do it, Mrs. Greenhow?" asked Morgan, interested.

"I believe I shall. It will be a challenging assignment. But, mind you, I can only be free to write as I choose if the true originator is clothed in complete secrecy."

"Veritas, it is; so be it," Buchanan said, raising his glass in a toast as the rest of them joined him.

"Then you are seriously considering running for president, Mr. Buchanan?" asked Bennett.

Buchanan sighed. "It is a great responsibility. But with the help of stalwart men from the North and the South," he bowed graciously to Rose, "and women as well, I might give it one more try."

"It will be the fourth try, Jim," said Rose, "and this time it will prove the magic to break the spell."

Their glasses having been refilled by an ever-attentive waiter, Mr. Morgan again raised his glass. "Let us hope so. Well, ladies and gentlemen, a toast to the future president of the United States."

"I'll drink to that," said Rose.

Rose and the three men drained their glasses. As he set his glass down, Morgan said, "This has been a most interesting evening. I declare, I am almost convinced that Mr. Buchanan is the best man to be our next president. I might vote for you myself, sir. Now, Bennett, don't you breathe a word of this to any of my good Republican friends."

The following day, Buchanan had a great deal of business to conduct in the city, and it was almost suppertime before he again saw Rose. She had left a message for him that she would be waiting in her room, and he went up to see her.

"Rose," he announced as she met him at the door and ushered him in, "I have decided to try for the nomination once again!"

"I am glad, Jim. I shall do everything that I can to help you realize your ambition."

She threw her arms around him and kissed him soundly. Then they paused and looked awkwardly at each other. It was the first time they had been alone since his return. A lot had happened since they had last seen each other. And the thought uppermost in both their minds was that Rose no longer belonged to another man in the holy bonds of marriage.

Slowly he placed his arms around her and drawing her to him, kissed her soundly. He held her in his arms for a moment, looking at her hungrily, then drew her close to him again and kissed her passionately, fervently. She returned his kiss and moaned softly, "It has been so long."

"It has, Rose. I have missed you greatly. I thought of you so much."

"The long wait has been worth it to hear you say that, Jim." She drew his head down to her and holding his face in her hands, kissed him several times on his forehead, his cheeks, and then affectionately on his lips.

Suddenly he pushed himself away from her. "My God, Rose, I only came up here to see if you would care to join me for dinner. I have been testing the waters all afternoon with Tammany Hall. I have been assured of their full support at the convention if I can come to an agreement with the chairman of the Tammany committee. I have a meeting with William M. Tweed in fifteen minutes. They have advised me he can only give me one half-hour. I wanted to tell you to meet me in the dining room in an hour."

Rose brushed his lapel and smiled. "I know it will be politics before pleasure for many months to come, Jim. Good luck!" She kissed him quickly and he left her.

She spent the hour preparing for her dinner engagement. At first she put on a long taffeta evening gown, then appraising herself in the mirror, promptly took it off. Since their dinner was to be strictly informal, she decided to wear a beautifully embroidered, perky silk paisley blouse with a fashionably low neckline and small pearl buttons to the waist.

This was dramatically offset by a loose wrap-a-round cotton skirt which she had purchased in a Mexican shop in California. She knew its gay colors could not be matched by the staid and formal fashions in the East, and she was fully aware of the possibility of accomplishing another coup with her outstanding attire. She threw a knitted shawl about her shoulders and surveyed herself in the mirror. She smiled. She could still look beautiful when she put her mind to it. She slipped the shoulders of her blouse down a fraction off her arms and went out to meet Buchanan in the dining room.

It was not the quiet dinner alone she had anticipated. Mr. Bennett had written an article for the *Herald* advising his readers of Buchanan's intentions to seek the Democratic nomination for president at their convention in June. He had mentioned that Mr. Buchanan had just arrived from London after completing his duties as ambassador to England and was staying at the Vanderbilt Hotel. During the meal people constantly came up to their table to wish Buchanan good luck in his quest for the presidency. It was while they were enjoying a frosted mint chocolate dessert that a short, stubby Irishman approached them and introduced himself.

"My name is Jimmy Murphy. I am captain of the thirty-third precinct, Mr. Buchanan. Boss Tweed has just advised me that we are supporting you for the presidency. I want you to know that I guarantee we will deliver the New York delegates to you at the convention."

Buchanan rose and shook Mr. Murphy's hand vigorously. "Thank you, Mr. Murphy. If we had loyal men like you in every state in this Union, I could be assured of victory."

"You'll get my people's votes on election day, too."

Mr. Murphy winked importantly and departed.

It was late that night before Buchanan finally accompanied Rose to her room and went in with her. He sighed and slumped on the side of her bed. "It's been a busy day, Rose. Back in our mother country two days and I'm already chained to the old political grind."

She came over and sat beside him on the bed. "You have missed it dearly, you can't deny it, Jim."

"I have, but it drains a man's strength so. Do you mind if I take off my coat and loosen my collar?"

"Of course not. It is unseasonably warm this evening." She helped him take off his coat and his waistcoat as well. He unbuttoned his heavily starched linen collar. He stretched his neck and unloosened his tie and was decidedly more comfortable. She ran her hand affectionately through his massive white head of hair, and she moved close to him. As she did so, her loosely wrapped skirt slipped apart revealing a goodly portion of her well-formed legs beneath her several petticoats. "I have thought of you often, Jim, since—Robert died. There have been many times I have needed your strength, your advice."

He wrapped his arm about her waist and smiled. "You have been in my thoughts more times than I can enumerate, Rose." He drew her close to him and holding her chin with his hand, gently lifted her face to him. He kissed her, at first tenderly, then more passionately.

"God, how I have missed you, Rose." She fell back comfortably on the bed and he leaned back beside her. He kissed her cheeks, her forehead, her hair, and caressed a good portion of her breast which lay exposed before him. As he pressed his body to her, he slowly slipped his hand beneath her blouse and underclothing and found her warm, bare breast. He pressed it firmly against her. Slowly he slipped her blouse further down her arms, clearly exposing the beautiful mound.

He leaned over her and pressing her breast with his hand, bent down and kissed it. As her heavy breathing moved her breast closer to him, he covered it with his open mouth and ran his tongue ecstatically about her nipple as it hardened beneath him. Gradually he slipped the other shoulder of her blouse down her arm. Reaching behind her he slipped her petticoats down and lowered her chemise to her waist. He unbuttoned her camisole and threw it to the floor. "Rose, you are so wonderful," he murmured. Both of her magnificent breasts lay completely exposed to him. Rising and falling, they pressed firmly against his body. He kissed her again and again. Then he lowered his head again to her breast and lovingly kissed it while he pressed her other breast and rolled it feverishly against her body. Presently he kissed her other breast and took it in his mouth while he pressed her other one hard against her body.

Finally he rolled away from her and lay calmly beside her. "Now you know my innermost secret, my Wild Rose."

She rose on her elbow beside him, her face flushed and panting as she murmured, "Are you telling me—?"

"Yes, my dear. You have given to me freely all that I want from any woman."

She leaned over and kissed him gently. "My poor Jim," she said softly. She kissed him again and he held both her bare breasts in his hands. Then he slowly rose. He buttoned his collar and tightened his tie.

"It's late, Rose. Regretfully, I shall have to leave you."

She helped him on with his waistcoat and coat and carelessly slipped her underclothing about herself. He turned to her, and taking her hand in his, bowed and kissed it. As he straightened up, she threw her arms about his neck and kissed him soundly. "You are a very sweet gentleman," she said smiling. "You will make a wonderful president."

He hunched his coat more comfortably about his shoulders and grinned at her in appreciation. "You are a very kind and understanding woman, my Wild Rose."

He kissed her gently and left.

No sooner had Rose returned to Washington than she went directly to her sister's house. She hardly entered the door before she asked sharply, "Ellen Elizabeth, where's Addie?"

"She isn't here."

"That simpleminded idiot!"

"Apparently you have heard."

"It came as a great surprise to me, Ellen. How could she marry that dirty little Douglas?"

"She loves him, Rose."

"My God, Ellen, why didn't you stop this before she became so involved?"

"I didn't realize how serious it was becoming, Rose. She has been seeing other young men as well as Stephen."

"Young men is correct. It is not bad enough that he is a mortal enemy to all we hold dear, he is old enough to be her father."

"What can we do?"

"Forbid the wedding. Prohibit her ever seeing him again."

"We can't do that. Stephen Douglas has become an exceedingly important man in this country."

"He is the leader of the antislavery movement in this country."

"I know, Rose. I have told her this. Addie's only reply is that she loves him and she is going to marry him."

"I shall not attend the wedding."

"You must, Rose. Not only for her sake but for what the Washington matrons will say if you snub your own flesh and blood."

"She is a spoiled, ungrateful child."

"She knows how dreadfully upset I am about her marriage to him. I have already warned her about the reaction she might expect from you."

"Doesn't she care about our position in this matter?"

"She says she cares very much and loves us all but she is so deeply in love with Douglas she will gladly face any of the

261

consequences resulting from their marriage."

"You have not been firm enough with her, Ellen. I shall never speak to her again, nor to him."

"Through all of our lives nothing has come between us, Rose. Think kindly of our predicament and don't take any action or say anything that you may later regret."

"I despise the man, Ellen. I would fight him openly with my bare fists and teeth for his bigoted, unmindful stand against slavery. Does not Addie realize this?"

Ellen sadly nodded her head. "She is determined, Rose."

Rose shook her head savagely and tears welled up in her eyes. "How could she do this to you? To me?"

"Believe me, Rose, James and I both have tried to reason with her, but she complains that we don't understand how much she really loves him."

Rose wiped the tears from her eyes with her handkerchief and turned abruptly to go. "She will regret this for the rest of her life after the first bloom of romance wears off. I warn you, Ellen, I shall never acknowledge that addleheaded daughter of yours or that egotistical ass whom she proposes to marry— never, ever again."

Ellen followed her as she stamped to the door. "Please relent, Rose, for all that we have meant to each other. I am hurt even more than you. But think on it, Rose, don't let this break up the close relationship of our family."

As Rose furiously opened the door, Ellen added pleading, "The wedding is next month, Rose. Please, please think on it more and find it in your heart to attend for all our sakes."

Without answering Rose slammed the door and walked away.

She did attend Addie's wedding to "that horrible monster," and she did relent and speak civilly to both of them, but for the rest of her life she never forgave her niece for "the dastardly predicament that she had forced upon her family."

XV

Campaigning

The Democratic convention was held on June 2, 1856, in Cincinnati, Ohio. Rose had fully planned to attend, and Buchanan had secured accommodations for her. However, two days before she was scheduled to leave, Gertrude had another severe attack of her malady, and Rose would not leave her.

She did make it a point to visit the *Washington Daily National Intelligencer* each day and closely scrutinize their incoming telegraph dispatches to learn what was happening at the convention. When the delegates started to vote for president, she visited the newspaper office twice each day. Buchanan was the first man to be nominated. Thereafter Stephen A. Douglas was named, as were several other prominent Democrats. For a while it seemed to Rose that there would, once again, be a stalemate, and a dark horse, whose name had not as yet been mentioned, would suddenly rise to the fore and sweep the convention. However, on the third day, Buchanan received the backing of a sufficient number of delegates, and on the seventeenth ballot he won the nomination as their presidential candidate. John C. Breckenridge was unanimously selected as his vice presidential running mate.

Rose promptly dispatched a telegram to Buchanan:

FOURTH ATTEMPT VICTORIOUS STOP
CONGRATULATIONS SAME GOES FOR FRIEND

She joyously rushed home to convey the good news to Gertrude and her other daughters.

Less than three weeks later Rose was appalled to learn that the new Republican party had selected the husband of her bitterest enemy, Jessie Benton Fremont, to be their standard-bearer for president. General John C. Fremont was nominated on the first ballot with 520 of the 568 votes. At first it troubled her greatly to think of her rival's husband facing her dearest friend. Then, with the fierce glint in her eye as of old, she vowed that she would relish the challenge. She would show Jessie Fremont once and for all who would win the final battle.

Again Buchanan became deeply involved in a political campaign and she saw very little of him. But this time she was equally involved, working behind the scenes to see that Buchanan became president and Jessie Fremont's despised husband was soundly defeated.

In a letter from her western friend, John Slidell, and shortly thereafter in another from Senator Gwin, she learned that it was questionable whether Buchanan would carry California. Almost at the same time she heard from Ed Pringle. He advised her that Limantour's claim was scheduled to come up in court and that he had requested that she testify at his hearing. Ed recommended that, because of her own Point Lobos claim, it would be in her best interest if she did so. She, therefore, suddenly announced to Buchanan and her family that she was setting out once again for California.

Hurriedly she wrote to her daughter, Florence, who had been urging her to visit them, that she would be leaving Washington in three days. She also sent off a hasty note to Colonel Keyes.

By now, the railroad had been extended to Kansas City. In addition, a man by the name of Pullman had invented a sleeper, which was being installed on one side of the passenger coaches, to bring the sleeping comforts of home to trains. Rose looked forward to trying one. She was amazed at its comfort and convenience. It made continual traveling by day and night an actual luxury. It was a far cry from horse-drawn coaches, and a great improvement over earlier train travel.

She went by way of St. Louis, where she had arranged a meeting with Dr. Morrison and other Missouri delegates who were to attend the Democratic convention. She secured wholehearted support from them and their assurance that they would mount an unprecedented effort throughout the state on behalf of Buchanan.

The fourteen-hundred-mile journey by stage coach from Kansas City was still an unnerving experience, and she was extremely fatigued when she arrived late one night in San Francisco. She was delighted to see her daughter, Florence, and her new husband at the coach depot to greet her.

"What a grueling journey," she said to them, brushing the outer surface of dust from her clothing. "I declare it will be a Godsend when the railroad is extended to the West Coast."

"It's wonderful to see you again, Mums," Florence said, hugging her mother. "We have redecorated our guest room just for your visit."

"I will not be staying with you, Florence. I have arranged for a room at the Brannan House."

"But, Mums," Florence protested, "we were planning on your stay."

"I am sorry, my dear, but I believe that fish and houseguests both begin to smell after three days!"

They laughed as Captain Moore helped the two women into his carriage. "You will stay with us tonight since it is so late, won't you?"

"I will be glad to."

As they drove off Florence linked her arm in her mother's and said, "Surely you can remain with us for two days. There is a reception scheduled for the new commandant of the Presidio the evening after tomorrow. We were hoping you would arrive in time so you could attend as our guest. It will offer you an opportunity to meet the officers and their wives and all the important members of our community."

"I would like that."

Rose was as much the center of attraction at the reception as the commandant himself. Senator Gwin and his wife, as well as John Slidell and his wife, Marie, were present and welcomed her heartily. They introduced her to several southerners who had come West and now lived along Stockton Street and South Park in the vicinity of Senator Gwin's mansion. All of them, as well as several of the Presidio officers and their wives, almost stood in line to meet the famous Mrs. Greenhow. She was happy to renew acquaintance with several southern generals, among them Irwin McDowell, William T. Sherman, Albert Sidney Johnston, and Winfield Scott.

She discreetly made it known to all of them that part of her mission to California was to promote Mr. Buchanan's quest for the presidency.

Mrs. Amelia Ransome Neville and her husband, Captain Thomas Neville of the British Army, both expressed their regrets that they could not vote for Mr. Buchanan in the upcoming election.

"Frankly, my dear," Amelia said confidentially, "I hardly think General Fremont is qualified to run your country. He has made such a deplorable mess of handling his own finances."

"He has?" Rose asked, concealing her surprise. "But I thought his Mariposa mine was so successful."

"It was in the beginning, but he has been forced to refinance his holdings, with the result that stockholders now own more of the mine than he does."

"It is what I would expect from the poor general."

"Their fortunes are definitely on the decline. Personally, I believe it is what prompted his sudden interest in the presidency."

"It would not surprise me," Rose smiled.

"Please don't mention it, however. I understand that they are in attendance this evening."

"I saw Jessie Fremont earlier but I have not spoken with her."

The Slidells came over to join them. "I do so hope that you can attend my reception tomorrow evening, Rose," Mrs. Slidell smiled. "I was not prepared for your arrival. It was such a short time ago that my brother-in-law, General Beauregard, advised me that you were visiting his family in Louisiana."

"I planned my trip rather hastily, but I shall be delighted to attend your reception."

Mr. and Mrs. Clement C. Clay joined them and Rose bowed graciously to the well-known couple recently arrived from Alabama. "I could not help noticing your gown," Rose said to Mrs. Clay. "It is absolutely stunning."

"Thank you, Mrs. Greenhow. The velvet was woven in Genoa. The material truly does make such a difference." Before the end of the evening, Rose had met a goodly number of the military men stationed at the Presidio and their wives. She was disturbed to note that Colonel Keyes not only was not in attendance, but had made no attempt to contact her since she arrived.

She mentioned his absence to Florence when they were alone for a few moments.

"Oh, didn't you know, Mums? He is away on maneuvers with his company. They are scheduled to be back in a fortnight."

Rose sighed. "Then he hasn't forgotten his old friend after all."

It was quite late in the evening when Senator Gwin came up and spoke with her briefly for a moment.

"Have you seen Limantour as yet?" he scowled.

"I have not. Ed Pringle told me he requested that I testify at his court hearing. I am meeting with Ed and him tomorrow concerning the case. I understand that the land commission has been dissolved."

"It has. They rejected Limantour's claims to the outside lands, including the islands, but they confirmed his titles in the

San Francisco area. He immediately placed them on the market and, I have it on good authority, he has already realized over three hundred thousand dollars. I cannot go into detail now, but he has been reluctant to organize a company with us to promote his lands."

"I don't understand. I know he agreed to form this partnership."

"He claims that he is in a position to finance his court battles himself now. He not only refuses to share any portion of his new-found wealth with us, but he will not discuss the matter."

"We shall see about that when I meet with him tomorrow."

"Do not jeopardize your own association with him."

"Mr. Limantour has far more at stake from our association than I."

The orchestra played until the early morning hours, and Rose, never at a loss for a partner, missed very few of the promenades. They returned to her daughter's house quite late.

They sat around the table for a late breakfast the next morning discussing the reception.

"It was a delightful affair, Mums, don't you think?"

"I had a very good time. I still love to dance. Now, tell me, Captain and Mrs. Moore, do you find that military life in California still agrees with you?"

"Oh, I love it, Mums."

"We are doing very well, too," Captain Moore joined in. "As you know, I have invested in some mining claims out here and they are paying off handsomely. I have wished to discuss this with you, but I hesitated to write for fear you might misunderstand. You must certainly feel by this time that I look upon you, dear mama, as if you were indeed my mother, and that everything I have is given as freely to you and yours as if you were all my own, so do not let any false delicacy keep you from letting me know your condition and prospects for the future . . . should the mines turn out as I expect, I will be well enough off to permit us to live comfortably."

"That is very considerate of you, captain. I assure you that I am presently in need of nothing. If Mr. Buchanan should be elected president, I am uncertain what additional expenses would be shouldered by me as a result of my increased activity in government affairs. I still have a small amount of money available for investment. Do you have any suggestions as to how it might best be utilized?"

"It is very difficult to recommend investments, mama. Regardless of how promising they might seem, they sometimes do not materialize as one might expect. I can only tell you that I have recently invested in Plank Road stock. I believe it has a tremendous potential."

"Then I shall do the same. I am seeing Ed Pringle today about several matters. I shall ask his assistance in securing some Plank Road stock."

"You are welcome to use our carriage, mama," Captain Moore volunteered. "The sulky is at your disposal. Do you wish to have someone drive you about?"

"That won't be necessary, but I would be grateful to you for the use of your sulky."

Moore hitched up his finest horse to the sulky and looked on in amazement at the competent manner in which his mother-in-law handled the sprightly thoroughbred.

Pringle was happy to see her. "I have so much to discuss with you. I have an appointment with Jose Limantour within the hour. I trust you will be able to stay to meet with him."

"I most certainly will. He does not seem to be much of a man of his word, judging from the way he is treating Senator Gwin and his friends."

"Jose has become a wealthy man, and it has affected his behavior and manners—which at no time were too gracious."

"I have heard that the land commission verified part of his claims. Which reminds me, Ed, you have spent considerable time on my behalf without compensation. It is now probable that it will be much longer before my claim is verified. I feel it is only fair that I share my claim with you in recompense for your efforts."

"That is not necessary, Rose."

"You have more than earned it already. Draw up the necessary papers granting one half of my Point Lobos claim to yourself and I shall sign them."

Pringle shrugged his shoulders. "O.K., boss lady. It will be done."

"You can start earning your fee, which still is not negotiable, by arranging to purchase some stock in the Plank Road for me."

"I will be glad to. I have heard that it is a very good investment."

"My son-in-law thinks so. I believe I could purchase at least two hundred shares. If you will determine the exact cost I shall issue you a draft for the proper amount. I trust that I will not have to spend too much time on Mr. Limantour's affairs, for I plan to devote my efforts while I am here on behalf of Mr. Buchanan."

"You will need to, Rose. As you are no doubt aware, the Black Republicans are betting against Buchanan in California. But it is too early to give up the ship."

"I am in the habit of fighting against great odds. And I also am in the habit of winning."

"Good for you. I certainly wish you luck."

Shortly afterward Limantour joined them. She hardly recognized the dapper man who jauntily strode into their office carrying a gold-headed cane. His long coat was made of the finest silk with a velvet collar and lining. He had grown a full beard in the fashion of the day, and his well-appointed morning attire was topped off by a tall silk hat and gray spats covering black patent leather pumps.

"Mrs. Greenhow, I do believe," he observed haughtily. "I had heard that you were honoring my fair city with your presence."

"I also have heard that your fortunes have taken a considerable turn for the better."

"Yes. Unfortunately some of my claims, which include your

270

grant, are yet to be settled. That is why I have been forced to appeal to the United States District Court to clarify what that stupid land commission left undone."

"It does seem, however, that they were more considerate of you than you have been of your partners."

"Whatever are you referring to?"

"I am referring to your agreement with Senator Gwin and his business acquaintances who advanced you the necessary money when you could not afford to do so yourself."

"Oh, that!" Limantour slapped his calfskin gloves which he had just removed, against the palm of his hands.

"Yes, that!" Rose jumped up from her chair and her eyes flashed in anger as she leaned on the table before her. "That, sir, is an agreement which you have with those good gentlemen to form a partnership with them to promote your lands."

Pringle remained silent as he watched Rose's actions and marveled at her courage.

"Please do not shout, madam. Remember whom you are speaking to."

"I know damn well whom I am speaking to," Rose shouted as she strode over and stood directly in front of Limantour. "It is the man my dear departed husband introduced to several of the most influential men in this city. It was mutually agreed that they would bail you out when you could go no further on your own. In return you agreed to form a partnership with them to promote your lands."

"Can you show me anything in writing?"

"You are well aware that it was a gentlemen's agreement. And you, sir, will honor it!"

"And what if I don't?" Limantour said contemptuously.

"Then I sure as hell won't testify on your behalf in court."

"You will only lose your Point Lobos claim if I do not win my case in court."

"I don't give a damn about my Point Lobos claim. And frankly I am beginning to wonder about all your claims. So many have come to the fore to testify that they are false. I

271

assure you, if you renege on your promise to my friends, I shall join the band that is so rapidly expanding against you. So help me, God, you will not be able to show your face in this or any other city in the state of California."

"Mrs. Greenhow, you are shouting like a charwoman. Please keep your voice down as befits a lady."

"It is a goddamned angry lady you see before you, sir."

"That is just it. I am not afraid of what you can say. Who will pay any attention to a hysterical woman?"

"This hysterical woman, as you say, has come to California on behalf of the next president of the United States." She was so close to him by now it seemed she would strike him as she raised her arm for emphasis. "If you dare to welsh on your agreement with these gentlemen, I promise you I will have you hounded in and out of the courts until you will not be secure anywhere in these United States."

"The next president you speak of is undoubtedly Mr. Buchanan, who is currently fighting for his political life. Let me remind you, dear lady, he has not won the election as yet. If the indications I perceive are correct, the day following the election you will only be the close friend of a defeated candidate. The sorriest of spectacles."

Suddenly Rose grabbed his coat. The quick action threw him off balance. Instantly he righted himself and pulled away from her. Rose clenched her fists in frustration and walked over to Pringle, who got up and stood by her side. She stared angrily at Limantour as he returned her gaze with disdain. Presently she spoke in a quiet, controlled voice. "Are you going to honor your commitment to those gentlemen?"

"Will you testify on my behalf?"

She pointed her finger menacingly at him. "My husband always advised me that in the legal profession a question in reply to a question is a sure sign of weakness."

"I repeat my weak question, Mrs. Greenhow." Again there was silence in the room as the two stared at each other. Presently Limantour came over to them. "What would you consider a fair arrangement with your friends?"

"First, that you form a corporation with them to promote your lands. All of your lands. Secondly, that you give them some portion of the proceeds you have already received as a token of your good faith."

"What portion do you suggest?"

"I don't know. I reckon at least twenty-five percent. What do you think, Ed?"

"I believe that would be an extremely fair amount."

"Extremely is the correct word for it, sir." Limantour came close to her and he, in turn, leaned his hands on the table between them.

"What would you say if I consented to all your outrageous demands and also agreed to give those gentlemen fifteen percent of all profits I have received to date?"

"I would say that I would testify for you and do all in my power to prove that your claims are legitimate."

"Very well, then." Limantour extended his hand. "Supposing we shake hands on it, Rose."

"It is quite obvious that your handshake is not sufficient evidence of your good faith." She turned to Pringle. "See that the proper papers are drawn up, Ed." Then she said sarcastically to Limantour, "I shall advise Senator Gwin and his associates of your most generous offer."

Rose spent the balance of the week traveling to the outlying districts of San Francisco, even going so far as San Jose, the state capital, organizing and bolstering the campaign of Buchanan for president. Senator Gwin had arranged a meeting with several political leaders for the following week, at which time they were to discuss the problems which confronted California and what steps Rose suggested that Buchanan would take to solve them if he were president. It was necessary to postpone the meeting since it conflicted with the date scheduled for Rose's appearance in court.

The courtroom was jammed with her friends on the morning of the case. Actually, the appearance of this powerfully persuasive woman was of more interest now than the claims of Limantour.

It became particularly intriguing when it was realized that Rose would have to reveal her age as she testified. Such a subject had been on the minds of many ladies and several of the gentlemen in San Francisco. She was still a beautiful woman, but with the Washington anecdotes she related dating as far back as the time of Dolly Madison, she must be—how old would one guess that she was?

By the morning of the trial, it was rumored that several wagers were being made by some of the younger men of the city concerning the nearest correct age of this famous woman who had already personally known eight presidents and was in California even now campaigning for a ninth.

She looked lovely in her dark purple brocaded dress as she took the stand. She might easily pass for a woman of thirty-five, but everyone agreed she must be older than that. Limantour's lawyer, James Wilson, stepped up to her and smiled kindly.

"State your name for the records, ma'am."

"Rose O'Neal Greenhow."

"How old are you, Mrs. Greenhow?"

There was not a sound in the crowded courtroom as everyone waited for her answer. She looked about the room with unconcern and replied simply, "Of sufficient age to testify."

Rose had heard about the wagers that were being made with reference to her correct age, and she smiled with satisfaction as she watched the audience's crestfallen reaction as it realized that this was one wager that would never be paid.

"Please explain to the court how you come to know the claimant."

"We met him at the French legation in Mexico City. When I speak of us, I mean my husband and myself. Mr. Limantour's visits were to Mr. Greenhow, not to me; I dined with him twice at the French Embassy and met him often."

"Have you been specifically advised of the boundaries of Mr. Limantour's claims?"

"My husband, Robert, took a map and designated the lands and islands Mr. Limantour claimed after his first visit to our house. He indicated the position of San Francisco on the map and pointed out Goat Island and Cedros in lower California."

"Have you any more specific knowledge of these claims?"

"I am sorry, I have never known or been shown the exact boundaries of the land which constitute Mr. Limantour's claims."

"That will be all, Mrs. Greenhow. Thank you."

Rose's testimony was not very helpful to Limantour's cause. Other witnesses later in the day proved most harmful. Several experts attacked his claims as forgeries. An officer of the territory of California before it had become a state questioned governor Manuel Micheltorena's right to deed the lands to Limantour. A clerk who had lived with Limantour testified, under oath, that Limantour had forced him to fake some of his records. M. Levasseur, who had since retired from the French Legation in Mexico, swore under oath that the official seal of the French Legation was fraudulently used by Limantour. Handwriting experts testified that the seals and paper upon which Limantour's claims were written were not authentic.

In summing up the hearing late in the day, Ogden Hoffman, the presiding judge, stated, "I have requested an advisory opinion by the United States attorney general as well as by Mr. Edwin M. Stanton, who has been officiating in California as special investigating council for the federal government, on land fraud cases. Their opinions are to be included as a matter of record in this court one week from today, at which time I shall render my decision."

It was a very serious Limantour who left the court that day. During the intervening week, Rose busied herself with as many meetings as she could with the influential local citizenry, persuading them to support Buchanan for president. Mr. Gwin's meeting was rescheduled, and Rose enthusiastically promoted Mr. Buchanan as the man who could do most for Californians should he become president. She was actually vitriolic in condemning the inefficiency of his opponent, General Fremont, and she questioned his ability to administer the affairs of the nation when his own financial affairs were in such disorder.

"What we need most in California to encourage its growth and economy," said John Slidell, "is a railroad through to the Pacific Coast."

"I strongly advocate this," replied Rose. "I have had occasion to travel across this nation many times. I know what the railroads have done for the East and the Midwest. Mr. Buchanan, as president, will be well aware of the necessity for such an extension of railroads into California."

"Do you believe Mr. Buchanan would write a letter before the election that we can publish supporting the Pacific Railroad?" cannily asked one of the gentlemen at the meeting.

"I can assure you that he will," replied Rose.

"If that is the case, I believe we can assure you of our support for him."

Amid cheers and shouts of "Buchanan for President!" the meeting broke up.

Many people who were following the Limantour hearing were becoming most suspicious of the smooth-talking dandy from Mexico. None of them, however, were prepared for the outcome of his latest appeal. There were not nearly as many persons in the courtroom the morning that Judge Hoffman gave his decision. Most of those present either had rival claims or were ready to deal with Limantour once his claims were clearly established. Rose sat quietly in the back of the courtroom accompanied by Ed Pringle. Everyone rose as Judge Hoffman made his appearance.

As the courtroom became quiet, the judge cleared his throat and plunged directly into his task. "As requested, I have received an opinion from Mr. Edwin M. Stanton, the U.S. government's legal representative, concerning the claims

276

herein presented by Mr. Limantour for verification. I quote: 'In the case of Jose Limantour, I have found irresistible proof of an organized system of fabricating land titles which has been carried on for a long time in California by Mexican officials!'"

"That does not associate me directly with any of those officials!" Limantour shouted from the table where he sat directly before the judge.

Judge Hoffman rapped hard with his gavel. "Counselor Wilson, will you kindly instruct your client in the proper procedure to address this bench. This court will not tolerate any such spontaneous or unauthorized outbreaks."

"Yes, your honor."

"Mr. Stanton has also provided me with the opinion of the U.S. attorney general, and again I quote: 'Jose Limantour's claims are soundly denounced as the most stupendous fraud. The greatest in atrocity as well as in magnitude ever perpetrated since the beginning of the world.'"

Limantour started to rise from his chair, but his lawyer hastily drew him back. Judge Hoffman continued. "As a result of testimony submitted in this court by qualified witnesses, I hereby conclusively reject Mr. Limantour's titles to any and all of the territory for which he lays claim. We have been honored by the testimony of several distinguished witnesses." He bowed in Rose's direction and smiled. "However, this court strongly condemns the unscrupulous and pertinacious obstinacy with which Mr. Limantour has persisted in these claims in which it is the opinion of the court he is wholly unjustified. In view of this, Jose Limantour, I have signed a warrant for your arrest, charging you with forgery and perjury."

Stunned silence followed the judge's stern pronouncement. Two bailiffs quickly strode over to Limantour, and standing on each side of him, placed their hands on his shoulders.

"Take your hands off me!" Limantour blurted out contemptuously.

Spectators began excitedly talking to each other and the judge again rapped his gavel for order. "I further stipulate that bail for the accused shall be set at thirty thousand dollars due to the seriousness of these offenses."

"I'll write a draft for that amount right now," shouted Limantour. "Whom do I give it to?"

"You may deposit bail with the clerk of the court. This case is dismissed."

While Limantour hastily scribbled a draft, Judge Hoffman rose and walked stoically out of the courtroom. Rose and Ed Pringle silently exchanged glances. Finally Ed said in a low voice, "The man is as clever as he is dishonest."

Rose sighed. "I was beginning to lose faith in him. My poor Robert would be greatly disillusioned to witness the sorry ending to this lengthy affair."

"I cannot understand how Robert could have—"

Rose quickly interrupted him. "Governor Micheltorena still backs Limantour's claims, as do several other worthy citizens."

Later in the day, Rose and Ed went to Limantour's office to talk with him. The door was locked, but a young Mexican boy whom Ed recognized as having worked for Limantour was sitting sullenly on the front step, his head slouched between his knees. As they tapped him on the shoulder he looked up at them through bleary eyes. It was obvious that he was quite drunk.

"Where's Mr. Limantour?" Ed asked him.

"Gone."

"Gone? Gone where?"

He shrugged his shoulders. "Somewhere. South of the border."

"He has fled to Mexico!" Rose said disgustedly.

"I guess this is the end of our Point Lobos dream," sighed Ed.

"I shall never cease my efforts to prove our claim.",

Rose planned to spend a quiet weekend at the Brannan House. Her many trips and speeches on behalf of Buchanan had tired her. In addition, the Limantour debacle had been most trying, and she was glad to rest peacefully and quietly in her room. She dined alone late in the evening and then returned to her room. She was deeply engrossed in a romantic short story by Louisa May Alcott, which had appeared in the latest issue of the *Atlantic Monthly*, when there was a knock on her door.

As she opened the door she was delighted to see Colonel Keyes standing before her, tanned and smiling.

"I just got back this evening," he said to her sheepishly. "I couldn't wait to see you. I trust I am welcome even at this late hour."

"You most certainly are," she greeted him cheerily. "Please come in."

As she closed the door, he placed his hands on her arms and held her steadily before him. "Let me look at you, Rose. You are exactly as I have pictured you these many months."

"Actually, I must look a fright. I am not prepared to receive guests," she laughed, tucking loose strands of hair into the knot on the top of her head.

"You look beautiful. Gad, how I have missed you."

"I've missed you, too. It has been so long."

He sat on the sofa and she sat down beside him. "It's been too long, Rose. I found myself thinking of you more and more while on maneuvers. Then when I heard that you had arrived I could not wait to get back. I'm afraid my training suffered. I found it difficult to keep my mind on my work."

"I was most disturbed when I arrived and found you were away."

"Are you staying West?"

"No. I must return to do what I can for Buchanan's campaign."

"I have heard that it is a very close race. His popularity seems to have increased considerably since you arrived. That was how I learned of your presence. Some of the men bringing supplies from the Presidio were speaking of your efforts on Buchanan's behalf. I also learned of Limantour's misfortunes.

That is unfortunate, Rose. Point Lobos is such a beautiful place."

"It may still be mine some day. I have not given up hope."

They were silent for a moment as they sat beside each other looking into each others eyes. Suddenly he moved closer to her and frowned in his seriousness as he spoke to her. "I wish you could stay here, Rose. Move out here. Bring your girls."

"I can't. There is so much for me to do in Washington."

"Can't you forget all that? Don't you ever plan to settle down again and—and marry?"

"If I ever did marry again—"

"If?—Is it that you don't care enough for any man to wish to marry again?"

"I care more for you than I wish to admit even to myself. It is just that—I can't leave Washington, particularly now, when the presidency is within Buchanan's grasp. He needs me."

"I need you, Rose. I'm asking you to be my wife."

She touched his cheek softly and patted his face. "I wish I could—there are so many obstacles. . . ."

"I love you! Won't that overcome any obstacles that might stand in our way? I know we would be happy together."

"I believe we would."

He moved beside her and gently putting his arm around her shoulders drew her to him. Suddenly she turned her head away. He took her chin in his hand and brought her face close so that he could look directly into her eyes. "Look at me, Rose. Can you honestly say that I mean nothing to you? Don't you believe, as I do, that we could find a happiness together that has evaded us since we were deprived of our first loved ones?"

"Oh—I do love you—I realized how much you meant to me when I came to San Francisco and found you gone. I—I was beside myself. Truly I was."

"Then it is so simple, Rose. What could possibly prohibit our marriage and being happy together the rest of our lives?"

She sighed. As she looked unseeing at the bare wall before her she spoke in a low voice. "I guess it is ambition. Women are not supposed to have this trait. I was blessed with an overabundance of it." She smiled wanly. "You can blame my father for that. He loved life. He wanted to get the very most from life that he could. That is what I wish also."

"But you can have that out here, Rose. Florence is extremely happy. San Francisco is growing bigger every day. You have many friends here. You are greatly respected. You could be a leader of our community the same as you are in Washington."

"It isn't the same. Out here everyone looks to Washington for the final answer—for direction as to what to do next—which way they should be guided. In Washington they make the rules—they tell San Francisco and the rest of the country what needs to be done—which way to go."

"The men of Washington are themselves uncertain now. They are as much torn asunder as if we were two separate countries."

"That is all the more reason I must go back. I want to help them decide what to do." She paused for a moment and did not look directly at him as she continued. "If I stayed here and Buchanan did not win this election—I would never forgive myself for the rest of my life."

"But if you died tonight, someone else would take your place."

"That is the reasoning of a loyal military man. One must always be prepared to die, to give his all—if it still is not enough, someone else will carry on in your spirit."

"It is true. You have a false loyalty to your country and what you believe to be right. You must have a loyalty to yourself and to your family and to me. Your loyalty should be to us, we come first."

"What I am doing is for my family, for myself. My ambition is to help make our country the most wonderful place in the world in which to live."

He turned away from her and slowly he rose. Looking sadly away, he said in a low, almost inaudible voice, "It is hopeless then." He started toward the door.

She jumped up and running, grabbed him and turned him toward her. "But it isn't. We still can be friends, can't we?"

"I hope so."

"Well, then, don't look so saddened. These are difficult times we are living in. There is much heartache throughout the nation. Others are finding happiness despite all this. We should find happiness, as well. Our friendship is too wonderful to wish otherwise."

He looked at her sadly, hungrily. "I desire more than friendship."

"So do I."

Slowly he slipped from beneath her arms which held him and walked away.

She grabbed him and drew him back. "Oh, come. We mean too much to each other for it to end this way."

"I don't ever want it to end."

"Neither do I. Dear, you take life too seriously. I have found that we must grab our happiness whenever we can, we must make the best of every moment—our moments together are too precious to waste!" She pressed her body against his and drew her arms about his neck. "Smile, please. Smile."

Gradually he put his arms around her and smiled down at her. "My Wild Rose," he said softly. Hugging her tightly, he kissed her. Then he kissed her cheek and her forehead. Her lips sought his and as they touched she pressed them rapturously against her own. She closed her eyes as his arms moved along her back making her flesh tingle. He kissed her again, ardently, wistfully. Slowly they slid down onto the side of the bed. Her negligee slipped away from her, partially revealing her beautiful legs. He ran his hands along her knees, then her limbs. Slowly she sank back onto the bed. He leaned over her and kissed her again, pressing his body against her.

Quickly, furtively she squirmed slightly away from him and moved her body until it rested along the length of the bed. He leaned over her and ran one of his hands caressingly through her hair which had fallen about her shoulders. She threw her arms about him and kissed him, moving her lips closer so that they were almost a part of him. She clung to him so tightly that he could not put his arms around her. She unbuttoned her negligee and it fell apart beneath her. Gradually he lay down beside her, returning her passionate kisses with the full warmth and tenderness that she gave to him.

He pushed her to the center of the bed so he could lie close beside her. Slowly she reached behind her and unbuttoned her camisole. He drew it down from her, revealing her gorgeous breasts. He bent down and kissed one of them and then the other. She closed her eyes and gave herself completely to the moment. She slid her pantalettes down and unceremoniously kicked them off. She lay beside him, breathing heavily. His hand shaking, he softly caressed her bare body as it lay before him. She lifted herself on her elbows and pushed him away, turning him about until he fell comfortably on his back beside her. She rolled over to him and gradually placed her body against him, lying on top of him. Carefully, deliberately she opened his belt and unbuttoned his pants. She was truly his Wild Rose as she brought him inside her, and then they were lost in an ecstasy of love. She moved in complete abandon as she deftly took up the rythmn of his body, and they made love in utter delight. They moved together as one being, kissing until it was all consummated in one glorious, ecstatic moment.

After the long moments of wonderful bliss she moved away from him and drew a cover over them both. They lay beside each other, completely spent. Entirely satisfied, they gradually dropped off to sleep.

Hours later he awoke. The gaslight was still burning brightly and the sun was shining even more brightly through the east windows. As he turned to her, she also awoke. "God, I love you, Rose," he said, kissing her.

She drew him to her and kissed him again, ravenously. Quickly he threw down the cover and jumped up from the bed. He looked down at himself, completely dressed even to his shoes. "I have never slept this way before."

"It was truly happiness," she said.

"I must see you again soon. Tomorrow night—I mean tonight. Glory be, I have lost all track of time."

"Time cannot be our master."

"I really must be going."

"I know."

"It would be too indiscreet for us to breakfast together. But may I meet you in the hotel dining room for luncheon?"

"Yes, but that is all. I must return to my room after that and pack."

"Pack?"

"I am leaving tomorrow morning for Washington."

"My God, Rose, you will surely drive me insane!"

"What do you mean?"

"I have just spent the most wonderful hours of my life with you and now you tell me it is suddenly all over."

"I never promised you anything else. I told you I am busy. I am needed back in Washington and I am faced with the busiest months of my life."

He straightened his disheveled clothing and casually ran his hands through his hair to smooth it down. As he slipped on his uniform coat, she reached down and grabbed her negligee, slipped it about her and got out of bed.

"I—I won't see you again then," he said.

"We were planning to have luncheon together."

"Is that the only time?"

"You may come to the coach station with me tomorrow, if you wish. I must warn you, however, that my daughter, Florence, and Captain Moore are taking me to the station."

"I meant—alone."

She smiled bewitchingly as she came to him. "There will be other times, I am sure." She threw her arms about him and pressing him against her body kissed him passionately. He returned her kisses with equal passion. Slowly he drew himself away from her. Reluctantly he bid her goodbye and left.

Book Two

XVI

Spring 1857

It was well into fall when Rose returned to Washington, and the weather was warm and muggy for so late in the season. Rose did not notice. She was immensely busy. Buchanan was on a campaign tour of the northeastern states, and shortly after her return she herself started on a tour of the southern states, visiting as many of her friends as possible to arrange meetings to solicit votes for him. It was nearly a month later when they finally met. He came to her house late one evening, tired and haggard.

"I don't think I can keep this up until election."

"Don't give up now, Jim, just when your chances look better than ever before."

"At this point, I don't care whether General Fremont or I wins. I just want to get it over with."

"Well, I care. You can't possibly harbor the thought of leaving this country in the hands of that incompetent fool and his wife."

He leaned his head on the back of the sofa and closed his eyes. "I'm not giving up. I just want to rest. Regardless of what happens, I think I shall spend two weeks away at Wheatlands after the election."

"You won't be able to, Jim. You'll be too busy selecting your cabinet and preparing to handle the country's business."

"I have not won yet, my dear."

"You have as good as won. Listen to this report I have just received from Ed Pringle." She picked up a letter on the table beside her and read: "I suppose we may say Hurrah for Buchanan, for we send him without doubt the vote of California, and the same influences that have given him this state must have given him a handsome vote at the East. . . . I hope you will not forget to enlighten me sometimes upon passing events in the world."

"You did a magnificent job in California, Rose. John Slidell reported that you can be credited with saving the state for our cause."

"We have their qualified backing, providing you write a letter to them in support of the Pacific Railroad."

"What?" Buchanan bolted upright in his seat and actually glared at Rose.

"That is no great obstacle. I promised John, and Bill Gwin and several of the most important politicians in the state that they would be able to publish such a letter before election."

"I will do no such thing!"

"Jim, you must. California's votes depend on it."

"It is impossible. If I should advocate such a measure, I would lose the support of Governor Henry Wise of Virginia and God knows how many other important southern Democrats."

"The Pacific Railroad is vital to California's future."

"But the Democrats, particularly in the South, will not stand for spending federal funds for a transcontinental railroad."

"I shall tell them what you propose to do. Perhaps I can soften the blow."

"I'm sorry, Rose. My mind is made up."

Rose's eyes sparkled as she raised her voice. "Then you will have to unmake it or lose the state of California."

He sighed and leaned his head back against the sofa. "Gad, I wish you hadn't promised them this."

"Write the letter they propose just before election. You will appease California and there will not be sufficient time for the South to form a united stand against you before election."

"They'll be damn bitter. They will undoubtedly see behind such a devious maneuver."

"But they will vote for you."

"All right, I shall do as you say. But such a move will gain me very few friends in the East."

"It will be too late for them to muster sufficient opposition to affect votes for you."

"Let us hope so."

"I am sure that Senator Wilson will sponsor such a bill."

"Damn it, don't let him introduce it before election."

"He won't."

Buchanan wrote the letter and it was published throughout California three days before the election. It would have done Rose's heart good if she could have seen Jessie Fremont, red-faced in her fury, as she read Buchanan's letter to the general.

"The scoundrel. The unmitigated scoundrel!" Jessie fumed.

"Buchanan is my opponent, Jessie. But I would not go so far as to agree with your description of him."

"I was referring to Rose O'Neal Greenhow!"

The night of election was a busy one. Rose was with Buchanan and other party stalwarts in the ballroom of the National Hotel. The first returns that came in by a special telegraph line which had been installed in the ballroom gave Fremont a slight majority of votes in several of the eastern states. But as the night progressed, votes from the big cities of New York, Boston, Columbus, Baltimore, and Philadelphia gave Buchanan a large plurality. Although the outlying districts, when they were reported, consistently whittled into his lead, it was not enough to counteract Buchanan's vast city vote. Shortly before dawn when they wearily decided to leave campaign headquarters, it was obvious that nearly all of the northeastern states would assure Buchanan victory in that section of the country. In the meantime, the southern states were also rolling up a vast plurity for him, no small thanks to Rose's efforts on his behalf.

Before leaving, Rose took Buchanan aside and holding both his hands said gleefully, "You will be the first bachelor president the United States has ever elected."

"And it would appear I shall also be the fourth president who has not been elected to this high office by a vote of the people."

Rose's face fell. "I don't understand, Jim. It is already apparent that you have garnered nearly one hundred electoral votes against Fremont's paltry sixty-five. We still have to hear from California, Illinois, Michigan, and the other western states."

"Have you tallied the peoples' votes? Fremont is well ahead in the total popular vote."

"Does it matter, Jim?" He looked sadly down at her. She patted his cheek and stroked his chin. "You are winning the electoral votes. You are being elected president of the United States by the due process of law established by our founding fathers. Does anything else matter?"

A faint smile brightened his somber expression. "I guess not. You are right. You are always right, my Wild Rose."

For the next few days the returns still favored Buchanan in the electoral votes of each state. When a report of the voting from California finally arrived, giving the total majority of that state to Buchanan, it was apparent that Buchanan would be the next president. Indeed, he had won 174 electoral votes, against 114 for his opponent. But a tally of the popular vote did not give him a total majority, as he had predicted.

A giant celebration was planned for the following weekend at the National Hotel. "I shall attend to all arrangements," Rose announced cheerfully. There was no time to complete a new dress for the occasion, but she did succeed in having a specially designed, wide-brimmed hat made. As she entered the ballroom of the hotel, she had the distinct satisfaction of noting that the incumbent president's wife, Jane Pierce, was wearing a similarly designed hat, as were several of the other important ladies who attended. Word had gotten about concerning Rose's singularly designed hat, and knowing her clothier, many ladies had placed orders for copies of the same unusual style. In the days that followed Rose was pleased to note the unique design appearing on more women in the capital. And it readily came to be known as the Greenhow hat.

It was obvious that Buchanan's victory was also a victory for Rose. It seemed only natural that many of the congratulatory messages that came pouring into the capital from around the country were addressed to Rose O'Neal Greenhow. She was receiving nearly as much mention in the papers as the president himself, not only in Washington but throughout the country. It gave her a strange feeling of strength—of power. At long last Rose had backed a winner. It was a unique feeling, and she was uncertain of the result, of how it would affect her life. But, in any event, she was extremely happy.

During her long career in the social life of Washington amidst the political activity at the center of the great building nation, Rose had hoped that she would be able to exert her personal influence on what direction the country should go. Was it possible that she could now be the power behind the throne? Only time would tell, but Buchanan was surely her very dear friend.

But Rose promptly decided that she needed more power to make certain that her ideas were indeed carried out. Whereas Buchanan now had more power in the nation, he would have to rely on others to see that his wishes were carried out in Congress. She would need the same. It was not difficult to determine who could best serve her in this august body. She had continued her close relationship with Senator Henry Wilson, and now she selected him to spearhead her many projects.

He, in turn, was most willing to become an accomplice to her every wish, by this time being completely smitten by her charms. That he did not always promptly do her bidding was probably not his fault. There were long periods when he did not see her, resulting in times of utter frustration for Rose. In true womanly fashion, she would complain to him and demand more attention for herself and her wishes.

"You say you care, but I have not seen you in many days. How can I believe I am still uppermost in your thoughts?" she wrote to him.

The following morning she received a note from him. "You know that I do love you. I am suffering this morning; in fact I am sick physically and mentally and know nothing that would soothe me so much as an hour with you. And tonight, at whatever cost, I will see you."

She smiled a most self-satisfied smile as she read his pleading note. Then he did not come. And so their relationship continued. Notwithstanding, her new status became evident only a few weeks after it had been confirmed that Buchanan would be elected at a meeting of the electoral college. She was resting at home one afternoon when a stranger came to her door. He introduced himself as Brunato Fari and requested a few moments of her time on a business matter.

As she showed him into her parlor, he sat down and came right to the point. "I am a shoe manufacturer, Mrs. Greenhow. I have a factory in my native Italy and also one in Poolesville, Maryland. I doubt if you have ever heard of it. It is not far from the city of Baltimore."

"I come from Poolesville, Mr. Fari."

"Is that so? I know many of the people of that community. We may have mutual acquaintances."

"I hardly think so. It has been a long time since I have been in Poolesville, but I shall never forget the town."

"Well, I would like to show you something that I have designed." He reached into a small valise he was carrying and drew out an exquisite lady's shoe. "It is made of highest quality leather. Note the sharply pointed toes, and the unique two-toned patent leather." He handed the shoe to her. "These shoes are handcrafted but can be produced by both my factories, as well as in many homes nearby my factory in Vigevano, Italy. That is not far from Milan." As he noticed Rose casually inspecting the unique shoe, he asked apprehensively, "What do you think of it?"

"It is beautiful."

"And unusual, yes?"

"I have never seen anything like it before."

"Aha! It is my masterpiece. I tell you, Mrs. Greenhow, nobody in the entire shoe industry has ever seen anything like it before."

"But what has this to do with me, Mr. Fari?"

"Oh, I am sorry. I had intended first off to congratulate you on the election of Mr. Buchanan. He is your friend, yes?"

"Yes."

"I have watched you establish the fashion in many cases. The Greenhow dress, the Greenhow hairdo, and just now the Greenhow hat. Only a lady as gracious and important as you could do such a thing."

"Why, thank you, Mr. Fari."

Fari took the shoe from Rose and held it up proudly before her. "Here is the Greenhow shoe!"

Rose looked at the shoe more closely. It was truly a masterpiece. "But you are aware that some of the fashions that I have established have resulted in the sale of many, many such products?"

"I know this, Mrs. Greenhow. Although this shoe is handcrafted, we are already producing many of them. Should this become fashionable, as I am sure it will, if I were able to say it had the recommendation of Mrs. Greenhow, we are prepared to have several thousand of the shoes on the market by Inauguration Day."

"Oh, I see."

"Is it not worthy of you, Mrs. Greenhow?"

"It is most extraordinary. And with the Greenhow recommendation you believe that you would undoubtedly sell many thousands of these shoes?"

291

"That is exactly the case."

"And if you do, you will make a great deal of money?"

"I readily admit it."

"And I—?"

"Well, Mrs. Greenhow, you will have the distinction of fostering another fashion that would soon be sweeping the country in your name."

"Tell me, how much would I be able to purchase down at the local fish market with this distinction?"

"Why—why—nothing."

"You are undoubtedly a good businessman, Mr. Fari. And I must admit I am well-taken with your exquisite design. But I am also a good businesswoman. I am sure that you have heard many times the expression that is uppermost in the minds of all good businessmen."

"What is that?"

"What is in it for me?"

"Well, really, Mrs. Greenhow. I was not prepared—"

"That is obvious by your surprised, I might say, astounded look. However, that does not alter the case in the least, does it? And have you given thought to the number of shoes you might sell without my recommendation?"

"You are not only a beautiful woman, but, as the Americans say, you are also astute."

"Thank you."

"I can offer you fifty cents for every pair of these shoes that my salesmen sell."

"That is not sufficient."

"I did not include any additional amount in determining the selling price of the shoe, Mrs. Greenhow."

"That is not my problem, Mr. Fari." As she stared sternly at the forlorn, wilting Mr. Fari, she felt sorry for him and smiled her most bewitching smile. "I know that you have a great deal at stake. I realize that production expenses are high and you must give salesmen's commissions and bonuses. Also, large stores will demand even higher discounts to purchase your shoes in quantity, but Mr. Fari, if I permit you to announce that I favor these shoes, and I would be most delighted to do so, I also have a great deal at stake."

He sighed. "I will recalculate my price so that I can offer you one dollar per pair sold."

"That is most generous of you, Mr. Fari."

"That is actually sold, mind you, not on speculation."

"I understand and I thank you."

"I shall have a contract drawn up accordingly."

"A confidential contract, Mr. Fari?"

"It will be so. I promise."

"And now if you will design a pair for myself, I assure you that I will wear them at the inauguration and the ball."

"These are for you, Mrs. Greenhow. I learned your size in advance. I thought that this would be all that was required—"

"To consummate the arrangement, Mr. Fari?"

He looked at her rather sheepishly. "Yes."

She smiled. "Doesn't it offer you a certain bit of pride for the good of our country to know that at least one of the advisers to the new president will be a good businesswoman?"

"Yes." He handed the delicate creation over to her. "Thank you, Mrs. Greenhow." Bowing gracefully, he departed.

Since she had not seen her Senator Wilson again for some days, she used the incident as a light hearted excuse to jog the senator out of his seeming lethargy.

"You will appreciate my recent experience with Mr. Fari, since you yourself made your mark in the commercial world as a shoe manufacturer, even being fondly called by your constituents the 'Natick cobbler' from the city in which you reside." Then she went on to briefly relate her experience with Mr. Fari, forcefully ending her note with the remonstrance that "You consistently tell me you love me, yet I do not see you. What is your Wild Rose to think?"

Again she received a prompt reply. "If fate is not against you, I will be with you this night. I long for your sympathy— for I need it. I am exhausted. I have been laboring hard and incessantly. My love is all yours and only yours."

Finally, he did come to her. They had a most enjoyable evening at Antoine's exclusive French restaurant. They laughed together over her most profitable deal which she had wheedled out of Mr. Fari. Then they returned to her home for a most enjoyable love tryst.

As she had expected, word soon spread concerning the spectacularly original shoes that had been designed for Mrs. Greenhow to be worn by her at the inauguration. By the evening of the inauguration ball, Mr. Fari dutifully reported to her that over eight thousand pairs of the spectacular shoes had already been sold—of course, forever to be known as the Greenhow shoes.

Rose planned the inaugural ball of March 4, 1857 in every detail, and it was truly her finest masterpiece. She had had the ballroom of the National Hotel converted to resemble an outdoor garden. Gaily colored paper flowers were profusely scattered about the massive room. Flags of the nations friendly to the United States were conspicuously displayed and their diplomatic representatives were all in attendance. A white muslin cloth was stretched across the entire ceiling, upon which golden stars had been mounted, and the gas lights were lowered to create the effect of an outdoor summer evening.

She had spent considerable time on her own attire, and the spectacular appearance that resulted made her undoubtedly the center of attraction. Her distinctive shoes offset her beautifully designed, long, flowing evening dress cut daringly low in front to amply display her splendid breasts. Her hair was wound high on the crown of her head in the famous Greenhow headdress. Throughout her black tresses small gold-studded diamonds were interspersed, and they sparklingly reflected their brilliance as she danced familiar Strauss waltzes with Delegate Lane, Senator Wilson, Colonel Keyes (who had come east to join in the festivities) and, by no means least of all, the newly sworn-in president of the United States, James Buchanan. Only one thing marred the perfect evening which marked the peak of her social career, and that was that Buchanan had been taken quite ill just before the inauguration.

When she danced with him she spoke about it with deep concern. "Would you rather rest than dance, Jim?"

"I'm fine. We must continue dancing."

"You are sick, you look pale and you are sweating."

"It is nothing."

"You have been ill for several days. You must be careful. I'm sure that you have been poisoned."

"Nonsense. The National Hotel and the army have both investigated the matter. The Hotel regretfully advised that they discovered that infected rats had fallen into the tanks of their water system. It has been completely drained and cleaned. There have been no further cases of illness reported."

"Of course not. Arsenic has been placed in your own water or your food. It is a dastardly plot by extreme abolitionists to get rid of you even before you take office."

"You are letting your imagination run away with you."

"Attorney General Black does not think so. He advises me that some of his men have discovered a plot to destroy you and several other members of your Cabinet. You should not have appointed Lewis Cass as your secretary of state. He has never forgiven you for your campaign against him at the convention before this."

Buchanan stumbled as he tripped over her foot. "Rose, how can you harbor such a thought concerning Cass? He has been one of my most faithful supporters throughout my campaign."

"I am sorry, Jim, but I trust no one in this vast morass of political wilderness."

"There will be no further investigation, Rose."

"But you must, Jim."

"I do not care to discuss it."

It was a tradition that the president of the United States did not call at private homes. In spite of this, Buchanan frequently called on Rose. Many times, if he needed a respite, he would

295

call upon Rose and they would promenade along the walks of the avenues in the city. She would have preferred to ride in a stately coach as she had so often done when she visited Mexico City. But it was the only time they could spend alone together, so she was content to bask in the glory of her association with him.

It was well that she could have those times with him for her days were filled with requests for her assistance. It was obvious that she had the ear of the president. Her authority was greater than it had ever been. Truly she was the power behind the throne. Important politicians and unknowns alike sought favors from her. She received a vast quantity of pleas from people throughout the country. "Will you intervene in my behalf to gain the post of melter and refiner in the California Mint?" "I respectfully request your assistance in achieving my appointment to the Supreme Court." "I will be forever grateful if you can help me acquire a cadetship at West Point, which has been my desire ever since I was a small boy." "You will note from my friend's accompanying credentials that he is well-qualified for an architect's commission to work on the new post office building in New York. . . . [signed by] William A. (Boss) Tweed." "Can you obtain an introduction to the American minister in England, since you are so well-acquainted with Mr. Seward?"

Many of these requests supplied material for several letters to James Gordon Bennett, predicting appointments and assignments. Readers marveled at how frequently Veritas's forecasts became actual fact. There were also letters from Veritas published in this center of the hostile North glorifying the fatherly treatment of slaves by large landholders in the South. "Who could be more fair and considerate of their slaves than Mr. and Mrs. James Chestnut, who own upward of one thousand happy and contented residents on their vast plantations in South Carolina?"

Buchanan remained ill for several weeks and one day told Rose, "It is necessary for me to drink several tumblers of unadulterated brandy to keep myself from entire physical exhaustion."

"Jim, you must get to the bottom of this monstrous plot."

"There will be nothing more said or done about it."

"But why?"

"Because startling facts would be laid open to the world, and I shrink from the terrible exposure."

Reluctantly, Rose did not mention the matter again, and eventually Buchanan recovered completely. "Fortunately; due to his strong constitution," Rose remarked to Attorney General Black.

Now that Buchanan was in command of the country, she began to prepare to utilize dear Henry Wilson as her own special envoy to the Senate. He was most attentive and continually showered her with gifts to prove his undying love for her. But it was almost impossible to have him visit her whenever she wished.

Did he really love her as much as he professed? And could she count on him to do her bidding? After not having seen him for several days, she hurriedly scribbled a one sentence note to him. "Since actions speak louder than words, I can only assume that you have completely forgotten one who remains your lonely, disconsolate Wild Rose."

Although she still did not see the senator, she received a plaintive reply to her appeal. "Your note caused me pain, because when I read it I realized how much you had suffered. You wish me to say whether or not I will be with you tonight and also to say that I love—I do say both. I am thankful to you for not doubting me. I am sick and suffering. If you knew how I suffered last night and am still suffering, you could find it in your heart to forgive me. I had a burning fever the whole night. I am now only able to sit up because I must be here. But sick or well I will be with you tonight—and then I will tell you again and again that I love you; as I now do, and that, too, most truthfully. Ever, your H."

Again he did not come to her and instead sent her a huge

bouquet of wild roses as a token of his undying love for her. It was not sufficient, but Rose was so busy she could not dwell on his uncertainness for very long. Her life had become one continual round of soirees, promenade concerts, and polka cotillions, interspersed with the business of the nation.

President Buchanan's niece, Harriet Lane, was the official hostess at the White House. She loved pomp and ceremony, and receptions at the White House took on a certain formal dignity. Rose cheerfully referred to Harriet's influence at the White House as "the court days." New furniture was brought in. Many oil paintings and portraits were added to serve as a reminder of important personages who helped build America. Guests were introduced with certain ceremony and protocol was strictly adhered to. Rose delighted in being introduced by a page as she was escorted into the banquet room on the arm of the president.

Since she was on the friendliest terms with Harriet, many of the social graces that were introduced at the White House bore Rose's own personal stamp.

"Harriet, dear, it would be most fitting if the household were moved to Soldiers' Home this summer. It will take your dear uncle away from the swampy poisons of the capital."

"I will suggest such a move to Uncle James. It will also give him an opportunity to get away from the incessant bickering and arguments which continue all day and well into the night, as you well know."

"Yes, and your affairs can proceed in a more relaxed informal atmosphere."

"I think it would be most appropriate for the summer months. And, of course, I will rely on you for your assistance in developing our guest lists, the entertainment, and the menus."

"I shall be delighted. I realize that your wild turkey and prairie hens and your partridge, quail and reed birds are most attractively prepared."

"Are you trying to tell me something, Aunt Rose?"

"Well, it might add variety to your menus if you were to include terrapin, oysters, and lobsters."

"I thought Uncle James did not like shellfish."

"On the contrary, he is extremely fond of them. But never serve any but those which come from the Rappahannock. You will notice the difference."

"I thank you for the suggestion."

"If you don't mind one further observation, Harriet, I have noticed that your uncle is being annoyed by several society women who are constantly trying to gain his attention. They are lovely ladies, and my best friends, but I'm sure he would find it a welcome relief if you did not invite Mrs. Clay, Mrs. Pryor, Mrs. Chestnut and Mrs. Slidell to every one of the receptions."

"But he has specifically advised that he wishes to have them in attendance."

"Oh."

"I shall try to alternate them at various affairs rather than having them all present at every reception."

Rose smiled bewitchingly. "Confidentially, it would be much more to my liking."

"I know."

"I am only human, Harriet."

"And sometimes a trifle jealous, Aunt Rose?"

"Can you blame me?"

"No. It's sickening the way they fawn over him."

"I agree most heartily."

"But he does make it most difficult when I suggest eliminating any attractive women."

"He doesn't realize what is best for him."

"I will do all that I possibly can."

"Thank you."

Rose was disturbed to learn from Senator Gwin, Colonel Keyes, and Ed Pringle that a depression had developed in her beloved San Francisco. "The gold rush days are over," Ed wrote. "In their wake are many bankrupt firms and great unemployment. Shipping, which was such a thriving enterprise, has been cut in half." She was pleased to read that the depression had not personally affected her close friends in the West. Whenever they visited Washington, which was becoming increasingly more frequent, she entertained them lavishly at her popular and informal dinner parties.

It was becoming more and more distasteful to her to visit the Senate. It had deteriorated into one continual session of angry debates. Additional security personnel had been brought in, and, on more than one occasion the sergeant at arms had been called into sudden service to separate feuding senators who, it would seem, were on the verge of resorting to physical combat to emphasize their strong stand. It appeared that a complete breakdown of relations between the North and the South was close at hand.

Buchanan was beside himself trying to appease both sides. Their positions were unalterable. "What can I do?" he asked Rose.

"You can do nothing. Let the situation take its natural course. What is to be, will be."

"But the country is suffering. Vital legislation has become bogged down as senators argue with each other—sometimes over trivial matters."

"It is entirely possible that the only solution *is* to permit each faction to go its separate way."

"But that would mean a breaking up of the Union."

"Is that such a horrible prospect if it restores peace to all parties?"

"No, I suppose not."

Rose found the atmosphere much more amiable at the many foreign legations and once again began entertaining the French and Spanish diplomats, and particularly the British ambassador.

She received with mixed emotions the information that British Lord Napier was being recalled. She liked Lord Napier very much, and they carried on many hours of lively conversations concerning the similar problems of the two nations. However, she knew that Buchanan had been most friendly with Lady Napier while he was in England. He had continued their friendship in Washington, and Rose was somewhat relieved to learn that the titled lady would shortly be removed from further competition where President Buchanan was concerned.

Senator Gwin had finally moved back to Washington and he and his wife staged a fancy-dress ball as a farewell party to Lord and Lady Napier. It was a magnificent affair.

Rose had invited Senator Wilson to go with her and had enjoyed several dances with him. However, at one of the intermission times, he had congregated with several other of the guests and had gotten into a heated discussion concerning the bills that were being introduced in the Senate. In a way she was happy to be alone, for she had found that, of late, a continual evening of dancing tired her considerably and she was happy to rest a bit. She was in such high spirits that she momentarily forgot her strong resentment of her niece as Addie joined her during an intermission between waltzes.

"You look positively radiant in the pale tints of the morning," Rose said to her. "You make a fascinating Aurora."

"Thank you, Aunt Rose. When I learned that Senator Pugh's wife was coming as Night, I decided I would be her opposite."

"Have you seen Mrs. Jefferson Davis?"

"No."

"She looks stunning as Madame de Stael."

"I must speak to her," replied Addie, then laughed. "Senator Gwin does an excellent impression of Louis Quatorze. He struts about exactly like the vain king himself."

Buchanan came up to them dressed in his usual formal dress coat and pants. "I almost wish I had come in costume," he said as he joined them.

"You should have, President Buchanan," Addie remarked. "It's so much fun pretending that you are someone else for a change."

"Harriet advised against it. She felt it would not be quite appropriate. But I am pleased to note that the ladies in costume are most charming."

"Thank you, sir." Addie curtsied slightly.

"Have either of you seen Daniel Sickles? I had gotten quite attached to the young man when he was secretary of the legation in London. I haven't had an opportunity to see much of him of late."

"He is here with his lovely Italian bride," Rose told him. "But you must be wary of her charms, Mr. President. She looks stunning in her costume and we American ladies have more than sufficient competition."

"I shall be on my guard," Buchanan smiled as he bowed and left them.

Mrs. Clay joined them looking splendid in her richly designed silk costume as Marie Antoinette. "I thought I saw the president speaking with you."

"He just left us. He was looking for Dan Sickles."

"I saw Dan at the refreshment table. He is not himself tonight. He is in a very disagreeable mood. His bride has left him alone most of the evening."

"But why?" asked Addie.

"Philip Key has been paying a great deal of attention to Dan's young wife. They have had nearly every dance together. Dan is furious."

"Who did you say has been dancing with her?" Addie asked.

"Oh, Philip Barton Key. You know, he is the son of Francis Scott Key who wrote that stirring poem, 'The Star Spangled Banner.'"

"Oh, yes," Rose remarked. "Philip is a very fine gentleman. He comes from Maryland."

302

"That in itself would promote him in your book Rose dear," Mrs. Clay smiled.

Before Rose could reply Mrs. Gwin joined them. "I trust everyone is enjoying themselves," she said, smiling graciously.

"It is a magnificent party, Mrs. Gwin," Addie said.

"I am sure Lord and Lady Napier will cherish it as one of their fondest memories of America," added Rose.

"I do hope so," Mrs. Gwin replied. "I have just been talking to Dan Sickles. I am afraid he has been drinking too much for his own good. I don't know whatever has gotten into the young man."

"We were just mentioning him," said Rose. "It seems Mr. Sickles has a bad case of jealousy. Philip Key has been paying a great deal of attention to his new bride."

"Now I understand why Mr. Sickles was so uncivil," Mrs. Gwin said. "He seemed to be furious."

"I am sure he has nothing to fear from Philip Key," said Rose quickly. "Philip is most unconventional and is attracted to all the ladies, but he really means no harm."

"Have you seen him this evening?" asked Mrs. Clay. "He looks really handsome—he's dressed as an English huntsman in white satin breeches and a cherry velvet jacket."

"I must confess he is most attractive in those lemon-colored boots," Addie commented. "And his silver bugle really tops off his costume."

"And he is such a flirt," Mrs. Chestnut added.

"Just innocent fun. But he had best be careful. Mr. Sickles is in no mood to be trifled with this evening," added Mrs. Gwin, and then broke into her most gracious smile as the president came up and joined them.

"Pray tell what is keeping so many beautiful ladies from participating in the promenade? I should like to invite you all to join me, but that is rather impossible, isn't it?"

"Quite," agreed Mrs. Clay. "However, you may choose any one of us and I am sure you will not be refused."

It was Buchanan's turn to smile. "Dear lady, I have not been a diplomat at the court of St. James for three years and a politician for over forty without learning to avoid taking sides on any extremely volatile issue—which includes selecting one fair lady from four beautiful contenders."

"I trust this is not your policy with affairs of state, Mr. President," said Mrs. Gwin.

"Absolutely not. I do strongly believe, though, that compromise on both sides can settle many thorny issues."

"But there are some matters that do not bow to conciliation, Mr. President," Rose said teasingly.

"I am not so sure. As yet, the final results have not been tabulated."

Suddenly a shot was heard from outside the ballroom. The dancers stopped and so did the music. In the horrified silence that followed, a second shot was distinctly heard and then a third.

Almost as quickly two armed soldiers came up to President Buchanan and placed themselves between him and the rest of the revelers. Facing the crowd, they both drew their revolvers and placed them at the ready slightly above the heads of the dancers.

"It came from the garden!" the president shouted. Turning to one of the guards he added, "Go see what has happened."

Without taking his eyes off the crowd the guard replied crisply, "I'm sorry, Mr. President. Our orders are not to move from your side."

At that moment, Senator Gwin came hurrying into the room. "Is there a doctor present?"

"What is it?" Mrs. Gwin asked.

"Philip Key has been shot," he replied.

"How dreadful," Addie murmured. "How could it ever happen?"

"I can guess," Rose said quietly.

"And I," Mrs. Gwin added.

304

Dr. McMillan, a prominent Washington physician, pushed his way through the gathering crowd and came over to the president. "Where is he?"

"He is in the garden. Follow me," said Senator Gwin hurriedly.

As both men quickly disappeared beyond the high French doors, Mrs. Gwin, a handkerchief pressed to her flushed face said, shocked, "What a dreadful thing to happen!"

"I shall see if I can be of any help," said Rose as she rushed over to the doors. As she started to go out, she was met by James Chestnut at the doorway. "Don't go out, Rose. Dr. McMillan is suturing the wounds. He thinks the man is dying."

William Yancey came running into the room. "Dr. McMillan has pronounced him dead."

He was followed by James Mason and Edwin Stanton, each of whom had an arm entwined in one of Dan Sickles's. "Let me have the gun, Dan," Mason said solemnly.

Sickles sullenly handed the gun in his hand to Mason. "I'm not sorry for what I did. I'm glad!"

Stanton turned to Rose. "Mrs. Sickles is understandably distraught, Rose. Perhaps you had better go to her."

"Yes, I must." Rose started to go out on the veranda, but Stanton stopped her.

"I shall have to take Sickles to the police. Someone must take her home."

"I will be glad to," Rose volunteered immediately. "Is it necessary to bring this matter to the attention of the police? It will be reported in the newspapers."

"I see no alternative," Stanton answered. "It is unpleasant, but I will attend to all legal matters. I will also defend Dan if he wishes me to." He looked at Sickles, who stood stoically glaring ahead of him with glazed eyes as if he did not see or comprehend anything that was going on about him.

"I'll send for your carriage, Rose," said Mason as he hurriedly left.

Stanton brushed his way through the crowd that had congregated about them and he and Sickles were soon lost from sight.

Rose noticed Senator Wilson standing on the outskirts of the crowd and went hurriedly over to him.

"Isn't this terrible?" he said, a startled look on his face.

"Dreadful. You will have to forgive me, Henry, but I must take his wife home."

"I'll go with you."

"No. It would only embarrass the poor girl."

"But we have had such a wonderful evening together. I had hoped that I could—"

Theresa Sickles suddenly appeared in the doorway. She was crying uncontrollably. She looked pale and so naive in her charming painted muslin shepherdess gown.

"This is an emergency, Henry."

"But it is so seldom we can be alone together. I thought after the ball we could go to your—"

"Tomorrow night, Henry. You do understand, don't you?" Without waiting for him to answer she rushed over to Theresa and put her arm around her shoulders.

"Come with me, Theresa," she said consolingly. "I shall accompany you home."

"It was all so horrible," Theresa said in very broken English. "It happened too quickly."

Reluctantly Rose left the gay party and escorted the poor young girl to her carriage, which by this time was drawn up in front of the mansion. She helped Theresa into the carriage and quickly drove off.

"It was so unnecessary," sobbed Theresa. "Philip was showing me the beautiful gardens, when—"

"Try not to dwell on it, Theresa."

"How is Philip? Is he hurt badly?"

"He is dead."

Theresa began to cry again. "Oh, poor Philip. My poor husband. It was not as he thought. Philip meant nothing to me.

306

It was not even, how you say, an innocent flirtation. It was nothing—Mrs. Greenhow."

"Call me Rose, dear."

"Oh, thank you, Rose. I shall never forget you for your help to me. I am forever grateful."

She rested her head on Rose's shoulder and sobbed quietly as the carriage drove on.

XVII

Summer 1858

On May 11, 1858, Rose sat proudly among the spectators in the Senate gallery when the State of Minnesota was unanimously accepted by the Senate as the thirty-second state. It was the last state to be carved out of the great Northwest Territory, and its acceptance marked the beginning of the expansion of the United States past the Mississippi River and ever closer to California and the Pacific Ocean.

At the same time, Stanton, who had been defending Dan Sickles for the jealousy killing of Philip Key, finally succeeded in securing Sickles's acquittal.

When Buchanan quietly told Rose that he was glad that Sickles had got off, she decided then and there to celebrate the twofold occasion.

She hastily summoned some of her good friends from both the North and the South to a quiet informal dinner party at her home. This in itself was a somewhat bold gesture, for feelings between northern and southern sympathizers were by this time so strong that very few hostesses would venture to have guests from both factions sit around the same table and break bread together. Although it was a spur-of-the-moment affair, Rose was able to offer much more than the traditional bread. Iced vichyssoise and quiche lorraine were served as appetizers. Her entrees included coquille St. Jacques, trout almondine, and filet of beef Wellington, topped off by crèpe Normande and walnut Viennese layer cake for dessert.

Dan Sickles was rather sullen as the guest of honor after his "horrible prison experience," as he spoke of it. His beautiful wife, Theresa, was overjoyed at being reunited with her new husband. She and Rose had become friendly during the ordeal of the trial.

President Buchanan was present with his official White House hostess, Harriet Lane. They both led the other guests in a toast to Rose, vowing that no other Washington hostess could serve as sumptuous a banquet on such short notice. Jefferson Davis, William Seward, W. W. Corcoran, the handsome southern widower, and Senator Henry Wilson all heartily agreed as they cheerfully raised their glasses. It was the one thing that the guests from the North and the South *could* agree upon. Strangely, the evening went smoothly, prompted along somewhat by the continual flow of Johannesburg wine and Virginia apple brandy.

During the summer, a new name began to be mentioned more and more frequently in political circles: that of a strange, homely backwoodsman Republican from the state of Illinois. Abraham Lincoln was jokingly being spoken of at receptions and soirees as a tall, ungainly man—and most unlikely to unseat Addie's husband, Stephen A. Douglas.

"I sometimes wish this Lincoln fellow would defeat the little giant. It would surely cut Douglas down to proper size," Rose confided to Buchanan as they promenaded down F Street one Sunday afternoon.

"Rose, you are speaking sacrilege. After all, Lincoln is a Black Republican."

"I don't care. Douglas's bitter denunciation of you for supporting Kansas's pro-slavery Lecompton constitution was entirely uncalled for."

"It is my opinion that the constitution will settle the tempestuous feuding in Bloody Kansas. The Little Giant believes otherwise."

"You must be wary of him, Jim. He will prove a mortal

309

enemy to you, even though he is a Democrat."

"He has been vitriolic on all legislation I have proposed of late."

"Ignore the little bastard."

"I can't. I need his support."

"Perhaps it will not matter if Lincoln should defeat him in their Senate race."

"If Lincoln should win, I fear there will be a stronger antislavery man in our midst."

"It might not be as bad as you imagine. We must wait and see. You know they have agreed to seven debates throughout the state. We'll soon know where they both stand on all issues."

Buchanan sighed. "We surely will. I shall watch those debates closely and note the reactions of the people."

Rose's eyes fairly sparkled with fury when she met Buchanan after the second Lincoln-Douglas debate on August 27 at Freeport, Illinois. "Are you aware of what your Little Giant has said? He advocates the people of a territory excluding slavery even before they have become a state!"

"He was forced to take that stand. This Lincoln is a shrewd one. He worded his question to Douglas in such a manner that if Douglas had given a negative reply, he would undoubtedly have offended many of his constituents, and ended up losing his seat in the Senate."

"But this is not in agreement with the Dred Scott decision as rendered by the Supreme Court! It is in violation of the law of the land."

"It is politics."

"I never had any use for the man. I warned Ellen her daughter would rue the day she married that dirty little bigot."

Buchanan smiled.

"Why are you smiling?"

"Addie has been married to Douglas for over two years— time to overcome most major obstacles to a happy marriage."

"You keep a sharp eye on him. He will do your efforts for

peace between the North and the South no good."

"If Lincoln is elected to the Senate, I daresay he will do me less good. This Lincoln is becoming nationally known for his clever remarks. There is no doubt of his feelings where the Union is concerned. 'A house divided against itself cannot stand.'"

"The man is a zealot. But perhaps he is manageable."

"We shall see."

Rose could not wait to meet Buchanan after Douglas and Lincoln had again debated in the flag-decked eastern Illinois town of Charleston on September 18. Hurriedly she had her buggy hitched up and drove straight to the White House. Buchanan was in his study mulling over several proposed bills.

She hardly waited to be announced before she rushed into his room swinging the *Washington Morning Chronicle* by her side.

"I told you this Lincoln isn't such a bad sort. Did you read what he had to say in his latest debate with Douglas?"

Buchanan looked wearily up from his desk and his eyes brightened with admiration. Regardless of the problems which beset him, he was always cheered by seeing the effervescent, enthusiastic Rose again. Her bubbling fervor buoyed his lagging spirits. "I must confess I have not had time to scan a paper this morning. What is the latest report?"

"This Lincoln might be more help for our cause than you think." She sat down on a chair beside his desk and continued excitedly. "He strongly denies that he favors equality of the races, and champions white supremacy. He said that he is not in favor of making Negroes voters or jurors or of qualifying them to hold office or to intermarry with white people. And listen to this." She found a place in the paper which she had previously marked and began to read. "This is a quote from him. 'There is a physical difference between the white and black races which, I believe, will forever forbid the two races living together on terms of social and politicial equality . . . while they . . . remain together there must be the position of

311

superior and inferior, and I, as much as any other man, am in favor of having the superior position assigned to the white race.'" She beamed radiantly at him as she finished, her eyes flashing in her enthusiasm.

"As I recall, the debate was held in the eastern part of Illinois."

"It was in Charleston."

"That portion of the state is as mildly antislavery as any other section of the north."

"But this is what he said."

"What would you expect him to say in such territory?"

"You are hard to convince."

"He did not say he was for slavery."

"It could be interpreted as such."

"We shall see. Of course, if he does not beat Douglas in the Senate race, we may never hear of the man again."

But they were destined to wait a bit longer before they were to know exactly where this man Lincoln stood. Douglas was swept into the Senate, once again, astride a Democratic landslide in the state, but Rose refused to admit that the best man had won—not where Stephen A. Douglas was concerned.

On February 14 of the following year, Oregon was admitted to the Union as the thirty-third state. Rose celebrated the occasion with a private dinner with that state's territorial delegate to the Congress, Joseph Lane.

Delegate Lane was his usual flamboyant self. "I've nursed my own dear territory since the settlement and treaty with Britain in August, forty-eight," he said proudly as he sipped an after-dinner brandy with Rose in her parlor.

"Do you know my dear late husband had a great deal of responsibility in the treaty of eighteen forty-eight with Britain?"

"Is that so? I met him on various occasions. I often wondered what he was doing out there."

"As a matter of fact, he plainly pointed out the United States' rights to the Oregon Territory in a book which he published."

"I never read it. But I'm grateful for anything that he did for my territory. Now, no disrespect to the dead, my dear, but the only way I can show my appreciation is to be downright considerate of his widow." He reached over, and before Rose realized what he was doing, he had grabbed her in his arms and kissed her soundly. She did not immediately resist him but gradually pushed him away. His eyes narrowed as he looked steadily at her.

"I know I can't compete with his memory, my Wild Rose, but I don't like thinking about the dead. It's only the living that counts, ain't I right, Rose, my darling?" He put his arm on the back of the sofa behind her and slid closer to her.

Rose looked away from him. "Of course you're correct. I—I can't help feeling sad whenever I think of him."

"I know it and it hurts. That is only proper, but we got to go on with the living. That's why you and me, we got to get the most out of living." Again he drew her to him and kissed her soundly. She responded to his crude passion and pressed her lips strongly against his in a desperate effort to forget all else.

He ran his hand through her dark hair and slowly down her back. "You're a lovely woman, you know that?"

She smiled and drew him over to her, kissing him passionately in return. Then quite suddenly she pulled away from him. "Well, tell me, Joe, what does this mean to you, now that Oregon has finally become a state?"

Surprised at her sudden change, he was determined that he would match her mood, whatever it was. "Why, not much of anything," he said swallowing the balance of his brandy in one gulp and slapping the glass hard against the table. "I'll just go back home and let the people know that I am now available to be their first senator."

"Senator Joseph Lane."

He beamed. "It does sound nice, don't it? Honey, now that I am a senator—"

"Not yet, Joe."

"You don't suppose there's any question, do you? As I was saying, being a senator now, or almost, that is, just as soon as I dispense with the formalities—don't you think you could show proper appreciation for being in such high company?"

"What do you mean?"

"Well, I'm tired. It's been a damn trying day, so, why don't we—well, why don't we celebrate, just you and me, by spending the rest of the whole doggoned night together."

"That would be rather difficult with my girls sleeping upstairs, even if I were of a mind to. Besides, why don't we wait until we get to know each other better?"

"How much better do we got to get?"

"Well, we should be sure that we have the same objectives. When you become senator, don't you think it would be nice if you represented a slave state?"

"Oregon? Rose, they don't know what slaves are out there."

"We could tell them what they are and spread the word about their advantages. Then, as their senator, you could at least introduce legislation to grant them the right to make their own choice."

"Yes, I suppose I could."

"And you will have great power now to influence others and vote for such vital legislation as the transcontinental railroad."

"Why, that ain't even come up."

"But it will. It was one of President Buchanan's campaign promises."

"I suppose I could vote for it if he wanted me to."

"And there are several other bills that he needs to have enacted in order to insure peace in our land."

"What sort of bills?"

"I'll be happy to go over them with you as they come up, once you are a senator, Joe."

"Are you trying to hamstring me, woman?"

"No man can hamstring you, Joe, let alone any woman."

"Well, that's right. And don't you ever forget it."

"You know I won't. When are you leaving for Oregon?"

"I'm planning to start back the end of this week. It's been a long time since I been home. That's what I'm trying to say to you, Rose. Time is short. I may not see you again for a good many moons, as my Indian friends would say." He moved close to her again and started to take her in his arms.

Gently but firmly she pushed him away. "No, Joe."

He shook his head sadly. "God damn, you sure try a man's heart and body. But I'm a patient man. I don't mind waiting."

He grunted as he slowly got up. Rose followed and he grabbed her in his arms and kissed her fervently. Almost savagely he pulled her to him and pressed her body close to his own. He kissed her again and then turned away as she slowly pushed him from her.

"I'll see you when I get back," he said jauntily. "And don't you forget it."

"I won't."

He waved to her cheerily and quite abruptly left.

On October 16 John Brown raided Harper'ss Ferry and took possession of the town. His purpose was to set up a central terminal within the very South where escaped slaves could be forwarded to safety and freedom in the North. Two days later Colonel Robert E. Lee led a company of marines in an assault on the arsenal where Brown had set up his headquarters and killed ten of Brown's men, and captured Brown and the rest of his little band. It seemed to be the breaking point of the mounting tension between the North and the South. While John Brown awaited trial in jail, fierce arguments erupted both in the Senate and the House, and in all sections of the country wherever thinking people gathered to discuss his escapade.

Undaunted, Rose chose this time when the issue was at its hottest to invite several guests from both the North and the South to a dinner at her home in honor of Joseph Holt, whom Buchanan had recently appointed as his postmaster general. Buchanan was unable to attend, being completely overwhelmed trying to work out necessary legislation with his advisers that would rescue and preserve the sacred balance between the unyielding North and the adamant South.

In addition to Mr. and Mrs. Joseph Holt, Rose had invited Mr. and Mrs. Charles Francis Adams of the distinguished New England family, as well as William Seward, Colonel and Mrs. John Magruder of Winchester, Virginia, and her dear friend Henry Wilson, the senator from Massachusetts.

It was a simple dinner by Rose's standards, consisting mainly of wild pigeon with, of course, shrimp and crabs from her beloved Rappahannock. All of this was accompanied by generous portions of her finest Madeira wine and was topped off after dinner by heated French brandy which had been sent to her by a former French ambassador whom she had befriended while he was stationed in Washington.

Rose had intended that the affair be free of any political encumbrances, but Abigail Adams thought otherwise. Shortly after they had eaten and were still seated about the table, Abigail suddenly remarked in a loud and distinct voice, "I feel so sorry for that poor John Brown, rotting unattended and unnoticed in his filthy cell."

Despite her previous intentions, Rose could not let this obvious provocation go unchallenged. "Sorry?" she asked, her eyes sparkling. "Whatever for?"

"His intentions were of the highest order. He was moved by a cause he so fervently believed in that he was willing to risk his very life and those of his sons to defend it."

Suddenly the room grew silent. Brandy glasses rested before each guest untouched, as no one felt comfortable about making the least unnecessary movement.

"Personally," Abigail went on, "I consider poor John Brown a holy saint and martyr."

Rose pressed her hand around the brandy decanter from which she had been serving until her knuckles became white. A slight frown creased her brow as she replied, "I have no sympathy for John Brown. He was a traitor, and must meet a traitor's doom." Quietly, in a low voice, Rose said to Seward, "You showed extremely good taste, Mr. Seward, when you repudiated all connection with John Brown in your latest speech."

Mr. Seward squirmed as he replied. "I have met the man only once. On that occasion Brown struck me as being a wild and visionary man, erratic in his ways and singularly striking in his appearance."

Mr. Seward ran his finger inside his thickly starched collar as he felt Abigail's firm, steely glare focused directly on him. "Brown impressed me as being a bold, truthful, and honest man. However, I consider him eccentric to a degree bordering on insanity. Actually, the raid merely confirmed my original suspicion that John Brown is mad."

Colonel Magruder carefully knocked the ash from his cigar as he spoke. "Mr. Seward, I must admit that I am prejudiced, being a close friend of Mrs. Lee, whose husband captured Mr. Brown. But I am strongly convinced that John Brown was guilty of prevarication, intimidation, and theft."

"John Brown must be hanged!" Rose said firmly.

Senator Wilson quickly spoke up. "Everyone knows that I am a stalwart antislavery man, as are most New Englanders. But I strongly criticize John Brown's raid—which I am firmly convinced had the backing of only the extremists in our midst."

Again there was deadly silence about the table.

Presently Mr. Seward spoke. "Well, now, this little affair is actually in honor of our new postmaster general, Mr. Holt. Tell me, Joseph, do you have any plans for speeding up delivery in our postal service?"

"I must wait until I have surveyed the situation, Mr. Seward. However, I am led to believe that service could be put on a more efficient basis." He laughed weakly, but when no one else joined him he quickly became quiet once again.

Shortly afterward Abigail rose from the table. "I am so sorry but, although it is an early hour, we must be leaving, for we have an extremely busy day on the morrow." Firmly she turned to her husband, "Isn't that right, Charles?"

Abruptly he rose, saying, "You are quite right, my dear." Then he turned to his hostess. "Rose, we must thank you for another magnificent evening." He bowed grandly and kissed Rose's hand as his wife glared coldly at him. They left, followed by all the other guests, with the exception of Seward and Wilson. Rose leaned her elbows on the table and bowed her head in her hands.

"I blame Mrs. Adams completely for raising the John Brown issue," Senator Wilson said softly.

"She ruined my dinner party," Rose sighed, without raising her head.

"The demonstration on her part was very ill-timed," Seward agreed.

"It seems the situation can no longer be avoided when northern and southern guests get together," Senator Wilson commented.

"I have learned my lesson," said Rose flatly. "The opposing factions shall never again sit down at my table together."

"You are wise, my dear," Seward concurred.

"It seems there is a strained feeling in Washington wherever you go these days," Wilson remarked.

"Exactly," Seward agreed. "Just like all hell is about to break loose." Shortly afterward the two men left together, and Rose went sadly to bed.

Rose was surprised when Buchanan reproached her two days later as he was relaxing beside her on the sofa in her parlor.

"Whatever have you been doing now, my Wild Rose?" he remarked casually as he took off his shoes and spread his feet on the ottoman.

"What are you referring to?"

"Do you not know that one does not openly challenge the sanctimonious Adamses of New England, particularly not Abigail?"

"Do you keep spies in my household?"

"Now don't get excited."

"Frankly, the incident greatly disturbed me. But I was not aware that the social engagements of so humble an individual as I would be brought to your attention."

"How you talk! Actually, I have heard it spoken of by five or six persons, who all greatly commended your spirit and independence."

"You have my word that never again will I have northern Yankees and southern sympathizers under my roof at the same time—never again."

"Let us not dwell upon it, Rose. It is so pleasant to have a place to come where I can be away from the affairs of state both petty and enormous."

"Could you bear to hear a word of caution about your dear niece?"

"My God, what has Harriet been doing now?"

"I fear she is seeing entirely too much of the new ambassador from England."

"You can't be serious, Rose. She has very specific instructions to be kind and courteous to all diplomats!"

"It is not necessary for her to single any one out for continuous personal attention."

"Might the admonition be tinged with a slight touch of jealousy? If she is paying Lord Lyons any special attention, she is only following the example set by our illustrious Rose."

"No one has reported that I shall be marrying Lord Lyons."

"Is that what they are saying about Harriet?"

"I have heard it spoken from many sources."

"I shall have to caution Harriet about this."

"I would urge you to do so. But please do not be too severe. I would not wish anything to come between either her relationship with you or our own relationship. I am happy that you still find some solace in my company."

"Not only solace, Rose. I welcome your counsel as well as your conversation."

"What is uppermost in your mind now?"

"There are so many problems, they vie with each other for immediate attention."

"I am glad the country has you as its leader. Thank the good Lord that you are as firm as the statue of Jackson in front of the Executive Mansion."

"You flatter me. If it is not your southern friends, it is our South American neighbors; if not them, it is the British."

She reached her arm along the top of the sofa and rested it on his shoulders. "Who has been agitating now?"

He leaned his head on her arm and looked at her wearily. "It would be more appropriate to ask who has not been agitating. The government of Nicaragua has someone waiting in my outer office daily concerning the Isthmus of Panama. Since we have transit rights across the Isthmus, a Frenchman by the name of Ferdinand de Lesseps vows he can build a canal across it. The little Frenchman, althought repudiated by his government, has made these silly people believe that he is going to dig a ship canal for them between ocean and ocean, a work which all the money in Paris would not accomplish. His plan is a subject of ridicule among capitalists both in England and in this country, but the Nicaraguans venerate him as a perfect prodigy."

"That is a minor problem. You can readily ignore their wildcat schemes."

"That is not hard to do. But with the British, it is a different matter. They are constantly interfering with American merchantmen who are suspected of carrying slaves. It is causing a great deal of ill will."

"But you are well-grounded in the ways of the British, having spent so many years as our ambassador there."

"Yes. I pride myself that I was able to allay a great deal of suspicion between our two nations while I was minister."

"You can greatly assist your secretary of state in binding up any differences that might arise."

"I have decided to go a step further. Lewis Cass is a

competent secretary of state, mind you; however, I have a more intimate knowledge of the British statesmen involved. I have decided to handle the diplomatic negotiations personally. When I so advised Cass he reacted very strongly against it. I suppose I would do the same if I were in his position. But that will not deter me. I personally am very happy that they selected Lord Lyons to replace Lord Napier. I wrote to Lord Clarendon advising that his mission here ought always to be filled by a first-rate man whose character is known in this country and whose acts and opinions will command respect and influence in England. Above all things, he ought to be instructed not to interfere on one side or the other in our party politics."

"You have spoken well."

"Cass insists that the wrong American has spoken. When I showed him my letter his face reddened. He said nothing, but I could tell that he was furious. I am sorry that he cannot see my position, but he will have to accept it."

"Do you mean to discharge him?"

"I will never discharge him. But he is a very independent man. If he chooses to resign because of my personal negotiations with the British, so be it."

"He must realize that responsibility for the good of the country still rests with you."

"Um-hum." His head drooped against her shoulder, and as she looked down upon him nestling against her arm, she smiled. He was fast asleep.

It was late in the evening three days afterward that the door gong sounded. Her children had long since gone to bed and she had dismissed her slaves, so she answered the door herself. She was surprised to see Colonel Keyes standing before her dressed in full uniform.

"What a pleasant surprise," she greeted him cheerily.

"I must apologize for the lateness of the hour, but I have just received news that I could not keep to myself."

"Pray tell, what is it that is so important?"

"I have received a transfer to New York."

"You mean you will be staying East?"

"Yes. General Scott has appointed me his military secretary."

"How wonderful!"

Colonel Keyes shifted his weight from one leg to the other as he stood in the doorway. "Well, aren't you glad?"

"You know I am. We will have so many good times together again."

"Rose, is anything the matter?"

"Of course not. Why do you ask?"

"You are acting strangely. You didn't mind my coming over at this late hour, did you? I was advised unofficially this evening while visiting General Scott and his wife. I was so delighted with the news I thought I would stop around on my way home to tell you."

"I'm glad that you did."

There was an awkward pause as they stood facing each other.

"Why don't you come over tomorrow evening for dinner?"

"Tomorrow evening?"

"Yes. It's so late tonight."

"Oh, I thought—well, that will be fine. I'll see you tomorrow evening, then."

He turned to go and Rose quickly grabbed his arm. He turned back. She drew him close to her. "It's so good to know you are going to be here indefinitely."

"It's good to hear you say that, Rose. I thought for a moment that—well, that you had forgotten."

"How could you think such a thing?"

"I don't know—I—"

She put her finger on his lips and stopped him. As she did, she leaned against him and drew him close to her. Eagerly, he grabbed her in his arms and kissed her passionately. She returned his kiss with equal fervor.

Quickly she drew away and smiled enticingly. "I'll see you tomorrow evening, then."

He smiled broadly. "I can't wait." He saluted her and departed.

She closed the door and went back into her living room. There, sitting slumped on the sofa, was the honorable senator from New York, William Seward. He had fallen asleep and was quietly snoring.

Rose casually walked over to him and sitting beside him blew gently on his cheek. At first he brushed his hand across his face as if shooing away a fly. She again blew in his face and he gradually roused up. Suddenly he was wide awake as he realized where he was.

"Jesus Christ, I must have dozed off."

"You were sound asleep."

"Well, you were gone for so long. Who in hell comes around to your house ringing door gongs at this ungodly hour of the night?"

"It was Colonel Keyes. He wanted to let me know that he has been transferred back East."

"Huh, more competition for your pleasurable company."

"Are you jealous?"

"It's getting so one needs an appointment to see you anymore."

She leaned close to him. "Oh, you know, senator, you can see me any time you wish. There's no one's opinion I value nearly as much as your own."

"Humph. Except when it comes to the slavery issue."

"Well, it wasn't very nice of you to say in your speech the other day that there would be a continual outward conflict until the United States became either all free or all slave."

"Dammit, that's the way I feel."

"Why can't our country live in harmony? You and I are on opposing sides but we get along marvelously."

"That's because I give in to you. You're not fooling me one bit, my Wild Rose. You're always buttering me up or plying me with those goddamned Queen Charlotte Cocktails so I'll forget my duty to my constituents back in New York."

323

She tugged playfully at his thick beard. "That is not true. You know that I consider you one of the most amiable of men."

"Yes, in the morning. I know what you said about me. 'In the morning he is the most tractable of men in the world.'"

"You see?"

"Yes, but son of a bitch, what else did you say? 'After supper and under the influence of the generous gifts which the gods provide, he is the most genial and confidential of men.' You can't deny it."

"I don't deny it. It is true. And all of it most complimentary."

"Hah! I'll wager you actually don't give a damn about me."

Rose placed her hand on his arm and leaned her head on his shoulder. "I think of you more than you will ever know."

"Well, it's nice to hear. And it is true I enjoy being with you. You set the best table in the city. And, I'll be a son of a bitch if them there Queen Charlotte Cocktails ain't the best I believe I've ever tasted."

"Will you have another one?"

"Hell, no. It's getting late. I've got to be going."

"I'm glad you came over, Bill. I wanted you to know how much I appreciated your support the other evening on my behalf when Abigail Adams made such a martyr of John Brown."

"Well, I spoke the truth."

"He is a wicked man and he deserves to hang for his treachery."

"That will be determined by his trial."

"It might help if you would talk to the judge who is presiding, Bill. You could set the matter straight with him and show him the law reads that such a crime is punishable by death."

"You want me, a senator from New York, to try to influence a judge in Carolina as to how he should conduct his trial?"

"It would be a distinguished lawyer with a national

324

reputation trying to assist some poor country judge in the finer points of law with which he probably is unfamiliar."

"Not on your goddamn life. Rose, you're out of your mind to think I would entertain such actions. We shall let justice prevail."

"I agree. Just so the traitor is hanged for his misdeeds."

"That's for his damn countrymen to say. Not you or me." Gruffly he got up from the sofa. "Now I've got to be going." Suddenly he turned to Rose and faced her directly. "Say, little lady, you know your way around this goddamned hell trap they call the nation's capital. What would you say if I were to tell you I was thinking of running for president?"

"Bill, do you mean it?"

"There's several members of the new Republican party that have been suggesting it."

"Well, I—I would say it would certainly be worth a try."

He looked at her quizzically. "That's a pretty damned awful endorsement, I must say."

"You surprised me, Bill. I was unprepared. Of course my first reaction would be to warn you that you would have to defeat some very formidable Democrats."

Seward tugged his own beard and squinted at her. "Would you have been any more damn encouraging if I'd agreed to go down and have a talk with the judge about John Brown?"

"Oh, Bill, how can you say such a thing? I don't mix politics and friendship."

"I know. Not unless you can gain your own goddamn aims one way or the other." He chucked her under the chin as he started toward the door.

"You wrong me, Bill. I'm sure you would make a very fine president."

"Thank you for your damned kind words of encouragement. Well, I just wanted you to know you could alert your friends about what I'm thinking. And, in the meantime, you keep inviting me over and I'll keep wishing you good luck where that damned John Brown is concerned."

Smiling mischievously at her, he opened the door and left. Rose watched him go with a deep frown on her brow. Senator Seward was a much more clever man than she had given him credit for. She made a mental note of that.

To Rose's satisfaction John Brown was found guilty by a jury of his peers and was hanged as a traitor at Charles Town on December 2, 1859.

Only a few short months later, Buchanan sat relaxed in her parlor and said, "Well, Lewis Cass did it. He resigned today."

"I'm not surprised. And I'm glad. I never trusted him really."

"He is a good man. I'll miss him."

"Nonsense. There are much better men."

"Who?"

"Do you know who would make a fine secretary of state? Jeremiah S. Black. He's reliable. As your attorney general he's tried very hard to enforce legislature concerning slavery."

"Which has been most unpopular."

"But he has stuck to his guns. You can depend on him."

"But then who do I appoint for attorney general?"

"I would suggest Edwin Stanton. He has been most successful in helping to clear up the land claim debacle in California."

Buchanan rubbed his chin thoughtfully. "You know, your ideas make a great deal of sense. I need the support of both of those men. They're hard workers, and you're right, I can depend on them. I'll do it!"

"That's what I admire so much in you, Jim. You are a man of decision."

Abruptly he got up, kissed her soundly, and said, "I must be going. I am meeting with my Cabinet first thing tomorrow morning, and I want their approval before announcing my new appointments."

She walked with him to the door and hurriedly kissed him goodnight. As he went down the steps of her house he turned back once, waving fondly, and was gone.

She smiled to herself as she returned to her parlor and drew a letter from her bosom. She read it again. "If we are ever to receive any benefit from our Point Lobos property, we must do something to counteract Jeremiah Black's adamant stand against Limantour's claims. His uncompromising attitude is difficult and the attorney general's decision carries great weight with the courts out here. Can't you get Buchanan to give him some other position in his administration? Ed Pringle."

Rose smiled to herself. Edwin Stanton should accept her suggestions much more readily than Jeremiah Black. Stanton had worked nicely with her when she was in California. Since returning to Washington she had gotten to know him quite well, especially during his defense of their mutual friend, Dan Sickles.

A welcome P.S. was appended to Ed Pringle's letter. "I am enclosing $250 from your Plank Road stock. That was surely a wise investment." She tapped the bank draft in her hand and hastily put it aside. She blew out the candles in the parlor, turned off the gas lights and went wearily upstairs to bed. As she laid her head on her pillow, she smiled. All in all, it had been a fairly successful day. She breathed a long, drawn-out sigh and slipped calmly into a deep sleep.

XVIII

Fall 1859

Although the national conventions were over four months away, prominent members of both parties were already seeking the best positions from which they could seek the presidency.

Rose had been attempting to coax Buchanan to run for another term. He was positive in his refusal.

"I will not consider running again under any circumstances," he said bitterly. "I am for peace. I am for compromise. It seems that both have become most unpopular choices."

"Not at all, Jim. The country will realize in the long run that you have been right."

"Right or wrong, I have had my share of inner bickerings and antagonistic slander that has been aimed at me in every move that I make. I doubt if I will run for any political office. I have had over forty years of service to my state and to my country. I deserve to retire to Wheatlands and watch other men resolve the sad plight of the country."

"But Jim, you need another four years to see the many projects that you have inaugurated come to fruition."

"I hesitated to run for president this time, you may recall, since I strongly believed that this president might see the nation resort to war. I was wrong. It has not come to open rebellion between the North and the South as yet."

"Thanks to your continued insistence that the two sides

seek a compromise that would finally end this dispute."

"I have only succeeded in putting the fateful day off. Neither side wishes a compromise. Both will settle for nothing less than complete victory."

"But, Jim—"

"There are no buts, Rose. My decision is final and irrevocable. I will not seek another term under any circumstances. Whoever embarks on the stormy ocean of politics must calculate to make a shipwreck of contentment and tranquility."

"You leave the Democratic party at a loss for a leader."

"Not at all. Breckenridge will be glad to take up the challenge. He is a much younger man than I. He is more capable of presiding over the battle that is inevitable."

"Are you saying that there will be war?"

"It is my firm belief that the only solution to the problems that confront the nation is for both sides to break apart and go their separate ways. Only then can they both win."

Rose was quiet for a moment. When Buchanan left the White House he would leave the power that was his behind him. He was happy to retire. She was *not* ready to retire, but all the glory and the power that she had experienced since he became president would be gone for her, as well. She wanted it to continue. But Buchanan was determined. He was through with politics. "Breckenridge is a good statesman," she mused, almost to herself. "And I have always been able to consider him my friend." Then she hastily added, "Of course, no one can take your place, Jim."

"Say what you wish, my dear. I don't care. I am through holding hands and nursing every politician who comes running to me crying that the opposition has thwarted his program."

As the date of the Democratic convention drew near, Rose heard Stephen A. Douglas's name being mentioned more and more as the outstanding choice for the Democratic nomination. She abhorred the very thought. In order to save face for her family, because of her niece, Addie, she did not outwardly oppose him. However, she worked furiously behind the scenes to promote Breckenridge's cause.

The Democratic convention was held on April 23 in Charleston, South Carolina. But those who thought that holding it in the heart of the South would appease the southern delegates were wrong. Buchanan attended the convention but took no active part in it. The incessant wrangling among the members of their own party seemed reminiscent of the halls of Congress. They could not agree on a platform, they could not agree on a single candidate, they could not agree on anything. Rose had succeeded in having her friend Joseph Lane (who had returned to Washington as Oregon's first senator), promise to keep her closely posted on the progress of the convention. Two days after they had gathered he sent her a hurried note. "The convention has divided; conciliation is hardly probable should they hold out as now, a southern man will be nominated, then we will have a triangular fight with the result doubtful. My room is crowded. Will see you before long. Yours, Lane."

At least Breckenridge was holding his own, Rose thought to herself as she read the note. She dropped into the office of the *Washington Globe* where she was surprised to learn that Senator Lane himself had also been nominated. However she also learned that the convention delegates were squabbling hopelessly.

Finally, a week later, she got a brief, forlorn letter from Senator Lane. "You will be delighted to hear that Douglas cannot be nominated. However, my name has also been withdrawn. In a bitter showdown your southern confederates actually walked out of the convention rather than support Douglas. Our wonderful party has been torn to pieces. What will happen now is anyone's guess."

Two days afterward she learned from the *Washington Globe* that the convention had adjourned, agreeing only that they would reassemble again in Baltimore on June 18 in the hopes that the intervening weeks would calm the delegates sufficiently to effect some rational compromise for a candidate.

The next week she saw Seward in his Senate office as he was preparing to depart for the Republican convention in Chicago with high hopes of being nominated as their presidential candidate. Rose had mixed feelings as she bade him goodbye. She knew him well, and confidently believed that, if he should win the presidency, she would still have access to the White House. But—"My God, he is a Republican!"

However, Seward was destined to be disappointed, and many others throughout the country were surprised when Abraham Lincoln, the Illinois backwoodsman, was suddenly glowingly nominated. Even more astonishing, on the third ballot he received a majority of the delegates' votes, whereupon he was unanimously nominated as their candidate for president.

Shortly afterward Rose received a pleading letter from Ed Pringle in California. "You told me of a reception that you had held when Joseph Holt was appointed postmaster general. In God's name can't you influence him to inaugurate a daily overland mail service? Communications between California and Washington are abominable. We sometimes have the feeling out here in California that we are a part of another country, communications are so slow."

Rose went to Buchanan about the matter and he sent word for Holt to come to his office while she was still there.

"Mrs. Greenhow advises me that her California friends are bitterly complaining about the postal service to their state," Buchanan said to him sternly.

"I know this, Mr. President. I assure you that we are seriously engaged in finding a solution to the problem."

"What in your opinion will be the solution?"

"I have been working with Mr. Cornelius Vanderbilt of New York. He has been most successful with shipping in Staten Island, as well as a freight and passenger service across Nicaragua."

"I am aware of that, Joe. What is the result of your discussions?"

"Well, sir, we do not have cost estimates completed, but, if you concur, we believe the most satisfactory solution is to inaugurate a series of pony riders to go from St. Louis, the end of the telegraph line, directly to Sacramento, California."

"How quickly could you deliver the mail?"

"We anticipate it would take about eight days."

Rose, who had been attentively listening, smiled broadly. "That is marvelous. It would truly be a pony express."

"It sounds like a great idea," Buchanan concurred. "When can you get started?"

"Within thirty days, sir. With your approval."

"You have it. Let's plan on the "Pony Express" before the end of this month."

So it was that in less than thirty days the Pony Express began to deliver mail along the last link of the transcontinental route. Rose sent a brief but exuberant letter to her daughter on the first batch of mail that went forth under the new system. True to their estimates, it arrived in Sacramento eight days later, marking the beginning of a new era in transcontinental communications.

It seemed that matters were fast coming to a showdown in the Democratic party. Still Rose was troubled by the continual mention of Douglas as the likely candidate when the second assembly of the convention drew near.

She visited John Breckenridge on several occasions, giving him suggestions as to how he could garner the nomination of his party. She went so far as to offer an alternate suggestion if Douglas should receive the nomination.

"You wouldn't want that rabid abolitionist to represent our party under any circumstances, would you?" she said to Breckenridge.

"Frankly, Rose, it makes my constituents in Kentucky get goose bumps every time the Little Giant's name is mentioned in connection with our great party."

"Then, if he should be nominated—and mind you, we should do everything in our power to keep that from happening—"

"Oh, I agree most wholeheartedly—but as you were saying, if he *should* be nominated—"

"I suggest that you lead the same group of southern delegates who walked out of the convention last time into doing so again. You could form a party of your own."

"An excellent suggestion. We could call ourselves the 'National Democrats.'"

"If you assume the lead in such action, they will surely nominate you as their presidential candidate."

"I must be prepared to suggest a running mate for vice president."

"I can think of no other man more qualified than Senator Joseph Lane."

"Do you think he would agree to run?"

"I am certain that he will. Let me discuss it with him."

"Gladly. If he will accept the vice presidential nomination, we will at least combine the efforts of our individual delegations."

Rose was quite certain of her friend Senator Lane. However, when she dropped him a note saying that it was urgent that he visit her as soon as possible, he replied: "I have had the pleasure of receiving your note and would go up and see you this morning but I am obliged to be with the committee on military affairs at ten this morning and may not be able to leave the Senate till late this afternoon, and of evenings you are crowded with company. I will see you before many days pass by."

Rose was most impatient when she read his note and sent her slave Randy over with a second note telling Senator Lane that there was a matter of great importance she wished to discuss with him concerning the coming convention.

He replied immediately. "Your note has been read. I would be glad to see you, but you must bear in mind that the Senate meets at eleven—committees meet at nine, and of an evening you are surrounded by admirers. To meet them affords me no pleasure, and besides I have no desire to be in the way of any one—understand me. I have no complaint to make but don't like to meet those above referred to. I may, however, call and see you at nine this eve (not certain, however)."

Rose caught a glimpse of her annoyed expression in the hall mirror as she read the note and carefully tucked a wisp of loose hair into the bun atop her head. Then she smiled. Senator Lane was insanely jealous of Senator Wilson—even more so than Wilson was of him. He did not come to her that evening. She learned from Breckenridge the following day that he had had a meeting with Lane and discussed their plan. Lane was not too enthusiastic about the idea, claiming that he was getting too old to go through the exhaustive activities of a national political campaign. Whereupon Rose sent Lane another urgent note telling him that this was the opportunity of a lifetime. He would have a hand in guiding the country at a most precarious time—one that undoubtedly offered all capable and willing men a place forever in the history of this great country. She ended with a stern admonition, "Pull yourself together, senator, for the glorious political battle that lies ahead."

He replied weakly. "You can hardly imagine how feeble I am and how unable to be on my feet. Still, if you insist, I will go. Believe me, my dear, I am not able to move about as a young man should. Please answer. Your Lane."

Senator Lane finally came to her house. They had a lengthy discussion, during which Rose reminded him of the accolades that would be his, and of the accomplishments he could add to his distinguished career if he was nominated and then elected. He finally agreed to go to the convention and work with Breckenridge to defeat Douglas. If this was not possible, he would join Breckenridge as Vice President on the National Democratic ticket.

As Rose had feared, when the Democrats met again in Baltimore on June 18, they quickly nominated Stephen A. Douglas as their candidate. She was delighted to learn from the telegraph dispatches in the *Washington Daily Globe* that the

334

southern delegates had again bolted the convention and set up a meeting of their own the very same day. The bolters promptly nominated Breckenridge as their candidate for president and Joseph Lane for vice president.

At least, poor Addie's despised husband would be thwarted in his quest for the presidency. Rose smiled as she thought, that if her friend Breckenridge and her very, very good friend Joseph Lane won the right to govern the country, her power on the national scene would be extended for four more years.

Rose was not able to dwell on the political situation for long, however. Gertrude's health was getting progressively worse. She continued to lose weight and now almost constantly ran a fever, sometimes quite high. Rose took her to several doctors, but still none could diagnose the malady, let alone offer any suggestions for a cure.

She took Gertrude away to the seashore of New Jersey during the hot summer months. She received a note from Ed Pringle, telling her how amazed he was at the strong showing by Douglas in California. He also teased her for hiding away in some out-of-the-way place called Atlantic City. "Write soon," he ended his letter, "and give me all the news to date; political, personal, scandalous, and have Atlantic City put in the next geography book."

Their stay in Atlantic City was doing Gertrude no good, so they returned to Washington. Gertrude was by now so sick that she could not attend parties, but she kept up a continual correspondence with Harriet Lane in the White House. She delighted in hearing about the visit of the future King Edward VII of England. Harriet wrote: "He is a charming little fellow, full of fun and jokes and wonderful in the admirable manner of conducting himself upon all occasions. It is unfortunate, however, that dignity is a sad obstacle in the way of pleasure. I am truly miserable, for the good prince has invited me to go to New York with him as his guest at a ball given in his honor at the Academy of Music and then on to Philadelphia to attend the opera with him. But, of course, I have refused. Uncle James was most emphatic in advising me. What would everyone say?"

On November 6 the country went to the polls to elect their president. The final returns were tabulated more quickly than in any previous election. In a matter of seventy-two hours Rose saw her hopes for a favorable administration—or at least one sympathetic to her southern cause—dashed beyond all hope of recovery. What she had not realized was that the hopeless split in the Democratic party caused by the emergence of Breckenridge and Lane left the entire nation wide open for Abraham Lincoln, the third opponent, who was sweeping the country. A letter from Ed Pringle clearly depicted the debacle that was unfolding. "What is to become of this forlorn country? I do believe that Lincoln has carried California. He is now thirteen hundred votes ahead of Douglas and nearly one hundred thousand votes counted and Breckenridge nowhere. Of course, the East has done likewise and elected him. What a breaking down in Washington! What nausea to you and to all your friends."

Douglas, the Little Giant, received only twelve electoral votes and Breckenridge secured seventy-two. Abraham Lincoln rode into office with a smashing one hundred eighty votes.

It was truly nausea! During the campaign Rose had found that, in spite of Lincoln's leanings toward inequality, he could never be counted on as a friend of slavery. He was truly the "Mammon of Unrighteousness"—to be dreaded, probably even feared. Now he was destined to be president of the United States. If she was to keep in contact with the upcoming government, she must make friends with him. Fortunately, she was already friendly with many stalwart Republicans such as Seward, Adams, Sumner, and, of course, Senator Wilson.

As she had received letters from every part of the country congratulating her when Buchanan was elected, she now received letters from throughout the nation deploring the overwhelming Lincoln victory. "What shall we do now?";

336

"You should know what we secessionists in South Carolina are planning to do."; "I am convinced that nothing now can stop the drift to war. Do you not agree?"

She quickly came to the conclusion that she could no longer gain her ends by working inside the framework of the government. She must prepare herself to act and work outside the normal bounds of the law. She lay awake one night going over it all again and again. She lit the gas light that hung over her bed and propping herself up jotted down her sad, disillusioned feelings in a poem:

> There is a feeling of the heart,
> A dreary sense of coming evil
> That bids all mirthful thoughts depart
> And sends enjoyment to the devil.
>
> A cloud that bodes the coming storm
> And partly wraps the heart in sorrow,
> And bids our feelings, bright and warm,
> Prepare a shroud upon the morrow.
>
> When all is sunshine to the soul,
> It turns its brightest hour to sadness,
> And grief with misty clouds will roll
> Above the sunniest scenes of gladness.

Turning out the light she tried to sleep, but so many thoughts kept running through her mind she remained wide awake. Whatever were the people of this nation thinking of? As far as she was concerned they could lie in the bed they had just made. But not her. She would take matters into her own hands. It was not for nothing that she had political and military friends in Washington—throughout the country, for that matter. She would still achieve her aims. It could easily be accomplished in Washington, for the nation's capital was actually more southern than northern.

Lincoln and his cronies could lay their plans—she would show them what Rose O'Neal Greenhow would accomplish without them. She began to attend secessionist meetings so she could know first-hand what was being planned. Senator Lane and Senator Wilson were both members of the Senate Military Committee. She constantly badgered them to learn the innermost plans of the military. What would the Union do if her beloved South rose up against the North, whose stubborn thinking seemed somehow to be spreading westward?

She determined that she would expand her vast circle of friends to include more men of the army and the navy. It would not be difficult. Surely, anyone would be flattered to be called to Mrs. Greenhow's house. Sure enough, military men and politicians alike began to vie with each other in making hurried calls to 398 16th Street. Most obligingly, they told her of their plans and the plans they knew the government was contemplating. Her southern sympathizers kept her posted on what they thought could be done to thwart the northern menace which was fast stifling the cause of their beloved South.

If it was open battle that lay ahead, she was prepared for it. She knew more of what went on in Washington, how the politicians and the military thought, than probably anyone else in or out of government. She would show the northern devils what they were up against!

XIX

Winter 1860

The weeks after Lincoln was elected were hectic for Rose. Sadly she watched her southern friends shutter their Washington residences to return to their homes down South. She was determined to stay. Although she still saw Senator Wilson infrequently, he had at least finally begun to give her information that might prove valuable in case actual hostilities should break out between the government and any of the southern states.

She kept accurate notes of the information, separate from her drawers of correspondence. Only four hundred marines were stationed at the marine barracks. One hundred enlisted men of ordnance were at the Washington arsenal. Volunteers were almost as few. The Potomac Light Infantry met in Georgetown and the National Rifles met in Washington. The Washington Battalion of Light Infantry consisted of one hundred and sixty men who drilled once a week.

"Wholly inadequate for the defense of the capital," snorted Wilson.

Rose nodded as though it worried her greatly, but said nothing.

In the midst of the fierce activity that was escalating in Washington and the worry over the health of her daughter Gertrude, Rose received an urgent letter from Pringle. "A new suit has been filed against the Limantour interests. Calhoun

Benham, the recently appointed United States attorney, is of a mind to press it. Make Buchanan help his friends a little before going out of office. Try to convince him not to sign Judge Ogden Hoffman's bill adverse to Limantour's interests. Without an appeal, proceedings will not be pushed. Must leave it to your generalship. It is of immense importance not to try it this term. Seriously, what is to become of the country? Bad enough for you in Washington, who used to be in the midst of a gay society where a Black Republican was a rare sight! And now you will be left alone to pay court to Mrs. Lincoln and Mrs. Hamlin, the vice president's dowdy wife. I despair of any solution. I sit and await the result as I do the result of the Point Lobos case."

Rose sighed. She would do her best, but matters in Washington presently required far more attention than her Point Lobos property in California.

Late the following evening Buchanan called at her home. He looked weary. He unbuttoned his coat and waistcoat and loosened his collar as he dropped upon the sofa and lay his head back. "General Scott came down from his New York headquarters to see me today. He is greatly disturbed concerning the city's inadequate defenses. I advised him that when Congress assembles in December, I will have the matter brought to their attention. But I hardly believe there need be an overhaul of the District of Columbia militia at this time."

"I certainly agree. If it should be attempted, the southern senators would surely defeat it."

"General Scott insists on moving his headquarters to Washington and I agreed. He was furious at the number of regular troops that have been distributed to the Indian country frontiers—Texas, Utah, New Mexico, and even so far away as Washington and Oregon."

"Isn't that where they are most needed?"

"That is why I did not countermand any of the orders as they came through. Scott only snorted that southern sympathizers have now had their wishes fulfilled. In case of emergency, he raged, it will take months to get our few thousand regular troops back here."

"Ordering them to Washington would be tantamount to mobilization. It would sadly affect the morale of the entire nation and result in an unwarranted crisis which our nation can presently ill afford."

"I believe that it is best to maintain the situation as it is."

"A wise decision, Jim."

"There shall be no secession if I can help it. Frankly, I deplore the very thought of it. I emphatically advised General Scott that no steps can be taken to garrison southern forts, for such a move would surely antagonize the South."

Rose poured him a glass of brandy, and since he quickly gulped it down, refilled his glass. "In my last message to Congress I am emphasizing that secession will be an illegal act on the part of any state."

"Jefferson Davis would argue with you on that matter."

"I shall probably infuriate him anyway by bringing this out in the open, but it is my belief and I owe it to my country to take a firm stand on this important issue."

Rose was silent as she listened to him. She knew how often secession had been discussed in the southern states. She knew that it was their belief that this was the only solution to their conflicts with the North. The South was weary of continual denial of their rights by the North. "For five and twenty years the agitation by the North against slavery has been incessant," she said quietly, almost to herself.

"I don't give a goddamn!" Buchanan banged his glass down on the table beside him. "The time for compromise has come, for the South as well as the North!"

Rose did not reply. They sat silently staring at each other, he overcome by the strife that was tearing the nation apart, and she pitying his efforts to maintain national unity, efforts which seemed so hopelessly thwarted. She did not agree with him, but she could not bring himself to outwardly challenge him. Presently he spoke in a more subdued voice.

"I'm sorry, Rose. It is just that I have heard your comment so often."

"I understand."

"You will be pleased to learn that I have not given up hope entirely. As you know, Kansas will soon be brought into the Union. I have submitted my recommendation to Congress that it be accepted as a slave state."

"My southern friends will be grateful."

For the first time, he smiled.

She poured herself a small glass of brandy, and sipping it, said to him, "I have heard from my California friends that the Limantour affair is again being brought up in the courts."

"Now is no time for this matter to be brought to the public's attention," he remarked impatiently.

"That is their feeling, but it is your attorney Benham who is pressing the case."

"I shall instruct him to drop it at once." He drew a paper from his coat and made a hasty note.

"The matter will be removed from the calendar of the courts if you do not sign Judge Hoffman's bill."

"God, must I take care of everything?" He frowned as he scrawled a second note on his paper and returned it to his inner pocket.

Rose did not let a week go by without visiting at least one of the military posts which Senator Wilson had listed for her. On the early evening of a bitter cold December day she visited the headquarters of the National Rifles. She was not certain which side they favored and aimed to find out.

"I am Mrs. Greenhow," she introduced herself to the commander of the company.

"I recognize you, Mrs. Greenhow." The tall, stately officer bowed to her. "I am Captain Schaeffer."

"Colonel Keyes of General Scott's staff advises me that your company is remarkable for its accurate and rapid drill and full ranks."

Captain Schaeffer beamed. "Thank you, Mrs. Greenhow. I

pride myself as a fine drillmaster. I was a lieutenant in the First Regiment of U.S. Artillery."

"I also understand that you hail from Maryland—my own home state."

"Yes, and so do a great many of my men. It is a good company, and I suppose I shall soon have to lead it to the banks of the Susquehanna!"

"Why so?"

"Why, to guard the frontier of Maryland and help to keep the Yankees from coming down to coerce the South!"

"I am happy to hear you say that, captain. You undoubtedly know of my strong sentiment for the southern cause. Am I to understand that you share my beliefs?"

"Most assuredly, Mrs. Greenhow."

"Good. And may I inquire if your company is up to full strength?"

"There are more than one hundred men on our rolls and I am daily adding to the number."

"That is encouraging to hear. Do you have sufficient arms for these men?"

"We do not, ma'am."

"That is why I am here." She took a small sheet of paper from her purse and a thick, clumsy pencil. "If you will tell me what you require, I shall see that you receive it."

"I'll be grateful to you, ma'am. Will you come to my orderly room? I have already prepared such a list."

Rose accompanied the captain to his room and sat down beside his desk. He quickly brought out a clipboard and began reading from it. "We will require one hundred more rifles with two hundred rounds of ball cartridges, and an equal number of sabers, revolvers, and ammunition. We also require two mountain Howitzers with harness and carriages."

Rose dutifully wrote his requirements down and then asked, "Where would you secure these instruments of battle?"

"From the chief of ordnance."

"Do you know if they have this material now in store?"

343

"Oh, yes ma'am. I have already checked with them."

"I shall arrange to have your supplies ready for you. An order from the secretary of war would permit them to be released to you, would it not?"

"Yes. But are you aware that the president has just appointed a new secretary, Mr. Joseph Holt?"

"I am, sir. He is a very good friend of mine. If these supplies are released, captain, can you arrange transportation for them?"

"Oh yes, ma'am. That is the least of my problems."

"Very well, then, I shall advise you when they are ready."

"I most certainly appreciate your efforts on our behalf, Mrs. Greenhow."

"It is the least I, a lone widow, can do for our cause. Keep your men in good shape, captain, in case you need them for protection against any overt action by our aggressive-minded Northerners."

"You may rest assured that I will, Mrs. Greenhow." He winked knowingly at her, started to bow, then stopped. "Oh, Mrs. Greenhow, I assume that you are planning to see the secretary of war, and—" he paused, cleared his throat and then continued. "Well, also President Buchanan himself at some time hence."

"Yes, you are correct."

"Well, I was wondering. I have been nominated by former Secretary Floyd for the commission of major in the District of Columbia Militia. I believe that it has gone forward to the president. Would it be too much trouble to ascertain—"

"I shall determine the whereabouts of your commission and if need be expedite it."

"Oh, thank you, Mrs. Greenhow. I'm deeply indebted to you. If I can ever do anything for you, just let me know."

"I shall do that. And for now, goodbye, captain." She waved cheerfully to him and left.

Rose wasted no time in going over to the war department and calling on Secretary Holt. Upon seeing her, he immediately ushered her into his office. After congratulating him on his new assignment she casually remarked, "Joe, I know that you have not had time to determine the needs of the military, but I have been talking with Captain Schaeffer of the National Rifles."

"A very good outfit, I am told."

"Very good indeed, except that they are undersupplied with necessary guns and ammunition."

"Is that so?"

"Yes. Captain Schaeffer advises me that he is sadly in short supply." She fumbled through her pocketbook. "I have the list of items he wishes to requisition."

"That won't be necessary, Rose. I am very familiar with Captain Schaeffer and his well-drilled company. I'll just write an order to the chief of ordnance advising him to issue all the ordnance and ordnance stores that the National Rifles might require."

"Captain Schaeffer will have his men call for them. When may I advise him they will be ready?"

"That depends on whether they are in store or not."

"He has already determined that the items are in stock."

"Then he can pick them up in three days at the latest."

"Thank you, Joe. Or perhaps I should say, Mr. Secretary."

"It really is not necessary, Rose. We must all work together in these trying times."

"We must, mustn't we?" She was about to leave when she turned to him. "Oh, by the way, Joe, I understand that former Secretary Floyd had nominated Captain Schaeffer for a majority."

"That is correct. I remember forwarding it to the president for his signature within the last day or so."

"I see. I shall speak to the president when next I see him. He has made an excellent choice for his secretary of war."

"Thank you, Rose. If I can be of further service, let me know."

"I shall do that." She breezed out of his office.

Immediately upon arriving home she jotted a hasty note to Captain Schaeffer. "You may pick up the supplies you require in three days. Incidentally, the order specifies that you are to be issued all necessary ordnance and ordnance stores for your company. Make sure that you requisition sufficient supplies for your entire company. Congratulations are also in order. Your majority has been forwarded to the president. I shall call it to his attention the next time I see him. Rose O'Neal Greenhow."

She also wrote another brief note to Senator Lane. Once again, it had been several days since she had seen him, and she had given him some assignments to carry out. He had promised to introduce the Pacific Railroad bill, and to steer it through committee and passage in the Senate. He had also agreed to bring her a copy of the latest military plans on which he was working as a member of the Senate Military Committee. He had not questioned her right to see the highly secret documents, and she was exceedingly anxious to know the government's plans. "You tell me that you love me," she wrote. "You say you cannot wait to see me again, but how can I believe you when you do not come, or comply with my simplest requests? Rose."

The following morning Rose received her reply. "I am happy to say that I feel particularly well this morning; and can well account for the favorable change. We are in the act of entering on the consideration of the Pacific R.R. bill. I will not fail you tonight and will bring with me the thing of which we spoke last time. Bless you always. Yours, Joe." But her errant senator still did not come. Rose was anxious to get more information on the actions of the military committee and wanted to see the railroad bill on its way before too many other pressing matters forced it aside, to be eventually forgotten.

She sent her senator a short but forceful note. "You have disappointed me beyond all forbearance. If our love means no more to you than this, I truly cannot forgive you. Rose."

His reply came to her quickly. "I feel conscious that you can scarcely forgive me—and yet I feel this because I know that you cannot know what I have had to encounter for some days and nights past. Indeed, I am nearly exhausted. Tonight, unless Providence has put its foot against me, I will be with you and at as early an hour as I can. That I love you, God, to whom I appeal, knows. Joe."

Although he did not come to her he sent her a most encouraging message the next day. "I will come tonight, but at what hour I can't say. This is the last night of the session and we will sit late. We are making one last effort to get up and pass the P.R.R. bill. But I will come, I repeat. Yours always."

Later that same day she received another message from him: "At ten o'clock tonight precisely expect me. I have but one moment. The Pacific R.R. bill is now being voted on, and you may know that I am all anxiety. Yours, Joe."

At ten o'clock that night he did come, to announce to her gleefully, "California shall have its railroad, my love. The P.R.R. bill has passed." He also brought her a copy of the military plans, which he dutifully left with her. They spent many glorious hours making love, and Lane was ecstatic.

Buchanan was sad as he delivered his last message to Congress. Congress was sad. The spectators who jammed the great hall, including Rose, were sad. There was a strained stillness in the air as he said, "The fact is that our Union rests upon public opinion and can never be cemented by the blood of its citizens shed in civil war. If it cannot live in the affections of the people, it must one day perish. Congress possesses many means of preserving it by conciliation; but the sword was not placed in their hand to preserve it by force."

There was no applause as he paused for breath. Instead, a few scattered boos were heard from the more radical listeners in the gallery. The president ignored them as he went on. "But may I be permitted to invoke my countrymen to pause and deliberate before they determine to destroy this, the grandest temple which has ever been dedicated to human freedom since the world began. . . . It is not every wrong—nay, it is not every grievous wrong—which can justify a resort to such a fearful alternative. This ought to be the last desperate remedy of a despairing people after every other constitutional means of conciliation has been exhausted."

There was scattered applause from members of Congress when he finished his speech. As he stepped down and walked past his fellow legislators, a few of the senators shook his hand.

Rose sighed. He had tried so hard to keep the country together, to mend its differences by conciliation. It was beyond conciliation. The die was cast, by both the North and the South, and in opposite directions. Buchanan would not admit it, but it was, no less, a fact. He was a leader. He had not shirked his duty. But he had lost.

Christmas was truly a solemn occasion in Rose's house, as it was in most other homes in Washington and throughout the nation. There were no parties. Families gathered but the celebrations were quiet and subdued. Rose made no plans for visiting on New Year's Day as she usually did. Nor did she attend any sort of celebration.

It was well that she did not. For finally, the inevitable—about which she had been forewarned—happened. On December 31, South Carolina passed an ordnance of secession from the Union.

Again, the week following, Rose was in the gallery of the Senate, now sitting with Varina Davis, when word was received that Mississippi had followed South Carolina in breaking away from the Union.

Senator Jefferson Davis stood up and strode heavily to the rostrum to speak. There was utter silence as he began. "Mr. Calhoun advocated the doctrine of nullification which he proclaimed to be peaceful, to be within the limits of state power, not to disturb the Union but only to be a means of bringing the agent before the tribunal of the states for their judgment. . . . Secession belongs to a different class of remedies. It is to be justified upon the basis that the states are sovereign. There was a time when none denied it.

348

"I am sure I feel no hostility to you, senators from the North. I am sure there is not one of you, whatever sharp discussion there might have been between us, to whom I cannot now say in the presence of God, I wish you well . . . it only remains for me to bid you a final adieu."

Rose cried unashamedly as Davis walked out of the Senate chambers, sometimes stopping to say a word to one of his fellow senators or shake someone's hand.

"He did not sleep at all last night," Varina whispered to Rose.

"His voice was so thin and taut," Rose replied, deeply affected.

"He was almost crying. What he was really doing was begging for peace."

"But no one heard."

"No one wants to listen."

Varina rose to go and Rose followed. They were forced to press their way through the huge crowd that had attended the session.

"We are leaving Washington, Rose," Varina said. "We are taking everything that can be moved back to our home."

"I am sorry to see you go. I shall help you pack your belongings."

The next two days she spent at the Davis home, helping them pack their clothing, silver, furniture, china, and bric-a-brac. It was sad. They talked very little, and then in somewhat hushed tones. The weather was cold and dreary. Everything seemed to be conspiring to make the situation as gloomy as possible, as if someone had died.

Rose bade them goodbye with tears in her eyes. "Promise that you will keep in touch with me."

"Yes, we must, Rose. I shall write to you at every opportunity." Then they were gone.

XX

Action

Spring 1861

Florida, Alabama, Georgia, Louisiana, and Texas quickly followed the first two southern states in seceding from the Union.

Buchanan was in a desperate state of mind as he came to Rose. "They are breaking up the Union. Seven states have seceded. What can we do?" he wailed.

"You can do nothing. What should you do? They have exercised their prerogative."

"We are witnessing the destruction of the Union."

"Do not blame the South. It is the North, arrogant, revengeful, and unmindful of the needs of the southern states."

"I am working with the congressional leaders who remain to establish a harmonious solution to the situation."

"Poppycock! Your Congress is idly sitting by, hoping, waiting, praying that no further action will be taken to upset the precarious ship of state. Surely you have heard both northern and southern sympathizers refer to them as the 'Peace Congress.'"

"Is peace such an odious objective?"

Rose was determined to gather as much information as possible now, for when she thought of the Union it was no longer 'we,' but 'they.' Senator Lane could give her vital information as to what steps the government planned as the emergency became acute. He did not come to see her as much as she wished. Actually, he seemed frightened. In answer to her urgent plea to come to her, he replied, on congressional stationery, "Your note is read. Believe me or not, you cannot be more wretched than I am. I cannot now explain. Let it suffice until we meet that for the last few days every movement and act of mine have been watched with hawk-eyed vigilance. For your sake more than my own I have been compelled to be cautious. But tomorrow morning at ten I will see you at all hazards. Joe."

Was he imagining that he was being closely watched? He was only performing his normal duties as a senator. Or was someone aware that he was giving her information concerning the military defenses of the city? She dismissed the thought lightly from her mind. No one could possibly know what transpired between the two of them. Of course, their friendship was common knowledge, but that was not a crime.

When he still did not come, she sent him a stern note demanding an explanation for his failure to see her and bring the information that he had promised. His plaintive answer came the next day. "I fully intended to come at the hour appointed this morning—but was not up until nearly the time—and then found three or four gentlemen waiting to see me on important business. You well know I love you—and will sacrifice anything on my own account. I have feared bringing you into trouble—for I repeat to you that spies are put upon me, but I will try to elude them tonight and once more have a happy hour in spite of fate. Joe."

Obviously, he was imagining spies all about him. She was closely attuned to all capital activity and she had heard nothing about the ferreting out of spies. Then a strange and startling event occurred. She received word that her long-standing friend, Senator William Gwin, had been arrested for espionage. It was a blow to her. She knew that he had been collecting military information for the South but had considered it perfectly harmless. Actually he was doing no more than she

351

herself was. He was fighting with all his strength for the cause which he thought to be just. So was she. But when she heard that he had been arrested and was actually being detained in prison, she had second thoughts about the casual attitude she had attached to her own activities. Perhaps poor Senator Lane did have cause to worry. She resolved that she would be more cautious. But how else could she serve as a martyr to the cause of the downtrodden South without doing so flagrantly, boldly, bravely?

Ten days later, Buchanan came to her early in the afternoon, his usually carefully groomed clothes in complete disarray.

"South Carolina shore batteries have fired on a U.S. ship," he blurted out.

"What would you expect if a strange ship ventured into its harbor?"

"We were only trying to reinforce Fort Sumter. The Senate is demanding that military action be taken against South Carolina."

"Any such action will surely lead to war!"

"This is why I have hesitated to order our ships to fire. But when they are fired upon—"

"Instruct your secretary of navy, Toucey, to forbid U.S. ships from entering all southern ports. There will be no need for confrontation."

"I'll do that. God, the pressure is becoming unbearable. Congress is clamoring that reinforcements be sent to Fort Sumter."

"If you send them, it will only prompt the South to meet the challenge with armed resistance."

"I realize this. If I am forced to arm any of our southern forts it will be a great mistake."

"Stand your ground. Do not make such a mistake. Every mistake is a product of all the mistakes before it. Both sides will pay for them dearly."

In the midst of the tense, almost unbearable situation in the country, Kansas was admitted to the Union on January 29,

1861 as the thirty-fourth state. Rose gave the matter only passing notice, for it was not admitted as a slave state as Buchanan had recommended, but joined the nation with a state constitution which totally forbade slavery. Rose had always been proud to witness the expansion of the nation by the addition of one more state. Now, she observed coldly to herself, it would just be another state to fight against the South.

Rose kept in touch with Varina Davis and many of her southern friends who had returned to the South. She knew from them before it became public knowledge that they had decided upon a meeting of southern leaders to take place on February 8 in Montgomery, Alabama. At that meeting they organized as a governing body, formally declaring the Confederate States of America! Rose could not know beforehand, but she soon learned that, on the following day, they unanimously selected Jefferson Davis as their president. She was delighted. They could not have selected a more capable man.

She continued to visit military installations and became familiar with officers at all of the depots in Washington. She was collecting a great deal of information concerning their personnel, their supplies, and their orders. In addition, she continually prodded Senators Lane and Wilson to learn what the Senate Military Committee was contemplating. General McClellan kept in constant touch with the senators, and she made it a point to see every letter that he wrote as well as the committee's replies. In an effort to appease her incessant demands, Lane finally agreed to give her daily copies of the committee's minutes.

She knew that the army was seriously disorganized, and she reviewed McClellan's scheme for complete reorganization.

"You should discourage this at all cost," she told Senator Wilson. "In these trying times such activities will surely be interpreted by the Confederacy as a belligerent act against them."

"The committee is unanimous in that they don't give a good goddamn what the Confederacy thinks! The public is demanding a strong armed force, and we are going to see that they get it."

She reviewed the current strength of the navy with the senator and asked about their plans for its expansion. "I suppose your committee will go along with the navy's plans for expansion on the same grounds."

"Positively."

"You will rue the day that you do. Mark my word."

"Already there is great dissatisfaction with Buchanan's orders to move our naval forces into northern waters to keep them away from southern ports."

"Does your committee want war? Is that it?"

"We wish to be prepared for any contigency."

"Little boys who strut around with chips on their shoulders usually succeed in finding a fight."

"Worse that the little boy has no defense for a fight if he should be confronted with an aggressor."

"The South will never be cast in the role of an aggressor."

"We shall see."

Rose had long since determined that her friend Ed Pringle in California agreed wholeheartedly with her southern sympathies. Now she received a letter from him. "How are you in these times that try men's souls? Perhaps after all, thanks to Seward and Wilson, you may do more with the incoming than the outgoing powers. It will do you well to make friends with the Mammon of Unrighteousness, for there is where the power will rest for the next four years. Get what we can out of anybody upon whom we can prevail. We must be Bohemians in politics.

"Bravo over the postponement of the Point Lobos case. It is a drop of comfort to have succeeded in one thing. Actually, Rose, I am not a disunionist per se, and I still believe reconstruction is possible. My own state of South Carolina will not go back, at least for a time, but the others might soon return on a good compromise. Although I do feel uneasy about war. War or no, I am coming east to visit my mother in South Carolina, for she is ill, and who knows how much longer she will be granted time on this earth."

Lincoln was inaugurated on March 4. He would have been somewhat disturbed and probably more careful to have Rose's activities closely monitored if he had read the letter that she sent to Varina Davis. "I saw foreshadowed what was to follow and I desired to obtain a thorough insight into the plans and schemes of those who are destined to become the prominent actors in the fearful drama, in order that I might turn it to the advantage of my country when the hour for action arrives. To this end I have employed every capacity with which God has endowed me and the result has been far more successful than my hopes could have flattered me to expect. I have verbatim reports of every caucus, of every Cabinet council, beginning with the hasty conclave convened on the morning of Lincoln's unexpected arrival in masquerade at Willard's Hotel; I am well aware that Mrs. Lincoln boxed the ears of a buxom chambermaid who inclined too amiably to receive the salute of her illustrious spouse."

Lincoln did not know that anyone except the few involved were aware of his change of trains at Baltimore to avoid a threat to his life. Nor did he imagine that Rose O'Neal Greenhow knew about his entering the capital at a different time than originally planned, covered with a black coat and heavy blanket to hide his true identity.

Rose had no intention of attending the inaugural or the ball that followed, mainly because Gertrude was too sick to leave the house, and the doctors had warned her there was little hope of her recovery. She sat by Gertrude's bed reading the accounts of the inauguration and the ball. She sighed as she thought of the many gay inauguration balls she had been so closely associated with.

Shortly afterward she received a letter from her son-in-law Moore which she found greatly disturbing. "As you are no doubt aware, I am for the Union, right or wrong, and I hope Uncle Abe will be firm and use force with the secessionists where needed. I will do all in my power to support the government as long as there is one state remaining to represent the confederation." How could the husband of her own flesh and blood be so blind? But neither he nor Florence must ever know of her true feelings. "Why not come out west, dear mama?" she read on. "My own situation is continually improving. I could assure you of two fine horses and eight to ten young officers to ride with you." Poor, misguided Captain Moore!

She made a courtesy call on Lincoln and wished him well. He was most civil to her, but it was obvious that each viewed the other warily, knowing full well that they were as far apart in their thinking as two human adversaries could possibly be.

Rose was quite disdainful of the women that the Black Republicans were bringing into the capital. Their husbands were to be the backbone of the new administration. "They are not of a class to shed much luster on the Republican court," she wrote to Buchanan, who had left the capital two days after the inauguration for a complete rest at his lovely Wheatlands estate. "The refinement and grace which once constituted the charm of Washington life has long since departed, and, like its former freedom, is now, alas, a tradition only."

She was even more disdainful of the way her niece Addie and the despicable Douglas so enthusiastically made friends with both Mr. and Mrs. Lincoln. "Addie is actually Mrs. Lincoln's strongest defender whenever anyone snubs or insults her," she fumed to her sister.

Colonel Keyes came to visit her later in March. She had attempted to secure information from him in his position as General Scott's military aide, but he flatly refused to give her any vital information. Their relationship had cooled considerably, but she still thought a great deal of him and had hopes of being able to use him to her advantage.

She greeted him warmly. "I have not seen you for so long,

356

I feared you no longer thought of me."

"No man would ever forget you, my Wild Rose, once they had known you."

"I have heard quite differently. A certain tall, handsome widow from Mississippi."

"Mrs. Bass?"

"The same. Not to mention the irresistible Mrs. Slidell."

"They are only passing fancies."

"Yes? How was your comment worded? 'As I conversed with her, I thought more of lutes and bowers than of guns and drums and camps.'"

Colonel Keyes's mouth dropped open in astonishment. "Rose, how did you—?"

"Do you deny it?"

"I only said that to my adjutant at headquarters. Have you been spying on me?"

"Of course not. But there was certain information I had to secure for myself since you refused to give it to me. In the course of my discussions at your headquarters, I cannot help it if the soldiers choose to offer me bits of gossip as well."

"Rose, you are treading on dangerous ground. Should there be a war—"

"There will be a war. In spite of your stubbornness, if you are wounded and captured, I shall bring you comfort in prison."

"That is most thoughtful of you."

"You do not have to serve. If you should resign, I am sure I can find a pleasant position for you right here in Washington."

"The army is my life."

"It is a dangerous life. Not only in battle, but there is such sickliness on the southern coasts in summer. You are subjecting yourself to all of these dangers needlessly."

"I have received advice from other sources encouraging me to transfer to the regular militia. I have been assured that nothing can kill me but a bullet."

"The encouragement, no doubt, of a northern damsel."

"Not as beautiful as you, my dear, but every bit as persuasive."

She leaned closer to him and put her hand on his arm. "You make light of the situation, but you should know the dangers you will confront, having experienced them in the Mexican War."

"It is no use, Rose. I have come here tonight to tell you I am resigning my assignment with General Scott. I fully intend to join an active military unit."

"Nothing that I can say will deter you?"

"Nothing."

"May I fetch you some brandy?"

"No, thank you, Rose. I must be going." He stood up and as he did so Rose quickly came to him. She put her arms on his shoulders and brought her body close to him.

He put his arms around her and drew her to him. Cradling her head in his arm, he kissed her soundly. Bending her backwards he crushed her against him and kissed her passionately. Slowly he raised his hand to her breast and in a circular motion squeezed it against her body. His lips found hers and he kissed her with the same soft, glowing warmth of long ago.

She clasped her hands in his and drew him toward the sofa. "Nothing can change your mind?"

He ran his hand softly over hers, then pushed himself away. "No, my dear. You are still a beautiful woman but I must do my duty as I see fit. I am going to fight for the cause that I believe is right."

"Even if you are wrong?"

He smiled. "It is my solemn opinion that beautiful women ought to be considered as contraband of war and captured wherever found and detained till after the fight under the guard of old persons of their own sex."

She shook her head fiercely. "Don't say that! You are making light of our beautiful love. Can't you see that you are breaking my heart?"

"No one will ever break your heart, my Wild Rose." He took her chin in his hand. "I found that out years ago."

"Then this is goodbye?"

"Goodbye, Rose. I hope that we will meet again under much more pleasant circumstances."

"So do I."

He kissed her again, passionately, and then he turned quickly away from her. He walked slowly to the door and she followed. As she opened the door, he grabbed her arm. "Be careful what you do, Rose."

"You will be in more danger than I."

"I wonder." He looked at her for a moment. He started to say something, then thought better of it. Turning abruptly, he left.

Later in that same month, Gertrude died. Although Rose was somewhat prepared for her death by her long illness, it still came as a shock to her. She cried incessantly, and donning the black clothes of mourning, she vowed that she would not wear anything but black ever again. She remained secluded in her home for several weeks. Pringle, who had been in South Carolina, came up to Washington to see her.

"Rose," he said, shocked at her sickly appearance as she greeted him. "Rose, you have been brooding over this for too long. It is unfortunate, but you can always know that you did all that you could to save her from suffering. No mother could ever have been more faithful and kind to her daughter. But there is work to do, Rose. Great work to be done. We must be ready for it. Prepare all your batteries. Get your arms in order."

She smiled at him. "It's good to see you, Ed. Your call to action does me good."

"Bosh, Rose. We are wasting valuable time. The crisis is upon us. We have a twofold purpose now. Our Point Lobos leases and our new country, as well. Both of them require all of our attention. I need a copy of the memorandum you

359

mentioned you were going to the Senate with."

"You mean the questions I planned to ask Senator Wilson?"

"Yes, and I need the map of Point Lobos. I have just met Black and had a long and rather satisfactory talk. Also, look among your papers for the letter from the Engineer Department to the War Department which gave a description of the government reserves. That information is going to be most valuable."

"Yes. I will, I will. Excuse me but a moment, Ed, and I will get the papers for you." She hurried upstairs and in a short time was back with the papers Ed had mentioned. "You are right, Ed. I can do nothing about the loss of my dear girl. There is much to be done. I can help, and I will."

"Good. This show of military strength in the capital is appalling, my dear Rose. It contributes nothing and only serves to antagonize all thinking people."

"It was a grave mistake to bring in poor old General Scott who is only resting uneasily on his laurels."

"I vow, ammunition vehicles and marching military companies in the streets of the capital are a menace."

"They imply a foreign enemy is at our very door. It is an insult to the good people of Maryland and Virginia."

"It will certainly strengthen the secession movement in those states."

"Buchanan would never have permitted this sword rattling."

"Nor would he have succumbed to the rabble-rousers' demands to reinforce Fort Sumter."

"I declare, this inept government seems to be purposely baiting our southern comrades."

"Stop it wherever you can, Rose."

"I have spoken to Senator Wilson and Senator Lane. They advise me that Senator Baker of Oregon has the ear of the president. I shall see him."

"Good. We must not let a single opportunity go by."

"You are right, Ed."

He left in a flurry of enthusiasm. Immediately Rose had her buggy hitched up and drove directly to the Senate, where she called on Senator Baker.

Despite the fact that they were on opposite sides, they chatted amiably about old times, when he had worked with her husband on many land claims in California. Then she adroitly brought up the subject presently uppermost in her mind.

"Why is the president so intent on strengthening the defenses of Fort Sumter at such a time?"

"Because it is sadly undermanned and undersupplied."

"Such a move will surely antagonize the southerners. It might cause open conflagration, which is to be avoided at all costs. The South will be so resentful that they may attempt to intercept the supplies. This could only result in military confrontation. The blood of both the North and the South would needlessly be shed."

"It is true a great many lives may be lost and we may not succeed in reinforcing Fort Sumter. But the president was elected by a northern majority and they are now becoming dissatisfied; and the president owes it to them to strike some blow by which he will make a unified northern party."

"Are you telling me that the die is cast—that there is no hope for a peaceful settlement of our differences?"

"I am only saying that the situation is grave. The president is doing what he believes is best for our country."

"Cannot you convince him to do otherwise?"

"I cannot, nor will I. I agree with him that a firm stand must be taken."

"Even if it should lead to war?"

"If blood must be shed in the performance of our duty, so be it."

"It may be your own blood, senator. You are Commander of the First Regiment of California Volunteers though you have moved to Oregon."

361

"Many lives have been lost in the building of our great nation." He looked at her gravely. "I can only say to you, thank God that we still have heroic men who are willing to die to protect our country."

Rose was saddened as she drove home. It was disastrous that the new administration was so stubbornly convinced it must show a strong, iron-fisted hand. She knew the feelings of her southern compatriots, who were just as firmly against such actions. The opposing forces were surely headed for open confrontation.

That night she wrote a sad, bitter letter to her old friend Bishop Kip in San Francisco, who had been such a comfort to her whenever she was faced with an unbearable burden.

"'Illinois first' may now be recorded of these United States. The old confederation is rapidly crumbling to pieces. Section division is widening, sectional hate growing stronger. The feeling, the language of the dominant, the aggressive party from the sterile coast of Oregon to the granite hills of New Hampshire is insulting and hard to bear. Coercion at the point of the bayonet or the cannon's mouth, or unconditional surrender are the mild alternatives offered us.

"Surrender this heritage of which the gods might be proud, to the Puritans, the wooden nutmegmaker, the Yankee peddlers of New England? Every feeling of honor, every feeling of humanity cries no. Then do you wonder that the South, with the alternative of national degradation before her, should choose the lesser of the two evils—and that the cry to arms should resound from the mouth of the Chesapeake to the Gulf of Mexico? That we should hold up our national flag and guard it as sacredly as the masters of old fighting for the sepulcher of Christ?"

Fort Sumter had become the focal point of the opposing factions of the North and the South. South Carolina demanded that it be handed over to them, since it was within their state boundary. When Lincoln became president, he proclaimed that Fort Sumter was United States government property, and as such formed a vital part of the federal government's defense. Efforts to reinforce the Fort were met with stubborn refusal on the part of the southern leaders. On April 8, in desperation, Lincoln advised Governor Pickens of South Carolina that he was sending a naval expedition down to provision the beleaguered garrison. Three days later General Beauregard replied that reinforcements would not be permitted and demanded that Major Anderson in command of the Fort surrender. The major flatly refused.

Rose wrote a hasty note to Buchanan. "We have the war upon us. Both nations will now be called to arms. The effort to reinforce Sumter will fail. In less than twenty-four hours Major Robert Anderson will have surrendered; and in less than thirty days Jefferson Davis will be in possession of Washington."

The following day, acting on orders received from the newly formed Confederate government, General Beauregard began the bombardment of the fort. It continued incessantly for thirty-four hours before Major Anderson was finally forced to surrender. The belligerent attitudes of both the North and the South had finally exploded head-on. The Civil War, or, as Rose excitedly called it, "the war between the states" had begun.

Rose read the *Washington Evening Star* of April 14, 1861, with bitter apprehension.

"PRESIDENT CALLS FOR 75,000 VOLUNTEERS," the headline blared. "Overwhelming force needed to fight the rebels," the news story continued. Then it went on to say that President Lincoln had ordered a blockade of southern ports to cut them off from supplies needed by the South.

So it was to be a battle to the end. The South would meet the challenge. The Mammon of Unrighteousness was determined to see blood running in the streets of Washington. The onus was on him. But the South would unite as a single body and fight him until victory.

Rose could be of great help to the southern cause and she was fully prepared to be. She would devote her every effort, her mind, and her body to helping the Confederate States remove themselves from the oppressive heel of the northern aggressors. She and they would defy the damned Yankees. She and they would win. The Union would soon learn what a formidable foe they had in the heart of their own capital when they matched wits with Rose O'Neal Greenhow!

XXI

Secrets

Spring 1861

Ten days after the ignoble fall of Fort Sumter and fairly late
in the evening, Rose was interrupted in her letter-writing by a
strange caller. It was a particularly warm evening and Rose had
left the front door open to allow a cooling breeze to blow into
the house. The stranger rang the door gong and then
impetuously knocked on the sill of the open door.

Rose quickly went to the door. "Yes?"

"Do I have the pleasure of speaking with Mrs. Rose O'Neal
Greenhow?"

"You do, sir. May I inquire who is addressing me?"

"Sorry, ma'am. I should have introduced myself right off. I
am Colonel Thomas Jordan."

"How do you do, colonel?"

They stood awkwardly staring at each other in the open
door. "May I come in?"

"I—I am sorry, colonel. Is it not a rather inappropriate time
for an officer to be calling unannounced on a lady?"

"It is that. But I can explain if you will give me a few
moments."

Rose hesitated. The man was tall and good looking.
Although he was dressed in the uniform of the northern army,
she was sure she could detect a decided southern accent.
"Please come in," she said shortly. She went into her parlor
and he followed her. With a slight feeling of trepidation she

announced, "I am not completely alone, you know. My slaves have not retired as yet. My personal slave is in the dining room shining our silver."

The colonel gave her a disarmingly warm smile. "I assure you, madam, there will be no need for you to call them to your rescue."

"I wasn't thinking of that. I am sure I can trust the honor of a military man. It is just that in these trying times one cannot be too careful."

"You are correct. And I urge you to continue to be most vigilant."

"Please sit down." She sat in her favorite armchair and motioned him to a lounge chair facing her. There was an awkward pause. "Will you have a drink of coffee? Or perhaps something more potent?"

"No, thank you. I can stay only a few moments." Colonel Jordan crossed his legs and again smiled at her. "I have been advised that you favor the cause of the South in this struggle that has been forced upon us."

"Is it the intention of the army to investigate every person who has ever expressed sympathy for the southern cause?"

"Don't let my uniform deceive you, ma'am. I am resigning my commission with the U.S. Army."

"Military life does not appeal to you now that your country has declared war?"

"The army is my life, Mrs. Greenhow. I graduated from West Point."

"Then I do not understand, colonel."

"While at the Point I roomed with William T. Sherman."

"Who has already resigned his commission to fight on the side of the South."

"I myself am joining the Virginia militia."

"That is most commendable. You are correct, sir, I am most critical of the high-handed attitude of the northern states in ignoring the plight of the South."

"Then you do favor the South in this unfortunate war?"

"I do. But it is not my intention to say or do anything that will incriminate me while I am still residing in the center of the enemy's camp, so to speak."

"I am very pleased to hear that, ma'am."

"What are you trying to tell me, colonel? What is your mission here at this late hour?"

"I believe you are, or were, friendly with Mr. and Mrs. Jefferson Davis while they resided in Washington."

"Varina Davis was one of my closest friends."

"Mr. Davis personally suggested that I contact you."

"Oh?"

"He said that no woman in Washington knew more statesmen, diplomats, officers, and businessmen, both from the North and South, than yourself."

"I am pleased to hear that Mr. Davis holds me in high esteem."

"If you do not mind my saying so, Mrs. Greenhow, Mr. Davis told me you are deeply involved with official Washington. It was he who vouched that you were dedicated to the Confederate cause."

"You have seen Mr. Davis recently?"

"I talked with him extensively less than a fortnight ago."

"Since the declaration of war?"

"Yes. I agreed with him that such assets as he attributed to you are admirable qualifications in my business."

"Just what is your business, Colonel Jordan?"

"I believe we can be quite frank, Mrs. Greenhow?"

"If you are as close an associate of Mr. Davis as you say you are, I assure you we can."

"Where the South is concerned?"

"Where the South is concerned."

"Good. Would you consider contributing your efforts to this cause?"

"I have already done so. I have determined the strength of several military installations in this area by personally visiting them."

"You have?" Colonel Jordan was silent for a moment before continuing. "Do you have this information available?"

"I do, sir. Would you care to see it?"

"I would be most happy to."

Rose went to a drawer of her living room table and reaching behind some other papers drew out a thick packet of closely written papers and handed them to him. He looked them over carefully, then whistled softly.

"This information is invaluable to the South. May I have these?"

"Why do you want them?"

He rubbed his chin as he looked directly at Rose, then, clearing his throat, spoke to her in a low voice. "This is what my business consists of, Mrs. Greenhow. I am engaged in ferreting out such information as this, sometimes at great risk, and forwarding it to the South for their use in developing their military plans."

"That is the activity of a spy."

He looked toward the rear of the house, then leaned closer to her as he asked, "Can your slaves be trusted, Mrs. Greenhow?"

"They have all been with me for years. Actually, they are considered a part of the family."

"My assignment for the Confederacy is espionage. Before resigning my commission I have established a group of agents in all parts of the city to collect the needed information for the Confederacy. We also have our people scattered over a large part of the entire country."

"You have already developed this system?"

"Yes. Mr. Davis said you were the best-equipped person to exact secrets from the Black Republicans. These papers indicate that you have already had such thoughts in mind."

"I knew that this information would be needed. I had not yet determined what should be done with it."

"Will you now officially join our operation, Mrs. Greenhow?"

"You mean spy for you?"

"Yes."

Without a moment's hesitation Rose broke into a broad grin. "I will be delighted."

"Good. Let me tell you more of our plans. I am leaving this weekend to join General Beauregard's staff. I shall be his adjutant general. You are to keep in constant contact with me, on a daily basis, if at all possible. But you must address your communications to Thomas J. Rayford, which is my alias."

"I will only be doing on a professional basis what I have been attempting to accomplish as an amateur."

"But, more than that, Mrs. Greenhow—"

"You may call me Rose."

"Thank you, Rose. We wish you to go even further. It is our desire that you head our operation in the capital."

Rose's eyes sparkled as she excitedly thought of her new assignment. "I will do so gladly."

"We shall instruct our agents to deliver their reports here at 398 16th Street. We will have a carrier come to you daily at the same time."

"How will I know them?"

"We will advise you of the names of each of them. In addition, they will give you the password. The password will be changed each month. During this first month the word is "managing," which must be answered by the word "affairs." Our agents have specific instructions not to pass on any information until both of those words have been spoken. You are to do the same."

"I understand!"

"All communications will be coded. The code will also be changed on the first day of each month. Our current code is simple. Let me show you." He drew out a paper and pencil and explained the code his people were presently using. "It is basically the same code that Julius Caesar used in his campaign. You will merely move each letter four letters down the alphabet. A becomes D, B becomes E, and C becomes F. If any communication passes into the wrong hands, it will make no sense. Without this key, no one will be able to read the message. You must use the code at all times." He took the paper upon which he had drawn the code, and twisting it into a long thin strip, touched it to a candle. Throwing it into a china dish, he watched until it was completely destroyed by the flame.

"When do I start?"

"You have already started, Rose. The information in these papers will go directly to General Beauregard's headquarters. They will be checked for their authenticity—"

"There is no need. I personally secured it."

"All information received is first checked. Many times one of our agents unwittingly gathers false information purposely made available to deceive us."

"I know my sources, colonel."

"That is fine, Rose. In this case it will only be given a casual check. Then it will be studied by our staff of military advisers and a dossier will be established of all places and persons mentioned."

"I may have additional information that could prove of value to you," Rose said enthusiastically as she went to her desk. Searching through her papers, she brought out a memorandum which she handed to Colonel Jordan.

His eyes widened as he read the brief message:

"Lt. General Winfield Scott
U.S. Army Headquarters
Washington, D.C.
Urgently require reinforcements. Have only forty-eight
(48) men total organization. Lt. Roger Jones."

"The message was sent by the commander of the garrison at Harper's Ferry," explained Rose importantly.

"We know of Lieutenant Jones. Rose, this is incredible! May I inquire how you came into possession of such a military document?"

"It never reached its destination. The man Lieutenant Jones gave the message to wanted no part of this war and he deserted. He gave the message to a friend of mine to deliver in his stead. The latter was a southern sympathizer who, knowing that I was collecting such data, gave it to me. I was not quite certain of its value, but I decided to retain it rather than forward it on to General Scott's headquarters."

"This information is priceless. There are several million dollars' worth of ordnance supplies stored at this important post."

"That is why Jones wishes reinforcements."

"Exactly. He does not have sufficient men to protect his garrison."

"It can readily be overpowered and the supplies captured."

"If we act promptly." Colonel Jordan quickly stood up, and as Rose followed, he took her hands in his and pressed them firmly. "Rose, Jefferson Davis was never more correct than in recommending you to head our operation in the capital. I am convinced that we have enlisted the most important link in our chain of espionage, which I now willingly turn over to your command."

"Thank you, colonel."

"I am immediately changing my plans. I shall start for Colonel Beauregard's headquarters tonight. This information will be in his hands before tomorrow night."

"I am glad that I can serve the southern cause."

"You will hear more of our operation from your newspapers. We desperately need those supplies, and now they are within our grasp. I am sorry that I must leave so quickly, Rose, but you understand the necessity for action as quickly as possible." He started toward the door then turned to her. "Your messenger will be a pretty young girl named Betty Duvall. You will recognize her by the code words that I have given you. Send all of your messages through her and see that they are entirely in code. Sign yourself ROG. We will recognize your initials."

As he opened the door and started to leave, she grasped his arm. "What type of information is most vital to you?"

"We need the names of ranking officers, starting with the rank of captain, and their addresses. We want mobilization and contingency plans revealing what action the military will take upon being attacked. We should have the precise location and significance of vital targets, including carefully hidden fortifications, mountain redoubts, storage depots, and command centers." He smiled as he watched Rose listening intently to him. "I doubt if you can remember all that I have said to you but I—"

"I have made a mental note of all of your requirements," Rose replied. Then she repeated word for word his entire list of vital information required.

Colonel Jordan listened to her in awe. "You are an amazing woman, Rose. I hope I may have the pleasure of knowing you better as our association progresses."

"Let us hope so, colonel." She smiled her most bewitching smile.

Early the next morning Rose left for the Senate chambers to see Senator Wilson. She was not going to leave their next meeting to chance. However, she was disappointed to learn that he had left his office the previous day with a sickly fever, advising his staff that he would probably not return for the balance of the week.

Seeing the disappointed look on her face, his aide quickly said to her, "If there is anything that I can do, I shall be glad to be of assistance."

"No, thank you," she said casually. "It is merely a matter concerning military personnel I had volunteered to contact for him."

"If it is military, Mrs. Greenhow, the Senate Military Committee has just recently opened an office at the War Department. Perhaps they can help you."

"Then I shall see them."

"They are located on the main floor in the rear of the

building by the archives."

"Thank you." She smiled at the young man. "I shall tell Senator Wilson how helpful you have been."

The aide smiled self-consciously. "Thank you, Mrs. Greenhow."

Hurriedly she went over to the War Department and found the Senate Military Committee's office.

She went into the room and confronted a young man seated at his desk near the door. Immediately he rose.

"I am Mrs. Greenhow," she introduced herself.

"Oh yes, Mrs. Greenhow," the clerk replied flustered. "I have heard the military committee speak of you often."

"I trust that it has been complimentary."

"Very much so." The young man's face reddened as he continued. "They were most flattering in their praise. I must say, however, if you will pardon me, ma'am, that they did not do you justice."

"Why thank you, Mr.—"

"My name is Callan, ma'am. John F. Callan."

"Well, Mr. Callan. Perhaps you can tell me where I might find Senator Wilson."

"He is not here. I believe his office said that he went home yesterday feeling ill."

"I am sorry to hear that. I thought perhaps—"

"Can I help you, Mrs. Greenhow?"

"Well, there was a project that Senator Wilson had requested that I undertake for him. He said that his office in the War Department might be of assistance."

"I shall certainly do whatever I can."

"The services are expanding so rapidly it is almost impossible to keep up with them. Senator Wilson pointed out that I have been derelict in my duties. You see I write to each one of our officers as they are mustered in. I have been failing to do so. I think it is important to offer a word of encouragement to our men who are being called upon to defend our country, sometimes at the cost of their very lives.

373

Don't you agree, Mr. Callan?"

"Yes, I do. This is most considerate of you, Mrs. Greenhow."

"You may call me Rose."

"Rose?" Callan replied, startled.

"Yes, that is my name."

"Oh, I—I—"

"Say it. It is not a difficult name."

"Rose." Callan almost breathed the name.

"That is fine. And I shall call you John. May I?"

"I would consider it an honor if you would Mrs.—uh, Rose."

"Now tell me. Do you know if there is an available list of the officers of our armed forces?"

"I myself have such a list. It is one of my duties to keep the list up to date, no small chore these days, I can assure you." He lifted the top of his slanted desk and drew out a sizable pamphlet and handed it to her.

She casually thumbed through the pages. Listed thereon were the names, rank, military addresses as well as home addresses of all of the officers of each command. "This is exactly what we had in mind, John. May I have a copy of this?"

"I don't know, Rose. It isn't classified, but there are only a few limited copies available."

"There is no harm in my having it, I'm sure." As Callan hesitated she quickly added, "If there is any question, you may contact Senator Wilson."

"Oh, no, no; it's just that—well, I guess it is all right for you to have a copy!"

"Thank you, John." She smiled her most disarming smile. "I shall make it a point to tell Senator Wilson how cooperative you have been."

"Thank you, ma'am."

She tucked the pamphlet into her large handbag and started to leave. "It has been a pleasure meeting you, John; I hope we may meet again in the not too distant future." At the door, she capriciously threw him a kiss.

Completely flustered and overcome by her companionable attitude, he absentmindedly waved to her as she left. Both of them knew that it was against military regulations as well as the law to distribute a list of military personnel. "But it happened so quickly," Callan mused to himself as he settled back on his high stool and tried to lose himself in his work at hand. "I really couldn't help myself."

When Rose returned home she was rather bewildered to receive a letter from Captain Moore. "Good for old James Madison Cutts, Jr. He has made Florence and myself both tremendously proud of him by joining the First Rhode Island Volunteers!" Rose crumpled the brief note in her hand and grimaced. Ellen had made no mention of her son's joining the Union army. She undoubtedly did not have the heart. Obviously Ellen had no control over her children. She had already proven this by standing idly by while her daughter married that Douglas person.

Slowly Rose smoothed out the crumpled paper and read on. "Would it be too much trouble, dear Mama, to use your influence in securing a colonelcy for myself with the Ohio Volunteers Regiment? I would also appreciate your securing President Lincoln's assurance that I will not lose my commission in the regular army if I switch to the Ohio unit."

Rose sighed. The poor dears were sadly removed from reality. They did not realize how matters had changed for her in Washington. A different party was in power distributing favorable assignments. Buchanan was gone. A second note was enclosed from her daughter. "Poor Moore is almost beside himself at having to remain here inactive whilst so many are earning laurels. But I thank God for it. Of course he will fight for the Union. And although of course, dear Mama, all my warmest feelings are enlisted for the southerners rather than the Yankees, still I do think the Union should come before all small state feeling, and I do think secessionists a little like traitors. Still, I most earnestly pray Moore may not be engaged in this terrible Civil War. But do what you can for the poor man. And again I say, Mama, it might be best if you and the girls came West and stayed with us until this dreadful conflagration ends." Rose frowned. Her own daughter speaking as a Union sympathizer. But she would do what she could for Moore; they must never know how deeply involved she was now becoming in the cause of the South.

She was interrupted in her troubled thoughts by the door gong. She had instructed her slaves that she herself would answer the door to all callers henceforth, and she went hastily to the door.

She opened the door to a pert, pretty little brunette with sparkling eyes, dressed plainly in a calico farm dress. "Mrs. Greenhow?" the girl asked innocently.

"Yes."

"I am Betty Duvall. I have been wanting to make your acquaintance."

"I don't understand."

"I have been told you were to instruct me in my managing."

"Ah, yes. Affairs. Do come in."

As they seated themselves in Rose's parlor, Betty smiled and asked, "Do you have anything for market today?" She then leaned over and continued in a soft almost-whisper. "Is there anyone within earshot of our conversation?"

"None that we cannot trust."

"Do you have anything for me to take?"

"As a matter of fact, I do." She went to her desk and drew out the pamphlet containing the names and addresses of officers. Can I be assured that this will be delivered to its proper destination?"

"Oh, yes, ma'am. You see, I drive my farm cart out of Washington every other day across the Potomac over the Chain Bridge. Although it is a two-day trip to Mr. Rayford, I spend the night at Lieutenant Catesby Jones's house in Virginia. He was formerly of the U.S. Navy, but is now one of us."

"I am sure that he can be trusted. I hope that we can be assured of the same devotion from our pretty little country girl."

"I was born and raised in Maryland, Mrs. Greenhow. Not so very far from your own village of Poolesville."

Rose smiled. She felt assured that this pretty young girl could be trusted. She handed the pamphlet to her. "You will note this is addressed to Thomas J. Rayford. I was instructed to send all of my messages in code. You can readily see it would not be practical to code this entire pamphlet."

"That will not be necessary. I shall merely throw it under my empty bags and bales with which I am to bring back the daily vegetables which I purchase."

"Oh, no, that will never do," Rose protested. "If you should be stopped it would be too easily discovered. You must hide in on your body."

"Oh, Mrs. Greenhow, that is not necessary."

Rose quickly secured a length of string from her desk as she admonished, "You cannot be too cautious. Now, lift up your dress, my dear."

"But Mrs. Greenhow—"

"Please do as I say, Betty," Rose said sternly.

As the girl lifted her skirt to her waist, her face reddened. "This is most embarrassing."

"All the more reason to believe that we have located a safe place for our message." Rose lifted Betty's petticoats revealing her plain ruffled pantalettes. Reaching underneath the tape that held the pantalettes, Rose placed the pamphlet against Betty's bare body. Quickly she wrapped the string about Betty's waist and tied it securely.

As Betty dropped her dress and petticoats in place she murmured uncomfortably, "Really, Mrs. Greenhow, I hardly think such precautions are necessary."

"It greatly enhances the safe deliverance of this packet."

"If it does not, my modesty will be sadly compromised."

Smiling saucily, she bade Rose goodbye and hurriedly left.

Very few days passed that Rose did not visit a military installation or two throughout the city. As she amiably talked with the officers at each fort, she made mental notes of the exact locations of the gun emplacements, ammunition storage, the number of personnel assigned to each post. Later, when she was alone, she wrote down the information she had gathered, and finally, at home, converted it to brief and concise coded messages.

She visited Salmon Portland Chase to request assistance in securing a colonelcy for Moore, only to learn that all officers' commissions had already been handed out.

On the third day after she had sent her first message through Betty Duvall, Rose was delighted to read that the garrison at Harper's Ferry had been attacked and captured by a contingent of the Confederate forces. During the surprise attack, the fort had been set afire, but most of the supplies had been captured intact.

On May 4, shortly before nightfall, Rose was interrupted while ciphering a message to be sent South, by a tall, stately-looking gentleman who greeted her by saying he had a message for her. A bit apprehensive, she showed him into her parlor and he immediately handed her a brief note. "This will introduce you to Colonel Thompson, a true South Carolina gentleman, who would be happy to take from your hand any communication and obey your injunctions as to disposition of same with dispatch." It was signed Thomas J. Rayford. She recognized his signature as authentic.

Rose casually slipped the note into the bodice of her dress. "Is not a southern gentleman placing himself in no little danger by flagrantly walking the streets of Washington, Colonel Thompson?"

"Oh, no, Mrs. Greenhow, I am a lawyer practicing in this city. I knew your late husband, although I regret not having had the pleasure of making your acquaintance. I presently live on G Street."

"Then you are safe in this city."

"Quite. My reason for this sudden visit is to seek your assistance in transmitting some important information I have received promptly to Richmond."

"But your note advised—"

"I know, Mrs. Greenhow. You see, ordinarily I travel quite frequently and I have several southern clients. So far my journeys have gone unnoticed. However, the material I have in my possession was received at a military conference of the reserves. Mr. Rayford has advised me that you have messengers readily available."

"I have someone calling here almost every day before going on to Richmond."

"Good. May I prevail upon you to forward this to our southern compatriots? You see, I am in the midst of a conference which will continue at least another three days."

He handed her two sheets of paper. They bore the present date of May 4 and were neatly written on the stationery of the War Department. "It is a detailed plan of organization for the increase of the regular army. You can readily observe that it is imperative that this reach our friends as rapidly as possible."

"Yes, of course," Rose agreed. Then she added, smiling, "This will be on its way before nightfall, Colonel."

"Thank you, Mrs. Greenhow."

"You may call me Rose."

"I shall be glad to, Rose. And now I must return to my conference before my absence becomes too obvious." He stood up and as Rose accompanied him to the door he suddenly turned to her. "By the way, are you familiar with William T. Smithson?"

"The banker?"

"Yes."

"I have heard of him but have never had the pleasure of making his acquaintance."

"He lives not far from here, on F Street."

"Why do you mention him?"

"He is one of us. I have been working with him. I can vouch

379

for his loyalty. You can expect a call from him this evening. He also has some data on the military defenses of the city which he is anxious for our friends to receive."

"I am not sure I will be able to recognize him."

"He will introduce himself by his given name although he prefers to be known as Charles R. Cables—for business reasons. He will also give you the password for this month."

"I shall be happy to oblige him."

"Thank you, Rose. I look forward to working with you in the future."

"I hope so, Colonel Thompson. We need all of the help we can muster."

Saluting her, he quickly left. In the days following, Rose worked very closely with both Colonel Thompson and William Smithson, getting to know them very well. They, in turn, introduced her to Frank Rennehan, who lived a few blocks from her house at 408 20th Street, and William J. Walker, a clerk at the main post office. Both of these men proved invaluable to Rose, with Walker going so far as to secure important military information by intercepting military mail sent through the U.S. postal system. He promptly turned over all plans that he received to Rose to forward to the Confederates.

She received a letter through the underground from Mary Lee, the wife of Colonel Lee, who was so valiantly distinguishing himself by his sudden and successful attacks on Union strongholds in the South. She told Rose how delighted the Confederate Army was at the ease with which they had captured the installation at Harper's Ferry. "Twenty thousand light arms were taken, together with tons of sorely needed ammunition and several million dollars' worth of ordnance supplies. It was truly a godsend, since, as President Davis told our Congress, we are without machinery, without means to protect our harbors and commerce on the high seas, and are threatened by a powerful opposition. But we do not despond. We have moved our capital from Montgomery to Richmond,

Virginia, to expedite our lines of communication with our armies. We have already sent agents to our good friends in Europe to buy small arms, guns, and ships, and several niter beds have been set up. Rose, there are going to be many bloody battles before this horrible conflagration is ended. It is a war which is criminally stupid, an unnecessary bloodletting brought on by arrogant extremists and blundering politicians. But it cannot be avoided. For the safety of your family, I beg you to close up your house and come down to our home until the battles are over."

She smiled wanly as she concluded Mary Lee's letter. Obviously she did not know that Rose was taking an active part in the battle between the states, and that her value to the South rested upon her staying at the center of the enemy's camp.

XXII

Turmoil

Summer 1861

Every other day, Betty Duvall came to Rose's house at approximately the same time. Ciphered messages were given to her addressed to Thomas J. Rayford, such as, "The first shipments of reinforcements are being shipped to southern forts via the southern railroad on May 16 exact destinations follow. ROG"; "Minutes of the Senate Military Committee of May 6 attached; received from H. ROG"; "Enclosed plans for new cast iron cannon being installed in all seaport military installations. ROG."

In return she received specific instructions from Rayford as to the information they needed. "Where are they first planning to attack? What is their present strength? Require exact number trained men. Are they fully equipped? Need plans of new army rifle reported invented. Thomas J. Rayford."

It was becoming increasingly difficult to see her friends, Senators Wilson and Lane. She began to rely more and more on the Senate Military Committee's clerk, John F. Callan. He was a good-looking, naive young man, not long away from a farm in Minnesota. Both his parents were active in the politics of the state, so they had had little difficulty in securing a coveted position for him with the Senate Military Committee. He was lonely for his home town and friends and imagined himself madly in love with the vivacious and still beautiful Rose, despite the fact that she was easily of sufficient age to have been his mother.

Rose liked the young man, and, because of the availability of the most secret of military documents, plans, and committee minutes to him, she used her every feminine wile to encourage his affection. Since she had a lifetime of experience behind her in the art of making men do her will, John was easy prey for her. He was a loyal Unionist, but since the way to Rose's heart was in the revelation of military secrets, he soon became her willing accomplice. What did a bit of stodgy military information matter, if a man could gain his goal through them?

One evening when he came to her home, he confided that he had always wanted to be an architect.

"I have a very good friend who is an architect. I am sure he will let you come to his office when you have free time and learn his business."

The friend was a stalwart southern supporter, and on many late evenings Rose accompanied Callan to the architect's office within a block of the War Department. Callan brought prints of northern installations and equipment from the military file with him, and her friend taught him to painfully reproduce accurate sketches of them. The following day each hand-drawn copy would be in the hands of Betty Duvall on the way to Thomas J. Rayford.

One evening they spent almost the entire night copying the Senate Military Committee map of red dotted lines of the army's route to Richmond. This she sent to Thomas Rayford with the coded comment: "thinking this might serve as a lesson to Confederate engineers."

She was overwhelming in her praise of John's natural talent and predicted that he would someday have a fine future in architecture. If he could not secure the documents, he would report their contents, and Rose and her friend would coax him to draw as much detail as possible from memory, a practice designed to promote strict attention to detail and commit the most minute points to memory.

On several nights after grueling hours of drawing sketches of military installations, John would walk home with Rose. On one particular day she had received a most difficult assignment from Rayford. "It is essential that we secure the Embassy Code Book. Our foreign agents abroad must decipher messages falling into their hands."

That night she was mixing a potent Queen Charlotte Cocktail for John as he settled himself comfortably on her parlor sofa, and she casually asked, "Does your office have occasion to refer to the Embassy Code Book?"

"Oh, yes. We have a single copy which is retained in the archives at all times."

"I should like to have a copy." She smiled as she sat down beside him and touched his glass in a toast. "To our happiness," she added.

"I'll drink to that, but I don't know whether I can get the Embassy Code Book for you." Then he startled her as he downed his drink and suddenly said, "You know, a lot of the work that I have been doing might be considered treason if it should come into the hands of the wrong person."

"But, John, all of the sketches that you have drawn have been given to me. You are studying to be a great architect. Some day you will no doubt be able to draw original sketches of such installations. You will be praised far and wide for your prowess and enthusiastic patriotism."

"There are great acts of treason being conducted by the North, Rose. I suppose any of these treasonable acts could be called enthusiastic patriotism."

As she filled his glass with another Queen Charlotte Cocktail, she asked, "What are you referring to?"

"Well, we have spies working for us in the South."

"Are you aware of any?"

"One of them reported to the Military Committee today. He's a colored man who has succeeded in ensconcing himself in the good graces of Jefferson Davis until he has become his personal man."

"He is now working for the rebel president?"

"Yes, and he reports to us on a weekly basis. He poses as a slave, but he is actually a freeman from the North who volunteered for this assignment."

"What is his name?"

"I only know his code name. He signs his reports 'Rufus.' That is the name he goes by in the Davis household."

"I doubt if he can secure much information of value from Mr. Davis's home."

"On the contrary. While pressing Davis's pants one day, he took his keys and had duplicates made before Davis missed them. He also stole the combination to his office safe."

"That could lead to a very serious charge of treason."

"You would rightly think so if you saw some of the reports which he has sent us. He has told us the names of all officers and their assignments. He has advised us what men have been sent to Europe to seek aid for the rebels and we are able to follow each of them closely."

"You can see now how important it is for me to have the Embassy Code Book."

"No, Rose, to tell you the truth, I cannot."

She moved close to him and put her arm about him so quickly he spilled a portion of his drink. Ignoring it, she drew him to her and pressed her partly exposed beautiful breasts against his body. "Because I have an uncontrollable curiosity to know what our government is relaying to the governments of Europe, justifying this bloody, stupid war." He hunched his shoulders self-consciously as she drew his face to hers. Slowly, softly, she took his face in her hands, and closing her eyes, pressed her lips to his. She kissed him gently, then passionately, until she could feel the warmth of his hot face. Her deft maneuvers inflamed his passions. Almost savagely he freed his arms from beneath hers and placed them about her, pressing her even closer to him as they met in a long, passionate kiss. He kissed her again and again with all the fervor of his youth. She could feel his body quiver as she gently took his arm and pressed it hard against her breast.

She was leaning over him now, running her hand through his hair and stroking his cheek. He ran his hands up and down her back as he pressed her even closer to him. Carefully, she moved away from him, and calmly taking his hand in hers, placed it in the opening at the neck of her dress. She slipped her dress aside and placed his hand on her warm, firm breast beneath it. Savagely he pressed his hand against her bare breast, rolling it in a circular motion as he moved his whole body against hers.

She drew his lips apart with her tongue and gave her body up to him as he moved ever quicker beside her. Suddenly she pushed herself away from him. Almost beside himself, he grabbed her, but as he pulled her to him once again, she firmly drew away.

"I—I love you, Rose."

"I love you, John, but we must not lose our heads."

"Why not?" he asked impetuously, as he reached out to draw her to him.

"It would not be proper, John."

"But I love you. I want you. God, I want to show you how much I really love you," he said, breathing heavily.

"No, John."

"Would you give me your all if I gave you the Embassy Code Book?"

"John, I do not measure our love by material objects."

"All right. All right! I'll get the Embassy Code Book for you. Then let us see what you will do for me."

She leaned close to him and kissed him gently. As he was about to take him once again in his arms, she drew away. Pressing her finger to his lips she smiled at him. "You are a sweet, lovely man, John." Slowly she took his arms in her hands and rose, drawing him upward with her. "Now you had better be going before I lose my head entirely."

Reluctantly he followed her as she moved toward the door. "But I want you to lose your head. Good God, I have completely lost mine."

"In due time, John."

He drew a long, weary breath, and stood listlessly beside her, the complete picture of dejection, before he finally spoke, "I can't wait. I must have you for my own, my Wild Rose."

"John," she said, surprised, "I didn't know you knew—"

"I have heard that other men have called you that. Now I know why."

He swallowed hard and opened the door.

"You do not think less of me for what other men might say?"

"I couldn't Rose, I love you. I—goodnight, Rose."

He jumped down the steps leading from her home and soon disappeared into the darkness of the night.

Before Rose retired she wrote a brief ciphered note for Thomas J. Rayford. "A slave in President Davis's household is a traitor. Called Rufus, he has a set of Davis's keys and the combination to his office safe. He is reporting vital secrets to the government here. The Embassy Code Book will follow. ROG."

In less than a week, Rose was able to forward the Embassy Code Book to Thomas Rayford. It was sent via Betty Duvall, tied securely by string around her middle, nestled against her bare flesh beneath her silk chemise, much to the discomfort and embarrassment of the poor girl.

Early in June, Ellen visited Rose to sadly announce that Stephen Douglas had died of typhoid fever.

"I am sorry for Addie," Rose said coldly, "but the end of his ceaseless tirades against the South will be a welcome relief."

"They have had five happy years of marriage, Rose. He has been good to her and she truly loved him."

"It would not be truthful for me to say I will miss him."

"I know, Rose. But be kind to Addie, will you? She loves you dearly and holds you in such high esteem."

"I shall do my best."

Later in the month Rose received a ciphered note from

Thomas Rayford commending her for a job well done. "Code name Rufus has been located and shot at dawn as the traitor that he was."

Toward the end of June, the city of Washington was suddenly in turmoil. Whenever Rose looked out her window she saw officers and orderlies on horses flying by; wherever she walked, the tramp of armed men was heard on every side; and martial music filled the air. Early in July, in her visits about the capital she witnessed field trains being prepared, transport and combat wagons being loaded. She made notes of it all, but she had nothing specific. Until now the war had been quiet. There had been none of the large battles and maneuvers that usually accompanied wars. Now, suddenly, it seemed that at long last something was about to happen. It irked Rose that she had as yet no knowledge of any impending operation.

In the midst of the turmoil, Senator Wilson came to visit her late one afternoon. "I have seen so little of you of late," he said, as he dropped down on her sofa and sighed heavily. "I thought I would surprise you, to be sure that the war has not inundated you with the ghastly horrors of which you have so often spoken."

"So far there has been no cause for alarm, my dear Henry."

"It has been quiet for all too long," Senator Wilson said, and then added importantly. "I assure you that the situation will change before too many days have passed."

"What in heaven's name are you referring to?"

"Aha. It is a military secret no inkling of which is to be divulged to the public in advance."

"Since when have I been considered the public?"

"Now, no offense, my Wild Rose. It is just that the fewer people who are aware of our military actions, the less chance that the enemy will get wind of them."

"Then a military maneuver *is* being planned."

"I didn't say that. But I can tell you this. We are strengthening our forces every day. We know that the rebels have twenty thousand armed men in Virginia, besides companies of volunteers. We are prepared at anytime, should they choose to strike."

"I am proud of the stand which the state of Virginia has taken in supporting the South, as well as the overwhelming number of their volunteers who have answered the call to arms."

"This is more than offset by your fine state of Maryland, which has remained loyal to the Union."

"My state is only being laggardly, my dear senator. They will undoubtedly answer the call of the Confederacy before long. I tell you quite frankly, sir, that I am doing all in my power to see that they do."

"My party will enforce its principles at the point of the bayonet if necessity demands it."

"Upon a poor defenseless state which by a fate of geography is placed at your mercy."

"We will put the iron heel on Maryland, crushing out its boundary lines, should she show any signs of abandoning our cause."

"Those who run may read the destiny reserved for Maryland. To make her an integral part of the North—and if her citizens resist, to raze her cities and blot out her boundary. I pity that once proud little state, which is now only a military department. I regret being only a poor woman at this crisis— but heart and soul, I am with this cause, and with all my poor ability will I serve it."

The senator's smile was more a leer as he spoke. "The country has been ruled long enough by the southern aristocrats."

"The break has been caused by the onerous oppression of the damned Yankees," Rose said heatedly, her voice rising.

"I fear you underestimate our perseverance. We are docile and slow to anger, but once roused we will not stop until we have achieved complete victory."

"If you do, it will be over the dead bodies of many of your fairest and finest young men."

"As we invade the South, we will conquer as we go." Wilson smirked proudly, revealing a new side of him which she had never before witnessed. "I expect that few of the Union men will return to the North, but they *will* be alive and well."

"You are speaking unclearly."

"Not at all. I am only suggesting that our men will have homesteads given them in the conquered country. Congress will apportion the land into quarter sections, and they will settle there and marry southern girls."

"Never, sir. But our Negroes will go north and marry yours as far more fitting helpmates," she replied defiantly.

"Oh, come now, Rose, I didn't come here to quarrel. It has been too long since we have been together." Quickly he got up and came over to Rose's chair. "Tell me, my Wild Rose, have you missed me?"

He started to sit on the arm of her chair and put his arm around her. Hastily she got up and stood glaring before him. "I am sorry, Henry. The differences between us have become too great."

"What are you saying?"

"Your tirades against the South have been too much to bear. You know how I have championed this cause. You have smothered my love for you in a sea of unfounded diatribes."

Slowly he rose and looked at her in astonishment. "After all that I have done for you, you now profess—"

"You have done little, senator, compared to all that I have given. I loved you. You are well aware of that."

"I am sorry, Rose. It was not my intent to break the ties that bound us together."

He put his hand on her arm. She quickly, angrily, pulled it away. "It is too late for reconciliation." They stood standing opposite each other. Presently he bowed his shoulders and turned away.

"I suppose this is goodbye, Rose. I shall always have many fond memories of our times together."

"I, too, Henry. I regret that they are in the past. But I am secure in the knowledge that it was not I who drove the final wedge between us."

"Goodbye, Rose."

"Goodbye, Henry," she said in a much more subdued voice. "We can still be friends, I hope. But that is all."

"Yes, I suppose so." He turned and silently walked away.

As he started down the stone steps outside the house, he turned back to her. "In a war opposing sides cut deep wounds."

"Yes, Henry, they do." He was gone, perhaps out of her life completely, but she felt no remorse.

No sooner had he disappeared from sight than she ordered Randy to hitch up her buggy. She drove furiously over to the Senate Military Committee office in the War Department building. She waited impatiently as John Callan conducted a discussion with a visiting officer. Finally John came over and bowed politely.

"I must speak with you," she whispered.

He looked hurriedly about him at others in the office, but no one seemed to be paying them any particular attention. "Not here, Rose."

"It is urgent. Walk with me down the hallway."

He threw some papers down that he had just received and accompanied her into the hallway.

"You have not told me of any military movement afoot," she said in a hushed voice, her eyes flashing in condemnation.

"But I do not know of any."

"There is action planned. The streets are full of armed men, officers riding, loaded transports, and combat wagons. Senator Wilson has confirmed that something is afoot but will tell me no more."

"It must be detailed in the daily military records."

"Why have I not seen them?"

"I do not have access to them. They are brought by special courier and immediately filed in the archives."

"It is imperative that I see them."

"They are locked inside the archive storage."

"Do you have a key?"

"Yes, but there is an armed guard stationed at the door twenty-four hours a day."

"Take me back there, now."

"It is impossible. We are closing down for the day. The guard will surely suspect some collusion if we attempted to go in at this late hour."

The hallway became filled with men leaving the building after their day's work.

Rose thought for a moment, then reaching in her pocket drew out several dollar bills. "Take these to the guard and tell him you must take me into the archive room."

"He is a military man. I doubt if he can be bribed."

"This is not a bribe. It is a plea from one man to another. Tell him that your wife has become suspicious of your affair with me and it is the only place that we can meet."

"But I am not married."

"The guard does not know this."

The hallway was gradually emptying until only a few stragglers remained.

"If you will act casually, he will suspect nothing."

"But I could take you to a hotel room."

"Explain to him that there are no hotel rooms available in Washington, because the city's overrun with both the military and civilians."

"My God, Rose."

"Go, now. Hurry."

Reluctantly he walked down the hallway and approached the guard. Rose leaned against the wall, her head bowed in complete abjection. The forlorn, lonely woman, uncertain of her hopeless plight. Presently he returned. His hand trembled as he took her arm.

"It worked, Rose. He thinks I am insane. So do I."

She placed her arm in his. As they walked past the guard and John unlocked the door with his key, Rose raised her handkerchief to her face, trying to hide herself in her feigned embarrassment.

Once inside the large, barren room, filled with unending rows of files, he hastily took her over to the drawers that contained the daily military memorandums. "We must hurry. The guard warned me that he tours the rooms every hour. We have less than forty minutes."

Already Rose was quickly and methodically drawing out folders and hurriedly scanning their contents. Most of the information had already come into her possession from other sources. Then suddenly she stopped as she read a message from military intelligence to the Senate committee. "General Beauregard is holding twenty thousand men at Manassas Junction, a vital railroad junction they wish to protect at all costs. The junction is approximately thirty miles from Washington." Another memorandum contained a list of requirements needed to bring one of McDowell's brigades up to full strength. Rose hurriedly made brief notes: seventy three-inch rifled cannon; eighteen four-and-one-half-inch; sixty thirty-two pounders; sixty ten-inch Columbiads; twenty nine-inch Dahlgrens; and thirty seven-inch siege Howitzers.

She hastily made a note of another message from General McDowell. "The president called for three-month volunteers. Enlistments are fast running out. Soldiers are leaving their stations. It is imperative that we take action as outlined in my memo of May 20 while our troops are still near full strength." What action was he referring to? Where was his memo of May 20?

As she frantically searched for his memo, the door to the archives opened and the guard appeared. Rose quietly closed the file drawer and threw herself into John's arms. The guard walked past the many aisles of file cabinets, loudly stamping his feet as he came. As he approached them, Rose hastily drew away from John's loving embrace. Flustered, embarrassed, she smoothed her hair and again covered her face as best she could with her handkerchief.

"I'm sorry, but you will have to leave. I am going off duty in a few minutes," he said quietly, almost apologetically.

All of the information she had gathered was written into a brief ciphered note and sent to Thomas Rayford the following morning when Betty Duvall came to her house.

In order to avoid suspicion, she decided that she would wait a few days before again visiting the archives. On the third of July she called on Callan at his office. For a few dollar bills the guard agreed to permit them to go back into the archive room. Once inside, she lost no time in locating General McDowell's memorandum of May 20. In it he suggested that an attack be made on the rebels at Manassas Junction, recommending that it be no later than the middle of July. By then, he estimated, his combined strength would total at least fifty thousand men. He ended the message with the note: "We can attack the enemy according to our plan outlined in our memorandum of May 1." Frantically Rose searched for the May 1 memorandum and finally located it. "I believe we can overwhelm the Confederate forces at Manassas," it said, "if we strike a surprise attack with superior numbers. We then can easily drive through their lines and proceed to Richmond."

Before the guard came in on his hourly round, Rose had made hasty notes, and walking arm in arm with John, led him out of the vast room. She smiled graciously as she passed the guard and leaned lovingly on John's shoulder.

The vital message was ciphered and ready for passage to Thomas Rayford. But Betty did not come. Rose was beside herself when she still did not put in an appearance. She seriously considered trying to take the information through the Union lines herself. Then she thought better of it, knowing full well that there was still much more important information to be secured and only she had the means of collecting it.

Late in the afternoon of July 10, Betty came to her home. It was a hot sultry day.

"I was worried for you, Betty. Where have you been?"

"I fear that I am being suspected," Betty said simply. "The

Union guards detained me for two days and searched me several times. I was frightened, but fortunately they did not find anything and finally let me go. I waited for further instructions before coming to you again."

"This justifies my own caution. I question if it will be safe to permit you to depart with this valuable information."

"Have no fear, Mrs. Greenhow. I have been instructed to take an entirely different route."

"When you arrive safely at your destination, tell the Confederates of your experience and seek their advice."

"I will. But I do not anticipate further trouble. After all, the guards have not seen too many of the weaker sex of late, and really, I am not too hard to look at." She pirouetted before Rose and flashed a disarming smile as she adjusted her dark curls on the back of her head.

"You are beautiful, my child. But this business is precarious enough without your taking undue risks."

"It is you I worry about, Mrs. Greenhow. What risks must confront *you* in securing such vital information."

Rose smiled. "With my additional years, I can assure you I have learned many ways to get what I want." Then she became serious as she brought out her ciphered message and gave it to Betty.

"Oh, this is no larger than a silver dollar." Betty smiled. "I will have no trouble concealing it."

"We will take no chances," Rose said. Then she folded it up in silk and sewed it into a tiny packet. "Your hair is beautiful, Betty, and it is so long it must be unnaturally held up."

"It is held with a tucking comb."

"Then please let your hair down."

"But Mrs. Greenhow—" Rose stood before her waiting for her to obey. "Oh, well, at least this is not as embarrassing as wearing it under my chemise." So saying, she drew out her tucking comb and flung her head sideways, loosing a beautiful head of black hair that fell down her back almost to her waist. Rose quickly placed the silk packet beneath the tucking comb and with Betty's help bound her hair once again on her head.

"I am sure this message will get through to Mr. Rayford."

"If I am stopped, I am also certain that no one will ever find it." Saying no more, she was off. Rose whispered a short prayer that Betty and her message would get through to its destination.

Rose had received another urgent letter from her daughter begging her to come out to California where she and her two younger daughters would be safe. Rose had to admit to herself that Washington was a dangerous place for secessionist families. Hastily she wrote a letter to Florence, advising that it was impossible for her to leave Washington at this time, and that, since little Rose was only eight years old, she was entirely too young to leave her mother. However, since her friends the Cottrells were going West by boat from New York on July 21, she would be sending Leila out with them to keep Florence company.

After posting the letter, she made her intentions known to Leila, who was delighted at the opportunity of visiting her older sister.

XXIII

Chaos

July 1861

Five days went by before Rose received word from Betty. She feared that perhaps the young girl had been caught on her vital mission, but Rose did not cease her efforts to secure additional information.

Accompanied by John Callan, she again went into the archives. By now they were well-known to the guard, and although she never spoke to him but shyly walked by on John's arm, she made sure that each time he gave the guard several dollars.

Once inside the room she closely scrutinized the latest military messages. She gasped as she read a brief message from President Lincoln ordering General McDowell to implement the previously approved attack on July 16 and requesting verification of the strength of his troops. She found a quick reply written two days later from General McDowell to the president, confirming that all was in readiness, and that fifty-five thousand fully armed troops would move forth on that date with three days' supplies in their haversacks. Searching further, she discovered the vital message she had been looking for. In it, McDowell told the president: "Our combined forces will commence on July 16, advancing from Arlington Heights and Alexandria on to Manassas, via Fairfax Courthouse and Centerville."

John pleaded desperately to accompany her home that

evening, but she put him off, telling him she was ill from the excitement of preparing for her daughter's departure. She promised him faithfully that they would spend an evening together, and alone, when she returned from taking Leila to New York.

Early on the morning of the sixteenth of July, a stranger arrived at her house while she was still sleeping. When he insisted that he see her, Randy finally went upstairs and knocked on her door. Sleepily she got up, and slipping on a robe, answered his incessant pounding. "Randy, I distinctly left word I did not wish to be disturbed."

"I'm sorry, Miz Greenhow, but there is a gentleman downstairs that won't go away until he sees you."

"What does he want?"

"He won't tell me nothing. I said to come back later, but he told me it was so important he just had to see you—now."

"Oh, all right."

Still half-asleep, completely worn out from the activities of the past few days, she wearily went downstairs.

The man took off his hat and saluted as she came to him. "Mrs. Greenhow?"

"Yes. Who are you, sir?"

"My name is George Donellan."

"Who sent you?"

"Mr. Rayford of Virginia."

"I must have further identification." She knew that the passwords for the current month were "material" and "witness," and she remarked casually, "Material."

"Witness," the man replied. "May I come in?"

"Of course."

"I have a message for you." He handed her a small piece of paper. On it were two ciphered words. Mentally she quickly deciphered the message: "Trust bearer."

As he sat down in the parlor Mr. Donellan said seriously, "I have heard of you many times, Mrs. Greenhow. I used to work for the Department of Interior, but I have never had the

398

pleasure of meeting you."

"Thank you. Did Mr. Rayford receive my message that McDowell has certainly been ordered to advance on the sixteenth?"

"He did, ma'am. That is why I am here."

"Where is Betty?"

"After learning of her close escape, we have advised her to temporarily cease her activity."

"Then she is all right."

"Definitely."

"I am glad that she got through for her sake as well as our own."

"Do you have any additional information on the proposed military strike?"

"I do, sir. When I did not see Betty, I wondered how I would get it to Mr. Rayford. As you are aware, the troops have started on their way today."

"President Davis has ordered General Joseph E. Johnson, with twelve thousand men who have been guarding the Shenandoah Valley, to join General Beauregard. General Holmes has also been ordered to move his force from Aquia Creek Landing."

"That is well, for General McDowell has fifty-five thousand men with him." She handed him her ciphered note.

Hastily he read it and uttered a low whistle. "This would have been a catastrophe, Mrs. Greenhow, if you had not secured advance warning for us." Casually he took off his right boot. Without ceremony he pressed the heel in a circular motion and removed it. It was hollow. He folded the message to proper size, and sliding it into the hollow heel, quickly screwed it back into place.

"It is imperative that this be delivered immediately."

"This message will be in General Beauregard's hands before midnight tonight. I have a horse and buggy waiting to take me down the Maryland shore of the Potomac. I have a boat waiting for me at Indian Head to ferry me across to Dumfries in

Virginia. There is a squad of cavalry couriers who will meet me there and rush the message to Colonel Jordan. I must be leaving at once."

"I wish you Godspeed, Mr. Donellan. You must be exhausted. Can I give you some nourishment before you go?"

"Thank you. I have some cheese and mutton in my buggy and a jug of water. That will suffice until I cross the Potomac."

"Then let me give you a portion of brandy." She hurriedly went to her liquor cabinet and poured him a generous amount of brandy and handed it to him.

He gulped it down in two or three swallows and started for the door. "I will be back tomorrow. I shall bring you a message if there should be any last-minute details we require." Smartly saluting her, he left.

The next day Rose waited impatiently for Donellan's return. By afternoon she could hardly contain herself, pacing impatiently back and forth across her parlor. Finally, shortly after two o'clock, he arrived, clearly exhausted from his journey to Virginia and the return.

"I have a message for you," he said, as he slumped into an armchair and dragged off his boot. Removing the heel, he drew out a small piece of paper and handed it to her.

Hurriedly she opened it and read: "Yours was received at eight o'clock at night. Let them come. We are ready for them. We rely upon you for precise information. Be particular as to description and destination of force, quantity of artillery, etc." It was signed Rayford.

"I shall go to my source immediately. Will you wait for any information I can secure?"

"With your permission, Mrs. Greenhow—"

"Call me Rose."

"Thank you. If I may, Rose, I shall take advantage of your hospitality and stretch out on your sofa for a brief nap. I have had little sleep in the past three nights."

"Better than that, you are welcome to my own comfortable bed."

"I do not wish to trouble you."

"Please do not stand on ceremony." She hastily called Randy and ordered him to show Mr. Donellan her bedroom and see that he was not disturbed. "When you return, hitch up my horse and buggy. Now hurry."

As she waited for Randy, she quickly gathered paper and pencil and stuffed them into a large handbag.

In her anxiety, she accompanied Randy as he hitched up her buggy. Impatiently whipping her horse, she drove directly to John Callan's office.

He appeared startled when he saw her, his face gradually losing its color.

"In God's name, what are you doing here now?" he whispered.

"I must see the latest military memorandums that have been delivered today."

"Someone might discover us."

She pushed some dollar bills in his hand. "Give these to the guard. Tell him that I am going away and this is our last rendezvous together."

"I hope it is. This way, I mean."

She followed him to the guard who hastily took the money. Then, as John told him of the emergency, he looked around to see that no one was watching and let them into the archive room.

She immediately went to the file which she knew contained the latest memorandums. She gasped as she started to open it. It was closed and locked with a large iron bolt and rod.

"We must break it open."

"What with?"

"A hammer. A crowbar. Anything. But we must open it." As John stood beside her gaping, she added, "Look for something, silly boy. Hurry. And we must have a cloth as well."

John went to the back of the building and Rose frantically started searching about. Finally she found a rock just beside the door. Grabbing it, she had started back to the file when she discovered a dirty turkish towel hanging from a low pipe. Taking it, she returned to the file and met John, who had found a fairly large chisel.

She wrapped the head of the chisel in the towel to muffle the sound of hitting, and handed the rock to John. "They'll certainly notice that it has been broken open," he said skeptically.

"We will worry about that later. Break open the lock. Hurry. We have lost a great deal of time."

John hit the lock but it did not budge. Although the chisel was covered, the muffled sound of hitting it with the rock got louder and louder as John hit harder. Finally the lock broke open. Rose hurriedly removed the bar and opened the drawer. At that precise moment, the door of the archive room opened. Suddenly the guard appeared and stealthily began walking up and down each aisle as he came toward them. Frantically she closed the drawer and quickly took off her dress. Then she removed her petticoats, her chemise, her camisole and her pantalettes, the last of her undergarments. She was stark naked.

"My God, Rose, what are you doing?" John asked in horror.

She only had time to pick up her petticoats and hold them before her as the guard rounded the tier of files where they stood. He gave a startled look, then turned away. "My sincerest apologies, madam. I thought that I heard a noise. Please forgive me." Hastily he beat a retreat and promptly strode out of the storage room.

Rose hardly bothered to finish putting her clothes on before she began to search through the file. She gasped as she read a hastily scribbled message to General Thomas W. Sherman from General McDowell directing him to drive full haste to Strasburg and destroy the Manassas Gap railroad between Winchester and Manassas, so as to delay General Johnson's move of reinforcements from the Shenandoah Valley.

Jotting down the brief message, she grabbed the broken lock

and shoved it into Callan's hand as she started toward the door.

"Purchase another lock like this one and replace it immediately."

"But I won't be through my day's work for another two hours!"

Suddenly she stopped and gave him such a withering look that he sheepishly added, "I'll go at once. I trust that I have sufficient money to purchase such a lock."

She thrust ten dollars into his hand, then quickly she took it back and whispered, "Go to the chief of ordnance and advise them the lock was damaged in moving the file. They will replace it."

As they neared the door, Callan said plaintively, "When will I see you again?"

"When I return from New York! Now hurry." With her heart beating so heavily she could feel its pounding against her body, she casually walked past the guard. He winked knowingly at her. She managed to blush profusely and lean her head against Callan's shoulder.

Once outside, Rose jumped into her buggy and dashed madly home. She rushed into the house and up the stairs and savagely shook Donellan from his deep sleep.

"They are aware of General Johnson's reinforcements to support Beauregard," she said breathlessly.

As Donellan jumped out of bed and slipped on his boots and pants which he had removed, Rose wrote a hasty ciphered note and handed him her third message on the important battle that was shaping up at Manassas. Quickly he grabbed it and slipped it into the false heel of his boot.

"Now that we are forewarned, McDowell will be confronted with thirty-two thousand well-deployed troops, instead of the twenty thousand he expects," said Donellan. With little further ceremony, he rushed down the stairs and was gone.

Three days later, Rose took Leila to New York and saw her safely aboard the boat with their friends the Cottrells. She smiled valiantly as she bade her daughter goodbye, but her countenance soon turned to a deep frown as she walked down the Collins Line dock on Canal Street. She was brusquely pushed aside to make room for a fully equipped United States battery of light artillery who were embarking on transports. There were six cannon, each drawn by six horses. A caisson, carrying ammunition and also drawn by six horses, accompanied each cannon. She readily identified the regiment and learned from one of the unsuspecting soldiers that they were headed for Washington, D.C. to protect the capital. She quickly made note of their number, equipment, and destination.

Returning to the Astor House, she was again delayed at Broadway and Courtland Streets, as they were completely blocked by a regiment of soldiers marching through. It was New York's crack Seventh Regiment, on its way to trains which would take them to Philadelphia. The crowds were cheering enthusiastically. Gradually the enthusiasm subsided, and Rose learned that the Massachusetts Sixth Division was, at that very moment, being forced to fight their way through Baltimore. The people of Baltimore were rising up against their oppressors, and the first shedding of blood in the war was upon them. Rose scowled defiantly at the news, and then she smiled bitterly.

Before she could move on and return to the Astor House, she learned that the rioting had been quelled and order had been restored in Baltimore. The cheering crowds about her once again became jubilant.

Then, as she entered her hotel, a bellboy rashly thrust out his hand and stopped her. "Have you heard about our first military victory?" he asked excitedly. "We have soundly defeated the southern rebels at Manassas."

Rose looked at him in horrified disbelief. "It can't be!" she said startled and left the surprised bellboy gaping at her in wonderment as she went up to her room.

She packed her valise late in the evening. She summoned a

bellhop to carry her luggage and went down to the lobby of the hotel. It was well after the dinner hour but she was not hungry. What had gone wrong? With all of the information she had been able to secure, George Donellan, yes, Colonel Jordan, as well, had assured her that they were ready. Had not her final message gotten through to them? Were they surprised by the attack in spite of all the information she had been able to provide? "It cannot be true," she mumbled to herself as she started out of the hotel. Her instinct told her that the triumph must be premature.

The scene that greeted her in the street was entirely different from that of the early afternoon. Men and women were talking among themselves in little groups. Jubilant cheers had been replaced by startled, apprehensive glances. She went up to one of the groups and asked, "What has happened?"

"It is awful," said one of the women in tears.

"We have just received word that our soldiers have been sorely defeated in our first battle of the war!" said one of the men excitedly.

The people were talking to each other and to other groups about them.

"Those filthy rebels have beaten our troops."

"I don't know how they could have done it. We had superior numbers."

"The *New York Herald* said that no one knew where McDowell was going to strike them."

"That's right! They said it would be a complete surprise."

Concealing her emotions, Rose entered a sulky to take her to the Pennsylvania Railroad Station. As she settled back in her seat, she smiled and thought to herself: This battle is as memorable in history as that of Culloden or Waterloo. And *I* have had no small part in its accomplishment.

She was even more elated as she watched the consternation of the passengers as she boarded the train and it pulled out of the station and headed south. The fear of the Yankees was manifested everywhere.

When the train stopped at Philadelphia nearly all of the women left the train. The conductor urged her to do likewise. "It will not be safe in Baltimore," he said frowning. "Those rebels of Baltimore will rise in consequence of the route of the Federal Army."

At that moment Lieutenant Henry A. Wise came down the aisle and stopped as he saw Rose. She had attended his wedding several years ago when he married Edward Everett's daughter Charlotte. "My dear Rose," he said, welcoming her with concern. "Whatever are you doing on this train which is headed for Baltimore?"

"I've told her she should get off the train, Lieutenant," the conductor said.

"He is right, Rose. Have you not heard the disastrous news?"

"I have, Henry. But I have no fears."

The Lieutenant and the conductor looked at each other, consternation plainly showing on their faces. "It is not safe to travel through Baltimore, particularly today." Lieutenant Wise leaned close to her to emphasize the seriousness of the situation.

"You forget, Henry, these rebels are of my faith. Besides, I fear, even now, I shall not be in time to welcome our president, Mr. Davis, and the glorious Beauregard."

The conductor shrugged his shoulders and went on to attend to the rest of the ladies in the car. Lieutenant Wise sat with her for the rest of the trip. There was no disturbance as they rode through Baltimore, but the lieutenant was still fearful for Rose's safety.

"I would be more discreet in boasting of rebel victory, Rose," he said to her.

"Why? Now is no time to hide my true feelings. I am sure that if the Yankees had been the victors, you would have been most enthusiastic in your praise."

"But your situation is different."

"How so?"

"Well, for one thing you are in the midst of enemy territory."

"A subjugated enemy at present."

"But this is only the beginning. There will be many more battles before the outcome of this war is decided."

"If there are many more as successful as this one, it should not be long before a rebel can again hold her head high in northern territory."

It was late in the afternoon of July 23 when Rose arrived in Washington. She was confronted with complete chaos. People in small groups in the streets were much more visibly shaken than the New Yorkers. "Why not?" Rose smiled as she boarded the carriage for home. "They know the victors of Manassas are only a few miles from them."

Much as she detested the Yankees she could not help feeling sorrowful as the wagons carrying the wounded from the battle began to arrive and were wearily drawn through the streets. Other wagons, piled high with the dead, skimpily covered with makeshift tarpaulins, moved slowly into the heart of the city.

The soldiers who only a fortnight before had proudly gone off to battle singing and marching in clipped, precise fashion, now skulked along, dragging muskets behind them which suddenly seemed too heavy for them to bear. Broken cannons, ammunition trailers, and dories muddied and covered with debris were rolling through the streets.

The people themselves were thoroughly demoralized. They roamed the streets with blank expressions on their faces, casting furtive glances about them. More than once Rose's carriage was blocked by the city's stricken defenders, who started at the clank of their own comrades' muskets.

She finally made her way through the tattered mob to her home. There she found a message for her. "Our president and our general direct me to thank you. We rely upon you for further information. The Confederacy owes you a debt." It was signed by Colonel Thomas Jordan, who apparently no longer thought it necessary to use his code name. She pressed the message fondly to her bosom and then read it again. Not only had her efforts paid off handsomely, but they were appreciated by those whom she had so tirelessly striven to aid.

That evening friends began to congregate to welcome her home and tell of the glorious victory. So many came that she did not have sufficient chairs to accommodate them. It did not matter. They cheerfully sat on the floor as they described the southern victory. "The heat and the dust were tremendous." "The confusion and panic on the battlefield—you cannot believe how desperate the enemy became!"

They laughed joyously as they described the behavior of senators and government officials. "They actually rode out to the hills overlooking the battlefield with refreshments and bottles of wine."

"They had envisioned a picnic as they watched their Union soldiers meet the Confederates and easily subjugate them!"

"Just like the royal courts of old watching the knights in tournaments."

"But with such sadly different results. The cream of the crop bolting in desperation."

"Their officers bolting in panic!"

"The very roads leading from the battlefield were blocked with discarded wagons, trundles, carriages, cannon, and equipment of all kinds."

"Knapsacks were piled in stacks in the middle of the road so the soldiers could retreat faster!"

"And the senators fleeing the melee in their carriages were reminiscent of some comic light opera."

"Senator Chandler and Senator Wilson were pitiful bragging to anyone who would listen how they bolstered the troops' morale, all the time scurrying away faster than anyone else."

"All they succeeded in accomplishing was to further clutter the roads."

Rose smiled. "If they were lacking in good blood, it appears that they surely had good bottom, for they seemed to be running with considerable agility."

"Colonel Ambrose Burnside was the most comical of all."

"Yes, he flounced into battle with two orderlies by his side carrying the flowers of victory which the comely wenches of the North had given to him as he left for battle."

"And on his return, he barely escaped leaving his hat and his shoes behind."

"I declare," said Rose quietly, "I have the urge to throw myself on my knees and give tearful thanks to the Father of Mercy for his signal protection in our hour of peril."

"And Secretary of State Seward has assured us in the newspapers that the Union need not worry. It will be all over in sixty days."

"If it is, and I hope that it is so," remarked Rose, "President Davis will be sitting in the White House dictating the terms of surrender."

"Did you read what the *New York Herald* warned?"

"They were most disturbed by the government maps and papers that were found left behind by General Bonham when he slipped away from the oncoming Union Army at Fairfax County Courthouse."

"I tore out the article," said someone. He brought out a torn sheet of newsprint and read, "What is the mystery of those important government maps and plans? We are at liberty to guess how Beauregard was so minutely informed of this advance and of our plan of attack on his lines as to be ready to meet it at every single point with overwhelming numbers. Could it be the work of one southern damsel who is well known to be in sympathy with the rebels' cause?"

"Whom do you think he is referring to?"

"I don't know, but it is obvious that henceforth no woman

with southern sympathies will be safe in this capital," said one fair damsel. "I am leaving for Richmond tomorrow."

"You too should leave, Rose," warned one of the men. "I shall gladly escort you to safety beyond the Union lines."

"I shall remain in Washington," answered Rose defiantly. "This is my home. No damn Yankee can turn me out by innuendos and incriminating guesses."

XXIV

Suspicion

August 1861

The startling defeat at Manassas had been so severe that
General McDowell was abruptly removed, to be replaced by
General McClellan. Rose was exuberant that her victory had
had such far-reaching effects in the northern military. She
readily transferred her careful scrutiny of McDowell's plans to
General McClellan's. Bolstered by her success, she increased
her activities in the next few weeks.

Rayford sent many different agents to her to act as couriers.
Both Thompson and Smithson delivered messages for her
many times. They also continually brought her valuable
information to be transmitted by her own couriers. It was
becoming more difficult to slip through the Union lines. But
more than this, Rose's constant flow of visitors made it
necessary for agents to be ever more cautious when
approaching her house. 398 16th Street was recognized by
Washingtonians as a gathering place of incessant activity. At
almost any hour of the day or night, shadowy figures would
appear on Rose's doorstep with information vital to the
southern military. She gathered it with painstaking care,
correlated it with her own messages, and sent it on to Rayford.

On July 31, just ten days after the victory at Manassas, Rose
forwarded her own observations of the situation in the North.
"All is activity. McClellan is busy night and day, but the panic
is great and the attack hourly expected. They believe that the

411

attack will be simultaneous from Edward's Ferry and Baltimore. Every effort is being made to find out who gave the alarm. A troupe of cavalry will start from here this morning to Harper's Ferry. Don't give time for reorganizing."

Later, on August 9, she sent a message that every road leading into the capital was being reinforced in order to resist an attack, particularly by way of the Chain Bridge. She said that McClellan was vigilant and alert, with over ninety thousand men surrounding the capital. She enclosed a map showing where camouflaged batteries were in position. She also forwarded a detailed list of the railroad schedules. "Many of the guns are rifles and great importance is being given to the artillery and cavalry."

Only two days later Captain John Elwood, commander of the Fifth Infantry Station of the Provost Marshal gave her detailed plans of the army's contemplated attack into southern territory. Captain Elwood was being more and more helpful, and incidentally ever more attracted by her charms. John Callan, not to be outdone by his competitor, brought her further information on the army's proposed attack and details of the forces that would be left behind to protect the capital. He gave her a map of the defenses and forts surrounding Washington. With the data at her disposal, Rose was able to forward a vivid picture of the Union's proposed operations, including the earthworks and specific data concerning their dimensions, the number of guns and caliber, how they were mounted, and their emplacement.

The data was enclosed in a package of several sheets, maps, and itemized lists, and it included her own assessment of northern defense. "The principal fortifications for the defense of Washington are in Arlington Heights and are of such a character that military men believe that five thousand men could hold them against ten times that number. A most formidable array of field artillery is being brought into service and upon its quantity, caliber, quality, and efficacy the most sanguine hopes are founded. From the neighborhood of

Arlington House to that of Alexandria, there are now between thirty-five and forty regiments, some of them in a state of demoralization, and fears are entertained that they cannot be relied upon in emergency. Sickness and insubordination prevail more or less in all the regiments, with perhaps twelve or fourteen exceptions." She then included a list of McClellan's thirty-two works surrounding Washington, with their locations.

This vital bit of information was forwarded to the South in the hands of Colonel Thompson. Rose left it to his own discretion as to how it was to be transported, not insisting upon placing it next to his skin as she had done in the case of Betty Duvall.

Army and navy officers were her constant dinner guests, intermingled with jurists, diplomats, and administration officials. So many visitors were bound to attract unwelcome attention. But without letup, Rose continued to secure more and more information, and Rayford valiantly attempted to send couriers to her who were not suspected or followed.

The password had become a vital part of their operation, for it was becoming impossible for Rose to know personally all of the messengers and informants who visited 398 16th Street. No couriers were given messages without identification. For the month of August the passwords were "true" and "blue."

John Callan continued to give her the minutes of General McClellan's private, secret conferences. She closely scrutinized McClellan's plans and entire operations. She knew his every move. From Lieutenant Rogers she obtained the dimensions and characteristics of a new navy gunboat while it was still in the blueprint stage.

The secret codes which Rose and her contacts used were becoming more complicated, and messages were garbled so that they could not be deciphered should they fall into enemy hands. Eventually, they used a series of hieroglyphics utilizing a system of squares, x's, dots, and sections of an enclosed cross.

Captain John Elwood was being particularly helpful. In fact, he was already vying with poor, lovesick John Callan for Rose's love and personal attention. He was much older than Callan, and more experienced in the ways of the world and the fairer sex. Callan was becoming insanely jealous of Rose's attention to the captain. It was an added problem for Rose, since she needed both men in her operations. She tried desperately not to show favoritism, but could not help being particularly gracious to Captain Elwood when he brought her the complete defense plan for the capital, should the Confederates invade it.

She quickly passed the plan on to Rayford with the request that he send someone to her qualified to assist in drawing up an effective counterplan.

Three days later, George Donellan appeared with an engineer from Richmond, Jarod Mansfield. They called on her while Lily Mackall was visiting her. Lily was a strikingly beautiful young blonde with whom Rose had recently become most friendly. Lily, as an active agent in the spy ring, brought her much vital information, and since she lived close by, was being used more and more frequently to assist Rose.

As the two men introduced themselves, Rose vouched for Lily's loyalty and the four of them sat about the table in Rose's parlor to work out a plan.

"In the case of invasion," said Donellan, "we must first cut all telegraph wires connecting military posts with the War Department."

"I can assist with that," volunteered Lily. "I have become most friendly with Sergeant Wainwright, who operates the message center at the War Department."

"Good," smiled Donellan. "Rose has previously given us the names and locations of the military posts. I shall assign agents to each of them."

Mansfield then suggested, "It will be necessary to spike the guns of Fort Corcoran and Fort Ellsworth."

"The guns at all defense points should be spiked," Donellan commented. "Rose, it will be necessary to secure the exact locations of all of these defenses."

"There are added defenses each week. Soon there will be forts on every hilltop surrounding the city. But I shall identify them for you and give you any other information I can secure."

"We must organize ourselves to be able to serve as a center of rebellion if invasion should come," suggested Lily.

"You mean when invasion comes," corrected Rose. Then she added, "You must tell us of strong military men or civilians in our midst, George, who are loyal to our cause. We can immediately contact them when the operation begins, in order to capture General McClellan, General Scott, and the Union Army's high command."

"A startling but not entirely unfeasible suggestion," said Donellan. "I shall give you a list of such men, and you may contact them in advance."

"If successful, such action will create still greater confusion in the first moments of panic."

The clandestine meeting broke up on a lighthearted, enthusiastic note. The South was going to win this war between the states, and here were four dedicated people united to see that it became a reality.

The day following their meeting William J. Walker brought Rose additional data which he had intercepted at his post office on its way to McClellan's subordinates. It detailed the movement of troops and ordnance munitions for the next two weeks. It specified what amounts were going to artillery placements and indicated specific artillery destinations. It included an enthusiastic letter exhorting the leaders to bolster the men's morale, which the general readily admitted was sadly deficient. A note indicated that the shortage of blankets was being taken care of and additional supplies would be forthcoming within a fortnight.

The very same day she received a brief note from Mrs. Philip Phillips, the wife of a Washington lawyer who had been a representative from Alabama. He and his wife had been friendly with Rose and her husband, and Mrs. Phillips was ever anxious to assist Rose in her operation. "I heard from a good source," the note said, "that a large force was to have been sent to Alquia Creek and under the protection of the vessel's guns land a large force and take possession. I send you this information as you may not have heard it. I think I heard Wednesday mentioned. Please make a note on't. Yrs."

All of this information was forwarded to the South by another messenger the next afternoon, with additional comments she had gathered since her last dispatch. "There are forty-five thousand Va. side. Fifteen thousand around the city, to wit, up the river above Chain Bridge, across Anacostia Branch, and commanding every approach to the city. If McClellan can be permitted to prepare, he expects to surprise you, but now is preparing against a surprise by you. Look out for batteries wherever you go. Their reliance this time is on an abundance of artillery which they have disposed formidably. At proper time an effort will be made here to cut their telegraph wires and if possible to spike their guns wherever they are left unmanned. A line of daily communication is now open through Alexandria. Send couriers and afford other facilities en route."

Early the next morning Lily came to Rose's house and pounded madly on her door.

Rose hurried to answer it. When she recognized her friend, she said astonished, "Good heavens, Lily, what on earth is the matter? I was expecting at the very least an invasion of my home."

Panting, Lily exclaimed, "It's Confederate prisoners from Manassas. Have you heard?"

"No."

"A crowd attacked them while they were passing Willard's Hotel. They hit them with stones and brickbats, and some pounded them with limbs of trees."

"Weren't they guarded?"

"There were not nearly enough guards. They have called out

416

a company of regulars to escort them to Old Capitol Prison. Some of the poor men are wounded."

"We must go down there. Those savages forget that these men are human beings even if they are the enemy." Rose threw a shawl about her and the two women hurried to Old Capitol Prison.

There they found the men huddled together in a large receiving room.

As they entered, they overheard Superintendent William P. Wood cursing the men. "Goddamn you swine, you got no more than you deserved. You should know better than to talk back to your captors."

"We wasn't talking back," said one of the men. "None of us said nothing. They just came at us as we rounded the corner. Before we—"

"Shut up, you son of a bitch, before I have you horsewhipped!"

"That is enough of such talk," Rose shouted as she entered the room.

Wood's face was livid as he turned to her. "And who are you?"

"I am Mrs. Greenhow, but my name is not important."

"Oh, Mrs. Greenhow, is it," Wood replied with mock politeness. "Well how do you do, ma'am, it is indeed a pleasure to meet the famed Mrs. Greenhow."

"How do you do?"

"I have heard it spoken on several occasions that our country would be better off if you too were one of my guests."

"Our personal opinions are of no import, sir. What does matter is the safety of these men who are under your charge."

"These stinking rebels have caused us no end of trouble at Manassas. Many of our brave boys lost their lives because of them. And I'll thank you not to be coming here interfering."

"It is not interference to demand that you treat these men civilly."

"How they are treated is my business! Now you, madam, get

out of here. We don't allow no visitors."

"I shall stay until I can determine if I can be of assistance to these prisoners!"

"You'll get out, I say. Both you women." Then turning away from them he shouted, "Guards!" Two men in uniform stepped hastily forward.

"And I say, sir, I shall report you to General Joseph K. F. Mansfield for your gross impudence."

Wood looked at her sullenly as he gestured for the guards to stand back, and then spoke in a low voice. "What do you want here, anyhow?"

"I am merely here to determine the present needs of these men."

"Well, go ahead and talk to them. But mind you, in the future no visitors will be permitted." He beckoned to the guards to take over, and as he walked away said in a loud, arrogant voice so that the prisoners could hear, "I was just telling our prisoners that any who don't take the oath of allegiance to the federal government will be hanged!" Scowling at Rose and Lily, he left the room.

As soon as he was gone, the two women quickly went to the men and made a list of what they needed most. As Rose approached each man, she pointedly told him, "Have no fear, gentlemen, the superintendent's threat was an idle boast. You have my assurance that the Confederacy will fearfully retaliate any violence against you."

Thus was added another duty to Rose's busy days. She and Lily brought clothing, bedding, and food down to the prisoners, although, true to his word, Superintendent Wood succeeded in having an order issued barring all visitors, specifically mentioning both Rose and her friend Lily.

Less than a week later as she was walking down the street on her way to Capitol Hill, Rose noticed that a strange man was following her. She immediately changed her route and went over to Lily Mackall's house. The man discreetly followed her.

As Lily opened the door Rose hastily entered the house.

"Lily, I'm being followed," she greeted her friend. Going to the window, she peeked out from behind the curtain. "Look, there's the man. He is stooping to fasten his boot."

Lily ran to the window and looked. "Oh, my God!"

"Isn't it exciting?"

"Exciting! Rose, we have been warned they are putting anyone whom they suspect in jail."

"Nonsense. They cannot arrest anyone without proper proof."

"Proof? You heard what Lord Lyons said at your dinner the other evening concerning Secretary of State Seward's frightening threats."

"You mean his arrogant idle boast?" Rose puffed out her chest and frowned pompously. "My Lord, I can touch a bell with my right hand and order the arrest of a citizen of Ohio. I can touch a bell again and order the imprisonment of a citizen in New York. And no power on earth except that of the president can release them. Can the Queen of England do so much?"

"But it is true, Rose. We must be careful."

But Rose was not listening. "Look, the man has walked to the corner and now turns and is slowly walking back." She laughed. "He is waiting for me to come out."

"Rose, you must take this more seriously. This is war. Both you and I are engaged in espionage. It frightens me what they could do to us."

"Only if they can know what we are doing and prove it. Lily, I cannot believe that the fragment of a once glorious government could give to the world such a proof of craven fear and weakness as to turn its arms against the breasts of helpless, defenseless women and children."

"You are feeling too secure, Rose. They are suspicious, or else they would not have assigned someone to follow you."

"I daresay it is that Pinkerton fellow or Major Allen or Mr. Hutcheson, I have heard say he chooses to call himself. He's the man who guarded Lincoln on his trip east, to establish a secret service department in the army. It is undoubtedly one of his men. He has need to show some activity to prove that he is on the job."

"If it is a Pinkerton man, it truly worries me. Perhaps we had better cease our activity for a time. If we explain the situation to Colonel Jordan, I am sure he will understand."

"Nonsense. Do you honestly believe they would dare arrest Rose O'Neal Greenhow? If they did, there would be a score of the most influential men in Washington clamoring at the door of the White House for my release. And they would be demanding an explanation."

As Lily again looked out the window, she exclaimed fearfully, "Look, Rose, he is not going away. For a moment I thought he had left when he turned the corner, but he has just reappeared."

"Of course. I told you he is waiting for me to come out. Let us give the man a proper fright."

"What are you going to do?"

"We'll leave by your back door, slip through the alley and enter the street directly in front of him."

"Oh, Rose."

But Rose was on her way out and Lily hurried to catch up with her. As Rose suggested, they emerged onto the street just as the man was turning back toward Lily's house. Rose went directly up to him and boldly confronted him.

"My dear sir," she said arrogantly. "Will you please advise me why you are following me?"

The man stopped and stared at her. "I—I—beg your pardon, ma'am?"

"Why have you been following me?"

"I haven't, ma'am," the man replied, obviously flustered. "I—well, to tell the truth, I am lost. I am a stranger to this city and—"

"Where do you wish to go?"

"I was looking for the White House."

"The White House, sir? It is two blocks north of here. It is plainly visible at the corner from which you just approached."

"Oh, oh, thank you very much." The man tipped his hat, and bowing slightly, quickly disappeared.

"The man was lying," Rose smiled smugly.

"Of course he was. Oh, Rose, do be careful."

"I shall. I was on my way to Fort Ellsworth, but I will postpone my visit for another day. I have several bits of correspondence that require answering. Perhaps it would be better if I returned home and attended to them."

So saying, she bade Lily goodbye and hurried home. She was not frightened, but it was most disconcerting to learn that someone was suspicious enough of her activities to have her followed.

Her apprehensions were not to be calmed at home, however. Shortly after her arrival she was surprised to receive a visit from Senator Lane.

"Welcome, stranger," she greeted him. "It is most unusual for you to visit me in the middle of the morning."

"I can only stay a moment, Rose. What in God's name have you been doing?"

"I don't know what you are referring to. I have been extremely busy—"

"Evidently. Rose, I came here to warn you."

"I don't understand."

"The Senate Military Committee has just received a letter from General McClellan's staff recommending that William Preston and yourself be arrested."

"That is ridiculous!"

"It is not, Rose. A member of McClellan's staff caught Preston in the act of stealing military maps from McClellan's war file."

"William Preston was Buchanan's minister to Spain. He would not stoop to such distasteful activities."

"He shall have to prove his innocence, because we have authorized his arrest."

"Do you have some trumped-up charge that will enable you to issue a warrant for my arrest as well?"

"No, I was able to convince the committee that such an act would be most inappropriate without definite proof."

"Thank you, senator."

"That is the least you deserve, Rose. But I must warn you to be most careful. You must avoid any disparaging remarks against the Union. As you know, Senator Breckenridge is retiring from the Senate and plans to address the full body when they convene tomorrow. I can assure you that if he makes one statement that can be construed against the Union, he will be arrested for treason."

"What a sad plight has come upon this once dear nation."

"It is war, Rose!" He took her hand in his. "I thought you should know of the seriousness with which our government is viewing anyone who is not wholly in accord with the Union cause . . ."

"Thank you, Joe." She leaned against him and kissed him. He hastily returned her kiss and left.

Rose immediately wrote a brief note to both William Preston and John C. Breckenridge, warning them of their impending danger, and hastily dispatched them by her trusted slave, Randy.

Both men heeded her warning. Preston hastily packed a few personal belongings and immediately left Washington for the South. Breckenridge delivered a farewell address that could be cited as an example of true loyalty to the glorious country which he had served for so many years. After his speech of loyalty, he, too, hastily left the city and returned to South Carolina.

Her agent, Frank Rennehan, sent a message to her that afternoon advising her that he had important information concerning action scheduled by troops at Evansport Landing, but that he suspected that his every move was being watched. He requested instructions as to how to best convey the secret information without chancing interception. The courier who brought the message suggested that he was in personal contact with Rennehan and would carry a reply back to him. While he waited, Rose jotted down a hasty ciphered note. "REGT. Evansport Landing. Send to Col. W. B. Bates, camp near Evansport Landing—ask him to send it to Chapmans by Mr. Ray of his REGT. Nat Chapman will deliver it to Dr. Wyvill who will bring it here so that I can get it."

On the evening of the same day, Captain John Elwood called on her. She mixed Queen Charlotte Cocktails which they both leisurely drank as they sat beside each other at her Duncan Phyfe table at the rear of her parlor.

"Have you brought the information you promised, captain?"

"I have that, my dear Rose." He reached into his inner coat pocket and drew out a map which he unfolded and laid it on the table before them. "What do you think of this?"

"What is it?"

"It is a plan of the fortifications both in and around Washington. It also designates a contemplated plan of counterattack."

"Oh, John," she beamed, as she threw her arms about him. "This is just what I have been hoping for. Show me what the markings indicate."

A fierce summer storm had come up and lightning flashed and thunder continually reverberated in the room. They hardly paid any attention as they reviewed the map. He pointed out the disposition of Union troops, the new fortifications that had recently been built. As he mentioned each one he told her the armed personnel assigned and she made a note of the numbers on the map. They poured over the precious map for nearly an hour until Rose clearly understood all of the information it revealed.

As they finished, Rose carefully tucked the map into a book and placed it on the table. "This is too valuable to chance leaving here. I shall hide it in my own personal library adjoining my bedroom." She came over to Captain Elwood and he promptly stood up.

"You have been most kind to bring me this information,

John," she said. Throwing her arms about his neck she drew him to her. Lifting her face to his, she smiled.

"My Wild Rose," he said to her softly. He ran his hands up and down her back, then brought her to him and kissed her softly, tenderly. Then as their lips met, he kissed her again, this time passionately, fervently pressing her body against his own, her lips hard against his.

Gently she drew away from him, holding his arms in her hands.

"It is such a deplorable night, John. It is not fit for anyone to venture out. Why don't you spend the night here with me?"

John sighed. "There is nothing I would rather do, but I must go back."

Softly she smoothed the lapels of his army coat. "Is it so important that you be there, John? I will miss you terribly."

"The very thought of leaving you is miserable to me, but I am in command of my station tomorrow. I will surely be missed if I am not at my command post before dawn."

"I'm disappointed."

He pressed her arms in his hands and drew her once again to him. "But I could stay for an hour or two. After all, it is not yet midnight."

"I'm glad, John." She drew away from him and said, "It's so dreary and damp in this room. I have a cheerful fireplace going in my room upstairs. Would you care to join me?"

His face was flushed and he swallowed hard as he said, "I would be delighted."

Never letting go of his hand, she led him up the stairs through her private library and into her bedroom. He started to sit in an armchair. She gently led him to her bed. Slowly she unbuttoned his army coat and slipped it down his arms. Eagerly hunching forward he assisted her in taking it off and threw it recklessly to the floor. She slipped his necktie down and drew it from around him. Then she unbuttoned his shirt and regulation undergarment until he stood before her bare to the waist.

She pressed his shoulders down until he sat on the edge of the bed. Without a word she unfastened his boots and took them off. She slipped his army socks from his feet and carefully laid them at the foot of the bed. Then, as she went to the head of the bed, she folded over one side of the silk spread and the covers until they lay beside him.

"This will be our night, John," she said to him as she stood before him, gently running her hands over his bare chest and shoulders. As his passion began to respond to her fond caresses, he grabbed her and pulled her to him. He put his arms about her and drew her down to him. He kissed her, then drew back and looked at her lovingly. He leaned his head against her body and sighed. She took his hands and brought them up to the shoulders of her dress. Slowly she drew them apart as the low-cut dress slipped down her shoulders, partially exposing her firm breasts.

He was about to kiss her again when she slowly turned away and stood motionless with her back to him. Presently she turned and said coyly, "Well, John, are you going to assist me?"

"Oh, yes, yes," he gulped. Feverishly, he began unbuttoning the long row of buttons on the back of her dress. As he drew it past her waist, he fiercely grabbed the dress and pulled it down until it fell to the floor. Smiling at his awkwardness, she stepped out of her dress and stood beside him. Madly, impatiently, he reached inside her chemise and unbuttoned her camisole. She wriggled both of them about her until they rested at her waist, completely exposing her breasts. Savagely he grabbed at her pantalettes and her petticoats and forced them to the floor. For a brief instant she stood before him completely naked. Then she drew away and slipped under the covers, pulling them up about her. She reached above her bed and turned out the gas light. Frantically he jumped up from the bed and almost ripped his pants and underpants from him and jumped into bed.

The faint glow from the fireplace silhouetted the two beside

425

each other, one bare body pressed snugly against the other. He
wrapped his arms about her and drew her even closer. He
kissed her again and again. Leaning down he pressed her breas
hard against her and kissed it. Then, slowly, he fondled it as he
rapturously took it in his hand and covered the tip of the
mound with his mouth. Slowly she began to sway against him
until he picked up her rhythm. Finally he pushed her onto her
back and deftly slid himself between her legs. They moved in
utter, complete abandon until he became part of her. Then, in
uncontrolled passion, they moved together again and again
until, in one glorious instant, they became one in pure love and
ecstasy.

Slowly he moved away from her and lay beside her
exhausted. Quietly she snuggled into his arms. They both
gradually drifted off into a peaceful sleep. Some time later he
roused up, and suddenly feeling her in his arms, said, startled
"My God, I must have fallen asleep. What time is it?"

She turned to him and murmured sleepily, "Does it
matter?"

"The post. My station. Good Lord, I've got to get back."

"You don't have to go right now, do you?" she said to him
cozily, pulling his head to her and finding his lips in the dark
She kissed him soundly. She found his hand and placed it on
her breast. He pressed it firmly against her and returned her
passionate kisses with his own.

"What the hell does it matter?" he murmured as he brought
her body to him and once more held her beside him until their
passions were finally completely aroused. Madly he pressed
her breast with his hand while he kissed her with all his being.
Then he kissed her breasts, her stomach, and her thighs, all the
time pressing her breasts feverishly against her body. Quickly
he moved ever closer to her, until they were one. They moved
in a gentle rhythm, ever faster, until once again in a frenzy of
ecstasy they became motionless against each other's body. He
lay against her for a brief time, again completely exhausted.
"My Wild Rose," he murmured. "I never realized anything on

earth could be so wonderful."

Slowly she ran her hand through his hair. Then she took his hand and pressed it to her breast. He leaned over her and kissed her gently. Then suddenly he pulled away from her, threw down the covers and jumped out of bed. "Jesus, Rose, where is the light? I've got to go."

Slowly she leaned over to the stand beside her bed, found a match and lit it. He took it from her and lighted the gas. She blinked in the bright light, then smiled. "I suppose all wonderful things some time must come to an end."

"It doesn't have to be forever." He smiled as he grabbed his disheveled clothing and hastily put them on. Quietly she watched him dress.

"When will I see you again?"

He came to the bed and sat down beside her. "God, I never want to leave you, my Wild Rose." He kissed her and slipping his hands beneath the covers ran them up and down her bare body. Suddenly he drew away and stood up. He sighed. "If I am not careful, I shall surely stay here beyond reveille, which could be my complete downfall. We would not want that to happen would we?"

She smiled up at him. "Now that we have gotten to know each other, I too, wish it never to end." Slowly she sat up in bed and as he saw her bare breasts he came back to her, and leaning down, kissed one of them. He put his hands on both of them, and pressing her down on the bed, kissed them. Then he kissed her passionately, and finally tore himself away from her.

"Please hand me my negligee," she whispered softly.

He handed it to her. She slipped it around her and slowly got out of bed. "You did not answer me, John."

"I hope I can be forgiven but I have completely forgotten what you asked me."

"When will I see you again?"

"We will be receiving our battle plans in a day or so. As soon as I have mine and can determine the movements of the other companies as well, I shall bring them to you."

"When?"

"In two days. Three, at the most."

"I can't wait."

"Neither can I." He kissed her, straightened his tie and coat, and they went down the stairs together, her arm lovingly resting in his. As he opened the front door a strong gust of wind blew rain against them. Rose stepped back.

"It is a dreadful night to go out. Won't you stay?"

"I can't. But after this memorable night, believe me, whatever I face is worth it." He blew a kiss, and turning, went out and started down the steps.

"Next time bring more agreeable weather," she shouted to him. They laughed and he left, soon disappearing into the dark, wet night. Shoving heavily against the storm, she closed the door, sighed, and smiled. She was completely contented.

She would not have been, however, if she had noticed the shadowy figure beside her porch, thoroughly drenched to the skin, his bootless feet firmly supported on the shoulders of another man so he could see inside her parlor. Major Allan Pinkerton had been watching their every move while they were in her parlor, and had patiently waited for nearly two hours with his assistant, Pryce Lewis, as their quarry exchanged loving embraces out of their sight in her bedroom above. The trespassers' observations, however, rewarded them for their long vigil. The exchange of data they had witnessed in the parlor of 398 16th Street provided them with the proof they had been seeking in their attempts to unravel the mystery surrounding the revelation of so many vital military secrets to the enemy.

Rose went into her parlor to extinguish the light and stopped short as she noticed the window slightly open at the bottom of the sill. Going to close it, she was startled to see that one blind in front of the window was opened. She frowned. Of late she had been meticulous in keeping her windows shut and the blinds securely closed, particularly at night.

She stopped for a moment looking strangely at the window.

428

How could this have happened? "Good heavens," she murmured to herself. "I trust I am not becoming absent-minded in my later years." She closed the blind and shut and fastened the window. Thinking no more of the matter she put out the lights and went up to bed. Soon she lay peacefully in a deep sleep, completely exhausted, but complacently happy.

While she slept, Captain Elwood trudged wearily along against the storm, his clothes very soon becoming thoroughly drenched. He was not nearly as wet as was Major Pinkerton, carefully plodding along behind him, his bootless feet squooshing the rain from his socks with each step that he took. It was so dark and the storm was so heavy that Pinkerton was forced to walk closely behind his quarry. Once Captain Elwood stopped and turned quickly to look behind him. Pinkerton stood motionless hoping that the heavy rain would conceal him. Apparently the captain had reassured himself for he continued on his way.

Pinkerton, thus assured, continued to follow. Suddenly the captain turned into a military building and Pinkerton, although caught by surprise, quickly followed him. There was a guard at the door of the building, and as Pinkerton stepped inside he was suddenly confronted by four armed men with fixed bayonets drawn and menacingly pointed directly at his breast.

He was unceremoniously ushered up the stairs and into a second-story room where the man whom he had been following stood glaring at him.

"Why have you been following me?" demanded the captain.

"I—I haven't been following you. I am new to the city. I have become lost and was trying to find my way home."

"What is your name?"

"T. H. Hutcheson, sir."

"Where do you live?"

"I am from Ohio."

"What are you doing out at this hour of the night? It is after two o'clock."

"I told you I am lost. I went out to see some of the sights of the capital!"

"At two o'clock in the morning?"

"I departed quite some time ago. I have been out in this damned rain for hours. You can see for yourself. I am thoroughly drenched to the skin."

"Where are your boots?"

"I don't know, sir. I—I lost them."

The captain started to ask another question, then thought better of it. Turning to one of the guards he said crisply, "Take this man downstairs and lock him up for the rest of the night."

"But, captain, I have done nothing wrong."

"We shall see about that in the morning. We certainly aren't getting anywhere at this hour. Lock him up, corporal."

"Yes, sir." The corporal nodded to him and the newly appointed head of the Secret Service of the United States of America was unceremoniously thrown into jail. He was wet, weary, and unhappy. To make matters worse, he found himself thrust into a large, unventilated room, with several vagrants, drunks, and a robber or two, all of whom had also been plucked that night from the streets of Washington.

XXV

Home

Allan Pinkerton spent the balance of the night in jail with
the riffraff of Washington as his companions. It was not until
early the next morning that he succeeded in bribing one of the
jailers into taking a note to Thomas Scott, the assistant
secretary of war, and his superior. In less than an hour word
came through to the military jailer to release the water-soaked
Pinkerton.

He returned to his house, where he stopped long enough to
take a hot, steaming bath, and don clean, fresh clothing. He
then reported to Thomas Scott, giving him a detailed account
of what he had observed the previous night. While Pinkerton
still remained there, Captain John Elwood was called to Scott's
office. At the same time Pinkerton's man, Pryce Lewis, was
dispatched to the captain's private living quarters, with orders
to thoroughly search them.

As Captain Elwood walked into Scott's office a surprised
look of recognition crossed his face.

"Good morning, Captain Elwood," Scott greeted him,
without smiling. "Won't you be seated?"

"Thank you, sir." He sat down opposite Scott. Pinkerton
remained seated by Scott's side.

"Captain, have you ever seen this gentleman who is sitting
with me?"

"I have, sir. That man followed me early this morning. I had

431

him arrested."

"Will you give me the particulars of the incident?"

"Gladly, sir. I had gone to visit friends. They live on the outskirts of the city. As I was walking home in a heavy thunderstorm I believed that I was being followed. I led the man—this man—to my station, and immediately ordered the guards to arrest him."

"Did you see anyone last evening who is inimical to the cause of the government?"

The captain's face grew pale and he nervously stretched himself against the back of the chair. "No, sir; I have seen no person of that character."

"Do you know this man?"

"I do not. We could get no information from him earlier this morning. I ordered him confined to prison until I could question him further."

"You did not continue your interrogation this morning?"

"I did not, sir. I was assigned command of my station. Having retired late last night, delayed somewhat by this man's questionable actions, I went immediately to my command post."

"Do you know Mrs. Rose Greenhow?"

"I—the name is familiar. Yes, I am sure I have met the lady. I have seen her at several military affairs—social affairs, that is."

"But you do not know her?"

"No, sir. I do not. I beg your pardon, sir, but may I ask what your objective is in this line of questioning?"

Mr. Scott turned to the man beside him. "Captain Elwood, I would like you to meet Mr. Allan Pinkerton."

Immediately the captain stood up, and bowing stiffly, saluted. Pinkerton did not move from his chair.

"Mr. Pinkerton is the newly appointed head of the United States Secret Service."

Flustered, Captain Elwood sat back down on his chair and nervously crossed his legs. "In that case, I owe you an apology for any inconvenience I may have caused you earlier this morning." Fidgeting, he bowed his head nervously in the direction of Pinkerton.

At that moment, Pryce Lewis entered the room and came over to Pinkerton. After a hurried whisper, both men rose and went over to Scott. Whispering to Scott, Pryce handed him some papers.

Scott looked at the papers casually and then stared at Captain Elwood. "Captain, are these papers yours?"

"I don't know, sir. I can't recognize them from where I am sitting."

"Will you please inspect them?"

Captain Elwood walked over to Scott, looked over the papers carefully, then threw them carelessly back on the desk. "These papers are not mine, sir. They have nothing to do with the operation at my station."

"These are manifests of naval ships leaving the ports of Baltimore, Cape May, and Philadelphia. They list the supplies that are to be shipped to our armies. There is also a manifest of all army personnel who are being transported, and their destinations."

"They are of no interest to me, sir."

Fiercely Scott rose, and leaning so heavily on his desk that the whites of his knuckles were plainly visible, shouted, "You are correct, sir! They should be of no interest to you. Now, tell me why they were found in your living quarters?"

There was silence in the room for a moment. Then Captain Elwood blurted helplessly, "I—I—they aren't mine. I don't know—"

Quietly Scott murmured, "Kindly surrender your sword, sir."

Without another word, Captain Elwood removed his sword and scabbard and placed them on Scott's desk.

"Arrest this man," Scott said simply. Lewis went over to the captain and silently escorted him from the room.

Scott turned to Pinkerton. "Mrs. Greenhow is obviously

becoming a dangerous character and must be attended to."

Pinkerton promptly rose. "Yes, sir."

"Put a trail on our lady twenty-four hours a day. I want to know every person she speaks to. I wish a report of what she does and where she goes."

"Yes, sir." Pinkerton started to leave the room.

"Oh, Allan—"

"Yes, sir?"

"Make that a daily report. I wish to know the names of everyone—I repeat, *everyone*—to whom she speaks. But for God's sake, be discreet. Remember, she is a most important person in this town. She has many friends in government."

"Yes, sir. You can count on me, sir."

Rose continued to be as active as ever. The name of every senator, congressman, diplomat, officer, and clerk who she saw was duly reported to Scott. She soon realized that, wherever she went, she was being followed. It did not frighten her. She found it was exciting. As she walked down the avenue with an official, a washerwoman with a basket of clean clothes would pass her by; while she was speaking to a foreign diplomat on the street, a kindly-looking old gentleman would smile at her; when she contacted John Callan at the War Department, a smartly dressed young man bowed to her. But there always seemed to be something wrong with the way these passers-by acted. They watched her too closely. So she knew that she was being observed, but each time it happened the slight chill that it gave her was almost pleasurable.

She wondered why she had not heard from Captain Elwood but had little time to dwell on his absence. She was too busy.

About a week after she had seen him, she was calling on some of the senators' wives with Mrs. Martha Wright Morris. Martha was the wife of Robert Hunter Morris, who had an important position on Seward's staff. Rose had decided it behooved her to be publicly noticed with loyal members of the government; it would help dispel suspicion.

As they were on their way to Martha's house, Rose remarked

casually, "But you, Martha, have blood ties with our southern enemy, do you not?"

"Oh, but of course, Rose. My sister's husband is on General Beauregard's staff. Poor dear, I often wonder how she is making out, and if she and her family are well. I have not heard from her since the outbreak of war."

"Well, Martha, I am a personal friend of Beauregard, and if you will bring me a letter, I will see that your sister receives it."

"Oh, will you, Rose?"

"I shall be glad to. You see, I keep in contact with several of my southern friends."

"This is so kind of you, Rose, my dear. If you would help me I shall be forever grateful."

"Bring me your letter. I shall see that your sister receives it."

Rose was quite pleased with the impression she had made on Martha Morris. It would be most helpful to have a friend who was the wife of one of Seward's staff. She would not have been so happy if she had witnessed the scene at Martha's home when Martha told her husband of the incident at the dinner table that evening.

"She offered to do what?" Robert Morris exclaimed, jumping up from the table, a mouthful of food still in his mouth.

"I thought it was most considerate of her, Robert."

Hastily Robert threw his knife and fork down, and leaving the table, grabbed his hat and coat.

"Robert, what are you doing?"

"I'm going to see Bill Seward."

"At this hour? But you haven't finished your dinner."

"I have lost my appetite. Martha, do not have anything more to do with that woman. Don't speak to her again."

"But, Robert, do you object to my sending a letter to my sister inquiring into her good health?"

"I most certainly do. Listen to me. I want you to promise that you will not send any letter by Rose O'Neal Greenhow or by any other means to Richmond for the duration of the war."

"Yes, I shall promise, if it means so much to you."

"It does. Better still, come with me, Martha, to visit Seward. Let him hear first-hand what you have just told me."

"I hope I have not harmed Rose in any way," she wailed.

"You did right, my dear. Now come with me."

On the way to visit Seward, Morris was silent. As he rang the doorbell, Martha said, "I fear I am a bit in awe of Mr. Seward. He seems always to be scowling at me as if he is looking right through me."

"You need not worry, Martha. Just tell Bill exactly what you told me."

Seward himself came to the door and ushered them into his parlor.

"I must apologize for visiting you unexpectedly, Bill, but I thought you should hear what Martha has just told me. Go ahead, dear, tell Mr. Seward."

"Always glad to have you call, Morris," Seward said as he seated himself and beckoned for the rest to do likewise.

"Well, I was out visiting with Rose Greenhow this afternoon and I was bemoaning the fact that I had not heard from my dear sister since the outbreak of war. She lives in Richmond and her husband—"

"Please get to the point, dear."

"It really wasn't anything, Mr. Seward. Rose told me she is a personal friend of Beauregard's, and if I wrote a letter to my sister and gave it to her, she would see that my sister received it."

"What?" Seward shouted, jumping out of his chair.

"She must be carrying on continual underground correspondence with the Confederacy," said Morris.

"Obviously. No one knows better than I the schemes this woman is capable of, nor how boldly she can accomplish her goals. Now I believe at last we have sufficient evidence to order her arrest."

"Oh, my goodness," wailed Mrs. Morris.

"My dear little woman," said Seward, coming to her and putting his hands on her shoulders. "We wish to thank you for the great service you have rendered your country, and to tell you you have had a narrow escape in not sending a letter to Richmond."

"Oh, thank you, Mr. Secretary. I did not mean any harm to Mrs. Greenhow."

"We will not harm her, Mrs. Morris. We have been suspicious of her for quite a while. However, the time has come to put an end to her bold adventures. I shall immediately order her arrest and a thorough search of her house."

"Oh, dear," fretted Mrs. Morris.

"I shall so advise Pinkerton tonight," concluded Seward.

Martha was almost in tears as they left Seward's house. "I never dreamed Rose was committing such a terrible crime, Robert."

"It is not so bad in itself, Martha. It is just the culmination of a long string of actions—all of them seeming to lead to Rose O'Neal Greenhow."

Early in the afternoon of August 23, 1861, Rose was strolling down 16th Street on her way home with Robert Bunch, the British consul at Charleston, who was visiting Washington. He had recently received a list of United States ships that were departing northern harbors, together with their sailing dates and the cargo and personnel they were carrying. The Union had agreed to submit such lists to the British to avoid interference or seizure by any British man of war cruising in the area. Bunch believed the information might be of value to Mrs. Greenhow, and had painfully copied the information and had just now given it to her.

"I thought you might be interested," he remarked as they strolled along.

"Indeed I am, sir. I appreciate your thoughtfulness."

She hurriedly folded the piece of paper into a small wad and pressed it in her hand. She had arranged to have William Smithson, her fellow agent, meet her on the street rather than in her house, to avoid possible interception of the exchange of messages.

"I hope you will be able to join me at dinner tomorrow evening, Mr. Bunch. I am giving an informal reception for Count Rigaldo, the new chargé d'affaires of the Italian Embassy."

"I would be delighted, my dear Mrs. Greenhow."

"And now, if you will forgive my abruptness, I shall be leaving you."

"But this is not your home."

"I am stopping off at Mrs. Watson's. Her little girl has been sick and I wish to inquire about her health."

"Oh, very well then." He took her hand in his, and bowing, kissed it. She smiled and patted him gently on the cheek.

"I shall see you tomorrow evening, then," she said as he turned to go.

"I look forward to it." He waved and departed.

Rose hurried to Mrs. Watson's house and knocked on her door.

Almost immediately, as if she had been waiting for Rose to come, Mrs. Watson opened the door and beckoned her to come inside.

"I can only stay for a moment, Miranda. I am expecting a caller."

"I am so glad that you dropped by, Rose. I was afraid you would go home unaware."

"Unaware of what?"

"Three men are watching your house. They have been there for nearly two hours."

Rose looked out the window. She could plainly see the men standing in front of her house talking. A balding, middle-aged man, a younger man in a Union Army fatigue uniform, and the third in mufti. "I see that I can expect a visit from official Yankee headquarters. I really dropped in to inquire about your daughter. How is she?"

"She's fine. Up and around. Young children can be

dreadfully sick one day and the next day completely recovered."

"I am glad that she is better. Oh, that we still had their recuperative powers!"

"I should say. It takes me a week to recover if I am down with a sickness."

"I had best be off to welcome my guests."

"I hope those men do not bode you ill."

"Don't worry, Miranda. I think I can handle them." Bidding her goodbye, she casually walked out. As she started toward her house, she spotted her accomplice, William Smithson, walking toward her. She pressed the message Robert Bunch had given her tighter in her fist. She had intended to pass the information to Smithson, but, being certain now that her every move was being watched by the men at her house, she retained it.

As she passed Smithson, she whispered, "I think I am about to be arrested. Watch from Corcoran's Corner. I shall raise my handkerchief to my face if they arrest me. Give information of it."

She moved on toward her house and casually took the message wadded tightly in her hand and slipped it into her mouth. Chewing it up as best she could, she swallowed it.

She approached her house and the older man walked up to her. "Is this Mrs. Greenhow?" he asked solemnly.

"Yes," she replied. "Who are you and what do you want?"

"I am Major Allen of the United States Secret Service. I come to arrest you."

"By what authority?"

"By sufficient authority."

"Let me see your warrant."

"It is verbal authority, madam, from the War Department, and the State Department as well." At this, Allan Pinkerton alias Major Allen beckoned to the other men and they moved forward halting on either side of her. She drew out her handkerchief and rubbed it across her cheeks. Looking in the direction of Smithson, she observed him watching her intently. He nodded and quickly walked away.

They started up the steps leading to her house. "I have no power to resist you, but had I been inside my house I would have killed one of you before I submitted to this illegal process," she said. As they walked into her parlor Rose said nonchalantly, "What are you going to do now?"

"To search," Allen replied bluntly.

"I will facilitate your labors." Rose went to her mantlepiece and drew a blue paper from out of a vase. It was dated Manassas, July 23. She handed it to Allen, who stood looking at her skeptically. "Well, read it."

"To Mrs. Rose Greenhow with the compliments of Colonel Thomas Jordan, who is well, but hard-worked," Pinkerton read out loud.

"I have shown this to Henry Wilson, Major Alexander D. Rache, Captain Richard D. Cutts and several other of my friends," she remarked proudly, then added, "You would like to finish this job, I suppose."

There was nothing but the heading on the letter, the rest having been torn off. Pinkerton disdainfully threw it aside. "It tells me nothing. If you are mentioning your friends' names to impress me, let me assure you, Mrs. Greenhow, it has fallen on deaf ears."

At that moment her door gong sounded. She moved to answer it but Pinkerton intercepted her. "I shall answer it," he said bluntly.

Six more men were at the door. Obviously they were from Pinkerton's staff, for he greeted them as they entered, "Start searching this place thoroughly, men," he instructed them. "Leave no stone unturned. Search every bed, drawers, wardrobes, libraries. Search through all her clothes, don't neglect her linens, even her dirty clothes. Get to it and be hasty about it."

Within an hour the books from Rose's main library lay opened and strewn in piles about the floor. Her parlor fireplace was methodically cleaned out and half-burned papers were studiously read and discarded indiscriminately about the floor if they contained no incriminating evidence.

As they completed their search of the main floor Allen started to lead his men upstairs. "Don't you dare touch any item in the first bedroom at the head of the stairs," she warned them. "That is my daughter Gertrude's room, which I have left intact since her recent death."

Allen looked at her disdainfully and told the two men nearest to him, "Watch her closely. Do not let her out of your sight for an instant." He then continued upstairs and directly into Gertrude's room. They methodically turned every bit of furniture upside down, cleaning out all of the drawers, searching through the bed linens and clothing.

Tears of anger and frustration rolled down Rose's cheeks. Hastily she brushed them away, fearing one of the detectives would notice and mistake it for weakness or fear. Presently one of the men came in to her as she sat dejectedly in her parlor. "I am Pryce Lewis, ma'am. I might say your correspondence is the most impressive I have ever seen. It does you honor. It is truly the most extensive private correspondence that has ever fallen under my examination."

"Thank you," said Rose in a low voice, smiling for the first time since they had entered her house.

"It is most interesting and important; there is not a distinguished name in America that is not found here. There is nothing that can come under the charge of treason, but there is enough to make the government view you as a most dangerous adversary."

"I am grateful that at least one of you recognizes the true value of my correspondence."

Presently Major Allen came down and called his assistants into the parlor. Pointing out six of his men, he said, "You men return to headquarters. The rest of us will continue the search upstairs. I must warn you gentlemen not to tell anyone of Mrs. Greenhow's arrest. If we can keep this matter secret, we might receive a bonus by a visit from some of Mrs. Greenhow's friends. They could very well be carrying vital communications that we can add to our dossier on this lady."

However, Allen was disappointed in his plans for secrecy, for, as his men left, they spotted Rose's young daughter perched high above the street on the branch of a tree in front of their home. She was chanting at the top of her lungs, "Mama has been arrested! Mama has been arrested!"

Allen raced out of the house and shouted, "Get that girl down."

Two of the men quickly went into the garden, and climbing the tree, dragged the little girl down. Pinkerton grimaced as he said, "Goddamned little kid is as arrogant as her mother." He was certain that his plans for keeping the arrest quiet had been thwarted. He was not as certain about whether the little girl had broadcast the news deliberately or just as a childish prank.

It was a dreadfully hot, sultry day, and Rose, in her deep black mourning dress and many petticoats, perspired heavily as she sat in her parlor sullenly watching the guards turning her household into a shambles. Their coming, although she had expected it after the events of the past few days, left her greatly distraught. Her captors would never have imagined it as they looked at the quiet, haughty woman, seemingly completely drained of all emotion. No one, least of all the Yankee invaders, would ever have the satisfaction of knowing that their actions, their presence in the privacy of her home, was having any effect on the orderly and well-planned life of Rose O'Neal Greenhow.

It was nearing five o'clock when the door gong rang and Rose jumped up to answer it. Captain Dennis, one of her captors, hastily stepped before her and quite forcibly shoved her back into her chair. Without a word he went to the door and opened it. Rose watched through the open double doors as Lily Mackall appeared. Seeing the uniformed officer, Lily quickly turned to leave, but Captain Dennis promptly grabbed her by the wrist, and none too gently, brought her into the parlor.

"I am sorry you came, Lily," Rose said quietly, then added in a helpless voice as she looked about her, "They have been here for nearly four hours. They have left nothing untouched."

Lily came to her and put her arm about her shoulder. "I am glad I came. You poor dear."

At that moment Pinkerton, alias Allen, came into the room. Glancing at the new arrival, he scowled, "What is your name?"

"I am Lily Mackall."

"A part of this operation, I assume."

"What operation?"

"Never mind. We shall attend to you later." Turning to Captain Dennis and Pryce Lewis, who had followed him into the room, he added, "Come upstairs with me and help with the search."

As the men started to follow Pinkerton, Lily asked, "Am I free to go?"

"Of course not," Pinkerton snapped curtly.

Rose did not move and Lily stood beside her. "What about these women?" asked Captain Dennis.

"Bring them upstairs with us. We can take no chances with Mrs. Greenhow, and the other one is probably of the same stamp!"

As Pinkerton started up the stairs and Rose still did not move, Captain Dennis went to her. He grabbed her roughly by the waist and lifted her bodily from the chair.

"Take your filthy hands off me!" Rose screamed as she wriggled to free herself.

Quickly she broke away, whereupon Dennis threw his arms about her and held her firmly. Rose screamed and kicked his shins with all her might. The harder she struggled, the tighter he held her, until she was pressed against his body and completely free of the floor.

Pinkerton shouted from the stairway, "Put her down!" Then, as Dennis let go of her, Pinkerton added in a calm but firm voice, "You have your choice, Mrs. Greenhow. Either come with us of your own free will or my men will pick you up bodily and carry you upstairs."

Sullenly, Rose started for the stairs as the rest of them followed. Walking up the stairs with Captain Dennis directly behind her, she haughtily turned to him and said, "If you dare touch me again, I shall report you to Thomas Scott, whom I know to be Major Allen's superior."

As they stood at the top of the stairs, Rose said contemptuously, "It is exceedingly warm. I would imagine that even ruffians like you will permit me to go to my bedroom for a change of clothing."

"Of course," Pinkerton replied coldly and nodded to the others.

Without further exchange of words, Rose went into her bedroom, and followed by Lily, closed the door. Slowly she started to remove her clothing, by now drenched with perspiration from her ordeal.

"Have they found anything incriminating?" Lily asked anxiously.

"Not as yet. I have a right to my own political opinions and to discuss the question at issue with whomever I choose— which is all that they have uncovered."

"Good."

"But as you know I have never shrunk from the avowal of my sentiments," she went on bitterly. "There is hidden here most vital information which I have not yet dispatched to Mr. Rayford. I have been ciphering the plan of the Washington fortifications that Captain Elwood recently gave me."

"Oh, my God, where is it?"

"It is lodged in the secret lining of a cover of a book in the top shelf of my personal library outside. But with the thoroughness of their search I am sure they will find it."

"I, too, have information. I was planning to give it to you."

"Oh, good Lord. Give it to me quickly."

Lily took a small packet from the inside lining of her wide

belt and gave it to Rose. Her dress still in her hand to conceal her actions, Rose glanced at the message. "Thank goodness it is in code. But we must destroy it."

Quickly she went to her bedside table and drew out a revolver. Holding the gun loosely, she twisted the papers into thin, long pieces. She grabbed a metal canister of rice powder, and dumping its contents on the floor, put the papers into the canister and burned them. As they turned to ash, she took them to the fireplace and threw the remains onto the grate. She threw the canister into a basket of wood beside the fireplace.

Suddenly there was a knock on the door. Covering her gun with her dress, she stood passively facing the door as it opened and Captain Dennis peered in. They stared silently at each other for a moment as she pointed the concealed gun directly at his heart. Seeing that nothing was amiss he turned away and closed the door.

"Good luck was with him," Rose said coldly. "I should have killed him. I raised my revolver with that intent; and so steady were my nerves that I would have balanced a glass of water on my finger without spilling a drop."

"But what are you going to do about—"

"Please do not mention it. I swear to you, if need be, I shall set the house on fire rather than permit them to discover those plans."

"Oh, Rose, I hope—" Lily stopped in the middle of her sentence as the door opened again. A fat, ordinary-looking woman came into the room and waddled over to Rose. Without smiling she announced coarsely, "My name is Ellen. I have been ordered to search your person."

Rose started to protest, then thought better of it. "Do so at your will."

Ellen took the dress Rose was holding revealing the gun still in her hand. "Please do not make any false move, Mrs. Greenhow. There is a guard just outside the door." As Ellen reached for the gun, Rose handed it to her.

Ellen turned the gun over to the guard outside. One by one

445

she removed each garment from Rose's body with the exception of her shoes and the stockings which drooped loosely about her ankles. Finally Rose stood proudly immobile before her, stark naked. "I am sorry for the inconvenience, ma'am," Ellen said as she carefully inspected each of her garments.

"It is only one more disgrace I have been forced to suffer since those hoodlums illegally entered my home."

"You may put your clothing back on," Ellen said. "I shall report that I have found nothing."

"Of course not," Rose replied bitterly. "What did you expect to find, a plot to blow up the city of Washington or perhaps to assassinate President Lincoln?"

Without another word, Ellen opened the door and left.

"Wasn't she homely?" remarked Lily.

"Her face is like an India rubber doll's. You were fortunate that you were not subjected to my embarrassment."

Rose slowly dressed, putting on a complete change of clothing. The clean white linens and silks were comforting to her.

There followed a long period of anxious waiting, while Rose tried to busy herself as best she could, not knowing what the men outside her door were doing or whether they had yet found any incriminating evidence.

Finally Pinkerton came into her room accompanied by a guard. He threw the door wide open and announced, "I am leaving for the night. I have ordered additional guards for your house both inside and out. We will be happy to entertain any guests who might come by with a thorough interrogation." Rose looked at him scornfully but did not reply. "This is your guard, who will remain in this room with you."

"You cannot do this to us."

"The guard will leave only when you advise him of your personal needs or wish to change your clothing, but your door must remain open at all times."

"We are entitled to some privacy."

"Frankly, Mrs. Greenhow, we cannot take any chances.

Before I leave I shall order whatever you wish for dinner and a guard will fetch it for you."

"I am not hungry."

"It is a long time until morning. I have left orders that under no circumstances are you to be permitted to leave this room. You would be wise to take advantage of our generous offer."

"I wish nothing, thank you."

Pinkerton shrugged his shoulders and turned to Lily. "Miss Mackall?"

"I do not wish anything, thank you. But why must I stay? Whatever you are looking for, you surely do not believe I can be of assistance to you."

"We shall decide that in due time, Miss Mackall. In the meantime you will remain right where you are. Now, do you wish us to order any food for you?"

"Nothing."

"Very well. I bid you goodnight, ladies." As he went to the door he smiled graciously. "Pleasant dreams, madam." He left.

The guard removed his rifle from his shoulder and leisurely slumped into one of Rose's silk-cushioned boudoir chairs.

Rose and Lily exchanged glances and settled down in chairs themselves. Both of them were nervous. Now, having to be careful of everything they said with the guard in their very room, the suspense seemed almost unbearable.

"Have patience, Lily. They are doing their utmost to unnerve us."

"They have succeeded where I am concerned."

"You must not show any sign of weakness. Remember, Lily, it is for a cause we both believe in."

The guard scowled as he glared at them but said nothing. The hours passed slowly. Finally, when it was nearly dark, the guard casually got up and lit two gas lamps in the room. None of them spoke. Presently the door gong sounded downstairs. There was movement on the floor below and eventually they heard voices and the footsteps coming up the stairs.

Lily ran to the open doorway, only to be stopped by the

guard outside the room. As the newcomers approached, she suddenly exclaimed, "Mother!"

Lily's mother and sister entered the room accompanied by a guard. "Lily, are you all right?" asked Mrs. Mackall.

"Of course I am, but why are you here?"

"We were worried when you did not come home to dinner," replied her sister.

"You shouldn't have come," said Rose.

"But—" Mrs. Mackall hesitated to talk as she eyed the guards. Then she continued, picking her words carefully as she spoke. "Whatever has happened downstairs, Mrs. Greenhow? It is a mess."

"Isn't it? They have been ransacking my house ever since early afternoon. They have found nothing, but they still continue to hold us prisoners and without legal authority!"

"Well—I suppose we can leave you now that we know you are all right, Lily," said Mrs. Mackall uncertainly. "I will go immediately to my lawyer to see what can be done to get you released."

She turned to go but the guard suddenly stood in front of her. "Madam, we have orders not to permit anyone who enters this house to leave until they have been cleared."

"You mean that we are now prisoners as well?"

Rose jumped up. "This is an outrage. Whatever you expect to find here does not concern these people. They are innocent."

"We are only obeying orders."

"We have sent to headquarters for further instructions," said the other guard. "Until we receive them, you will have to stay here."

"Make yourselves comfortable, Mrs. Mackall. I can see that in time of war this poor deprived nation has no consideration for either defenseless woman or child."

Sighing, the four women sat down. Being extremely conscious of the guard who sat close by staring at them, they looked blankly at each other.

The clock above the fireplace mantle showed twenty minutes after eleven when Rose walked over to the guard.

"Do you drink?" she asked.

"I beg your pardon?"

"Do you enjoy liquor?"

"I do ma'am."

"I have entertained most of the leaders of this nation in my house. Diplomats and even royalty from many of the kingdoms of Europe have been guests at my parties."

"I know, ma'am. I have heard that you are one of the greatest party throwers this country ever knew."

"I pride myself on my wine and liquor store. Would you care to sample some of the brandies and rums that heads of state have drunk?"

"It is against regulations to drink on duty."

"The hell with that. What harm can it do? Four helpless women confined to one room. Surely this does not require too stringent surveillance. It may be some time before I entertain guests freely again. It seems a shame to let my stock of fine liquors go unsampled."

"I suppose a taste of your fine liquors wouldn't do any harm."

"I'm sure it wouldn't. And with a guard posted outside our bedroom there is little chance of our attempting to escape."

"Of course, I'd have to bring Roger into the deal, too."

"Roger?"

"He's the guard outside the door."

"Certainly you must include him. Tell me, is Pryce Lewis still here?"

"No, he left right after dinner."

"Good. My liquor cabinet is in the rear corner of the dining room. I have several bottles of ten-year-old Courvoisier brandy in stock. Go down and help yourself. You will find glasses on the shelves above the cabinet. Take as much as you wish. Give the men downstairs a treat."

"Well, now, I don't know—"

"It's going to be a long night, officer."

"I am not an officer. I'm just a corporal."

"You have the makings of a fine officer."

"Well, thank you ma'am."

"It is still many hours until dawn."

"I know it. I hate guard duty at night."

"It must get terribly monotonous."

"It does for sure. Let me go out and talk to Roger."

"By all means."

The guard started for the door. As he was about to leave, he turned back and warned, "Now no shenanigans while I am gone."

Rose gave him her most capricious smile. "What could we possibly do?"

"Yeah, that's right." He disappeared.

They could hear the guards talking between themselves. Their voices became louder as they discussed Rose's offer. Rose whispered, "This is worth a try. I have got to get those plans of the Washington fortification or we are all doomed."

Mrs. Mackall put her hand to her mouth and gasped. "Oh, dear."

"If I do not retrieve them, I vow, I shall burn my house down."

"Oh, dear," repeated Mrs. Mackall, more startled than before.

Presently the guard returned. "Roger was not hard to convince. We shall be glad to sample your brandy."

"Very good judgment, corporal."

"Is it true that it is the brandy that Napoleon drank?"

"He never went into battle without a goodly quantity of it in his quarters and inside himself."

"I'm going downstairs. But Roger will be coming into your room while I am gone."

As the guard left, Roger entered their room, grinning from ear to ear. He sauntered over to a vacant chair beside Rose's bed and plopped himself down with a smug air of anticipation. His smiling countenance soon changed, however, as the minutes passed and his fellow guard did not reappear.

Finally, after nearly half an hour, Roger suddenly jumped from his chair and menacingly grabbed his rifle. "How long does it take to get a bottle of brandy? That damn Irishman's jolly well helping himself, that's what."

Rose smiled at his sudden outburst. "You're English, aren't you?"

"Yes, and mighty proud of it."

"You had trouble with the Irish back in the old country, didn't you?"

"Yeah, that's right. I always said you can't trust an Irishman out of your sight."

Just then a loud cheer rose from below and some of the men began singing. Scowling, Roger ran out of the room and started down the stairs. Suddenly he turned, and looking back at the women, returned to the head of the stairs. Hanging over the banister he shouted, "Hey, you damned Irishman, what about me?"

"I'm coming up. Just hold on to your horses!" came the shout from below. Presently the guard came thumping heavily up the stairs and greeted Roger with a resounding whack on the back.

"What's the idea of leaving me stranded here while you celebrate without me?"

"They wouldn't let me go."

"Where's my brandy?"

"I forgot it. But there's plenty more downstairs. Go help yourself," smiled the guard cheerfully as he came into the bedroom. Then, bowing to Rose, he added, "That is, with our gracious hostess's permission."

"Of course," Rose smiled.

As Roger started down stairs, he threw his rifle to the other guard and shouted, "Goddamned no-good Irishman."

The Irishman rushed to the top of the stairs. "What do you mean by that?" Then he looked at his charges, and mumbling to himself, came back into the room.

"The English are not noted for their sense of humor," Rose said sympathetically.

"That's right," agreed the guard. "My father always said they never show no emotion so's no one will know how stupid they really are." Then he laughed uproariously.

So the first night of Rose's imprisonment wore wearily on. The monotony of the ordeal was greatly relieved as the guards freely imbibed Rose's rare brandy and rum. The two upstairs guards almost came to blows on more than one occasion, arguing nationality differences and accusing each other of staying downstairs for too long.

Eventually, in the early morning hours, they wearied of their drinking and it became a major problem to remain awake. Finally Roger slumped in his chair and dozed off. Rose jumped up and whispered to Lily, "Now is my opportunity to recover the plans. If he rouses, call me."

The guard outside her room was sleeping so soundly he was snoring. She tiptoed out of her room and quickly climbed to the top bookshelf where the plans were securely hidden in a book. Ripping them out, she hid them under her dress and slipped back into her room. As she entered, Lily put her finger to her lips and pointed to Roger, who was still sleeping, with his chin resting heavily on his chest.

"You will undoubtedly be released before I. Take these plans and dispose of them."

"Where can I hide them?" Lily replied, frightened.

"When Ellen searched me she did not search my shoes or stockings. Take off your stockings."

Quickly Lily removed her shoes and stockings and the two women frantically slipped the telltale papers into the soles of the stockings. Lily then replaced them and her shoes.

452

"No one would ever suspect," said Mrs. Mackall.

"If they should search you as you leave, immediately come back to me. Tell them you wish to share the honors of the conflagration."

Once again they continued their monotonous wait, though now Rose felt more secure, with the telltale evidence removed.

XXVI

Prison

Shortly after four o'clock the following morning, another contingent of guards marched into the house to relieve those on duty. The latter tried valiantly to cover up the evidence of their night's celebration by appearing uncommonly alert and attentive. The replacing guards also brought word that Lily and her mother and sister were free to go.

Lily promised to visit Rose later in the day and she and her family quickly left the frightful scene. Wearily, Rose removed her shoes and slipped into bed, while a new guard sat stealthily watching her from inside her door. In spite of his sullen glare, she was so exhausted that she soon dropped off to sleep.

Fairly early in the morning, Rose was roused from her few hours of fitful sleep by guards resuming their search. Now they thoroughly inspected her own personal library. Robert's books, many of them priceless and written in foreign languages, were rudely pulled from their shelves, thoroughly searched and recklessly thrown on the floor. Some that they suspected might conceal evidence in the covers were torn apart. As she sadly watched the ransacking of her husband's prized possessions, she smiled bitterly to herself. At least she had succeeded in outsmarting them. The telltale evidence that could incriminate her was out of their reach.

The search continued for days. Her papers were wrapped in bundles, packed in boxes, and taken away to be closely scrutinized for evidence against her.

Every bit of furniture was overturned. Drawers were emptied of their contents in the hopes of discovering secret hiding places. Her beautiful wardrobe, which had grown through the years as her exclusive fashions were added, was searched, then carelessly thrown in heaps on the floor.

Rose was glad that Lily was permitted free access to her home. She visited every day. On more than one occasion, Rose was able to slip vital evidence to her under the very noses of the guards. At first she instructed Lily to destroy it all. Later, as they both grew more bold, Rose decided that, since many of the items contained valuable information still important to the southern military, Lily should pass it on to one of Rose's agents. Lily began to bring her additional military data. It seemed that once again they had outsmarted Rose's captors. They could continue their clandestine operation even though Rose was a closely guarded prisoner in her own house.

Both Rose and Lily were fairly secure in the knowledge that nothing incriminating had been discovered. One day, however, Lily casually picked up a blotting paper still resting on Rose's writing table, and wide-eyed, pulled it off and showed it to her. There, plainly visible, was the imprint of Rose's vital message of July 16 concerning the preparations for Manassas.

Without attracting the guard outside the bedroom, the two women tore the blotter into bits and hid them in the soles of Lily's stockings.

"Thank God I discovered it before they did," Lily whispered.

"Just another evidence that Providence watches over me as a humble instrument in a glorious cause."

Their new system for conducting spying operations was being accomplished so easily that Rose had misgivings about it. She finally realized that Lily was being followed, and that several arrests were directly traceable to missions that she had sent Lily on. First, there was the information about the disposition of troops which Rose instructed Lily to pass on to

Frank Rennehan for delivery to Richmond. Lily did so, and before nightfall Frank was arrested—before he had an opportunity to pass on the information. Then, she discovered the note she had received when Michael Thompson had introduced himself to her. Fortunately, the detective police had not yet discovered it. She gave the message to Lily with instructions to take it to Thompson and warn him of the danger he was in. Lily smuggled the note out of the house in the bodice of her dress, since the guards gave her only a cursory inspection as she departed. She promptly delivered the incriminating note to Thompson and warned him. Early the next morning he was awakened by the detective police, who, upon searching his house, discovered the telltale note and arrested him. Finally William J. Walker was arrested, shortly after he had given Lily important military information he had intercepted at the post office.

They immediately abandoned their latest procedure. Lily could not be used as a courier, for obviously she had been granted free access to Rose's house so that she would lead the police to other members of their organization.

Within a week, a strange man visited Rose, offering to deliver messages to the South. He seemed authentic enough, having a decidedly southern accent and actually giving her the secret password. However, Rose politely declined his offer, feeling certain that he was simply an agent from the provost marshal's office sent to spy on her.

Lily and Rose actually laughed in spite of the situation as Lily brought her word of the effect her arrest was causing in government circles. The letters from 'H' brought a certain senator under suspicion and caused him several embarrassing meetings as he assured government officials of his own innocence. Many of Rose's papers were discussed privately at a Cabinet meeting. Several Republican officials were called in to explain their association with the lady as revealed by her correspondence. Black Republicans, Democrats, judges, lawyers, military officers, clerks, even Cabinet members were extensively questioned concerning their activities with Rose. Few prominent men in the capital were not questioned with regard to their associations with the notorious Rose Greenhow. Although she was confined to her home, which had now become her prison, she gloried in the massive investigation that was being conducted by the government to try and unravel the vast chain of espionage with which she had been involved. Through it all, they found little with which to convict her of outright treason.

"Lincoln and his Cabinet were greatly disturbed at the accuracy of some of the drawings of fortifications that they found," Lily reported. "Their unanimous opinion was that they could not have been drawn by a woman."

"They are correct. I hope that they do not trace them to poor John Callan. But they know that I was involved, and their obvious distress does justice to the zeal with which a southern woman can execute her patriotic duty."

"They actually deliberated whether you should be publicly tried for treason and made an example of."

Rose's usually calm demeanor was suddenly shattered as she looked at Lily with a startled expression. Remembering Senator Gwin, who was still lodged in jail, and the recent arrests of several of her contacts, she asked almost fearfully, "Lily, do you believe that they will go so far as to bring me to public trial?"

"Not at present. Lincoln's Cabinet decided against it. Your social position is such that they dare not."

"Their fears have elevated me to a most dangerous eminence. Truly, Lily, I have many devoted friends in their own ranks, a fact of which they are well aware."

As the days dragged on, it seemed that her captors were endeavoring to try Rose to her utmost. She was never allowed to be alone; while she slept, a guard watched over her in a nearby chair. When she changed clothes, she was permitted the privacy of her room, but her door was kept open at all times, while guards peeked in to watch her as she changed.

457

Their leering glances mortified her, but never once did she give them any indication of her discomfort.

Through every trying day, she continued to receive messages from her many agents, and by devious means, to still send vital information on its way to Richmond.

Lily's visits were a godsend. She kept Rose abreast of current activities. They both chortled gleefully when Lily told her how piqued the adminstration was at her continued ability to thwart their every move to isolate her from outside contacts.

Less than a month after the fateful August day of her arrest, she sent a comprehensive report to Rayford. "Our friends here all are ready to cooperate and carry out what I planned. I have signals, take care that the cipher does not fall into their hands. I destroyed it and every paper of consequence, but oh my God, with what danger, with twenty detectives following my every step.

"McClellan is fast making the army efficient; it has been in a deplorable state. They look for an attack and are greatly puzzled to know what is the plan. They make blunders every day. The appointment of the French princes was one. Foreign ministers all sympathize with us. Spies are employed to every class and more is spent on the secret service than ever before. Destroy the cipher; thousands are offered for it and for weeks the most skillful detectives are at work at it. As yet nothing has been made of it.

"Artillery is constant and severe, about sixty thousand troops are surrounding, including McDowell's command. They come in slowly and badly equipped. Meigs asks for private contributions of blankets. You are losing golden moments. Bitter feuds in sections of the party. I am sorry to see that Lincoln is going with the strongest party—that which opposed interfering with slavery. They speak of the mild and beneficent institution, etc. etc. Think of me with guards at my chamber door with bayonets; how long is this to last? Enclosed is a list of the forts, it is a work of the wise."

Late in September it appeared that Rose might be freed. The

horrendous job of tracking down and overseeing the great number of southern spies and sympathizers was becoming too great for the fledgling detective police and what military personnel could be spared. More and more spies were being released upon swearing oaths of allegiance to the Union. Rose was elated at the thought of being released from her dreadful existence.

Then Lily brought word that shattered her hopes.

"The authorities still do not know what to do with you. But Mr. Pinkerton is well aware of their leniency and has written a strong letter to Provost Marshal Porter warning him of the great mistake they would be making if you were to be released. He told them that you are the head of the southern spy ring that encompasses spies throughout Washington, and, in fact, all over the country. He has submitted a list of all the names of the persons with whom you have had correspondence. He advised Mr. Porter that you openly engaged, for months before your arrest, in giving aid, comfort, sympathy, and information to the enemy. I could not secure the report, but I did get a portion of it from John Callan, who, incidentally, sends his sincerest wishes for your early release. He hopes that he may see you again soon. Now, here is a copy of part of Pinkerton's report."

Lily handed her a closely written sheet of paper and Rose read: "She has made use of whomever and whatever she could as mediums to carry into effect her unholy purposes. She has not used her powers in vain among the officers of the army, not a few of whom she has robbed of patriotic hearts and transformed into sympathizers of the enemies of the country which has made them all they were.

"For a great many years Mrs. Greenhow has been the instrument of the very men who now lead in the rebel councils and some of those who command their armies; they have successfully used her as a willing instrument in plotting the overthrow of the United States government, which she, no less than they, had desired to accomplish; and since the commencement of this rebellion this woman, with her uncommon social powers, her very extensive acquaintance among and her active association with the leading politicians of this nation, has possessed an almost superhuman power, all of which she has most wickedly used to destroy the government. She, as have other traitors, has been most unscrupulous in the means she has chosen. Nothing has been too sacred for her appropriation, so long as by its use she might hope to accomplish her treasonable ends."

As Rose finished reading the excerpt from Pinkerton's report, she breathed a long sigh and pressed the paper against her bosom. Slowly, carefully, she folded the sheet and tucked it beneath her dress against her breast. She smiled. "It is almost worth the hardships and degradation I have been subjected to to know in what high esteem that little bastard holds my unceasing activities for the cause which is dearest to my heart."

Lily smiled and shook her head. "It is a sound case against you, Rose."

"It is that. I would never release any prisoner who has been credited with such talents."

She smoothed her long strands of black hair that were becoming streaked with gray, drew them on top of her head and knotted it all in a bun. For a moment she was the proud, haughty, and distinguished Rose of old. "Thank you for bringing me this, Lily. It has tremendously boosted my morale which has suffered so greatly in these trying, tedious days I endure."

All hopes of release were forgotten. After Pinkerton's glowing denunciation of her, she did not expect any. "My castle has become my prison," she wrote to Varina Davis in a letter she was able to smuggle out to the underground. "The detective police have blasted every hallowed association of my home. They have stooped so low as to take poor Gertrude's trinkets!"

Pinkerton was beside himself as he realized that information was still being transmitted to the South. He credited it to his comely prisoner, Mrs. Greenhow. He knew that Lily Mackall had to be involved, as well.

It was a sad day in September when Lily visited Rose and announced, "This is my last visit. They have forbidden me to call on you again."

Rose's lips quivered in fury. "I shall protest this. They are only being spiteful in denying me this one bit of womanly companionship."

"It will do no good to protest, Rose. Pinkerton has succeeded in having his order countersigned by Secretary Seward."

"They are bound and determined to make my life miserable. But I shall not let them. I shall rise above this as I have all else!" Suddenly Rose glared fiercely at Lily and her eyes widened as she whispered. "Better still, we must retain contact with each other. Every day at precisely the same time—I suggest three o'clock in the afternoon—walk by my house. Be on the alert for a message from me. I shall be watching from my daughter Rose's room—it faces the street."

"But how can we communicate?"

"Spell the letters of the deaf and dumb. Are you familiar with them?"

"I am aware of them. I don't know—"

"Watch me closely," said Rose eagerly. Hastily she went through the letters of the alphabet and Lily followed her every motion. Lily enthusiastically repeated nearly all of the signs over and over to be sure that she knew them.

Thereafter, every afternoon at three, Lily walked by her house on the opposite side of the street, and Rose and she exchanged messages.

Thus Rose was able to carry on her work. She made her every gesture count, and many times even succeeded in whispering messages through her barred doors. Her daughter, little Rose, now eight years old, took no small part in her contacts. Young Rose had enjoyed unsupervised freedom since her mother's arrest. She often played in front of their house on the sidewalk. She became an ideal courier, and Rose thoroughly implanted in her the need for secrecy.

One of the agents carefully slipped a note beneath the young girl's dress, cautioning her not to give it to anyone but her mother and to do so when no one was watching. The note said: "Samuel F. du Pont is sailing from Fortress Monroe on October 23 with seventy-seven vessels to land forces commanded by Thomas W. Sherman."

Rose diligently sewed the message inside the sole of her daughter's shoe and then instructed her to deliver it to Lily, making sure not to arouse the suspicions of the guards.

Soon thereafter, Rose received another message. "General Ambrose E. Burnside is leading a naval expedition from Fortress Monroe for Albemarle Sound, North Carolina, about January 1." This information she conveyed to Lily, by means of her visual code, like a continued story, over a period of three days.

Outraged at the continued flow of messages going forth from 398 16th Street, Stanton ordered that Rose should be barred from her daughter's front bedroom. Henceforth, Rose was to be confined to her own bedroom at the rear of the house. Fortunately Lily thought to walk down the side street from where Rose's window was visible and contact was continued. When the messages did not cease, Rose's bedroom window was locked and covered with huge iron bars through which only shallow slits of sunlight could permeate.

Lily sent word to her that Rose's house was now known as Greenhow prison, and that she could expect other female prisoners to join her at any time.

The detective police were replaced by military men, most of whom were of a more refined and gentlemanly manner. Lieutenant Sheldon was in command, and a total of twenty guards was assigned to Greenhow prison. Rose lost no time in making the acquaintance of Lieutenant Sheldon, and she tried her best to use him to her advantage, as she had done with so many other of his fellow military officers. But she soon learned that, although he was always polite and actually kind to her, she could not undermine his loyalty to the Union.

As Lily predicted, other guests began to arrive. Mrs. Philip Phillips was among the first, but Rose's cheerfulness at the thought of having female companionship was short-lived. They were not permitted to communicate. Mrs. Bettie Hassler was the next to arrive, and Rose frowned uncertainly as she watched her being escorted into her home. Bettie was one of her trusted couriers. Rose wondered how many others the Secret Service were discovering.

Apparently, upon searching Mrs. Phillips's home, the detective police had discovered incriminating evidence that involved her whole family. Two days later Mrs. Phillips's daughters Caroline and Fanny were brought into the prison and locked in one of the downstairs rooms.

Less than a week later, a Mrs. Medora A. Onderdonk came to Greenhow prison. Rose received a clandestine message that this good lady was a common whore from the streets of Chicago. She never did learn what her offense was, but when she was assigned to Gertrude's room, Rose screamed at the top of her lungs for Lieutenant Sheldon. That good man hastily came to her. When he learned of his error, Mrs. Onderdonk was summarily assigned to another room at Greenhow prison.

Rose thought of still another means of communication and advised her captors that, since she had so many idle hours, she would like, once again, to take up the art of tapestry. Agreeably, the provost marshal's office provided her with innocent balls of wool. These she promptly converted into a system for conveying information to her outside contacts. Red indicated that it would be dangerous to contact her. White specified that the coast was clear. Green meant that she had a message for which she desired someone to contact her. Yellow advised that her daughter Rose would have a message to be picked up on the following day. The symbols were painstakingly worked out with Lily. Contact was also maintained by embroidering the alphabet of the deaf and dumb on her patterns and smuggling them in and out.

One fall day Stanton visited her house. Lieutenant Sheldon told Rose that Stanton was arranging for the release of Mrs. Phillips and her daughters. He had also secured safe escort for them through the Union lines to the South. Remembering her association with Stanton in the many land claim trials in California and his brilliant defense of Dan Sickles in the jealousy murder of young Philip Key, she begged the lieutenant to deliver a message to Stanton before he left her house.

"Tell him I wish to secure his assistance in drawing up a writ of habeas corpus in order to secure my release from prison."

Lieutenant Sheldon left to deliver her message. He returned a few minutes later, his face flushed, to inform her that, "Mr. Stanton sends his deepest regrets but advises that he is unable to comply with your request. He shall be glad to assist you in any other way that he can."

"Poppycock!" exclaimed Rose, turning hastily away to hide the look of disappointment that crossed her face. A short time later she sadly watched Stanton go down the stairs accompanied by Mrs. Phillips and her two daughters. As Stanton departed, he did not once look in her direction. As he disappeared from view she sadly wondered to herself if he knew it was she who had recommended that he be Buchanan's attorney general.

The following day she received a vital message concerning an imminent attack. Hastily she wrote a ciphered message and placed it at the center of a ball of pink wool. She advised Lieutenant Sheldon that she was in need of exercise, and he assigned a guard to accompany her on a stroll through the streets. She made it a point to pass by Mrs. Phillips's house. As she noted an open window, she went up and called. When Mrs. Phillips came, Rose said casually, "Here is the yarn you left at my house." Throwing it into the open window she went on with her walk, laughing and talking with the guard who accompanied her. Mrs. Phillips took the yarn with her to the South. In spite of being searched at Fortress Monroe, she still had the yarn when she arrived in Richmond.

Mrs. Phillips immediately called on President Davis, and told him about how Rose had thrown the wool into her window. She then gave it to him. He unwound the wool and at the center found Rose's message: "Cape Fear River; Smithville, are to be the real points of attack."

Under any circumstances Rose would have been a constant thorn in the sides of the northern leaders. She had known many of the Black Republicans on an intimate basis, and Seward, Wilson, McClellan and many other advisers to Lincoln were aware that she could embarrass them no end if she cared to divulge their many secrets. In addition, her continual spying despite all precautions they took to discourage her, made it difficult for them to decide how best to handle this indomitable woman.

A new inmate was brought into Greenhow prison by the name of Miss Ellen M. Poole. She constantly checked into Rose's every move, as well as those of her young daughter. To make matters worse, she reported everything she saw, or sometimes imagined, to the guards. It grew particularly irksome and Rose complained to Lieutenant Sheldon. "The miserable existence that I am forced to endure is not degrading enough," she said to him. "You now take sadistic pleasure in bringing that Poole woman here to spy on my every move and dutifully report to you."

"That is not true, Mrs. Greenhow. We do not encourage her to spy on you. She is doing this of her own free will."

"Well, keep her away from me."

"It is impossible in the small confines of your house." As Rose glared at him, he added, "We will do our best to separate her from you."

She knew that every letter she wrote was not only censored but closely studied for any clues that might lead to her methods of disclosure. Knowing it would not be safe to use coded messages, since the War Department had now broken all the codes they had previously used, she resorted to garbled messages which made no sense to any but the intended receiver. Lily smuggled a note to her by young Rose advising that the provost marshal's office could not believe that such a clever woman as Mrs. Greenhow should write such nonsensical drivel. In the same note Lily provided her with specific information about a vast naval maneuver which was to take place in two weeks.

Rose desperately needed a messenger to convey the information to the South. She spent many hours devising an innocuous message that she was sure would pass through the hands of her guards and the office of the provost marshal. "Tell Aunt Sally that I have some old shoes for the children and I wish her to send someone downtown to take them and to let me know whether she has found any charitable person to help her to take care of them."

Two days after she had mailed her letter, William T. Smithson, the banker who was not yet suspected, dropped by her house to inquire concerning her health. Learning that she was in good spirits, he asked if he could see her. The guards permitted him to visit her for fifteen minues. This was sufficient time for him to cheer her up and receive the vital message from her, again directly under the noses of her captors.

Lily unceasingly sought Rose's release by every means that occurred to her. She spoke to each member of Lincoln's Cabinet, and finally, late one afternoon, was granted an audience with President Lincoln himself. Plaintively she begged that Rose be released and sent beyond the Union borders to the South, like so many other sympathizers.

Lincoln looked at her impassively as he rose from his desk and said, "That woman has had too much good treatment already. She has done more to damage and bring my government into disrepute than all the rest of the darned rebels together, and by God, she shall never see me again if I can help it." Lily bowed graciously and left him, unable to withhold the tears that streamed down her cheeks. Her last hope for Rose's release was shattered.

Shortly thereafter, Lily caught a severe cold, and, her resistance low from her exhaustive efforts, she soon developed pneumonia. Mrs. Mackall sent Lily's brief message to Rose through her other daughter. "I am deathly ill. Please come to me."

Rose wrote a pleading note to Seward begging his permission to visit her dear friend. The following day Lieutenant Sheldon showed her his reply. "The provost marshal will please inform Mrs. Greenhow that, in consequence of her correspondence with the general commanding armies now besieging Washington, her request to visit the house of Mrs. Mackall cannot be complied with, as it would be an interference with military arrangements."

Rose bowed her head. Slowly she stood up and looked directly into the lieutenant's eyes as she said, "Although I am sadly grieved that I will not be permitted to visit my very dear friend who is so ill, Mr. Stanton's denial is actually a compliment to my prowess in espionage, which he obviously greatly fears."

Three days later, on the second of October, Rose received word that Lily Mackall had died. For the first time since becoming a prisoner, she threw herself on the bed and cried uncontrollably.

During the weeks that followed, Rose was thrust into a deep depression. She ate sparsely and stared speechlessly before her for many hours at a time. She missed the contacts with the outside world that she had been able to maintain through Lily, despite all efforts to disrupt them. Now, they were gone. Lily was gone. Rose was despondent—desperate.

In order to shake herself out of her melancholy and to help herself regain some of her old defiant mood, she began to write down the events that had befallen her since she had been made prisoner. As she reviewed her notes, she determined that the nation should know of her plight and of the suffering that she had encountered at the hands of her captors. She wrote a scathing letter and addressed it to President Lincoln. Then, believing that Stanton was primarily responsible for the treatment that she had received, she changed her mind and addressed the letter to him.

On November 17 she was able to smuggle the letter out of her prison, together with a copy to Thomas J. Rayford. "I defy you to imprison my soul, if you dare," she wrote bitterly and felt better putting the words onto paper. She angrily condemned the invasion of her privacy, of having to change her very clothing within full view of her guards. She described, with dramatic force, her rough handling and the drunken brawls that went on in her home which was her prison. She denounced the seizure of her private papers: "The Iron Heel of power may keep down, but it cannot crush out the spirit of resistance in a people armed for the defense of their rights. It is your boast that thirty-three bristling fortifications surround Washington. The fortifications of Paris did not protect Louis Philippe when his hour had come."

She was delighted to learn that her letter was published in the *Richmond Whig* and reprinted in the *New York Herald*. She heard that Stanton was furious, Lincoln was embarrassed, and many of her old friends cried out in her defense. But the letter and its widespread publicity doomed her to even more stringent regulations.

"That woman must be silenced," raved Stanton, his face livid with rage. But still he did not dare move too swiftly. He could not punish her too severely, particulary since her letter had caused such great anguish in the hearts of many chivalrous men.

Her old friend James Gordon Bennett did not agree with her, however, and called attention to the disastrous results of her possible release. "Grant all the personal rights of freedom of speech and action which Mrs. Greenhow demands in the midst of this great rebellion, and we may as well abolish our armies and turn over the country to unrestrained ruffianism; for under this system of liberty we should all be at the mercy of ruffians and robbers."

As Christmas drew near, her sister Ellen finally visited her for the first time, accompanied by her daughter Addie. It was a joyous reunion, for Rose had not seen either of them since her imprisonment, nor had she heard from them. They brought her a cake and Addie had several small presents for little Rose.

"Thank you, Ellen. Thank you, Addie," Rose smiled with tears in her eyes. "It has been so long."

"You are making it hard for yourself, Rose," said Ellen, putting her hand on her arm. "Graceful submission will end it all."

"I realize you do not concur in my thinking. I know that you condemn my actions. But please grant me the right to submit to my instincts as I gladly grant you yours."

Addie shrugged her shoulders. "If you will only relent, Aunt Rose, we have many friends who will mediate in your behalf."

"Such thoughts are inconsistent with my own feelings and derogatory to my honor."

"But you must think of little Rose," begged Addie. "Your own safety is in danger if you continue to alienate every member of our government."

"Do you wish me to repudiate my principles? Are you asking me to deny everything for which I have stood and worked incessantly?"

There was silence in the room for a moment. Then Addie faced her squarely and looking directly in her eyes, unflinching as her aunt glared at her, replied calmly, "Yes."

"Never!" shouted Rose.

The guard came into the room. "I am sorry, ladies, but you are only permitted fifteen minutes and your time is up."

Ellen and Addie kissed Rose and her daughter goodbye, and crying unashamedly, left.

The day before Christmas, another cake was delivered to Rose, but upon close inspection it was found to contain several bank notes. One of the guards came up to her room, and waving the bank notes before her, jeered, "Look at all the bribe money we have discovered. We will save you the trouble of dispensing it. It's in the hands of its intended without our having to grovel to do your bidding." Further examination of the cake revealed a note: "Take heart. Your escape and conveyance into Virginia is at hand."

The number of guards was increased and Rose was no longer permitted any visitors. Although Ellie Pool had been released, Rose and her daughter were henceforth shadowed wherever they went. A note reached her just after Christmas, warning her that she was being transferred to Fort Warren.

She asked Lieutenant Sheldon about it.

"No, Mrs. Greenhow, you will not be going to Fort Warren. But you are to be transferred."

"Where?"

"It has not been decided."

"Oh, yes. They dare not hang me, are afraid to release me, and would like to encourage me to escape in order that they might catch me and spirit me away."

"I have heard it said that your punishment would be most lenient if you would but agree to dispense with all activity against the Union."

"Never, sir. I demand my unconditional release, indemnity for my losses, and restoration of my papers and effects."

"Then I cannot help you, ma'am."

"Freedom is sweet, and although I have suffered much, there are many things dearer to me and I will not compromise a principle even though I am detained as a prisoner for the duration of the war—the sentence, I learn, which is already pronounced against me."

Lieutenant Sheldon solemnly bowed and left her.

That afternoon Rose defiantly sent another message carefully sewn into the sole of her daughter's shoe, with instructions to her to take it to William Smithson. "Twelve hundred cavalry supported by four batteries of artillery will cross the river and get behind Manassas cutting off railroad and other communication. For God's sake heed this. It is positive. They are obliged to move or give up. They find me a hard bargain and I shall be, I think, released in a few days without condition but to go South. It seems my case shall form an exception and I only want to gain time. All my plans are nearly completed." She instructed Rose carefully as to how to elude followers.

On January 18, after she had continued to send messages to the South for over five months without the Union ever being able to stop her, Rose's house arrest was ended.

Major Allen suddenly appeared early one morning followed by Lieutenant Sheldon looking pale as marble. Two guards strode directly behind them as they entered her bedroom.

"You are to accompany us downstairs, madam," Allen said coldly.

As Rose got up and walked toward them she smiled mischievously. "To what do I owe this sudden visit from the chief of the Secret Service?"

Ignoring her Allen strode over to her desk and ripped up her blotting pad, grabbing all of the loose papers on her desk.

"What are you doing? The paper you are taking is all that I have for my writing journal."

"You will have no need for paper or ink or pen where you are going."

She looked at Lieutenant Sheldon, startled. "Where am I going?"

"Why, to Old Capitol Prison, of course," said Major Allen. "Where you should have been detained from the very beginning."

"You cannot deny me my writing materials."

Allen leered at her. "You are to have no paper, ink, pen, or newspapers. Let us see how many messages will get through to the South now."

"This is an outrage. I demand my rights."

471

Ignoring her Allen turned to the guards. "Search the room. Go over all her dresses as well. If you find any concealed pockets, bring the dresses down to headquarters."

"You cannot take my personal clothing."

"We can and we will. We will have no more of your fancy little tricks with secret pockets."

She turned furiously to Lieutenant Sheldon. "Lieutenant, am I not to be permitted my very own clothing?"

The lieutenant looked at her for a brief moment, then turned away from her steady gaze. "When the guards have determined what clothing should remain, I have received orders that you may select the clothing you wish to take with you," he said.

"Now come with me, madam." Allen strode out of the room and the lieutenant bowed gracefully, gesturing for her to follow. Leaving the guards behind, the three went downstairs and into the parlor.

"You might as well sit down," Allen said crisply. "I'll bring these papers down to headquarters and have them thoroughly inspected." The two men were silent as Rose quietly strode over to her sofa and sat down.

Then Allen spoke to Lieutenant Sheldon. "She is to be removed before noon. I shall send a covered wagon for her with an armed military guard." He looked scornfully at Rose for a moment, and then broke into a narrow grin that was more of a sneer. Turning again to Sheldon he said, "Thank you for your cooperation, lieutenant."

Lieutenant Sheldon smartly saluted and opened the door for him. After he left, the lieutenant returned to Rose.

"Must I be taken from my home in a common prison wagon, lieutenant?" she asked him plaintively.

"I am sure that I can arrange a carriage for you. I shall attend to it." Then he came close to her. "Here are some personal mementos I have rescued for you." He handed her a small family Bible, some cherished daguerreotypes of her family, and her personal rice powder case. "There can certainly be no items of sabotage in these, Mrs. Greenhow."

She looked up at him and smiled wanly. "Thank you. You may call me Rose."

Shortly before noon Lieutenant Sheldon escorted Rose and her daughter to a waiting carriage and helped them into it. She carried a small valise with some of her personal belongings and he threw a small amount of her clothing onto the seat beside them. Then he jumped up into the carriage himself. "I have assumed personal responsibility for your delivery to Old Capitol Prison, Rose," he smiled.

A crowd was beginning to gather about the carriage and the guards hastily forced them a safe distance away. Rose recognized some reporters from the Washington papers. Several of them tipped their hats to her. She ignored them. She leaned forward in her carriage and waved instead to some of the guards who had been kind to her and considerate of her daughter. "I trust that your next duty will be a more honorable one than that of guarding helpless woman and children," she said to them.

She turned back and looked for the last time at her beautiful brick home which was now Greenhow prison. She wondered when she would visit 398 16th Street again.

As the carriage started off and they headed for Old Capitol Prison, she patted Lieutenant Sheldon on the knee. "I thank you for the kindness and courtesy you have shown to me."

Lieutenant Sheldon looked at her without smiling. "It has truly been an onerous assignment, Rose."

"I am sure your courtesies to me proved embarrassing to you with your superiors at times."

"I truly wish I could have done more."

"I understand. Perhaps if we had met under more agreeable circumstances, our relationship could have been entirely different."

She patted his cheek. He swallowed hard and his face slowly became flushed as he looked at her. For a moment—for a fleeting moment they were not on opposite sides of a dreadful war, but simply a man and a woman.

XXVII

Capitol

Winter 1862

As the carriage drew up to Old Capitol Prison, Rose shaded her eyes from the glare of the noonday sun. She did not see the forbidding walls with heavy iron bars nearly covering each of the windows. She clearly imagined the stately old mansion of happier days. She probably knew Old Capitol Prison better than any other living person. As she looked at the many brick chimneys rising majestically from the roof, she could envision each room from which they arose, for this had been her first home in Washington. This forlorn, weatherbeaten old building was where she had once listened to the political discussions of the leaders of their day as they dined in leisure at her Aunt Hattie's boarding house.

She thought of the many grand balls to which she had gone from this very house when she was a young, carefree girl. What was it she had once proudly vowed to herself? "Someday I will influence the destiny of this great nation. The leaders who determine the future of this country assemble here and someday they will listen to me and let me guide them." She had known many important men since those days. Many of them had vied with each other to do her bidding. And now—?

Lieutenant Sheldon jumped out of the carriage and helped her and her daughter to the street. He handed her valise and few clothes to a guard and turned her over to the superintendent of the prison, who had personally come out to oversee the arrival of his latest charge.

"Well, Mrs. Greenhow, we meet again, and under somewhat different circumstances."

"How do you do, Mr. Wood?" Rose replied unemotionally, ignoring his stinging greeting.

Superintendent William P. Wood waved Lieutenant Sheldon off as he started to escort Rose up the steps. "She's my prisoner now, lieutenant. Thank you for delivering her to me."

The lieutenant hesitated for a moment then solemnly saluted him. "Yes, Superintendent Wood. I entrust her to your care." Turning to Rose, he said simply, "Goodbye, Rose."

"Aha, Rose, is it? No wonder you have had so much trouble with her."

Lieutenant Sheldon jumped into the back of the carriage, and as Rose turned to watch him go, Wood brusquely grabbed her arm and shoved her carelessly toward the prison door. "You will find that we treat prisoners differently here at Old Capitol. Come on, get inside—"

As they entered the worn, run-down brick building, little Rose looked up at Mr. Wood and announced defiantly, "You have got one of the hardest little rebels here that you ever saw."

Wood frowned at the elder Rose, then bent down and addressed the little girl. "If you get along with me as well as Lieutenant Sheldon, you will have no trouble."

Rose put her arm around her daughter's shoulders as they walked into the prison. "You must be careful what you say here, dear," she said in a low, even voice.

Wood escorted them to a large room just off the hallway and motioned them inside. As he stood in the doorway, he said, "This is our search room, where all new inmates' baggage must be examined."

Rose and her daughter went in and Mr. Wood left them, but not before stationing a guard at the doorway.

They seated themselves on a bench along the side wall. It

was the only furniture in the room. They had not been seated very long before Rose suddenly put her hand to her mouth and gasped. This was the very room in which she had nursed and comforted John Calhoun in his dying hours, only twelve years ago!

Rose was not long with her thoughts before a young guard came in, casually inspected her clothing and valise, and directed them to follow him. He led them up the stairs and into a small room at the rear of the building, whose original use Rose could not remember. As the guard threw her meager belongings on the straw bed, she silently paced the length and breadth of the room. "Ten feet by twelve feet," she murmured. "Not very sizable quarters for one person, let alone two."

"It is not spacious, ma'am, but quite adequate compared to the general quarters of the rest of the prisoners who must be content with bunks three tiers high," said the guard.

"It is also conveniently located so that one cannot see or be seen from outside the building," Rose remarked.

The guard left them alone and Rose looked apprehensively about the cell that was to be their home. The nearly bare room contained a plain wooden table, two wooden chairs, and the straw bed. There was a small mirror on the wall in which Rose could hardly see her whole face. Little Rose was impatient to explore her new surroundings. When she attempted to leave their room, a guard stopped her.

"Do you mean that we are both to be confined to this room?" Rose asked increduously.

The guard sadly shook his head. "I am only following my instructions, ma'am."

Rose sighed and busied herself putting her few belongings in the tiny closet. It did not take long. She carefully arranged and rearranged them. When this was completed she listlessly sat in one of the chairs and tried to entertain her daughter, who by now was fretting at her inactivity.

The day dragged gradually on and Rose shuddered when she thought of the prospect of every day passing in the same manner for an indefinite period of time. She could see into the prison yard from her single barred window. She spent a great deal of the day watching other prisoners exercising below. But she was not to be permitted this diversion for very long. Later, in the afternoon, wooden boards were nailed across the outside of the window. Only thin streams of light could now find their way into the dismal room.

In the days that followed Rose was appalled at the continual flow of strangers who passed by her open door, stopped, curiously gaped at the two occupants, and then smiled unashamedly as they nodded and passed on. After more than two weeks of this incessant flow of sightseers, Rose indignantly demanded to speak with Superintendent Wood.

He came to her late one evening, well after she had sent for him so that she would know he was not waiting to do her bidding.

"What is troubling you, Mrs. Greenhow," he said, smiling. "Do our quarters not please your fancy?"

"I have no fault with them, Superintendent Wood. It is the constant flow of tourists who pass by our door. It is as if they were witnessing strangers from another world. This is not a menagerie, you know."

The superintendent sat on the edge of her bed and for the first time spoke in a serious, almost civil, tone. "I am truly sorry about this, Mrs. Greenhow. Believe me, it is not of my doing. You are an important person. It seems that everyone who visits Washington secures a pass from their congressmen to visit Old Capitol and get a first-hand look at its famous occupant."

"This is deplorable. Can it not be stopped?"

"I'll do my best to halt it. Actually, it poses a great problem for us security-wise."

"I should imagine so. You can never be sure one of your guests might not join the visitors and walk away with them unobserved."

"I hope that you are not thinking of attempting it,

Mrs. Greenhow."

"Of course not."

"I have learned from my many years in this business that thoughts voiced many times generate action."

"Please stop this flagrant invasion of my privacy, Superintendent Wood. I beg of you as a fellow human being."

"I will try. Do you know I have been offered as much as ten dollars to permit visitors to come and view you without a pass?"

"How degrading."

"It is that. Of course, I assure you I have never accepted money from any of them."

"Thank you. While you are here, is it necessary that we both be constantly confined to this one room? My daughter is suffering from such inactivity. She is only a child and should get exercise."

"I see no reason why she shouldn't be allowed a certain amount of freedom. That is, within the confines of the prison."

"Of course."

"I shall advise the guards. Our prisoners are granted a certain amount of time in the exercise yard. You will be permitted the same privilege."

"That is considerate of you, superintendent."

He left. Thereafter the flow of sightseers subsided considerably, but it never did cease completely. The following day, her guard advised her young daughter that she was free to leave their room. Happily, little Rose went out walking about the halls and into the exercise yard in the rear of the building. She was not gone long before she returned to her mother, crying.

"Rose, what on earth is the matter? I thought you would be overjoyed to be able to go out."

"They are all niggers here. One of them said that you were responsible for his kin being killed. Then a lot of them began to shout at me, 'Your mommy is a killer! Your mommy is a killer!'"

"Oh, dear God!" Rose sighed aloud. Sitting on the edge of

her bed, she drew her daughter to her and wrapped her arms about her. "Don't pay any attention to them, dear. Remember you are superior to these Yankees whether they are white or black."

"I know, Mommy. But I slapped one of them and a guard hit me with the butt of his rifle and dragged me away from them."

Tears of frustration welled up in Rose's eyes. She pressed her daughter so close to her she could feel the beat of her little heart against her breast. "We will have to bear this, Rose darling. Let us hope that it is not for long." She ran her hand through her daughter's hair and wiped her tears away. "Try not to have anything to do with those other prisoners, my darling."

"I won't, Mommy. We'll show them won't we?"

"We surely will."

The days were harrowing for Rose. She was bored. She could not sleep. She, who had always been so active, even during the months that she was a prisoner in her own home, was now limited to doing nothing—absolutely nothing, day in and day out, within the bounds of one small ten-by-twelve-foot room. She had encouraged young Rose to go about the prison and the yard. She would question her about the activities of the other prisoners whenever she returned. It was the only interest in life that was left to her. She learned that her upstairs quarters were almost completely inhabited by Negroes. The white prisoners were on the floor below. The black prisoners spent their days playing cards and simple games. As the days wore on, young Rose told her mother that most of the "darkies"—they didn't like to be called niggers—were being kinder to her now. Two of the men who played checkers every day were teaching her how to play. Sometime they danced, and more than once Rose returned to report that the guards had been forced to break up a fight or two amongst them. Her joy at young Rose's activities turned to horror one day a short time later when her daughter returned to report more private activities being practiced in the section.

"They were kissing each other, Mommy," young Rose reported innocently.

"You mean a man and a woman were together?"

"Oh, they are all together. All the men and the women. And today this one man, his name is Washington, he pulled this young girl to him and began kissing her. Then he took her away from the rest of them. He pulled her dress down and began kissing her all over. She didn't cry out or anything. She just smiled as if she liked it. Then he pulled her dress off her completely and then—"

"Oh, my God! Rose, you mustn't go down there with them anymore."

"But they are fun, Mommy. And I'm learning a lot. You told me I must always be learning so that I can improve my mind."

Rose sighed and looked away. She could not deny her daughter the one bit of pleasure available to her. However, she could not see her subjected to the harsher realities of life, either.

"Please, Mommy, let me go down to them again."

"You shall go down every day, my dear. But I shall go with you."

"Oh, Mommy, it will be good for both of us."

"I am sure it will. Particularly since we have absolutely nothing to do."

Only a few days later the guards brought up a desk, a sewing machine, a trunk, and some writing materials and books!

"Oh, thank God!" Rose exclaimed. Then, as she fondled the few pieces of furniture and the books, she shouted in amazement. "Why, they are mine!"

"That's right, Mrs. Greenhow," said Superintendent Wood, who had followed the guards into her room. "Lieutenant Sheldon sent them to you."

"How gracious of him!" Rose smiled and added, "Thank you, superintendent, for letting me have them."

As Rose started to lovingly rummage through the drawers of

her desk, Wood came over to her. "We discovered a pistol in one of those drawers, but, since there was no ammunition, we decided it would do no harm."

"I hardly think I will have need for it. I am well protected here without resorting to firearms." She drew the small pistol from one of the drawers, caressed it, and put it back.

Superintendent Wood's face cracked into a strained smile. "I knew you were getting pretty bored here."

She came over to him. "Would you be so kind as to convey my thanks to Lieutenant Sheldon and let him know how much I appreciate his thoughtfulness?"

"I certainly will. In return I must ask a favor of you."

Rose looked at him warily. "What is it?"

"You and your daughter are looking very pale these days. It is undoubtedly due to your confined existence. Now, being my prisoners, it is my responsibility to see that you do not become ill. You are not getting sufficient exercise and the guards have reported that you are hardly eating at all. I have ordered Dr. Stewart to place you under his personal care."

"But isn't he the man I see strutting about every day inspecting the prisoners?"

"Yes, Brigade Surgeon W. D. Stewart. He conducts daily sanitary inspection to see that all of our prisoners keep in good health."

"I have observed his inspections, Superintendent Wood. I will not have him inspecting us."

"You must, Mrs. Greenhow. If anything should happen to you—"

"Nothing will happen to us. We are of strong stock, I assure you. He does not inspect those poor women, superintendent, he molests them. I will not allow that pompous ass to enter our room."

Wood's face became red and his eyes narrowed. "It is not for you to say, Mrs. Greenhow! You are my responsibility; I have been specifically cautioned concerning the well-being of both yourself and your daughter. If any harm or illness should befall you, it would be a matter of national concern."

"That charlatan is obviously a vulgar, uneducated man bedizened with enough gold lace for three field marshals."

"Madam, you are speaking of our brigade surgeon!"

"Brigand surgeon is more like it. He will not attend to us. I demand my own family physician."

"Of course. So you can carry on your illicit correspondence as you did while confined to house arrest. Not on your life."

"I shall not have Brigand Surgeon Stewart attend to us. Not on *your* life."

"We shall see."

The prison doctor continued his daily rounds in the building but he did not inspect Rose or her daughter. However, fate seemed to take a hand in the matter, for shortly thereafter, young Rose became seriously ill. When Superintendent Wood learned of it, he immediately ordered Dr. Stewart to attend her. Unannounced, and with a certain bit of trepidation, for he knew full well how Rose felt about him, Dr. Stewart suddenly appeared early one morning.

As Rose saw him standing on the threshold of her room, she raised her head haughtily and her eyes blazed as of old. "You are not to enter this room, sir."

"Your daughter is ill, madam. Superintendent Wood has requested that I look in on her." He walked over to young Rose lying in bed and felt her head. "This child has a fever." He sat on the side of the bed and took Rose's wrist in his hand.

Immediately Rose strode over to him. "Take your hands off my little girl."

Dr. Stewart jumped up facing Rose squarely. "I will not quit your room; I am here by order of Brigadier General Porter."

"I don't care if President Lincoln himself has ordered you here. I will not have you molesting my little girl. Get out of here, I say."

"Don't you care for your little girl? Are you not concerned for the well-being of your own flesh and blood?"

"Of course I am. That is why I order you away from her."

Completely ignoring her, he said to young Rose, "Let me see your tongue, little girl."

As young Rose stuck out her tongue, thickly coated, he leaned over and slipped her nightgown off her shoulder. Rose grabbed his arm and savagely pulled it away. "Why, this girl has camp fever. Do you wish me to write a prescription that will cure her, or don't you?"

Rose eyed him sullenly for a moment, then let go of his arm. "Do so by all means."

Casually, with as much dignity as he could muster despite the awkward situation, he sat down beside the table and scrawled a prescription. As he handed it to Rose, she hastily glanced at it and threw it in the air. "Why, this is written in English. You, sir, are not equipped with the fundamentals of the most common doctor. You probably do not know Latin! I doubt if you *are* a doctor. Sir, I command you to get out! If you do not, I will summon the officer of the guard to put you out."

Dr. Stewart looked at her scornfully. "Your prejudice is standing in the way of the well-being of your daughter, madam." He turned to young Rose and started to pull the covers down from the sick child. Rose, outraged, stamped over to him and stood between him and her daughter.

"At your peril but touch my child. You are a coward and no gentleman, thus to insult a woman."

"I will not go out of your room, madam! It is my duty—"

Rose, livid with rage, strode over to the door and called, "Guard!"

The poor guard quickly appeared at the doorway, apparently prepared for being summoned. "Yes, Mrs. Greenhow?"

"I demand that this man be removed from my room."

The guard gulped helplessly. "But he is an officer, ma'am. I'm only a sergeant."

"It is your duty to protect helpless women and children although they may be prisoners. Take this man away."

The guard walked over to the good doctor and took hold of

his arm. "Please, sir,—" he said plaintively.

"Oh, all right. I'll leave, sergeant." Slowly Dr. Stewart walked to the door. "You are endangering the very life of your little one by your stubbornness," he said bitterly.

"I prefer to trust my child's life to the care of the good Providence which has so often befriended me."

Without another word the doctor left her room.

Fortunately for all concerned, Rose got better. With the great resilience of the young, she was up and running around two days later.

True to her promise, Rose took her daughter out in the exercise yard at least once every day. She hated the visits, for Rose's choice of companions were smugglers, felons, blockade runners, and rebellious soldiers. None of these were of the type of person Rose had associated with in her entire life; nor did she choose their company even now in her dire need for companionship. She did make friends with a man called Charlie who drove into the prison yard each day with a load of fresh produce for the prison. He was a likable old man with a large handlebar mustache and a gay Irish wit.

"If I can ever do anything for you, Mrs. Greenhow, just let me know," he said to her on one of his early morning rounds.

"Do you mean that, Charlie?"

"I sure do. You been a heroine of mine for these many months." Then, leaning close to her, he whispered, "I admire your spunk. It did my heart good the way you kept shaking up the hoity-toity in this city."

"Why, thank you."

"They think they're so high and mighty, right next to God. So help me, some of them act as if they are above Him!"

Rose laughed at his seriousness. "Then you might consider doing me a favor that could be considered against the rules?"

"Just try me, ma'am."

She smiled at him graciously. "I have a small pocket revolver—a .22 Derringer. The prison officials let me keep it since they know I do not have any ammunition. The situation makes me most uneasy. A poor defenseless woman and her young daughter at the mercy of this rugged band of ruffians here."

"Aw, and it's a crying shame, it is that. I truly wish I could help you."

"You can."

"How?"

"You could get me some ammunition for my revolver." His eyes grew wide at the suggestion. She hastily added, "You need not feel obligated, Charlie. I wouldn't wish you to do anything that might trouble your conscience."

"Mrs. Greenhow, do I look like a man who wouldn't help a lady in distress?"

"That is why I value your friendship so."

He winked at her slyly. "I'll have them bullets for you in jig time. It may not be on my next visit, but it will be soon."

"I can wait, Charlie. I am not going anywhere."

Charlie guffawed loudly and slapped his horses madly as he drove on. Three days later, he brought her a handful of .22 caliber bullets. He slipped them to her as he talked about the weather. "Thank you, Charlie," Rose said, hastily wrapping them in her handkerchief. "If you will advise me their cost, I shall repay you."

"I wouldn't think of it! Just say they are compliments of the produce man."

"But Charlie—"

"Besides, you've already paid me what they cost."

"But I've paid you nothing."

"Neither did I. I stole them." Laughing uproariously, he slapped his horses and drove on to the prison kitchen. Rose quickly returned to her room and loaded her small revolver. For the future protection of myself and my daughter, if the need arises, she told herself.

A few days later, she was complaining to Charlie about the drabness and loneliness of her stay in prison. "Nothing ever happens!" she moaned. "There's no one to talk to."

"My God, you've got a whole prison full. The place is bursting at the seams with people."

"They are the dregs of society, Charlie. They're not like you."

"Yeah, a pretty seamy lot. Well, I might brighten up your day a little. If you want to try something different, I could give you a ride on my wagon to the prison kitchen."

"Oh, that would be exciting. Would you really?"

"Hop on."

Swiftly, Rose jumped up and rode with him to the kitchen.

As he started to slow down at the kitchen entrance, she said quickly, "Oh, Charlie, this has been so wonderful. Why not drive around the yard?"

"I don't know. I might get in a lot of trouble. This prison account means a lot to me, Mrs. Greenhow."

"Call me Rose."

"Well, I don't mind if I do, Rose."

"You could let me have the reins. If someone complains, tell them I grabbed them from you and you couldn't help yourself."

Charlie's eyes sparkled at the prospect. "It's a deal!" he said as he slipped her the reins.

Joyously she slapped the horses, not once but several times, and the animals leaped forward at a faster clip than they had gone in a long time. "I'm off for Dixie!" Rose shouted as she stood up and drove the horses around the yard.

As the creaking old wagon careened around the yard, the other prisoners cheered them on. They passed a group of women prisoners who shouted, "Give us a ride too, Mum."

"Sure!" Rose shouted back in a most unusually gracious mood. She slowed the wagon down and several of the women hopped on. Then she whipped the horses again and they sped about the courtyard. Immediately all windows were filled with inmates shouting and cheering them on. Those in the yard cheered and ran after them yelling encouragement. Rose's face was flushed. It was exhilarating! "Hooray for Charlie!" she shouted and the other women in the wagon took up her cry. Pandemonium reigned in the yard. A guard came rushing forward and shouted for them to stop. When she did not, he rushed away for the officer of the guard.

That good man ran out into the yard, and taking the situation in at a glance, hollered frantically, "It's an escape! Call out the guards! Post them at every exit!"

Superintendent Wood was immediately called, and as he entered the yard, he shouted, "Stop that vehicle!" By now the horses were so excited that it would have been difficult to stop them, and Rose was enjoying herself too much to even consider the idea. Prisoners clapped their hands. One of them started playing a harmonica and several of them began to dance.

Superintendent Wood was shouting orders at the top of his lungs, but he could not be heard above the music and the din. Finally Rose noticed that the guards had hurriedly been issued bayonets and were aiming them dangerously at the wagon. Breathlessly, she drew the horses up beside the prison gate and brought them to a halt. As Wood came running up to the wagon, the other women hurriedly jumped off and ran away.

"What in Christ's name got into you, Charlie?" shouted Wood.

"I'm truly sorry, superintendent," Charlie said dejectedly. "The horses just got out of hand. Mrs. Greenhow is a fine horsewoman, sir."

"What the hell is she doing up on the wagon, anyway?"

"She saw that I was in trouble, sir. She offered to help me calm my mares. If it hadn't been for her, sir, we might have had a serious accident."

Wood eyed Charlie skeptically. "Well, see that it never happens again. If you have to, get another rig."

"Oh, yes sir, I will. But I am sure it will not happen again. Just look at them poor beings, all sweating and frothing at the mouth. I'm certain they have learned their lesson, sir." He

jumped off the wagon and helped Rose off. "Thank you fo
your assistance, ma'am. I don't know what I would ever hav
done if it hadn't been for you." Turning to Wood, he sai
humbly, "She's sure a fine horsewoman, sir."

"I'm sure she is, Charlie. But it is against regulations fo
prisoners to be driven about the compound."

Rose looked at Wood impishly. "Can you quote me th
regulation, superintendent?"

Wood ignored her. "Get over to the kitchen and deliver you
goods, Charlie." Then he turned to the rest of the prisoner
who were standing silently by watching them and shouted
"All of you, break this up. I don't want any more disturbanc
do you hear me? If I hear one shout, I'll have you all confine
to your rooms for a week! Do you hear me, goddammit?"

Several of the prisoners nodded as they walked away. Ros
laughed recklessly as she noted that all of them were smiling

Less than a month later, Charlie brought her word of th
Union Major General John A. Logan's defeat at Fort Donelson
Once again her spirits were revived. She decided to celebrate
At dusk that evening she bolted her door and lit a candle in th
window. Almost immediately a guard outside noticed it an
shouted, "Put out that light!"

Rather than obeying his terse command, Rose rummage
through her meager belongings, and finding several scraps o
nearly spent candles, lit them all and placed them on th
windowsill.

"Douse those lights, damn you," shouted the officer of th
day. She heard guards running up the stairs and along th
hallway. The officer of the day came to her door and tried t
enter. When he found that it was barred, he shouted, "Ope
this door, madam." Rose leaned against the windowsill an
smiled mischievously.

"It's a signal," he shouted. "Call Superintendent Wood!"

Other prisoners began to shout. Quickly word was passe
from room to room that the special prisoner in the little room
at the head of the stairs was teasing the guards again. Prisoner

began shouting words of encouragement, none of them knowing exactly what was happening.

In a very few minutes Superintendent Wood came storming up outside her door. "What the hell are you doing in there now? Open this door." As Rose made no reply, he screamed, "This is Superintendent Wood speaking. Open up, I say, or I'll order the goddamned bolt shot out."

"She has that gun, remember, sir?"

"Yes, but it isn't loaded." It suddenly became quiet outside her door as the guards waited for their next order and the prisoners breathlessly tried to anticipate the outcome.

Quietly Rose tiptoed to the drawer of her desk and drew out her gun. She quickly wrapped it in a handkerchief and pinned it beneath the folds of her dress onto one of her petticoats.

"Damn you, Greenhow," Wood shouted as he pounded on her door, "if you don't open this door I warn you I'll order the guards to fire into your room." Rose did not move or speak. "I mean what I say!" Wood screamed. "You are making signals and must remove your lights from the window."

"But it suits my convenience to keep them there," Rose calmly shouted back.

"We will break open your door if you don't open it!"

"You will act as you see fit but it will be at your peril."

"Do you suppose she has ammunition, sir?" she heard one of the guards ask apprehensively.

"How could she?" Wood asked exasperated. Then suddenly in a firm, loud voice, he shouted, "Stand back, men. Break down the door!"

A heavy thud sounded against the door. Then another louder and heavier. "Son of a bitch, fire the bolt!" Several shots were fired and the door finally broke away from the sill, falling to the floor. Several guards came rushing into the room. Instantly they put out the candles. Wood madly rushed to the desk and pulled open each drawer. "It's gone!" he shouted. Savagely he turned to Rose, "Where's your gun?" Rose looked at him expressionlessly. "I shall have you punished if you do not tell me. Son of a bitch, give me your gun." Frantically he looked about the room. It was obvious there was no place that she could hide it. He strode over to her, his face livid with rage. "You are trying me beyond control. I know you have a gun. Give it up, I say!"

"You have searched my furnishings. Obviously it is not there."

"You are hiding it on yourself. I warn you, madam, give me that goddamn gun or I personally will tear your clothes off until I find it!"

"You would accost a poor defenseless woman?"

He came closer and stared viciously at her. "I would! And I shall!" Roughly, he grabbed her arm and pinned it behind her as he grasped her dress at the shoulder.

"Wait!" She shuddered as she pulled herself away from him. With an outward courage that she did not feel, she calmly turned away from him, and lifting up the front of her dress, unpinned the handkerchief and handed it to him.

Frantically he opened it. As the gun dropped into his hand, he slipped open the barrel and six bullets fell into his hand. Slowly his face paled. "My God, the gun is loaded!" Beads of sweat gradually formed on his brow. Rose could see his hand tremble as he handed the gun and bullets to a guard and turned back to her. "Where did you get these bullets?"

"What does it matter? You have them in your possession. They are of no use to me now."

He wiped the perspiration from his forehead and looked helplessly about the room. "I—I—goddammit woman, I'll certainly be glad when they order you out of here."

"So will I, superintendent."

"What in God's name were you trying to do?"

"Nothing, really. I merely lit a candle to find something in my trunk. Thereafter your guards made a mountain out of a molehill."

Wood shook his head and with a great show of calmness for the benefit of his men said sternly. "Return to your posts, men. And double the guard at her door until it can be fixed in the morning."

"Yes, sir."

"Tell the carpenter to leave the bolt off the inside of the door."

"Yes, sir."

The incident bolstered Rose's morale for the next few days. But it was short-lived, however. As young Rose got into bed a few nights later, she groaned plaintively.

"What is it, dear?"

"I'm hungry, Mommy."

"You're hungry? Didn't you eat your supper?"

"It was nothing but mush and gruel. I can't eat any more of that horrid stuff, Mommy."

Rose sighed. "Oh, dear God—" A tear slowly trickled down her cheeks as she sat beside her daughter. Then, suddenly, she sat bolt upright and jumped up. Quickly she went to the small closet in her room and knelt down on the floor.

"What are you doing, Mommy?"

"If I remember correctly—come help me, dear. When I lived here, there were some loose boards in this closet. Aunt Hattie was forever going to have them repaired. I wonder if she did?"

Young Rose joined her mother and soon they succeeded in pulling up three of the boards in the flooring. "They were never repaired," Rose said joyously to her daughter. They could see into the room below, and several men were visible sitting around a small table and lamp.

"Psst," Rose called to them. "Can you hear me?" The men stopped what they were doing and looked about the room.

"Up here in the ceiling," she whispered.

As the men looked up one of them gasped, "My God, it's Mrs. Greenhow."

"Shh," she cautioned. "Please do not attract the guards."

"Oh, we won't, ma'am. What do you want?"

"You might be able to help me. Do you have anything

491

to eat?"

"EAT!" shouted one of the men and then was quickly hushed up by the others.

"Yes. My little girl is hungry. I have just learned that she did not eat any supper."

"I don't blame her," said one of the men. "That godawful stuff aint' fit for cows."

"I got some fruit my wife brought me," said one.

"I've got some cake my mother baked for me," volunteered another.

"Sure, we can give her something," said another. "How can we get it up to her?"

"I don't know."

Quietly the men brought a chair beneath the hole in the ceiling and one of them stood on it. The ceiling was still quite a distance away from him. He jumped down and they quietly brought the table directly under the hole. They were closer to the ceiling now, but still could not reach her.

"Could you lower her down to us?" suggested one of them.

"I—I—could try."

"Good." Three of the men jumped up on the table. As Rose cautiously lowered her daughter, they firmly grabbed her legs and carefully slid her down amongst them. Then each of them hastily went to his bunk and brought out some of his hoarded food and gave it to her.

Rose watched them, smiling. "I don't know how I can ever thank you," she whispered to them.

"Do you want some, ma'am?" one of the men whispered up to her.

"No, thank you. But perhaps some other time my daughter may be able to take advantage of your generosity."

"She can do it anytime," said one of the men.

"Tell us what she likes best and I'll get my wife to bring some down to me."

"Oh, thank you, so much. I shall never forget your kindness, gentlemen."

"We're just in here to be of service to damsels in distress," said one of the men and the rest laughed.

After a few moments, Rose whispered, "Please gentlemen, don't give her any more tonight. You will make her sick."

"Anything you say, ma'am." When young Rose finished what she was eating, the men lifted her up again and as Rose caught her, they boosted her up into her room.

Thereafter, little Rose was provided with an abundance of good, wholesome food whenever she felt she needed to supplement her prison diet.

A few days later Rose was writing a lengthy letter to her daughter Florence when she noted a considerable amount of activity in the hallways. Prisoners were washing down the walls and scrubbing the floors painstakingly, directed by the guards. As one of them passed her doorway, she asked, "Pray tell, what is the cause of all this sudden interest in cleanliness?"

"We're having visitors tomorrow. General Fremont and his staff are inspecting our facility."

"General John. C. Fremont?"

"The very same, ma'am."

"My God, the Union has sunk so low as to resurrect that poor derelict from the forgotten past."

The guard looked at her quizzically. "I beg your pardon, ma'am?"

"Never mind. Good luck with your inspection tomorrow."

"Why, thank you, ma'am."

Rose returned to writing her letter. It was difficult for her to concentrate. One could plainly detect from the frown on her brow that the mention of General Fremont brought back many unpleasant memories to her.

XXVIII

Trial

March 1862

That afternoon as she was walking in the exercise yard while
her daughter played, Charlie drove his wagon up to her. They
had been careful not to speak to each other for any length of
time since her escapade in the courtyard, but he seemed
nervous as he brought his wagon to a halt.

Bending over, he whispered, "Just act casual, but I got
something for you."

"Whatever is the matter, Charlie? You seem—"

Charlie put his finger to his lips and frowned. "Here, quick.
Take this apple and orange. They are for your daughter, with
my compliments."

"Thank you, Charlie."

"Slice the apple carefully before you give it to young Rose,"
he said mysteriously. "There's a message from Mrs. Baxley.
She said you would take care of it. Give my love to your little
girl, Mrs. Greenhow." He waved cheerfully to her and was off
to the prison kitchen.

Rose tucked the fruit under her bonnet which she was
holding in her hand. Presently she called her daughter and
they went back to their room.

"Charlie has brought you some fruit, dear. Here, peel this
orange while I cut up your apple."

Rose carefully started to cut into the apple with a rusty table
knife which she had been permitted to retain. At the bottom of

494

the apple was a crudely cut hole with a piece of paper partially protruding from the core. It was a most amateurish disguise. She drew out the paper and unfolded it. On it was written a single sentence in a lady's neat handwriting:

"Eighth Infantry and Third Iowa Cavalry together with six other batteries are converging at Elkhorn Tavern, Arkansas, on March 5."

Rose looked up from the message and frowned. Carefully she folded the tiny piece of paper and placed it in the bodice of her dress. She was flattered that Mrs. Baxley and Charlie still had faith in her ability to contact the South. But it was no longer possible. She had not communicated with Colonel Jordan since she had been a prisoner at Old Capitol. She peeled the balance of the apple and gave it to her daughter. Slowly she walked over to the window and peered through the small shafts of light that shone between the wooden slats. Once again she had information which would be vital to her Confederate allies, but she was helpless to pass it on to them. For the first time in her long imprisonment she felt completely powerless. A tear slowly trickled down her cheek. She swallowed hard, and savagely brushing it away, turned to her daughter. "May Mommy have a bite of your apple, darling?" she asked casually, unconsciously pressing her hand to her bosom where the vital information protectedly rested.

The next day the prisoners were marched out into the courtyard and Superintendent Wood gave them an enthusiastic speech advising them that they were having important visitors sometime that day. General Fremont was conducting an inspection of the prison. It would be to their advantage if they remained on their best behavior, for the distinguished general was in a position to grant additional funds for the prison if he believed they deserved them. If all went well, and they did receive more funding, he promised them it would be reflected in more rations for them.

His speech worked wonders with the inmates. Rose sadly shook her head as she noted the strange silence that fell over the prison. There was no shouting, no squabbling or bickering that day. Shortly after the noonday meal, she learned that General Fremont had arrived. Rose sighed as she heard the crisp military steps of the guards marching to and fro in the hallways, and the quiet, subdued, yes, even polite answers that the prisoners made to any inquiry directed at them. As she sat alone in her room, embroidering a cape for young Rose, she marveled at the failings and foibles of mankind. The entire prison, both guards and prisoners, were being hoodwinked by an incompetent nincompoop because he bore the title General before his name.

She would not be a party to this inane adulation. She was facing the open door and gradually became aware that someone was standing in the doorway. She looked up and gasped as she saw Jessie Benton Fremont smiling down at her. Rose did not rise. Calmly she laid her embroidery down on the table beside her and returned her visitor's smile.

"Hello, Rose." Jessie walked slowly into the room.

"Hello, Jessie."

"Superintendent Wood said I would find you here."

"I have been here for quite some time."

"So I have heard." The two women stared at each other, Jessie looking down and Rose returning her insolent gaze with unflinching steadiness. "Well, aren't you going to invite me to sit down?"

"Of course."

Jessie silently walked around the little table and sat down in the only vacant chair in the tiny room. "The general is inspecting the prison facilities."

"So I have heard."

"I decided to accompany him on his visit."

"I had not heard of that."

There was an awkward pause as the two women measured each other. Presently Jessie looked about the room and sighed. "Not too attractive surroundings."

"Oh, but this is a private room. You should see the other

prisoners' quarters."

"I have. Quite a change since you lived here with your Aunt Hattie."

"Yes. It has deteriorated sadly since the Union took it over. The walls are crumbling, the paint is peeling. Loose boarding is apparent throughout the building. The Yankees don't seem to notice some of the finer amenities of life."

Again there was silence in the room. Occasionally a brisk military command could be heard in the distance as men marched through the hallway.

"Discipline is surprisingly evident," said Jessie. "The general was quite impressed."

"He should be. It is for his benefit."

Jessie continued to smile as she drummed her fingers on the bare table between them. "You don't look well, Rose. You are pale. Your cheeks are sunken."

"The accommodations are not too conducive to good health."

"They could be better. The General has advised me that your situation would be greatly improved if you were not— well—"

"Stubborn?"

"No. The way he put it was, 'If you would only be more cooperative!'"

"If I would renounce everything that I have held dear to me all my life. If I would bow down to that Mammon of Unrighteousness and freely admit that they are right and I am wrong."

"Not necessarily. The country is at war. The least our leaders can expect is loyalty."

"You mean blind, unfaltering worship! I shall never bow down to their arrogance and deceit."

"You haven't changed a bit, Rose."

Rose's eyes flashed as she quickly retorted, "And I never shall!"

"It will wear you into an early grave."

497

"Are you visiting me in an official capacity? Do you represent the government in some sort of a scheme to advocate a compromise to me?"

"Of course not. I only dropped in to inquire about your well-being."

"Let us not pretend, Jessie. You don't give a damn whether I am dead or alive."

"You truly wrong me."

"The hell I do. You have come here to gloat over my unfortunate situation."

"Oh, my dear, you do me injustice."

"I know you. Remember? I've known you since you were a little girl. You and I have always been on opposite sides. You resented it every time I won in a skirmish with you. I had the pick of the young men we knew, you had to be content with those who did not fit my fancy. I fought you and your general for the presidency of the United States—and I won that, too!" Rose's eyes flashed as of old as she leaned on the table between them and glared at her.

Jessie glared in return, raising her voice as she spoke. "But it looks as if I am going to win this last round, doesn't it?"

Rose jumped up from her chair. "Is that what you have come here to tell me?"

"I don't have to tell you that. Observe my position in life and look at your own. I have won this last and most important battle of our lives. I just want to see you admit it."

"Never!"

"You don't have to, really. It is obvious to everyone in the whole country that I have won and you—you, Rose O'Neal Greenhow, for the last time have chosen the wrong side." Jessie pounded her fist on the table as her voice grew harsher.

Rose looked at her silently for a moment. She was breathing heavily, her face was flushed. Slowly she sat down and leaning back in her chair became calm. "If that is what you have come here to tell me, I will thank you to leave."

Jessie smiled scornfully as she realized that she had at last

ucceeded in bringing her enemy to bay. "You can't order me
o go. I can stay here as long as I see fit and you can't do
nything about it."

"I admit I am a prisoner of this depraved government. But I
do not have to listen to your degrading insults." Jumping up,
she angrily pointed to the door. "Get out."

"I'll go when I get damned good and ready!"

"Get out, I say. Get out of my room. Get out of my life!"

"I haven't said all that I want to say to you yet."

"I will not listen, do you hear me? I demand that you go!"

A taunting, sneering grin came across Jessie's face as she
looked up at her adversary. "No, I won't!"

"You—you—bitch!"

Slowly Jessie rose. "Only a defeated adversary would stoop
to such lowly, foul epithets." She walked slowly, deliberately
toward Rose. "You have poisoned every unfortunate soul you
have ever known. Poor Senator Gwin sits rotting in prison
because of you. And simpleminded, naive Colonel Keyes—
everyone knows that his love letters were found in your
possession when your treachery was revealed. Although he is
still free, I know how valuable he was to you in your dastardly
deeds. I know how he betrayed his own country for a few
moments of illicit pleasure in your arms."

"You lie!"

"I speak the truth. And you can rest uneasily, Rose O'Neal,
never knowing whether or not I will reveal the facts that will
put your poor, misguided lover behind bars, disgraced by the
very military he holds so dear."

Rose ran to the door and shouted frantically. "Guard!
Guard! GUARD!"

"God knows how many more innocent souls you have
brought to untimely disgrace by your foul deeds and your
treason!"

A guard suddenly appeared at the doorway, his bayonet at
the ready before him. "What is it, Mrs. Greenhow?"

"Mrs. Greenhow, indeed. I leave you now, Mrs. Greenhow!

To dwell in your solitary confinement and carefully mull over both our destinies. Weigh the differences in our lives now and be honest with yourself, Mrs. Greenhow. Have you won over me again, or have I, at last, won over you?" She turned to the guard and slipped her arm in his. "Shall we go now, officer?"

The guard turned to Rose. "But Mrs. Greenhow—"

"It was nothing! Just a personal matter between Mrs. Greenhow and myself."

As Jessie strode out into the hall, she turned and smiled sweetly at Rose. "Goodbye, my dear!"

Rose turned back into her room and slowly walked to the table. Completely exhausted, she slumped into her chair, and throwing her head in her arms on the table, cried. Her body shook with bitter, uncontrollable sobs.

It was sometime later when young Rose came up to the room from the downstairs hallway where she had been playing. A guard was with her to announce that everyone was to eat in the main dining room that night. They were to be provided with a feast of terrapin and pigeon pie to celebrate their tremendously successful inspection. There was also to be a dessert. When Rose saw her mother, distraught and red-eyed, she came running to her. "What is the matter, Mommy?"

"It is nothing, dear. Just a fit of despondency."

"Are we going down to the feast?"

"No, dear, not tonight."

"But, Mommy, I am hungry. And it has been such a long time since I have had pigeon pie."

Rose smiled lovingly at her daughter. "You go, dear. Mommy is not hungry." Turning to the guard, she said, "You wouldn't mind accompanying my daughter to the dining room, would you?"

"No, of course not. Come with me, little lady." As she watched her daughter put her arm in the guard's, Rose choked with emotion. Her hand went involuntarily to her bosom. As she unconsciously rubbed her breast, she felt the message concealed beneath it. Suddenly a bitter thought struck her.

Running to the doorway she called, "Guard, Guard, please come back." As he hastily returned she asked, "Has General Fremont completed his inspection?"

"Oh, yes ma'am. Him and his staff has left long ago."

"Good. Will you please tell Superintendent Wood that I must see him immediately?"

"But, Mrs. Greenhow, the superintendent is dining with the guards this evening. It is a special occasion."

"Tell him it is urgent! It is a matter of national importance."

"All right, I'll tell him." He left, looking back at her questioningly as he accompanied her daughter down the stairs.

In a very few moments, Superintendent Wood came hurriedly into her room. "What is it, Mrs. Greenhow? Officer Sloan advised me it was urgent."

"It is, superintendent. You will see what I mean when you read this." She reached inside her bodice and taking out the message handed it to him. As he read, his eyes widened and he muttered quietly, "My God!"

"My days of espionage are over, superintendent. Apparently some of my accomplices do not realize this."

"Who gave you this?"

"I have had only one visitor the entire day."

"But that was the general's wife, Mrs. Fremont!"

"Yes!"

"You don't mean—Jesus Christ Almighty, it can't be!"

"The message speaks for itself, does it not?"

"Yes—yes—Oh, my God—my God."

"You will note that the message is clearly in a lady's handwriting."

"Yes—yes, I see that. Oh, wait until Colonel Doster learns of this. Oh, my God—my God. . . ." He left the room, seeming almost to be in a stupor.

It was not until the next night, when she was lowering young Rose down to the men below, that she heard the news. "Have you heard that General Fremont's wife has been arrested?"

"Oh, my good heavens," Rose said surprised. "Whatever happened?"

"Something about betraying military secrets. We didn't get the whole story, but everybody's talking about it."

"What a dreadful thing to happen. And to the good general. The poor man. I feel so sorry for him."

"Military police searched their home, but they found nothing."

Several days later Rose learned from her friends below that Jessie Fremont had been released. Rose smiled. It seemed that they did not have sufficient evidence to implicate her. "But it sure looks mighty suspicious to me," said one of the men.

"It does to me, too. I don't care if she is a general's wife." Rose smiled bitterly. She wondered if Jessie was now so sure that she had won their last battle. She didn't care. She had had a few moments, a few days of wonderful revenge, and at the expense of her hated lifelong rival, Jessie Benton Fremont!

It had been several months since Rose was brought to Old Capitol prison. She had tried many times to enlist the aid of some of her former friends to secure her release, but her efforts had been to no avail. Then on the fifteenth of March Superintendent Wood came to her to announce that she was being taken to the provost marshal's headquarters.

"For what reason?"

"Why, for a trial, of course. Better bundle up well, it's a bitter day outside."

"I welcome a public trial, sir. I want the country to know the facts in my case. There will also be many revelations which heretofore have remained secret."

"This is not to be a public trial, Mrs. Greenhow. You are to have a private hearing before General Dix's commission."

"Are you referring to General John Adams Dix?"

"The same. Do you know him?"

"He has dined at my home on several occasions. He was President Buchanan's secretary of the treasury. I find him to be a most kind and genteel man."

Superintendent Wood shook his head in disbelief. His most distinguished prisoner, whose indomitable will had sustained her through nearly a year of grueling imprisonment, was surely one of a kind. She amazed him!

Rose was driven through the snow and sleet of a blustery, cold March storm. She was chilled through by the time she reached the provost marshal's office. She sat in an unheated room for nearly an hour and tried valiantly to hide her nervousness. More than once she wondered if they had forgotten her. By the time two soldiers finally came for her, she was numb with cold and shivering. They took her to the commissioner's office and directed her to a seat at a long table opposite the two commissioners. She recognized both General Dix and Judge Edwards Pierrepont. She had known them well in happier times. Chilled, and shaking from the cold, she looked about the room and frowned imperceptibly. She recognized the bleak and barren room as the once glorious parlor of her old friend, Senator Gwin. She sighed as she recalled the many gay soirees she had attended in this very room. As she approached the two men they both stood up.

"Gentlemen, resume your seats," she remarked casually as she seated herself. "I recognize the embarrassment of your position. It was a mistake in your government to have selected gentlemen for this mission. You have, however, shown me but scant courtesy in having me kept waiting your pleasure for nearly an hour in the cold."

"I am sorry, we did not know that you had arrived. We were reviewing the facts in your case, Mrs. Greenhow," said General Dix apologetically.

"You have previously addressed me as Rose," she reminded him.

The general cleared his throat. "We must maintain a certain decorum in this investigation," he said.

"Of course!" Rose replied, then added sarcastically, "Since this is only a mimic court, I assume that I shall be permitted to answer your questions or not as I see fit."

Judge Pierrepont scowled at her. "You are charged with aiding the enemy with military information!"

"Do you have proof?" She was startled to note that one of the soldiers who had escorted her into the room had seated himself beside the two men. He was furiously writing down every word that was being spoken.

Jumping up she said bitterly, "If it is your object to make a spectacle of me and furnish reports for the newspapers, I shall have the honor to withdraw myself from this court."

"Please sit down, Mrs. Greenhow," hastily commanded General Dix. "An official record has been requested by the War Department."

"Why is this necessary?"

"You must recall that at the time of your arrest certain papers containing information on military operations were discovered in your possession."

"That is false! I had no occasion to destroy any papers. I had removed all the papers I desired to have removed before I was arrested."

"Madam, please be seated," said General Dix in a firmer tone of voice than he had ever before used in addressing her.

Slowly Rose seated herself and looked directly at her accusers. "The letters those brigands illegally confiscated were written long before the outbreak of war."

"What about the letter to Seward and its publication in a Richmond newspaper?"

"You must ask Mr. Seward about that! And while you are about it, you might advise the gentleman that the lady in question deems it an outrage to allow a private letter of hers to find its way into the public print."

"What about Manassas?" asked Pierrepont gruffly.

Rose straightened herself in her chair and fiercely looked at both of the men before speaking. "It is certain that if I had the information, I should have given it. I should consider that I was performing a holy duty to my friends."

"If you were behind our enemy's lines, would you then consider yourself bound by the laws of war?"

"Of course not. This is my home. I have been taken from my home and carried to a prison, to be insulted and subjected to treatment of the most outrageous kind. Every association of my home has been broken up and destroyed. If the government designs to send me across the lines as an exile, I have no alternative but to go as such. But if this is to be the case, will I be forcibly exiled or permitted to go of my own free will?"

"Would it be exiling you to send you South among your friends?" questioned the judge.

"It is exiling me to use any force to send me South, away from my home."

The judge nervously tapped his pen on the table before him. "I suppose it is hardly worthwhile to ask you to tak the oath of allegiance or give your parole of honor?"

"You would blush to do that," she replied harshly, "because I belong to a religion and a section of the country which makes an oath binding. If I took the oath of allegiance, no matter how galling it might be, I should consider myself as being bound by that oath."

"Have you any peculiar religion?" Pierrepont snapped.

"None but that which relies on the mercy and goodness of Providence."

Frustrated, Pierrepont turned to the general. "General, I think you had better talk to Mrs. Greenhow. You are an old friend of hers."

"I don't know as I have anything to say."

"You both see how pleasant it is," Rose quickly interrupted them.

Pierrepont suddenly thrust a paper before her. "This, madam, is a dispatch listing the number and disposition of troops quartered around Washington! Do you deny that this was in your possession?"

Rose looked at the paper before her for a moment, obviously flustered. "I—I do not recall it. I think that is false. I won't

505

swear it is. I have been in the habit of entertaining guests in my house. So far as I myself am concerned, I pronounce it unequivocally false."

Pierrepont rose and glared at her furiously. "The charge is not that you wrote those letters but that it was through your agency that they were transmitted."

"That I pronounce to be false. I am no one's agent. They might have been there, and they might not have been there. I am not to be made accountable for my guests."

As the two glared at each other, General Dix interrupted. "Please sit down, judge." Then he turned to Rose. "You know, Mrs. Greenhow, that in a contest like this, while the very existence of the government is in danger, the communication of such information as this, which tends to subvert the interests of the government, should certainly be considered a very serious offense."

"I do not consider it so when that government is dictated to by the unscrupulous Mammon of Unrighteousness." In a calmer voice, she continued. "Gentlemen, I beg you to consider the situation at that time. I had lost my child a short time before. I was not out in the world during that time; therefore, any information I may have got must have been brought to my house and brought to me. Brought to me by traitors, as you call them. If Mr. Lincoln's friends will pour into my ear such important information, am I to be held responsible for all that? Could it be presumed that I would not use that which was given to me by others? If I did not, I would be unjust to myself and my friends. It is said that a woman cannot keep a secret. I am a woman; and a woman usually tells all she knows."

"If you got this information as a secret, what then?" asked Pierrepont.

"That doesn't make any difference. I haven't any intention of working against my friends. I have written as much as any man against the party now in power; because I believe it is this party that has brought all the present trouble upon the country. The government is gone. You can never reestablish it. I can see no treason in any action that I have taken."

"I don't think you are bent so much on treason as on mischief," Pierrepont smiled sardonically at her.

Rose's eyes narrowed as she leaned closer to him to reply. "Let me tell you, I have studied the Constitution and the laws of this country. I have informed myself about the Constitution as well as I have about my Bible. Your government ought to be ashamed of itself for allowing me to be so scandalously treated, for allowing such scoundrels as it did to get my letters, and read them, and laugh over them. I have been made the victim of every kind of villainy. It has sent its emissaries to betray me."

Pierrepont frowned at her as he replied. "The question is not as to whether you have only written the letter, but, also, whether you have a right, knowingly, to try and subvert the purposes of the government."

"I look at it in an entirely different light. I have a right to write what I please. I always did so."

"You are charged, madam, with holding communication with the enemy in the South."

"If this were an established fact, you could not be surprised at it. I am a southern woman, and I thank God that no drop of Yankee blood ever polluted my veins; and as all who I have ever honored or respected have been driven by ruthless despotism to seek shelter there, it would seem the most natural thing in life that I should have done so."

"How is it, madam, that you have managed to communicate, in spite of the vigilance exercised over you?"

"That is my secret, sir; and, if it be any satisfaction to you to know it, I shall, in the next forty-eight hours, make a report to my government at Richmond of this rather farcical trial for treason."

"Why do you continue in your villainous tirades against our government? Do you not have relatives risking their very lives for the North?"

"I have a son-in-law and a nephew in the Union Army.

Unfortunately, I have a great many relatives who are benighted on the subject." Again there was silence in the room as the two men carefully studied her and she studied them. "What proof do you have that I am continuing these villainous tirades against your government?" she added triumphantly.

General Dix picked up a piece of pink writing paper and handed it to her. It was the letter that Rose had so recently written to her daughter Florence from Old Capitol Prison. "Read this, madam."

"Why should I read it? Obviously you are still stealing my own personal letters to my loved ones."

"Read it aloud. Look at it from an impartial point of view and see if you do not conclude that this letter is equal to declaring determined hostility to the government."

Rose glanced at the letter before her, undeniably written in her own hand. "I don't—" she started to say, then thinking better of it, read her letter to them: "My God! You cannot conceive the outrages practiced here. I will have my revenge, and I bear these outrages better on that account. I have no feeling but hate toward this detested, demoralized nation, and I thank God that it is in its last throes. McClellan has got his congé, having served the purpose of killing off Scott. Stanton has been brought forward to get rid of McClellan, and he will be put aside in his turn. These men let their vanity blind them as to their real position, and content themselves with the applause manufactured in advance to suit the role they are intended to play, and they lose sight of what a light observation should point out to them: the necessity of making a party. Stanton is now fooled to the top of his bent. He writes magnificent orders for Lincoln and lords it in the most approved fashion; he does not see what others see, that his own fall is not distant.

"The abolition policy is now fully avowed. Fremont has been again galvanized into prominence; if he was a man of talent and nerve, he would be the first American dictator; as it is, he will be the cat's paw to draw the chestnuts out of the fire

508

for somebody else to eat. I am pressed for time, darling. The naval engagement has been a glorious victory to the Confederate States, unprecedented in daring in any age. The retreat from Manassas was also a most masterly success, and I don't wonder at the howl of indignation of the whole North at being so outwitted. I shall try to give you a full account of things here. I shall publish an account of my experiences. I do not care to speak of Mrs. Cutts. I am now seven months a prisoner, and in that time, she and Addie have been only once to see me. Only once during that whole period have they ever sent me the smallest thing, and that was on Christmas, as an ostentatious display. But I am content. I shall send you some colored clothing for yourself and Leila; as for myself, I shall never lay aside my mourning.

"God bless you, darling. My love to dear Leila and Minnie. Your devoted mother."

General Dix scowled as she finished reading. "Now, how would you judge the author of that letter?"

"I should have been the meekest, lowliest Christian in the world if, after being smitten on one cheek by the government, I should have turned the other. Well now, have you any other letters of mine?"

"Mrs. Greenhow, you must know that we have considerably more letters in our dossier on you," said General Dix solemnly.

"The government knows what my feelings have been and always were. I have not changed them. I have no other feelings than those now."

General Dix sighed audibly. "Judge, I don't know as we wish to ask Mrs. Greenhow any more questions."

Rose glared at him. "In these war times, you ought to be on some more important business than holding an inquisition for the examination of women. I look upon this as nothing more than an inquisition." Neither of the men chose to answer her. After a strained moment of silence, Rose looked at the two impatiently. "Well, gentlemen, am I free to return to my dungeon?"

"Yes." General Dix turned to the clerk who had been

recording their conversations. "Call the guards. Instruct them to return Mrs. Greenhow to Old Capitol Prison."

As the clerk rose and disappeared from the room, Rose looked impassively at each of the men. "Am I to be advised of the disposition of my case?"

"Of course," replied Pierrepont. Rose looked at him expectantly. "After we have conferred on all the issues brought to light."

As the guards reentered the room, Rose stood up and watched them as they took their positions on either side of her. Then she turned dramatically to the two men who had sat as her judges. "On examining this evidence, you can but smile at the absurdity of the charges. I have, however, sir, to return my most sincere thanks to you and your colleagues for the delicacy and kind feeling which have characterized your bearing toward me, and to congratulate you upon the conclusion of a task which can be but little in unison with the feelings of a gentleman."

Almost daily Rose inquired of Superintendent Wood as to the outcome of her mimic court trial. Finally, more than a week later, he told her that he had heard that she was to be ordered South. "However," he warned, "I have received no official notice as yet."

The following day one of the men in the room below showed her an announcement in the *Baltimore News*, claiming that Rose O'Neal Greenhow had made a full confession. "Is it true, Mrs. Greenhow?" the men asked.

"It most certainly is not. I categorically deny it! I shall advise the *News* of their error."

Hastily she scribbled a brief message to that newspaper.

"I have made no confession of treason or treasonous correspondence; neither was I subjected to an examination intended to bring to light my sources of information. I but claim the right which our fathers did in '76—to protest against tyranny and oppression."

But the months dragged wearily on and she still received no

word as to the disposition of her case. Sloan, a guard who had taken a liking to young Rose and attempted to make her stay in prison less distasteful, said to Rose, "I have it on good authority that you have been ordered South, Mrs. Greenhow."

"Then why have I not been released?"

"General McClellan has countermanded the order."

"Oh, my God, I will never be freed from this infested hell hole!"

Rose waited impatiently for news, but, gradually, as the weeks dragged on into months, she began to lose all hope of ever being released. During these trying weeks of waiting, she was even more disturbed at the news she received intermittently concerning the progress of the war. New Orleans had fallen to the enemy. Norfolk had been evacuated, the great southern ship *Virginia* had been severely damaged by gunfire and sunk with a great loss of lives. This was that ship's second life, since it had been reconstructed from the old *Merrimac*. One rumor claimed that Richmond had been evacuated, but this was quickly denied.

On May 28, a group of Confederate prisoners was brought into the prison, and news spread quickly that they had been captured in a great battle that had taken place on the outskirts of Winchester, Virginia. But, more important, they brought news that, although they personally had been captured, Stonewall Jackson had won a smashing victory.

The following day, while she was still joyously reveling in the first bit of good news she had received in a long time, Superintendent Wood came to her early in the morning. "You are to be released and sent South, Mrs. Greenhow!"

"When?"

"As soon as transportation can be arranged for you."

"I am glad that it is over."

"Details for your trip south should be completed within a week."

"Thank God!"

XXIX

Richmond

On a beautifully sunny day which gaily welcomed the summer month of June, 1862, Rose got up early in the morning and painstakingly dressed. Superintendent Wood had himself visited her late the day before to advise her that she was scheduled to leave Old Capitol Prison early the next morning. She dressed in a light-weight gossamer dress with an almost unnoticeable hoop. She had been told that the day was going to be hot, and she had learned that the wide hoop skirt was no longer in fashion.

Young Rose, aroused by her mother's bustling about the room, was also dressed in the finest clothes that had been brought with her to the prison. Rose topped off her exuberant feeling on her day of liberation by donning a tight-fitting pair of black kid gloves. As they looked at each other's immaculate and gay appearance, they both laughed.

"You look beautiful, Mommy," said young Rose.

"And you, my dear, are the epitome of grace and loveliness!"

"So we are ready, now what do we do?"

"We shall wait until someone comes for us."

"Awwww, waiting again!"

"After months of nothing but waiting, my child, I am sure a few more hours will matter not at all," said Rose as she seated herself stiffly on the bare wooden chair.

Young Rose sighed and sat herself down on the side of the bed. "No, I suppose not, but I am anxious to leave this hell hole."

Rose's eyes widened. "Where did you ever hear such language, young lady?"

"That's what all the darkies call this place. I heard you say it more than once, Mommy."

"You must never say that again, Rose. Remember, we are leaving this life behind us when we go out that prison door."

"Yes, Mommy."

Shortly after eight o'clock, Superintendent Wood appeared in the doorway. He was dressed in a dark blue uniform surprisingly similar to the military uniform of the Union Army. Rose stood up as he entered the room, unable to conceal her surprise.

"Why, Superintendent Wood, you look positively handsome!"

"Thank you, Mrs. Greenhow. But your obvious amazement almost offsets your compliment."

"You took me by surprise, superintendent. This is the first time I have ever seen you in uniform."

"I must say you two ladies look exceedingly beautiful for this momentous occasion."

The two Roses curtsied grandly and Rose said teasingly, "I did not expect that a farewell visit would warrant the full regalia of your office."

"It is not farewell. I am going to accompany you."

"Oh?"

"I am escorting you personally to the borders of the Union."

"I will be pleased to have such a distinguished official escort us."

"Pleasure and duty, ma'am. It assures our country that there will be no deviltry while you still remain in northern territory."

"The leaders of our government have thought of every contingency, haven't they? When do we leave?"

Wood held out his arm. "Immediately, if you are ready."

She took his arm and holding young Rose's hand walked out of the room that had been her home for so many months. Word spread rapidly that they were leaving. As they walked down the hall every doorway they passed was filled with prisoners.

"Goodbye, Mrs. Greenhow." "Good luck to you." "Remember us to your southern friends." "Take good care of yourself." "Get plenty of fresh air." "Get out in the sun, you need to brighten up those pale cheeks." "You should erase that prison pallor as quickly as possible." "Goodbye!" "Goodbye!"

As she descended the stairs she turned to Wood and asked politely, "May I bid goodbye to the men who occupy the room below ours?"

"Of course."

As they came to the doorway, the men broke into a wild cheer. Her eyes glistened as she shook each of their hands. "Rose and I shall never forget your kindness to us."

"It was a pleasure, ma'am. We were glad to help you."

Superintendent Wood tilted his visored cap as he scratched his head. "Now what could these men have possibly done for you?"

"That is our secret, superintendent." She turned back to the men. "I shall send you packages once I am settled."

"Why, thank you, Mrs. Greenhow."

"That is, if Mr. Wood will permit it."

"Certainly. But I do not understand why—"

Rose smiled mysteriously. Waving to the prisoners, she bade them goodbye. As she walked down the hall, prisoners on every side waved to her and shouted words of encouragement.

The sun was shining brightly as they entered the exercise yard. A loud cheer arose from the prison. Every window was filled with enthusiastic prisoners, waving and bidding her goodbye.

A military coach waited inside the courtyard by the prison door. Six beautiful white horses neighed and stomped restlessly, pulling at their bits. Twelve cavalry men sat at attention on their horses, sabers by their sides, six before and six behind the carriage.

A young lieutenant jumped down from the carriage to assist her. She turned to him before entering the carriage. "Sir, before I advance further, I ask you, not as Lincoln's officer, but as a man of honor and a gentleman, are your orders from Baltimore to conduct me to a northern prison, or to some point in the Confederacy?"

The officer looked at her, wide-eyed with amazement. "On my honor, madam, my written orders are to conduct you to Fortress Monroe and thence to the southern Confederacy."

"Thank you."

She got into the carriage followed by her daughter and Superintendent Wood. The procession solemnly drove out of the yard and into the streets of Washington.

As they rode along, she looked sadly about her. She could faintly see the Capitol and the many government buildings that had been so much a part of her life for nearly forty years. Now she was leaving all this behind her—perhaps forever. Washington had been her home, the center of her activities. She had made her mark in the halls of government and on the social scene, as well. It was with mixed feelings that she realized she was bidding farewell to that part of her life.

They drove directly to the Washington railroad station where they were met by a contingent of foot soldiers armed with fixed bayonets. "I am honored," she said to Wood, "but is all this ostentatious display of military might necessary?"

"It is, madam. Frankly we have taken every precaution to prevent your communication with sympathizing friends."

But it seemed to be of no avail. As they arrived at the station, a large crowd was gathered there to see her off. A cheer went up as she stepped out of her carriage. Hands reached out to touch her as she walked to the station platform. "God bless you, Mrs. Greenhow!" "Godspeed!" "Good luck!" "Remember us to our southern friends!" "Give the rebels our best!" "God be with you, Rose."

A lump welled up in her throat as she boarded the train. She turned and waved farewell to the crowd which followed her until the guards prevented them from entering the car.

No one was permitted in her private car, except her daughter, Superintendent Wood, and her military guard.

Immediately the train pulled out of the station and headed for Baltimore. A short time later, as they pulled into the station at Baltimore, Rose jumped up excitedly and started down the aisle. Two of the guards quickly crossed their bayonets before her.

"What is the meaning of this? I wish to get off."

"We will get off, madam. But not until the other passengers have left."

"Baltimore is the center of a great many uprisings," Wood hastily explained. "We would like to avoid any demonstrations, if at all possible."

Finally, as the platform was cleared of all other persons, they left the train and marched to the street and a waiting carriage. They quickly drove to Gilmore House, where the party was to stay overnight.

They walked into the foyer of the hotel and Rose stepped haughtily up to the registering clerk. As he placed his guest book before her, she signed her name with a flourish. No sooner had she completed signing, however, when General Dix came rushing up to them.

Without greeting, he turned abruptly to the hotel clerk. "That name must be stricken from your book, sir. We must take all necessary precautions."

"Yes, sir," said the clerk meekly. Sadly disappointed, he hurriedly erased the famous lady's signature before the ink had dried on the page.

"Why, General Dix," Rose beamed cheerily. "It is a pleasant surprise to see you here."

"I am to accompany you to your destination, Mrs. Greenhow."

"How nice, but why not call me Rose for the remainder of

516

our trip?"

General Dix coughed nervously, and ignoring her suggestion turned quietly to the guards accompanying the party. "We will have guards stationed at the entrance of the hotel on a twenty-four-hour basis until Mrs. Greenhow leaves. We must avoid any overt uprising."

"Yes, sir."

Early the next morning, they drove to the docks of Baltimore, where Rose was to board the ship for Fortress Monroe.

As she alighted from her carriage, a large crowd suddenly converged on the small party. A loud cheer rose up as she started to walk toward the pier. The crowd followed her. Military guards pushed the enthusiastic crowd away to make a path for her. Women madly waved handkerchiefs at her as she walked by, calling "God bless you!" "Good luck!" "Remember us to the rebels!" "Tell them all is not lost!" "Take heart, the Confederates are winning at Seven Pines!" "The Yankees have been beaten back at Fair Oaks, too!" "Don't worry, Rose, Richmond is safe for you!"

Tears welled up in her eyes at this spontaneous expression of sympathy for her. For so many months she had been alone in the midst of the enemy. Now, in the center of the enemy's territory, sympathizers were rallying to her side. She turned and waved her handkerchief, and a sudden quiet came over the crowd. "God bless you all!" she said loudly. Although there were tears in her eyes, she smiled joyously. "May we hope and pray for an early victory!" she shouted defiantly. A spontaneous cheer broke from the crowd, and Rose was hurriedly ushered onto the waiting ship.

As the mooring lines were cast off and the ship trumpeted its departure with a fierce blow of its deep, foghornlike whistle, another cheer rang out from the crowd. Shouts of good wishes and "Bon voyage!" continued until they were well into the harbor.

It was only a short trip to Fortress Monroe. As the imposing fort came into view, General Dix walked over and stood by her side. "Superintendent Wood and I will be leaving you now. We have seen you safely to the end of Union territory."

"You have been most gracious, General Dix."

Superintendent Wood came up to her and shook her hand. "I hope you will not think too badly of our association, Mrs. Greenhow."

She smiled at him. "We have had many differences, haven't we, superintendent?"

"That we have, ma'am. I have never housed a spunkier prisoner. Nor one more ladylike."

"Thank you." She patted him on the cheek. "You know, superintendent, I shall miss you."

He smiled good-naturedly. "I can understand that. You won't have anyone to take issue with you."

"Rose shall never be at a loss for confrontations," interrupted General Dix, touching her arm. "There is always someone with a mind of his own to keep her from doing exactly as she damn well pleases. And, take heed, my Wild Rose, there always will be." He bowed and kissed her hand.

"It has been a long time since anyone called me that." She smiled.

He straightened to his full six feet and remarked affectionately, "I do wish you Godspeed, Rose."

"Thank you, General Dix."

Nervously, the general cleared his throat. "And now, there is one more official duty which I must perform before I free you to go South." He drew out a paper from an inside pocket of his uniform.

Rose frowned. "I shall not sign an oath of allegiance," she warned.

"I would not be so foolhardy as to suggest it. I do believe, however, that you will see fit to sign this." He handed her an official-looking paper. She read it. "Upon my word of honor, and in consideration of my being set at liberty beyond the lines

518

of the U.S. Army, I will not return north of the Potomac River during the present hostilities without the permission of the secretary of war of the U.S."

"I shall gladly sign this, general," said Rose cheerfully as she signed the paper. "Of course, you realize that this document is null and void should President Davis and General Lee take command."

He did not reply. He clicked his heels and turning away, said, "Captain Barstow, I leave you in command to release this prisoner." He left her, followed by Superintendent Wood. As the two men disappeared into the ship's cabin, Rose said sadly, "Goodbye." She would miss them both!

General Dix's aide-de-camp, Wilson Barstow, remained by her side accompanied by a single guard. "Now, Mrs. Greenhow, where do you wish to go?"

"To the capital of the Confederacy, wherever that might be."

"It is still Richmond, Virginia, although it might well be in northern hands before you arrive."

"I shall take my chance on that."

Rose and her daughter, accompanied by Captain Barstow and the guard, leisurely walked across the deck to the captain's cabin.

Captain Van Valkenburgh, who had stood by his cabin witnessing the strange scene which was taking place, saluted her as she came up to him.

"Mrs. Greenhow, it is a pleasure to have you aboard, and on such a joyous occasion."

"Thank you, captain."

"I have had a luncheon prepared for you. Will you join me?"

The two Roses entered the captain's cabin followed closely by the two United States soldiers. There, on a mahogany table covered with an Irish linen tablecloth such as Rose had not seen for many months was a sumptuous luncheon laid out for them. There was cured ham, terrapin, and a saddle of mutton, together with stuffed mangoes and oysters. There was champagne, too. Rose could not remember the last time she had tasted champagne. The captain filled her glass. She raised it high above her head and said fervently, "To Jefferson Davis and the Confederacy!"

Captain Barstow, standing at attention beside her chair, quickly turned his back to her as did the guard.

Late in the afternoon Rose and her party boarded the small excursion boat that was to take them to City Point. The sun was particularly warming, and she stood on the deck gazing at the scenery, cooled by a mild sea breeze. The *Monitor* was lying at cumbersome anchor at the north end of the Chesapeake Bay which led into her beloved Rappahannock River. She heartily expressed her disdain at the intrusion of the "low, black ugly thing." A short distance beyond, they passed the Union battleship *Congress*, party submerged in the lower bay.

A few hours later they sailed up the James River and docked at the port of Richmond. As Rose left the ship, she kneeled down, kissed her hand and placed it lovingly on the first Virginia soil she had touched for longer than she wished to remember.

She was ceremoniously welcomed to Virginia by Colonel W. S. Ash and Major G. W. Alexander. They drove directly to the Ballard House. As she alighted from her carriage, a small army band struck up the lively strains of "Dixie." General Winder, the commandant of the City of Richmond, strode briskly over to her, bowed deeply, and kissed her hand. "I have taken the liberty of removing the necessity of a formal report to me, Mrs. Greenhow, by personally calling on you."

"Thank you, general." She smiled graciously.

Later in the evening, while she sat in the lobby of the hotel surrounded by well-wishers, Jefferson Davis called on her.

As he bowed and kissed her hand, he could not conceal the startled look that came into his eyes.

"You seem surprised, Jefferson. Has my appearance altered so?"

"I cannot help but note the changes that your long imprisonment has made in you, my dear. You have suffered greatly on our behalf. Your nerves, no doubt, are shaken by the mental tortures you have been forced to bear. We are forever in your debt. But for you, fair lady, there would have been no Battle of Bull Run."

She smiled. "All that I have endured has been worth hearing your gracious words of thanks. I shall ever remember this as the proudest moment of my whole life, to have received the tribute of praise from one who stands as the apostle of our country's liberty in the eyes of the civilized world."

For the next few days she rested luxuriously in her hotel suite. Several times during the day, she and young Rose went out to feel the luxury of freedom, to once again breathe deeply of the fresh, flower-scented air. She could go wherever she pleased! Often she would smile and bid a cheery "Good day" to complete strangers she passed along the way.

Richmond was a different city than the Richmond she had known. Prices of food were extremely high, and the necessities of life were becoming scarce. When she arrived, the enemy was pounding at the very doorstep of the city, and only after a week of furious fighting at Seven Pines and finally Malvern, were the Union forces soundly defeated and driven off. Rose, and the people of Richmond, breathed a sigh of relief as the siege of the city was ended.

As could be expected, after two weeks of complete, refreshing rest, Rose began to feel the need for greater activity. She decided that she would write a book about her gruesome experiences and began collecting and sorting out the remnants of correspondence which had been left to her by the marauding military police. She reread her diary, which she had meticulously kept during every day of her imprisonment. She wondered if Colonel Jordan had retained any of the many messages she had sent. She sent a note asking if she could see him at his convenience.

He immediately replied, inviting her and her daughter to be

his guests for dinner at the America Hotel where he was staying.

It was a touching reunion, and Colonel Jordan was expansive in his praise of the work that she had done.

"You have substantially aided our cause, Rose; more so than any other person since your imprisonment!"

"Thank you, colonel. My only regret is that it could not have continued longer."

"It is our regret that you were forced to pay so dearly for your loyalty."

"I am well rewarded to know that my efforts are appreciated by those for whom I sacrificed. Now that I am free, I have decided to write a book about my experiences. I am wondering if you have kept any of the messages which I sent you, and if you would loan them to me for review."

"I most certainly have kept them—all of them. I shall collect them and bring them to you. I will also give you my own correspondence and notations concerning the valuable information that you forwarded to us."

"I am sure that it will refresh my memory in many instances. I find that as I—"

Excitedly, young Rose attempted to get her mother's attention. "Mommy. Mommy. Do you know—?"

"Hush, child. Can't you see that Colonel Jordan and I are discussing business?"

"But this is important, Mommy!" Rose insisted.

It was not like her daughter to interrupt her elders when they were speaking. Impatiently, she turned to her. "What is it that is so important, dear?"

"Do you remember Pryce Lewis who helped guard us when we were prisoners in our home?"

"Of course. He was one of the few men on Pinkerton's staff who was civil to us. But what is so important that you should interrupt our discussion?"

"Well, don't look now, but I am sure he is sitting at that table yonder, talking to that man and woman."

Rose glanced at the table her daughter had indicated and gasped. "Good heavens, Colonel Jordan, it is Pryce Lewis— one of Pinkerton's men—in the uniform of a Confederate soldier!"

"Are you sure?" asked Colonel Jordan.

"I am positive."

"So am I!" remarked young Rose.

"I shall attend to this immediately. Please excuse me."

Hastily he left their table and was gone only a short time before he returned and sat down with them again. "That was most observant of you, my dear little girl," he said admiringly. "The Confederacy can be proud that we have another loyal supporter who is following in her mother's footsteps."

At that moment three armed soldiers came up to Pryce Lewis and whispered to him. He immediately got up, as did the two persons who were with him and they were quietly escorted out of the dining room.

"We shall interrogate them at military headquarters."

"What will you do with them?"

"It depends on what they tell us. Frankly, the information that they might give could be more important than their capture. Holding them only increases our burden; there are so many of them."

"I might be able to encourage him to talk, Colonel Jordan."

"I would appreciate your assistance. And I shall report your daughter's aid in this matter."

Rose patted her daughter's cheek. "I am proud of you, darling."

Shortly afterward, Colonel Jordan saw them off in their carriage, promising to deliver the messages and notes concerning Rose's activities within the next day or so.

The following day, Rose went to military headquarters. Learning that Pryce Lewis was still being detained, she asked to see him.

He smiled wanly at her as she entered his cell. "I was afraid that you had recognized me last evening."

"It was my daughter who noticed you."

"The young lady is as alert as her mother." He sighed. "Well, we meet again, under different circumstances."

"Wars have a way of engulfing us in strange circumstances."

There was an awkward pause as Lewis lowered his gaze. Presently he spoke, still without meeting her eyes. "I suppose it would be fruitless to ask you to intervene in my behalf."

"On the contrary, I might be able to help you."

He looked at her eagerly. "Would you?"

"When we were your prisoners, you were courteous and considerate. Now, Mr. Lewis, if you will tell the authorities all that you know—your mission—your contacts—I believe I can persuade them to return you to northern territory."

"I would be forever grateful, Mrs. Greenhow. I was sent down to locate Timothy Webster. He is one of Mr. Pinkerton's ablest assistants, and suddenly he disappeared."

"You have not located him?"

"I learned last night he is a prisoner here. The man and woman who were with me are—"

"Don't tell me, Mr. Lewis. Tell the military interrogators. But mind you, it must be the truth."

"You can rely on me, Mrs. Greenhow. I don't believe I could ever be a very efficient spy. I—I am not cut out for this kind of work."

Rose smiled and bade him goodbye.

Three weeks later, after he had told the authorities everything he knew and it had been verified, Rose was successful in having him released. When he departed to go back North, Rose gave him some warm clothing and fruit and condiments to deliver to her friends at Old Capitol Prison. She sent them other packages from time to time, working through a new mercy organization that a woman named Clara Barton had formed. Unfortunately, Timothy Webster would tell his captors nothing, and the following week he was hanged for his espionage activities.

Rose diligently began work on her book. As the months went by, however, she found time to visit many of her old friends. She called on Varina and Jefferson Davis often and soon was closely embroiled in the affairs of the Confederacy, as she had so often been in those of the northern government before the war.

"The blockade is slowly draining us of our resources," Davis lamented. "We have cotton and tobacco bulging at the seams of our warehouses, with no market."

"But what of our markets before the war?"

"We need ships to deliver to those markets. We need arms and ammunition to protect the ships. We must have money and gold to buy them. Gold is becoming increasingly scarce. Our bonds are going begging."

"Have you contacted our old customers?"

"How? Our best customers reside in the North."

"What about England and France?"

"Relations with them are not too good. With every defeat that we suffer, they move further away from us. John Slidell and James M. Mason, our commissioners in Europe, are doing their best, but—"

"Why not utilize our underground to increase our commerce?"

"We have tried, but with only limited success."

"May I help alleviate the situation?"

"You are most welcome to try, but I can't imagine how—"

"I had issued a power of attorney to William T. Smithson, the Washington banker who is sympathetic to our cause, shortly after my imprisonment. He has one hundred twenty shares of my railroad stock, which I shall instruct him to convert to Confederate bonds."

"That is most generous of you. But how can you arrange the transaction?"

"I shall work through the underground."

"Good luck, Rose. We are desperate enough to attempt anything."

Rose immediately sought out Colonel Jordan and through him established a direct connection with banker Smithson. When her own transaction was successfully completed, she extended her operation to other sympathetic friends in Washington and in many parts of the North. Couriers were continually traveling from Rose through Colonel Jordan to banker Smithson, who, for obvious reasons, preferred to be known as Charles R. Cables.

Jefferson Davis was astonished and delighted at the increasing amount of Southern securities and bonds for which Rose was finding buyers. Banker Smithson acted as Rose's northern representative as thousands and eventually hundreds of thousands of dollars of sight drafts were negotiated in Richmond. Great quantities of Confederate bonds and notes were sold at the unheard-of lucrative rate of eight percent.

Davis was enthusiastic in his praise of Rose's financial operation. "You have brought us more cash and credits than all of our southern bankers combined," he told her.

She smiled proudly. "Thank you, Mr. President. I realize that this is a small portion of what is needed, but I believe we can increase our yield from the North and from Europe, as well."

"I cannot imagine how it can be done."

"Cotton and tobacco, which we have in abundance, are salable commodities. On the other hand, we are in the market for all of the ships, ammunition, and finished textiles we can procure. Why not eliminate these cash transactions and effect an exchange of our needs for theirs?"

"We cannot accomplish this without money or gold."

"I believe we can."

"How?"

"By simply issuing cotton and tobacco certificates from our treasury redeemable at the markets where we deliver our goods."

Davis thoughtfully rubbed his chin. "By gorry, it sounds like an excellent idea! It might just work. I shall have to speak to Judah Benjamin, our secretary of state, and to our secretary of the treasury about this."

Two days later Davis called on Rose while she was working on her book.

"Forgive my intrusion, Rose, but it was urgent that I speak with you."

"A visit from you, sir, is never an intrusion."

"I see you are deeply involved in your book."

"Yes, I have the first draft almost completed."

"Good. What is it to be called?"

Rose shrugged her shoulders. "I haven't thought of a proper title as yet. Since it is the story of my imprisonment, I suppose something like that would be appropriate."

"It is also a reflection of the first year of Abolition Rule."

"Yes. *That* is an ideal title. I shall call it "My Imprisonment and the First Year of Abolition Rule at Washington."

"An intriguing title." Suddenly Davis came to her and put his hand on her shoulder. "I have been so engrossed in discussing your book I completely forgot to tell you the purpose of my visit."

"I distracted you. I am sorry."

"Don't be. I wanted you to know that both Benjamin and our secretary of the treasury think your cotton and tobacco certificates are an excellent idea. We are going to try them. As a matter of fact, I have authorized a printing of the certificates to be available to purchasers of our goods without a formal exchange of money."

"It will simplify the transaction. When will the certificates be available?"

"Within one week. I am so advising our European commissioners Mr. Mason and Mr. Slidell. Now all we need to complete the transaction is to successfully deliver the goods by ships!"

"That is your responsibility, sir."

"We will do our best, but with the blockade becoming more effective each month, there are bound to be a certain number of goods delivered to the bottom of the sea rather than to their destination."

"But the certificates will not be valid until the actual goods are safely delivered."

"Of course."

During the bleak winter of 1863, Rose enthusiastically promoted the cotton and tobacco certificates. Many of the bales of goods were intercepted by the enemy, but the profits on those shipments safely delivered were so great that these losses were readily offset. Rose began to purchase great quantities of cotton and tobacco herself, becoming her own broker. Before spring, she had allotted a great portion of her personal monies to this operation, and it had become a thriving business.

She still managed to spend a few hours each day writing her memoirs. By early summer, drafting and rewriting were completed and her manuscript was ready for publication. With the unsettled condition in America she wondered if her book would be more successful in the European market. The more she dwelt on the idea, the more attractive it seemed. Then another thought struck her. If she delivered her manuscript personally, she would be assured of its safe arrival. In addition, her presence would make it more convenient if any revisions were required.

An ocean voyage could also be helpful to the Confederacy. She could promote tobacco and cotton certificates on the Continent. Then too, such a trip would be good for Rose. Her daughter's long imprisonment had left its mark on the impressionable child. A stint in one of the competent finishing schools in Paris would be highly desirable for her. Even greater rewards could be expected if Rose were enrolled in a convent. Her religious training had been sadly neglected in recent years.

Young Rose was thrilled at the prospect. "You mean I shall travel in a big boat just like grownups?"

"They are called ships, dear. Your education suffered while we were imprisoned. It would be augmented considerably by a year or two in a fine convent in Paris."

"A convent, Mommy?" young Rose asked dubiously.

"It is simply a finishing school for young ladies. They are called convents since they are operated by religious orders."

"Oh."

"You will learn to speak French fluently and your grammar and history will improve."

"You mean it's a school?"

"Yes, but more than that, you will learn how to conduct yourself properly, and you will be prepared for the joys and pleasures of a well-organized social life."

"Well, I guess it will be fun, the ocean voyage and Paris and all."

"I am sure it will be most rewarding."

At about this time, Rose received a letter from her oldest daughter. It was the first time she had heard from Florence in many months. She bemoaned the fact that she had not seen her mother in such a long time. She told her that several of Leila's friends had gone to a boarding school in Pennsylvania, and, since Leila had begged her to go with them, she was now enrolled there. Florence missed her and was lonely. Since Moore's mining interests had now made him quite wealthy, he had suggested that she take a trip back East. She hesitated because of the unsettled conditions brought on by the war. However, when their latest dividends proved to be considerably more than they had anticipated, he suggested that she take a trip to Europe. Florence told her mother that she did not require much convincing, and that when Rose received this letter, Florence would be sailing on the high seas, bound for Paris. She enclosed the address of where she would be staying. She ended her letter on a somber note, lamenting the fact that she knew not when they would see each other again.

Florence's letter finally made up Rose's mind. She and Rose would go to Europe, and they would meet Florence in Paris.

In midsummer, Rose approached Davis with her plan. Now was an opportune time for her to personally visit Europe. Help from France and England was desperately needed. Ships and military supplies were being consumed faster than they were being replaced. But because of recent reverses, relations with France and England were continuing to worsen. By visiting London, Rose could not only oversee the publication of her book, but she could also promote the cotton and tobacco certificates. She would do everything within her power to gain additional support for the Confederacy from the governments of France and Britain. Davis was well aware of the many European diplomats Rose had known, all of whom she had entertained many times in her home.

When the great battle of Gettysburg was lost, Davis was convinced that Confederate prestige abroad would suffer even more. Thus he readily agreed to Rose's suggestion. She would sail to Europe as an unofficial representative of the Confederacy. She was authorized to sell cotton and tobacco certificates in exchange for ships, ammunition, and other supplies sorely needed by the Confederacy.

Immediately Rose made necessary arrangements, booking passage on a recently built swift privateer, the *Phantom*. She sent a hasty note to Florence advising her of her plans and telling her how overjoyed she was at the prospect of a reunion with her in Paris.

When Varina Davis learned that Rose was scheduled to sail on August 5, she suggested to her husband that he sponsor a cotillion in her honor to wish her bon voyage.

At first he hesitated. "It is such an unnecessary expense, my dear. We can ill afford such frivolity at this time."

"Nonsense!" Varina replied emphatically. "Our people need a bit of gaiety to take their minds off this horrible conflict, if only for a few hours."

"Perhaps you are right. Our nation could surely do with a bit of encouragement."

So, official word went out that the Davises were sponsoring a farewell cotillion for Rose. The ballroom of the America Hotel was engaged, and Varina herself supervised the preparations. The night of the cotillion was warm, and both the ballroom and the adjoining patio were gaily decorated with silver candles and low-hanging paper lanterns.

Rose had received permission from the captain of the *Phantom* for young Rose to go aboard ship with her new nanny several hours before sailing time. Consequently, they arrived late in the afternoon of August 5 with their baggage, and Rose was able to see her daughter comfortably settled in their cabin before going on to the America Hotel and the cotillion.

Flushed and excited, she advised Varina and Jefferson Davis who greeted her at the hotel entrance that she must leave at eleven-thirty since her boat sailed promptly at midnight. Before they entered the ballroom, President Davis gave her a letter for John Slidell and another for James M. Mason, advising those gentlemen of Rose's mission and requesting their cooperation.

On that memorable evening Rose was once again the center of attraction. She had not bought any new clothing for the cotillion and was still dressed in black mourning, but she was beautiful as she entered the ballroom on the arm of the president of the Confederacy.

Jefferson's entire Cabinet and their wives were in attendance, as were as many of the general's officers, and government officials who could be spared from duty. Two orchestras alternated playing, so that dancing was continuous. Rose was radiant as she danced to the popular tunes of "Lorena," "Bonnie Blue Flag," and "Dixie." She had completely lost her prison pallor and looked years younger as she twirled about the ballroom floor.

Through it all, however, she never lost sight of her responsibility to the Confederacy. While dancing with General W. H. C. Whiting, she was astonished to learn that he was presently without a command.

"It is inconceivable that your vast experience is simply going to waste because of your inactivity."

"But I have not been offered any command."

"Pish, general, our nation needs men desperately. Since you are one of the greatest cavalrymen of our day, you would attract many competent men to battle under your command."

"Do you really think so?"

"I know so. You must know many well-qualified cavalry-men."

"Yes, I am familiar with several experienced horsemen!"

"Then why not organize a cavalry brigade, general?"

"I'd have to promise my men commissions."

"Of course. I am sure that can be arranged. Let me speak to President Davis."

"Well, if the Confederacy will offer commissions, I would certainly seriously consider it."

Rose reached up and boldly kissed General Whiting on the cheek. "The Confederacy needs more brave men such as yourself," she said smiling her old bewitching smile.

Within the hour, Rose had Davis's promise that any men General Whiting enlisted for his proposed brigade would be granted commissions. Quickly relaying this information to General Whiting, she succeeded in securing his promise that he would begin to organize a cavalry brigade at once. He told her that in her honor he would call it the Rose Brigade.

"And I shall send you a rose for each of your officers when you receive your first order to battle," she said proudly.

At the hour of eleven, Jefferson Davis stopped the orchestra and stepped up onto the bandstand. "Ladies and gentlemen, may I have your attention." As the noise subsided, he continued. "We are gathered here tonight to honor a great lady of the Confederacy, Rose O'Neal Greenhow. I ask her to join me now on the stand." A burst of applause began and gathered momentum as Rose, smiling, wended her way through the crowd and came to him.

It was several moments before the spontaneous accolade subsided sufficiently to permit him to continue. "Mrs. Greenhow has served our nation well, and in so doing, has suffered much on our behalf. She has spent many months in unmerciful captivity at the hands of the enemy. Her efforts aided us in many battles; foremost amongst them being our great victory at Manassas. It is because of her undying loyalty that we deem it appropriate to give her some tangible token of our appreciation. With this thought in mind we have dug deep into our limited and somewhat strained funds to present her at this time with a Confederate draft for twenty-five hundred dollars!"

Amidst thunderous applause and cheers, Rose took the draft and pressed it to her bosom. As the din subsided, she smiled graciously and said, "This is indeed a surprise. As many of you know, I am leaving tonight on another mission for our great country. I promise you that I will use this money to our country's best advantage as I travel through the capitals of Europe in an effort to win their greater support for our cause. The successful conclusion of this battle against tyranny and oppression is uppermost in my heart and forever shall be. Thank you for your kind generosity."

Again the guests applauded, and it was several moments before Davis could continue. "The time has come," he said, "to say goodbye and bid this great lady a fond bon voyage. Rose, we wish you every success in the publication of your book, and may your efforts on behalf of the Confederacy meet with equal acceptance." He signaled to the orchestra, which began a favorite Strauss waltz. Davis took Rose's hand and led her onto the dance floor. He waltzed her around the ballroom as the guests looked on. Then General Lee tapped him on the shoulder and he, in turn, danced with her. He was followed by Generals Beauregard, Whiting, Samuel Cooper, and Carpot Posey. As one distinguished guest danced with her about the ballroom, he was followed by another—Roger A. Pryor, Clement C. Clay, Judah P. Benjamin, James A. Seddon, Joseph E. Johnston, Colonel W. S. Ashe, Colonel Jordan, Major G. W. Alexander, Stephan R. Mallory, and Louis D. Wigfall—until every one of the leaders of the Confederacy had danced with her and wished her Godspeed.

As the dance finally ended, Rose, exhausted and still flushed from the accolades of her well-wishers, hurried toward the door.

"I must go," she smiled radiantly, "or the ship will be leaving without me."

"On to the blockade, your next conquest!" someone shouted.

"I sincerely hope so," she laughed. "Actually, this is my first visit to Europe. The Yankees are reported as being unusually vigilant, a double line of blockaders block the way. I hope by the blessing of Providence to get out in safety."

"You will, my dear." "Goodbye." "Good luck!" "God Bless you!"

She waved to them fondly as she stood at the doorway of the great ballroom of the hotel. She spoke to the Davises and the others standing nearby. "And now, my dears, I must say goodbye. I can never sufficiently thank you for your kindness to me. As I depart I can only say, may He ever guard you all and keep you in health. This is my most fervent prayer."

Eager hands helped her into her carriage and she was off. Waving from the window, she soon disappeared into the night.

XXX

Europe

Winter 1864

It was late in the afternoon when the boat docked at London.
Rose took her daughter's hand and carried a small valise in her
other hand. She was followed by young Rose's nanny with a
second satchel. Rose frowned.

"It is almost four o'clock, it will be hours before we get
through customs and on our way."

"I'm hungry, Mommy."

"I'm afraid it will be a long time before we are able to dine.
You must think of something else, dear."

"What?"

"Well, isn't it exciting? Here we are at the port of London,
the gateway to a whole new world. We are about to step on the
soil of the greatest and most powerful nation in the world."

"It looks the same as any other place to me."

"Oh, Rose, you must imagine all the wonderful adventures
that are in store for you."

"I'd much rather be settled somewhere in a nice cozy
home."

"You'll be settled soon enough. Come along now."

As they walked down the gangplank and stepped onto the
London pier, a distinguished-looking gentleman came up to
them. He tipped his bowler hat as he smiled at them and said
cheerfully, "May I be of any assistance, madam?"

Rose turned to him startled, until she recognized an old

friend. "Why, Lord Lyons, how nice to see you." Dropping her valise, she threw her arms about him and pressed her cheek to his. "How wonderful to meet a dear friend upon arriving in a strange land!"

"I had a feeling that my sudden appearance would please you."

"It surely does, Lord Lyons. It is getting so late in the day and we still have to go through customs."

Lord Lyons looked at young Rose, and brushing the windblown hair out of her eyes, said, "And is this your youngest daughter?"

"Yes. Rose, this is a dear friend of ours, Lord Lyons."

As Rose curtsied, Lord Lyons remarked, "Gad, how she has grown. She was nothing but a babe in arms when last I saw her." Then turning to Rose he asked, "Where is the rest of your luggage?"

"A porter is taking it off."

"Do you have tickets for it?"

"Yes."

"Give them to me, if you will."

She reached into her bag and finding the tickets, gave them to him. "I don't understand."

"My man will take care of your luggage. Of course you will be staying at our town house while you are in London."

"I have reservations at Claridge's."

"But I insist, Rose."

She put her arm through his. "Lord Lyons, there is an old precept in our family: 'Fish and house guests both begin to smell after three days.'"

Lord Lyons guffawed. "Jolly well, then. But surely you will stay with us tonight."

"Of course."

"Shall we go?" He started toward the pier terminal.

Rose stopped abruptly. "But I have not cleared through customs."

"Please come with me," he said rather firmly. He started out and Rose followed him.

As they came up to the long line of passengers waiting to have their baggage inspected, Lord Lyons wended his way past the line until he came to the inspector's table. Catching the eye of the chief inspector, he said casually, "This is the lady and her entourage I spoke to you about."

"Oh, yes, Lord Lyons." Immediately the inspector left his post and came over to them. "Will you open your bags, please?"

"Of course." Hastily Rose opened her bag and instructed the rest to do the same.

The inspector gave them a rather perfunctory glance as he lifted up their clothing and other contents and said briefly, "Thank you, madam, you may pass through."

Amazed, the little party started on. As they came to a wide staircase leading to the veranda and the upper floors of the customs building, Lord Lyons pointed to them. "This way please."

"But aren't we going to your home?"

"Of course. But first you are wanted in the harbor master's quarters."

Rose could not conceal the startled look that came into her eyes. "Lord Lyons, is anything wrong?"

"Be at rest, my dear. Just a matter of protocol."

As they opened the glass-paneled door of the harbor master's quarters, they could hear loud talking and laughter. They quickly walked through his deserted office. They went out into a large room overlooking the pier facilities and the Thames River. Rose gasped. There was a long table at the far end of the room covered with sandwiches, hors d'oeuvres and canapes. At closely spaced intervals, bottles of chilling champagne rested in heaped buckets of cracked ice. Beside each bucket stood a liveried footman.

But it was not the vast quantity of delicacies that had

startled her. Rose walked into the room and a loud, spontaneous cheer rang out. "Welcome to her Majesty's islands!"

As Rose looked about, it seemed that the room was filled to overflowing with all the British friends she had ever known and entertained in her home. Lord and Lady Russell, Lord and Lady Napier, Lady Franklin, the Duke of Argyll, and many new faces whom she did not immediately recognize.

"You must be famished, my dear," said Lady Lyons as she came up to them. "Come, join us in a bit of sustenance." She led them over to the well-stocked table.

"My dear, my dear, how nice to finally see you," said Lady Georgiana Fullerton. "We waited so long, we had to send out for more ice for the champagne."

Small china plates were quickly passed around and the guests helped themselves to the bounteous display of food piled high on the table. Servants poured champagne and distributed it, and everyone began to gather around Rose.

"A blooming sight for sore eyes," said Lord Palmerston as he came up to her and threw his arms about her.

"It's nice to see you," Rose replied cheerfully. "It's so good to be here."

"We are glad you are here, too," Lady Franklin said, joining them.

"Oh, Lady Franklin, thank you for meeting me."

"I appreciated your letter when Sir John was lost. It was a most comforting message."

"Your husband was a great man, Lady Franklin."

"He was that." Lady Franklin sighed. "He gave his life for a good cause."

"There is nothing more important to either of our continents than the discovery of a Northwest Passage."

"You must look me up during your stay in London."

"You may be assured that I will."

Lord Lyons came up to her with a tall, stately-looking woman by his side. "There is someone I especially want you to meet, Rose. I am pleased to present to you Miss Florence Nightingale."

Rose smiled and took her hand. "This is an honor, Miss Nightingale."

"This great lady saved more lives in the Crimean War than any other person alive."

"I am well aware of your tremendous efforts to alleviate the plight of the wounded. Your courageous leadership is sorely needed in the war in which our country is engaged."

"Thank you. I hope I may have the opportunity of speaking with you about the plight of your wounded during your stay here, Mrs. Greenhow."

"I would consider it an honor if you would call me Rose."

"I shall be glad to, Rose."

"And I assure you I shall find time to talk with you during my visit."

Lady Russell joined them on the arm of a young-looking older man. "You must meet my very dear friend, the renowned author, Thomas Carlyle." Carlyle bowed low and kissed her hand.

"Yes, Mrs. Greenhow. I understand that a new writer will soon be joining our ranks."

"I am not sure that my writing can be classed in such distinguished company as Thomas Carlyle's, but I am in hopes of having my book published while I am over here."

"I am very interested in the war in your country. It is heart-rending when a nation is torn asunder and blood brothers must choose opposing sides."

"An unfortunate circumstance, sir, brought on by the lords of abolition."

"You are referring, no doubt, to Mr. Lincoln's administration."

"Mr. Lincoln and his unmitigated cronies, Seward, Wilson, and Stanton."

"You know them, I assume."

"If you knew them as I do, you would be opposed to their

539

tyranny and oppression as I am."

"Your observations are no doubt reflected in your book, Mrs. Greenhow. What do you call it?"

"'My Imprisonment and the First Year of Abolition Rule at Washington.'"

"Obviously a propaganda piece on behalf of the southern cause. Similar, no doubt, to Miss Stowe's *Uncle Tom's Cabin*."

"Yes, excepting my book is more fact than fiction."

Carlyle pursed his lips and rolled his eyes. "I can see that the south has in you a most ardent supporter. I can only hope that your book will be as successful over here as *Uncle Tom's Cabin*."

"Thank you, Mr. Carlyle. I believe it would be well worth your while to write an article on the southern revolution."

"I might just do that. I should like to talk to you about it sometime."

"I can provide you with a great deal of information, much of which is not included in my book."

"Many of my literary friends are interested in your cause. I shall be delighted to bring you down to Cheyne Walk sometime to talk with them."

"I look forward to it, Mr. Carlyle."

They were interrupted by Lady Fullerton who joined them on the arm of a tall, distinguished gentleman with a heavy, neatly trimmed beard and mustache.

"Rose, my love, you must meet my dear brother. This is the second Earl of Granville, George Leveson-Gower Granville. May I present Mrs. Rose O'Neal Greenhow."

Lord Granville bowed low and kissed her hand. "This is a pleasure I have looked forward to for a long time, Mrs. Greenhow. But I would much prefer that I be known to you as just plain George."

"I am delighted to meet you. I shall be happy to call you George, sir, if you will return the compliment by calling me just plain Rose."

"Rose it is, then. And a beautiful one, I might add. My sister has spoken of you so often I feel as if I know you already."

Lady Fullerton patted him lightly on the shoulder. "That is only a half-truth, Rose. George has asked me practically every day since he learned that you were coming over if you had arrived as yet. There's nothing more boring than a lonesome widower. I tell him that he must get about and meet more people. But he has been reluctant to do so." Lady Fullerton's eyes widened as she took Rose by the arm. "That is, until he learned that you were coming to visit us."

"Well, my dear, it isn't every day that one has the opportunity to meet a famous American. One who has even served a term in prison for her political beliefs."

The afternoon quickly passed as Rose made many new friends and renewed old acquaintances. Gradually, as the guests began to leave and it became quieter, Rose sat comfortably in an armchair, going over the many fond memories she shared with her British friends. It had been an exhausting trip, and this reception upon her arrival had been a glorious but tiring one.

Young Rose, sitting beside her, was leaning against her almost asleep. Lord Granville came over, and smiling, sat down with them.

"She must be exhausted from the trip and your strenuous welcome," he said softly.

Rose smiled. "So is her mother. But it was a glorious reception. It was so kind of you all and so considerate."

"Lord and Lady Lyons deserve the credit. It was their idea. But I am most grateful that I was invited."

They were quiet for a moment as Rose watched the servants clearing the tables and rolling the dishes and trays away on wagons. Presently Lord Granville spoke. "The ocean voyage must have been an exciting adventure for your daughter."

"She enjoyed it immensely. It has truly been an education for her."

"I understand that you will be conducting certain business transactions while you are here. Will she be going along with you?"

"No. I am taking her to Paris to enroll her in a convent. I haven't decided which one it will be."

"There is only one convent in Paris, Rose. That is the one conducted by the Sisters of St. Vincent de Paul. They are one of my sister's chief philanthropies. As a matter of fact, she is planning to bring the sisters to England and establish them here."

"Well, then I shall enroll Rose in their convent."

"If I am not too assuming, I know Sister Angelina, the Mother Superior, well. I will be glad to accompany you to Paris and assist you in enrolling your daughter."

"I would appreciate your help."

"Let me know when you plan to go."

"It won't be immediately. I have some business to conduct here in England first."

"I know, the publication of your book."

"Yes. Lord and Lady Napier assisted us in securing a publisher for one of my husband's books. They have already offered to take me to their publisher again. I am dubious, however. There was a bit of misunderstanding concerning our last book."

"Why not let me take you to Richard Bentley. He is publisher in Ordinary to Her Majesty, and I am sure he will be most receptive to the suggestion that he publish your memoirs."

"Thank you kindly for your help. It appears that I am to be indebted to you before we are even established in your fair city."

"Not at all. I am doing this because I want to help an old, dear friend of Georgiana's. Of course, I have an ulterior motive. You see, it means I will be spending quite a bit of time with you, and—well, while I am with you, it will discourage any of the many other candidates for your attention." He placed his hand on her lap. She smiled and pressed his hand.

They made arrangements to visit Richard Bentley, the

publishers, two days hence in order to give Rose a day to settle into her living quarters at Claridge's.

Mr. Bentley seemed most agreeable to the prospect of publishing Rose's book, but "of course," he said, almost apologetically, "I must have one of my editors read and review it." He advised them to return in three weeks for further discussions concerning the book's publication.

During the intervening weeks, Rose met with several southern compatriots who were also abroad promoting the southern cause. She was thrilled to renew the acquaintance of Commander Matthew Fontaine Maury, the noted oceanographer whom she and Robert had known when he was head of the National Observatory in Washington. Calhoun had considered him a man of great thoughts, and Rose heartily agreed. The commander had already endeared himself to the South, after his resignation from the Observatory, by mining the rivers and harbors of the Atlantic from Virginia southward. He had brought considerable money over with him to London to purchase Confederate ships and had already bought the *Georgia* and the *Victor*.

Rose readily convinced him that it would not be necessary to spend sorely needed capital if she were able to promote cotton and tobacco certificates. Whereupon he took her to Liverpool, where he introduced her to James Spence, who was engaged in the sale of Confederate bonds.

"But I can see the great advantage to your certificates," Mr. Spence volunteered. "Particularly for a nation at war." He agreed to serve as Rose's representative for western England in promoting the certificates. "With the high commissions you offer, I am sure George McHenry and Henry Hotze, your southern compatriots in eastern England, will soon find a ready market for them."

Lord Granville introduced her to a close friend of his, Lord Wharncliffe, who became so enthused by her glowing praises of the Confederate cause that he agreed to organize a sympathetic group to promote it. "We shall call it The Society for Obtaining the Cessation of Hostilities in America," he said happily.

"You can meet in my hall at 215 Regent Street," Lord Granville volunteered.

"I do wish you every success, Lord Wharncliffe," Rose said, touching his arm. "Our nation will forever be a friend of the British Lion if it will only help us during these harrowing days."

"I'll do my best. Perhaps you could come and talk to our group when I arrange a meeting. I am sure your presence and eloquent persuasion would win many hearts to your cause."

"I shall be glad to. I have been most encouraged by my reception by the cotton trade."

"You won't have to worry about the trade, Rose," said Lord Granville. "When war was first declared, they were beside themselves when the Union announced that all shipments of cotton were being seized on the high seas."

"The press raised such a commotion at the stubbornness of the Union, our papers have been on the side of the Confederacy ever since," Lord Wharncliffe remarked.

"You will find most of the peerage favors the South," said Lord Granville. "Of course, there is the Duke of Argyll and such men as Richard Moncton Milnes, Richard Cobden, and John Bright who are siding with the North. They have become particularly friendly with the American minister to England, Charles Francis Adams. I am sure your paths will never cross."

"I would not see him even if he had not been appointed by that simpleminded Seward. Mr. Adam's wife, Abigail, and I have had little in common since that madcap John Brown met his doom. Abigail was discourteous enough to make a political issue of that traitor at a dinner in my home. I have never forgiven her for it."

"They are not too well thought of in British circles, my dear," said Lord Wharncliffe, shaking his head vigorously. "That is why I believe we can make great inroads with the working class."

"I wouldn't be too sure," interrupted Lord Granville. "They seem to be adamant in their stand for the Union. You know, they are just like a flock of sheep. Give them one strong leader and the rest will blindly follow."

"All the more reason I think we might be able to sway them," retorted Lord Wharncliffe. "If we can get them to listen to us—and to Mrs. Greenhow." He bowed graciously at the mention of her name.

"Thank you, Lord Wharncliffe, but please call me Rose."

"I will be delighted."

Three weeks later, Lady Fullerton went with Rose and her brother when they returned to see Bentley, the publisher.

"What is the opinion of your editors, Richard?" Lord Granville asked expansively as they sat down in Bentley's private office.

"It is an exceedingly well-written book, Mrs. Greenhow," said Mr. Bentley, bowing to Rose.

"Thank you, sir. I value this appraisal deeply, coming from your professional editors."

"I have read the manuscript as well, Mrs. Greenhow," replied Mr. Bentley. "I do note that it is bitterly vituperative and sarcastic."

Rose's eyes suddenly flashed. "No wonder if my nature grew harsh and vindictive, and if the scorn and wrath that was in my heart sometimes found vent in my tongue or from my pen."

"I also have read your manuscript, Rose, my dear," interjected Lady Fullerton. "Your frantic sense of bitter wrong alarms me. Would it not be more acceptable to the public if it were, well—toned down, you might say?"

"Never! I want the British people to see the lords of abolition in their true light."

"But you are so intense in your hatred, Rose," said Lady Fullerton. "It is not good for you to be so overwrought!"

"I am disappointed that I have not convinced you of my sincere dedication to the Confederacy. I vow that I shall live and die for the southern cause!" Rose said fiercely.

"It will be well if your dedication does not drag you down to early madness, my dear," retorted Lady Fullerton, kindly but firmly. "Such devotion could be beyond the realm of human endurance."

Lord Granville, seeing how disturbed Rose was becoming, quickly interrupted. "Well, tell me, Richard, what is your final decision on Mrs. Greenhow's manuscript?"

"I shall be delighted to publish it!" The three visitors smiled at each other. "We are not in the habit of publishing such sensational personal confession stories. I had hoped that I could persuade Mrs. Greenhow to delete some of the more lurid passages, but I can see that she is most firm of purpose."

Rose shrugged her shoulders and looked apprehensively at Lord Granville. "I readily admit that I used men without scruple. But the situation was desperate. I have only revealed the truth."

"Bravo for you, my dear Rose. I admire a woman who describes life as it is."

"Thank you, George." Rose smiled at him, then reaching into her purse, she drew out a small piece of paper. Turning to Mr. Bentley, she handed it to him. "I am truly grateful to you for deciding to publish my book. With your permission I should like to include this dedication."

Bentley took the paper and read it aloud. "To the brave soldiers who have fought and bled in this our glorious struggle for freedom."

"It is most appropriate, Mrs. Greenhow. I shall give it a full page following the title."

"Very good. When do you think it can be published?"

"It will be ready for distribution in one month."

"Excellent!" Lord Granville chimed in. "I shall start telling them down at the club about it. I am sure it will have a wild reception here in London."

"And the rest of England as well, Georgie," Lady Fullerton added.

They left and Lord Granville insisted that they drop in to the Balmoral, a private little drinking and dining house, for a celebration.

In a gay mood, Rose ordered a Queen Charlotte Cocktail. When she learned that they were not familiar with the drink, she instructed them how to make it and they all ordered one. By chance, Commander Maury and James Mason were there, and Lord Granville insisted that the two men join them. They too were celebrating, for Commander Maury had just negotiated the purchase of several sorely needed iron rams to be shipped to the Confederacy.

"I have also perfected a working model of an electric mine," he announced proudly.

"It is a tremendous breakthrough," added Mason.

"Thanks to the superior research facilities which have been put at my disposal by some of our British friends," said Maury modestly.

"With these successes we have high hopes of persuading the emperor of France to recognize the Confederacy," volunteered Mason.

"Then this would be an opportune time for me to visit Paris and seek an audience with him," said Rose.

"It would indeed," Mason agreed. "John Arthur Roebuck is planning to announce to the House of Commons that the emperor will recognize the Confederacy if England does."

"Marvelous!" exclaimed Rose excitedly. "I shall go to Paris within a fortnight. I am taking my daughter with me to enroll her in a convent."

Arrangements were hastily made and Rose sent a note to Florence telling her of her plans to visit Paris.

The following week, Rose sailed across the English Channel. With Lord Granville's assistance, she was able to enroll young Rose in The Sisters of St. Vincent de Paul Convent. Her daughter was happy to be with so many young ladies her own age, and when Rose promised to visit her frequently, she quickly kissed her mother goodbye and left to join her new-found friends.

Florence did not meet them, having gone to Germany to enjoy one of the famous spas there. She had not received Rose's message, so Rose forwarded another note to her in Germany.

It was several days before she could secure an audience with the emperor, and she utilized the intervening time visiting French bankers and renewing acquaintance with French diplomats whom she had entertained at her home in Washington. She was very successful in arousing interest in the cotton and tobacco certificates.

Lord Granville was her constant companion and as they came to know each other, they found they had a great many things in common. She liked him immensely. She found herself thinking more and more about him. She was thrilled at the thought that once again a man had come into her life, a possibility that had not entered her mind for many months.

He was most attentive and considerate and shared her enthusiasm at the fine reception the cotton and tobacco certificates were receiving. Lord Granville knew Paris as if he were a native of the city. He delighted in showing her its beautiful landmarks as they rode along the Champs Elysées and drove through the Arc de Triomphe in an open carriage. They visited the Church of the Sacre-Coeur, the French Academy, and the Pantheon, so gorgeously lighted at night. The Bastille had a strange fascination for her as she recalled her own imprisonment and compared it with the unfortunate Marie Antoinette's. They spent a full day touring the famous Luxembourg Palace and Gardens, and finally, the Louvre.

At last, after two weeks of glorious sightseeing and dining in Paris's most famous restaurants, Rose received word that the Emperor would see her in an informal audience.

She met him in a small salon in the Tuilleries. He was seated on an ornate throne at the far end of the spacious room. His lovely wife, the Empress Eugenie, sat by his side on a gilded throne slightly smaller than the emperor's. As Rose was presented to the royal couple, she bowed deeply and waited for His Majesty to bid her rise.

Instead, he came down from his throne, and taking her arm, ushered her over to a small circular table at the side of the room and gestured for her to be seated. "For you see, this is to be an informal meeting," the emperor said, grandly gesturing for the empress to join him.

"I am deeply honored that you have granted me this interview, Your Highness," Rose said, sitting in a chair opposite the emperor.

As the empress sat down beside her husband, she smiled and said in perfect English, "It is we who should be honored, Mrs. Greenhow. Comte de Sartiges has spoken of you often. We were most impressed with your unofficial position in the halls of government—that is, before your great war."

"The war," said the emperor, "it is uppermost in the minds of all Americans now."

"It is my reason for being here, Your Majesty."

"Ah, yes, but my ministers tell me you have been in Paris over a fortnight. Surely you have taken advantage of all the glorious sights that Paris has to offer."

"Most assuredly, Your Majesty. The beauties of Paris are thrilling to the citizen of a nation embroiled in a desperate battle for its very existence. Your magnificent monuments, your splendid boulevards, are among the most beautiful in the world."

"And the lighter side of Paris," beamed the emperor. "The theaters and the luxurious shops."

Rose smiled. "I have visited many of them since coming here. Before the war, in better days, I bought many of my dresses from the shops of Paris. Truly, it is the fashion center of the world."

"True—true." The emperor nodded in agreement. Then suddenly he became serious. "But you have kept abreast of the progress of your war since you have been staying here?"

"Oh, yes. I read the latest accounts every day in the reading room of the Grand Hotel, where I am staying."

"Then you know that your situation is not too encouraging!"

"No one can deny the great loss we experienced at Gettysburg."

"But there have been others. The battles of the Wilderness, Spotsylvania, and Cold Harbor. Your nation has been defeated in all of them."

"It is not for our soldiers' lack of valor. They fight bravely but they sorely need guns and ammunition, which are in plentiful supply on this side of the ocean."

"And many ships are required to transport them to your shores," the empress joined in.

Rose smiled at the empress. "I see that you are well acquainted with our situation, Your Majesty."

"Commander Maury has been most persuasive in pleading your cause before us," she replied.

"Then you are convinced that our cause is a just one and your help will greatly bolster it!"

"Oh, but most definitely!" agreed the empress emphatically.

The slightest frown appeared on the emperor's brow. "But, unfortunately, the empress does not make the decisions for France."

"The British are seriously considering coming to our aid," Rose continued hastily. "Commander Maury has been successful in securing many iron-clad rams which have been forwarded to the port of Liverpool for shipment to our country."

"Those rams have been impounded, my dear Mrs. Greenhow. By now I am sure the British government has issued orders to forbid their shipment to your country."

"I was not aware of this."

"It has not been announced as yet."

"But I was under the impression that the British government was about to recognize the Confederacy. John Arthur Roebuck was prepared to announce—"

"Mr. Roebuck has already announced that I would recognize the Confederacy if England did so."

"Yes, I was sure that he would."

"I have denied this emphatically!"

"You are against our cause, Your Majesty?"

"Not at all. But you must recognize that your situation is progressively worsening!"

"But these defeats can readily be turned about if our men can be properly equipped on the field of battle. France's position in the New World might well be greatly affected by a Confederate victory. International relations between Mexico, France, and the United States—"

"Leave much to be desired. I am well aware of this," interrupted the emperor quickly.

"Surely the Archduke Maximilian of Austria can confirm the many advantages of supporting our cause in return for the benefits you will receive when the Confederacy has won the war."

"Commander Maury has pressed his friendship with Archduke Maximilian to the utmost to secure our recognition of your government."

"I am sure that they have both made you well aware of the possibility of separating California from the Union and restoring it to Mexican sovereignty."

"If you should win the war."

"Yes, when we win the war."

"It is a most enticing plum that you offer, Mrs. Greenhow. One, no doubt, that has completely influenced the archduke in our country's behalf."

"Thank you, Your Highness. Are you saying that there still is hope that you will consider granting us recognition?"

There was a moment's pause as the emperor looked directly at Rose and she unhesitatingly returned his steady gaze, never flinching from his burning eyes. Without taking his eyes from her he smiled and said quietly, "It is too late, my dear!"

"But it is not, Your Majesty," Rose pleaded, partially rising

551

from her chair. "The war is far from lost if we can only get your ships. British sympathy is ever rising to our defense. I personally have sold many cotton and tobacco certificates since coming to London. All of these are to be redeemed by us in return for ammunitions, arms, and finished goods. Goods that are sorely needed by our country. Even now they are piled high in British ports. With sufficient ships to take them to our shores, you shall see, the tide of war will change. We will win! I will gladly stake my life on it!"

"Your country was well advised to send you to plead their cause. Frankly, you are most convincing." Slowly he rose from his chair.

Rose immediately jumped up, and leaning on the table before her in her eagerness, said earnestly, "Our country has had every right to entertain hopes of favorable results from France because of the close ties that have bound us together in the past. May we not hope that you will dwell further on the subject and reconsider your position of neutrality?"

"I did seriously consider it, madam. I was sorely tempted to grant you our support—our assistance—"

"Well, then—"

"That was before Gettysburg—before Spotsylvania and Cold Harbor."

"But don't you realize, Your Majesty, that these losses were due to our lack of equipment? All of this can be changed if we can but count on your aid."

Slowly the emperor shook his head. "It is too late!" he repeated.

"But it is—" Rose began, then stopped in the middle of her sentence. She realized that further pleading would be useless and might jeopardize the feeble ties that still bound the two nations together. Slowly she curtsied deeply to the emperor. "You have been most gracious, Your Majesty, to listen so patiently to my plea."

"I am sorry, Mrs. Greenhow."

"I understand."

As Rose curtsied before the empress she could see tears well up in her eyes. "I am aware that you sympathize with us, Your Highness. I hope that you will never cease trying to convince the emperor that our cause still is not lost."

"I admire you for your faith, Mrs. Greenhow," the empress said, extending her hand. "Let us hope that the courage of your convictions and the strength of your will brings aid to you from many sources."

Rose bowed again to the emperor and the empress and quietly left the room.

She was silent as her carriage took her back to her hotel. Lord Granville met her in the lobby. He took one look at her distraught countenance and said quietly, "You were not successful?"

"He is adamant in his conviction."

"Deplorable." He sighed and then brightening, added, "It is well past the dinner hour. Come into the dining room with me and tell me about it."

"I don't feel like eating, George." She leaned her head on his shoulder. "Please take me to my room."

"But what will people—?" He stopped and putting his arm about her waist escorted her up the wide carpeted steps leading from the foyer of the hotel.

Stopping before the doorway to her room, she brought out her key. Without a word, he took it, and opening the door, went inside with her.

He lit the lights and helped her take off her coat and hat. She walked over to the sofa and sat down. He sat down beside her. She looked up at him, then blankly at the walls of her room. Suddenly she began to cry. He put his arm about her and she dropped her head on his shoulder sobbing uncontrollably.

It was several minutes before he attempted to calm her. Then he raised her head, and taking his handkerchief, gently wiped the tears from her cheeks. "Was it so terrible, Rose?"

"They were most polite. The emperor was very considerate. I could see that the empress was favorable to my plea, but I could not persuade the emperor to change his stand of neutrality. He was emphatic. He was immovable."

"I am sorry, Rose. I know how much this has meant to you."

"If he would only agree to give us ships. We have been successful in getting munitions and other materials from your country. Oh, George, I feel so desolate and alone."

"You must never feel alone, my dear Rose, for I will always be by your side."

She smiled at him and patted his arm which was still around her shoulder. "You have been so helpful, George. I don't know what I would ever have done if I hadn't had you to turn to." Silently they looked at each other. As she turned toward him and looked softly into his eyes, they were close. He faced her directly and slowly drew her close to him. Their cheeks touched, then their lips met in their first kiss. Slowly she put her arms about him and kissed him soundly, passionately. He pressed his lips to hers and kissed her again and again. Her bosom pressed against his body and she closed her eyes, thrilling to his warm touch.

Suddenly he jumped up and, looking at her fiercely, started to walk away. Quickly she rose and followed him. "George, what is it?"

"I must leave, Rose. At once."

"But why?"

"I—it is for your sake, dear Rose. I fear I cannot trust myself alone with you. Rose, I—I love you."

She rushed over to him and turned him to her. "But I am glad, George." She threw her arms about his neck. "I don't want you to leave. I want you near me." She pressed her body fondly against him and kissed him. It had been so long since she had been in a man's arms. It was ecstasy.

He threw his arms about her and savagely pressed her closer to him. "Rose, Rose, my darling Rose. I love you. I do love you so!"

They were leaning against the bed now. Slowly she sank down on the side of the bed and he dropped down beside her, never releasing his hold on her. She pressed her cheeks to him and rolled her lips against his, moving her body closer to him. Slowly she took his arm and brought his hand to her breast. Closing her eyes, she kissed him madly, passionately. Running his hand over her breast, he rolled it fervently against her body, returning her kisses with equal passion.

Suddenly there was a short, hesitant knock on the door. Instantly he dropped his arms and looked toward the door. She turned his face back to her and brought his lips to hers. "Let them knock!"

He drew himself away from her. "You can't do that. It might be important." There was a second, louder knock.

"Oh, George," she sighed. "It was so wonderful."

"It was heaven, my dear. Truly the answer to all my dreams."

There was a third knock on the door, louder and more insistent than before. Slowly Rose got up and opened the door.

There, standing in the doorway looking radiantly expectant, was her oldest daughter. "Mums!" Florence shouted as she threw her arms about her mother.

"Florence! Oh, Florence, how good it is to see you at long last." They kissed each other several times and hugging her tightly, Rose said, "Do come in. Oh, Florence, you look so lovely."

Florence came into the room smiling cheerfully. Suddenly she stopped short and gasped as she saw Lord Granville, who had jumped up and stood watching the joyous reunion.

"Oh, Florence, I want you to meet Lord Granville. A dear friend of mine. George, this is my oldest daughter about whom I have told you so much."

Lord Granville bowed grandly.

"How do you do, Lord Granville," Florence curtsied. "I'm sorry, Mums, I didn't mean to break in on you unannounced, but I couldn't wait to see you."

"Of course, my dear child. Oh my, it is so good to see you. I had about given you up, with you traipsing all over Europe.

Where have you been, you naughty girl?"

"I've been to Baden-Baden taking the baths. Don't I look wonderful?"

"You look positively enchanting," Lord Granville volunteered.

"Oh, thank you, Lord Granville. I must sound terribly conceited."

"On the contrary, you do look dashing."

"Actually I never felt healthier. Those baths work wonders. But I left immediately when your notes finally caught up with me. I received both of them within two days."

"I say, I feel as if I am intruding. Perhaps it would be better if I left," volunteered Lord Granville.

"Please don't go, George. I want you to get acquainted with my daughter."

"I was hoping you would say that," Lord Granville smiled. "This does call for a celebration. I'll ring for champagne." Going to the wall he yanked the wall pull vigorously.

Lord Granville ordered champagne and hors d'oeuvres. They all seated themselves around the small table and talked for hours.

In spite of Rose's disappointment over her interview with Emperor Napoleon, the next few days were gloriously exciting. Florence assured her mother that she definitely approved of Lord Granville and the three of them toured Paris and the outlying countryside together. They visited young Rose several times at the convent, but the young lady was so engrossed in her new surroundings and friends she scarcely had time to meet with them. Once or twice they took her with them as they visited the Chamber of Deputies and the Latin Quarter. She seemed interested and watched the many famous landmarks politely as Lord Granville pointed them out to her, but it was obvious that she was anxious to get back to the convent.

Several times Florence and Lord Granville would accompany Rose as she visited important bankers and diplomats to interest them in Confederate cotton and tobacco certificates. They would wait outside while she called on her prospects, but both of them gleefully shared her enthusiasm at her many successes.

It was nearly a month later that they received word from publisher Bentley that the first copies of Rose's book were coming off the press and he was distributing them to critics and key newspapers. He suggested that she might make herself available in London a few weeks hence to help increase public interest.

That evening, as they were bidding goodnight to Lord Granville, Florence suggested going back to London with them. When they both appeared delighted she announed to Lord Granville that he would not be able to meet them the next day until late in the afternoon, because she was planning a surprise for both of them.

Rose got up fairly late the following morning, for Florence had made an appointment to meet her mother at ten. When she arrived they had a hasty breakfast and Florence announced her surprise.

"It is time, dear Mums, that you dispense with those horrid mourning clothes."

"I have worn them so long, Florence, that I feel they are almost a part of me."

"That is just it, Mums. But you are entering a new life now. You will be meeting important people to interest them in your book and you will be very much in the public eye. The time has come to treat yourself to an entirely new wardrobe. You must do it while we are still in Paris to take advantage of the latest fashions."

"Oh, but it will be so expensive, Florence. My trip has been costly—"

Florence put her hands on her mother's shoulders. "Mums, you have not let us do anything for you in a long time. Moore and I wanted to help but we did not know how best to do it. Now we are going to buy all your new clothes."

"Oh, but Florence—"

"You will be attired in the latest fashions, Mums. Come now, you must look chic for Lord Granville's sake, if for no one else."

Rose smiled. "Isn't he a dear?"

"He is Mums. He is not only the perfect gentleman, he is so considerate of you."

"I am really quite taken with him."

"You are in love with him, Mums."

"I didn't know it was that obvious."

"Do you remember when I first fell in love with Moore? You said, 'A girl in love wears her heart on her sleeve.'"

Rose looked away from the steady gaze of her daughter. She could feel the warmth of her own flushed cheeks. She sighed. "I guess we are all girls whatever our age when we fall in love."

"It becomes you, darling. Now, let us hurry to Vincent le Moie's. We will start there."

It was late in the afternoon before they had finished shopping. Florence saw to it that her mother got a complete new wardrobe and insisted that she and Moore purchase it. They bought morning dresses, day dresses, and evening dresses with the newest flounces. They purchased warm winter coats and summer slip-ons. Nor did they stint on the many soft silk underthings. By the end of the shopping spree, Rose was completely exhausted but deliriously happy. She had forgotten how wonderful it was to be dressed in the latest fashions and gay colors.

When they met Lord Granville for dinner that night, he stood boldly staring at Rose, his mouth agape. "I never realized how truly beautiful you really are," he marveled. Both women laughed at his complete abandon of British reserve.

The following week when they attended the opera, all eyes turned to the mysteriously stunning woman as she entered her box. Dressed in a dark purple satin well-off-the-shoulder evening dress with flounces and hooped skirt topped by a fashionable bustle in the rear, she looked every bit a queen.

Word had been received that Rose's book was popular reading in London, and French society was already clamoring for copies. She wore a red rose in her hair, and Lord Granville had given her a cluster of rubies and diamonds which she wore on her breast. A thin black band was wrapped about her throat fastened in front by a pearl and ruby brooch. As they were seated in their box, several of the gallants began to politely applaud her and she smiled at the orchestra below. Once again she was the center of attraction, and on the arm of Lord Granville, with her oldest daughter by her side, she was deliriously happy.

On the first of the following month, Rose returned to London with Florence and Lord Granville. Rose had become a celebrity. There were requests for her to speak, not only at literary teas but political functions, as well, where she enthusiastically begged her listeners to come to the aid of her beloved Confederacy.

The Society for Obtaining the Cessation of Hostilities in America had increased to over five thousand members. Rose addressed as many of their meetings as she possibly could. She went to Liverpool, Manchester, and Birmingham to help organize additional clubs. The demand for her to speak at bazaars and meetings was so great that it became necessary for her to list her appointments well in advance. Florence helped her establish an itinerary so that she could make the best use of her time. One day she would be in a crude meeting hall addressing British workers. The next day she would be addressing a staid group of bejeweled women in a Victorian drawing room. British statesmen sought her out to ask her opinion of the American situation. She gladly organized charitable affairs whose purpose was to collect money and clothing for the hard-pressed rebels.

She dropped in to visit her publisher from time to time, and each time he diligently settled his account with her. At their first meeting, he placed nearly two pounds of solid gold British sovereigns in her hands, the first royalties from her book.

"And by the looks of it there will be many more," he commented.

"I knew that it was a winner!" shouted Lord Granville gleefully. "What else could it be coming from such a wonderful and talented woman?" He squeezed her closely to him.

"We are receiving orders from America, too. Not only from the South but from the North, as well. Do you know a Colonel Doster?"

"I most assuredly do. He was appointed provost marshal in charge of prisons when Stanton became secretary of war."

"He has purchased a copy of your book. He must have been most anxious to read it, for he sent us sixteen dollars in gold for his copy."

"Well he might be, for he wishes to know what I have had to say about Old Capitol Prison. He will learn that I have said plenty!"

The months slipped by in an almost blinding whirl. Rose sadly rued the fact that her dear Confederacy was not nearly as successful on the battlefront as she was in her contacts with the British public. She began to believe more and more that their cause would succeed only if the South could report some outstanding victories. Eventually she decided that she must return to America and report directly to President Davis. Help was forthcoming, she was sure, if the Confederacy could only show that they could support their demands for recognition as a new nation with resounding victories on the battlefield.

She finally announced that she would make a quick trip back to America. It would only be for a short time, she told Lord Granville, and she promised him that when she returned they would be married.

"You have made me the happiest man in the world, my dear Rose," he said to her, his eyes shining. Then he turned away. "If only—"

As he hesitated, Rose took his chin in her hand and turned his face toward her. "If only what, Georgie?"

"Well I—forgive me, my love, but I would feel more confident of our life together if only you could be more forgiving and less vengeful toward your enemies. Your intenseness and outrage might some day drag you to devastation."

Rose looked at him quietly for a moment without speaking. Then smiling, she reached up to him and kissed him gently on the lips. Patting him on the cheek she said calmly but firmly, "I have given you my heart, dear Georgie, but I shall never give anyone my mind!"

They did not discuss the matter further.

Passage was booked on the three-funneled steamship the *Condor*, which was making its first trip to the Confederacy. A few days before sailing Rose received word from Alexander Collie, a British shipping magnate, that he must see her on important business. Knowing that he owned the largest fleet of blockade runners in the British Isles, she promptly visited him.

He greeted her expansively as she sat down in his mahogany-paneled office. "You and I have a lot in common, Mrs. Greenhow," he greeted her. "I, too, have done a great deal for the Confederacy."

"I know. You are operating a vast fleet of blockade runners to our country, sir."

"Yes, but are you aware that in three months my ships have run out over two hundred thousand pounds sterling in cotton?"

"I was not, Mr. Collie. That is magnificent!"

"I agree. I am willing to do even more. That is why I wanted to see you before you sailed for the Confederacy."

"Oh?"

"I wish you to take this draft on my London bank for ten thousand dollars and present it to President Davis."

"But what is this for?"

"Tell him he can use it in any manner he wishes—it is my contribution to southern charities."

"That is most gracious of you, sir."

"It is only the beginning, Mrs. Greenhow. You might advise President Davis that I shall send him ten thousand dollars' worth of goods each month for the next six months. They will be transported in my ships as they sail for America."

"Your generous offer leaves me speechless, Mr. Collie. I—I do not know why—"

"Yes, I have helped the cause of the Confederacy greatly. But I freely admit my endeavors have been most profitable for myself, as well."

"True, but we ask nothing more of you than to continue to deliver goods to us in your ships."

"But I seek something of you, madam."

"Oh?"

"I shall come straight to the point. I have—or I should say I *had*—the services of a most competent agent handling my interests in your port of Wilmington, the only open port remaining for commerce to the South. Theodore Andrea; perhaps you have heard of him."

"I believe I recognize his name. He has been most active. What do you mean you had had his services?"

"It seems he was unduly ousted from the city of Wilmington for—well, as North Carolina put it, for 'bringing the state of North Carolina into violent collision with the general government.'"

"Was he involved in any wrongdoing?"

"No, of course not." Mr. Collie turned his eyes away from Rose's stern glare. "That is to say, he might have been a little overzealous in the performance of his duties. But aren't we all, Mrs. Greenhow—when the situation demands extra effort, as in the case of a fearful war."

"I suppose we are, yes."

"I am glad you see it my way. We need Mr. Andrea to continue his activities in Wilmington. I need him to look after my interests, you need him to help you in filling the demands of your cotton and tobacco certificates, and President Davis and his government need him to expedite shipments to and

562

from Wilmington to the outside world."

"I agree his presence will be helpful to us all."

"It is for this reason that I seek your support in settling this matter."

"I—I shall do all that I can, Mr. Collie, I assure you."

"Good." He handed her a legal paper. "I have had a power of attorney drawn up in your name."

She took the paper and stared at it and then at Mr. Collie. "But is this necessary?"

"Mr. Andrea advises me that it is. It seems that there are certain penalties and fines that will be connected with the settlement of his case."

"What limits do you place on this power of attorney?"

He looked at her carefully for a moment before he spoke. Then he leaned heavily on his desk and said simply, "None!"

"None?"

"I hope you will forgive me, Mrs. Greenhow, but I have had you thoroughly investigated on both sides of the Atlantic. I know of your dedication to the southern cause. I know how you have suffered for it. I have even read your book, Mrs. Greenhow. It is the first book I have read since I attended school. It is an excellent representation of the southern cause."

"Thank you, sir."

"It also reveals the character of a true martyr. I know of no other man or woman whom I would rather trust with this vital mission than yourself."

"You are most generous in your compliments."

"My compliments do not come easily. I need your help. If this situation cannot be resolved, my whole operation might be ruined. I need Theodore Andrea back at his post in Wilmington. If he is not reinstated, it will be a great loss to me. Oh, I can withstand the loss, I am an extremely wealthy man, Mrs. Greenhow, but can your country withstand the loss of his and my services?"

There was silence in the room as the two looked seriously at each other. Presently Rose slowly stood up. "I shall personally attend to this matter immediately upon my arrival in America, Mr. Collie."

"Good. Do what you can."

"I shall go beyond that, sir. I assure you that Theodore Andrea shall be reinstated."

"Thank you, Mrs. Greenhow. I will make it worth your while."

"That is not necessary. As I see it, the Confederacy stands to gain as much in this matter as you yourself, sir."

"I knew that I had selected the right person." He rose from his chair and extended his hand. They shook hands. "When are you sailing?"

"On August 10. Two days hence."

"I caught you just in time, didn't I?"

"You most certainly did, sir."

"Good luck, Mrs. Greenhow."

"I shall let you know when the matter has been settled—to your satisfaction, sir."

"It is a pleasure doing business with you, madam."

On August 10, 1864, exactly one year after her arrival in England, Rose set sail from Greenock, Scotland, for the Confederacy. She wore a large heavy leather reticule suspended by a long chain around her neck.

As she watched the shores of Scotland fading in the distance, she unconsciously fondled the leather reticule and looked down at it lovingly. It contained three hundred English sovereigns, over two thousand dollars in gold, the accumulated royalties from the publication of her most successful book. There were more English gold sovereigns sewn in the folds of her dress. They were heavy, but she did not mind. It was undoubtedly the safest place the valuable cargo could be stored.

Epilogue

The trip across the ocean had been uneventful. They had encountered several early fall storms, but the *Condor* was superbly adapted for her trade. She had great carrying capacity and drew only seven feet of water. She sailed majestically through all types of weather, as swift as a sea swallow. Rose had early become acquainted with her captain, Admiral Samuel S. Ridge. He assured her that the ship's crew of forty-five stalwart men were the ablest-bodied men available and well capable of taking the ship neatly through the northern blockade.

Admiral Ridge was the youngest son of the sixth earl of Buckinghamshire and knew Lord Granville well. He and Rose had many conversations during the voyage, and Rose felt completely at ease in the hands of this gallant, experienced seaman who on many occasions had skippered Queen Victoria's own yacht.

During the entire voyage, while promenading the deck, dining with the admiral, dancing in the gilded saloon, in fair weather or foul, Rose always kept the heavy pouch of gold securely fastened about her neck.

On September 7 the *Condor* docked at Halifax, where James B. Holcombe and his deputy, Lieutenant Wilson, came aboard. Holcombe had been assigned to Halifax as Confederate commissioner to the North American Colonies of Great Britain. Holcombe and Rose had several lengthy conversations as he brought her up to date on the progress of the war. The news that he brought her was worse than she had imagined. The plight of the Confederacy was by now desperate.

They remained in port in Halifax for several days, and finally Rose inquired of Admiral Ridge the reason for the delay.

"We are waiting for the moon to wane," he replied simply. "A dark night is much to be desired for running a blockade."

"It makes us ever aware of the dangers that confront us."

"There is little danger, Mrs. Greenhow. Although the blockade is becoming ever more effective, it will offer little trouble to us if we can sail into port in complete darkness."

"When do you expect conditions to be right for our sailing?"

"We will up anchor on September 24."

"Seventeen precious days which I had not anticipated lost completely."

"I am sure you will agree that it is better to be safe than sorry."

Early on the morning of September 24, the *Condor* sailed out of the harbor at Halifax so that they would come into the southern port of Wilmington in the black of night. The next week passed quickly as they steamed down the United States coast, well out at sea beyond the Union blockade.

On the thirtieth of September, Admiral Ridge advised Rose they had safely navigated past Union territory and were again heading westward toward Wilmington Harbor. She went to bed early that night, and although she was excited at the prospect of finally passing through the Union blockade, she soon dozed off into a sound sleep.

At four o'clock the following morning of October 1, she was savagely tossed from her bunk and rudely awakened by a tremendous crash aboard ship. The *Condor* shook from stem to stern and then abruptly stopped. A raging northeaster had come up and it was raining heavily, with the wind blowing almost a gale. Slipping a coat about her, she quickly rushed up on deck, and passing Admiral Ridge as he too hurried to the pilot house, she asked, "What is wrong, admiral?"

"Only a minor problem," he muttered hastily. "The pilot

called me. He has run aground."

"Oh, dear! Where are we?"

"We should be off Cape Fear."

Admiral Ridge hurried on to the pilot house with Rose following close behind him. As he entered the cabin, he shouted, "What happened?"

"The hulk of a sunken ship stood in our way, cap'n. I shifted course to avoid it when we ran aground on New Inlet Bar."

"God, man, we've almost reached our destination. If it is New Inlet Bar, we are within two hundred yards of the Confederates' Fort Fisher."

"You are correct, sir. I have checked the chart."

"Ring the engine room for full speed astern."

"Aye, aye, sir."

The ship bell rang and the vessel shuddered as it suddenly plunged into reverse. It strained and rocked but still remained solidly grounded on the bar.

"Ring for quick forward then reverse speed."

"Aye, aye, sir."

At that moment, a burst of rockets spewed forth into the sky, seeming to come from just behind them.

"My God, we've been spotted," shouted the admiral. "Here, give me the wheel!"

Almost at once, batteries from Fort Fisher began to open fire.

"We're caught right in the middle, goddammit!" said the admiral bitterly.

Rose gasped, and running wildly out of the cabin, groped her way to the deck's outer railing. Braving the fierce lurching and rocking of the ship, with the rain beating relentlessly against her, she finally returned to her cabin. Drenched to the skin, she threw off her nightgown and hurriedly dressed. Shortening the long chain about her neck to make it more secure, she grabbed a heavy winter coat and went back on deck.

Guns were still firing from Fort Fisher, and in the first faint glow of dawn she could make out another ship off their stern and starboard, less than three hundred feet away.

She entered the pilot house, using every bit of strength to shove the cabin door closed against the furious wind. "You had better stay in your cabin, Mrs. Greenhow," Admiral Ridge hollered.

Ignoring him, she shouted back, "There's a ship bearing up on us, admiral."

"I know it. I make out the Yankee *Niphon* with my glasses."

"Oh, my God!"

"She's pulling away, cap'n," yelled the pilot.

"Thank the good Lord," breathed Rose aloud.

"The fort's shells are hitting too close to them for comfort. She's pulling away to safety. We're sitting on this inlet like a dead duck."

"Will they attempt to capture us?"

"The won't dare with the fort's guns protecting us. They'll wait out the day and attack us at nightfall."

"But we are practically at our destination, admiral. We can save ourselves by going ashore."

"Not in this storm! The seas are coming over our decks on the port side."

The door opened and James Holcombe burst hurriedly into the cabin followed by his deputy, Lieutenant Wilson. "The sea is frightening, admiral. Are we safe?"

"Of course, we are. This ship has every protection developed by man."

"What about that ship behind us?"

"She's pulling off. The guns of Fort Fisher will protect us at least until tonight."

"What then?" asked Holcombe. The wind was blowing so loudly he could not make himself heard. He repeated his question, this time shouting loudly. "What then?"

"God knows. I don't. If we sit tight, the worst we can hope for is to be attacked and seized by the *Niphon*."

"I will not be captured," shouted Rose fiercely. "I want to go ashore!"

"It is impossible. We are safer here than to make one false move against this raging sea. We could endanger our very lives."

"I have been a prisoner of the Yankee masters once, sir. It shall never be my fate again!"

"You have no choice until the storm subsides."

"We can go ashore!"

"That is madness! You can't hope to survive in this holocaust."

The entire length and breadth of the ship was suddenly ferociously rocked as a mountainous wave crashed over the decks. They were thrown against each other and frantically grabbed the railings to right themselves.

Rose groped her way beside the admiral and shouted above the roar of the winds, "Admiral Ridge, we are official representatives of the Confederate government, returning to report to our president!" The storm was raging so loudly by now that it was necessary for them to shout every word at the top of their lungs in order to be heard.

"I well know that."

"We have messages for him that are urgent. I demand that you supply us with a boat to take us to shore!"

"It is impossible."

"Nothing is impossible!"

"Even if it were possible, it would be foolhardy. I shall not take the responsibility."

"It is not your responsibility, sir. It is mine!"

"Mrs. Greenhow, you do not know how treacherous the sea can be in a storm such as this."

"I know the cruel boot of my enemy and I shall take my chances with the lesser evil."

"You are safe from the seas on the *Condor*. You are protected from your enemy by your own Fort Fisher. In a dinghy you will be protected from neither."

Rose clutched the heavy chain around her neck and swayed as the boat lurched. "It is my decision that we will be safer on shore."

"You are insane, madam!"

"And you, sir, are defying the wishes of your passengers. You yourself do not know what will happen to this ship in the next hour."

"I only know the safety of my ship and the perils of a small boat in these mountainous seas."

"I repeat, sir. This is only one man's opinion! I choose to think otherwise." They stood glaring at each other as the wind howled about them and the rain beat against the cabin windows. Fiercely, Rose grabbed his arm and yelled, "I demand that you launch one of your boats and send us ashore to safety!"

He watched this lonely woman standing before him, drenched to the skin, demanding that she be transferred to a small boat in this raging storm and slowly shook his head. He had done all that he could. He had used every means of persuasion to make her change her mind. But she was correct. She was his passenger. He had been hired to do her bidding. Sullenly he turned to the pilot and shouted close to his ear, "Choose two volunteers and loosen the lifeboat furthest astern. Swing it out and launch it to port."

Rose patted his shoulder. "Thank you, admiral. I have brought with me four dispatch bags to be delivered to the Confederate government. I request that they also be put into the boat with us."

"Very well." He beckoned to his pilot, indicating he was to do as she requested.

It was nearly an hour later when they had succeeded in loosening the lifeboat and securely seating Rose and the other two passengers in it. As several crewmen slowly lowered them into the treacherous sea, the tiny boat was battered several times against the *Condor*'s sides. Finally it was successfully launched into the water and freed of the mother ship.

Rose did not look back as the men strained at their oars and headed toward shore. In the gradually increasing light of day, they could faintly make out the walls of imposing Fort Fisher on the shore ahead. The wind savagely beat the rain against their faces. The two emissaries of the Confederate government looked sadly at each other and then sorrowfully at Rose. She glared fiercely back at them.

Suddenly they sank into a trough of water so deep that they could no longer see the *Condor* behind them. They were completely surrounded by waters high above their heads. Then, as suddenly, a huge wave came rushing toward them and crashed over the boat. Rose screamed and clutched her coat closer about her in a futile effort to protect herself from the fury of the wind and the lashing rain. Helplessly the men at the oars struggled to turn the boat sideways to the wave. But it was too late! As the men tried to keep the boat upright another wave crashed over them and turned the boat upside down, throwing the passengers and the contents of the boat into the sea.

The boat's bow shot quickly out of the sea and then settled upside down on the surface of the water. The two oarsmen and the pilot grabbed the bottom of the boat and clutched madly at the centerboard.

As Holcombe and Lieutenant Wilson were helplessly swept by, the sailors frantically grabbed them and dragged them up beside them. Quickly the seamen swam and scurried to the other side of the boat to balance it so it would not sink. They could not see Rose.

As Rose was flung out of the boat, a second wave picked her up and threw her clear away from the boat and the other passengers. She could see the men clinging to the overturned boat as the sea savagely pulled her further away from them.

In a quick, flashing moment, she thought of her daughter Rose in a French convent. Of Leila, safely ensconced in boarding school, of her older daughter Florence, who had happily bade her goodbye, and the beautiful wardrobe of new clothing she had bought for her. Who would wear them now? She thought of dear Lord Granville and her promise to marry him when she returned. In sudden retrospect she envisioned Robert Greenhow, Jim Buchanan, Ras Keyes, poor Henry Wilson, and yes, General Lee, valiantly struggling to lead his men to victory. She saw Jefferson Davis and his wife waiting for her triumphant return from Europe. She could plainly see General Whiting as he ordered his cavalrymen into battle, frowning because she had not sent them the roses she had promised.

Pushing desperately against the surging waves, she raised her head above the water. She tried to scream, but salt water rushed into her mouth and muffled her voice. Slowly she sank back into the swirling inferno. The hundreds of heavy gold sovereigns about her neck dragged her relentlessly downward beneath the surface and plunged her helplessly toward the bottom of the sea. As she struggled and gasped for air, she felt the terrible pressure of the water that was fast engulfing her. Her lungs were bursting for want of air.

Suddenly she saw a great white light rising before her—not colored as a sunset, but pure white, as if she were approaching a great magnificence. She sighed, for she realized that, truly, she was. The light began to shine ever brighter and rapidly spread itself larger before her. Quietly, calmly, she closed her eyes and gave herself up to the sea—her first and final master!

READ THESE MEDICAL BLOCKBUSTERS!

BLAZING CIVIL WAR SAGAS

SOMETHING FOR EVERYONE—
BEST SELLERS FROM ZEBRA!

WHAT PRICE LOVE by Alice Lent Covert   (491, $2.25)
Unhappy and unfulfilled, Shane plunges into a passionate, all-consuming affair. And for the first time in her life she realizes that there's a dividing line between what a woman owes her husband and what she owes herself, and is willing to take the consequences no matter what the cost.

LOVE'S TENDER TEARS by Kate Ostrander   (504, $1.95)
A beautiful woman caught between the bonds of innocence and womanhood, loyalty and love, passion and fame, is too proud to fight for the man she loves and risks her lifelong dream of happiness to save her pride.

WITHOUT SIN AMONG YOU   (506, $2.50)
by Katherine Stapleton
Vivian Wright, the overnight success, the superstar writer who was turning the country upside down by exposing her most intimate adventures was on top of the world—until she was forced to make a devastating choice: her career or her fiance?

ALWAYS, MY LOVE by Dorothy Fletcher   (517, $2.25)
Iris thought there was to be only one love in her lifetime—until she went to Paris with her widowed aunt and met Paul Chandon who quickly became their constant companion. But was Paul really attracted to her, or was he a fortune hunter after her aunt's money?